I am the end of all things.

UNDERWORLD PUBLISHING HOUSE

Underworld Publishing House LLC

Dark Magic

The Chronicles of the Underworld

Copyright @ 2021 by Raluca Narita

Summary: When the Devil escapes his prison in Hell, the Goddess of Death must team up with one of the fabled Grimm Brothers to hunt Lucifer down and prevent his murderous rampage.

ISBN: 978-8-9876762-1-9 (Paperback)
ISBN: 979-8-9876762-0-2 (eBook)
ISBN: 979-8-9876762-2-6 (Hardcover)

Cover design by Dede Yusup

Interior design and typesetting by Marcy McGuire

R.E.Narita

THE CHRONICLES OF THE
UNDERWORLD

BOOK ONE

DARK MAGIC

RALUCA NARITA

Underworld Publishing House

To my family,
thank you for your never-ending
love and support. This book is dedicated
to my sister, Kristine.

THE UNDERWORLD

Oasis

Acheron

Management
and Operations
Headquarter

Reaper
Barracks

Oasis

Goddess of
Death's Palace

Military
Base

Lethe

God of Life's
Palace

Elysium
Administration
Building

ELYSIUM

Oasis

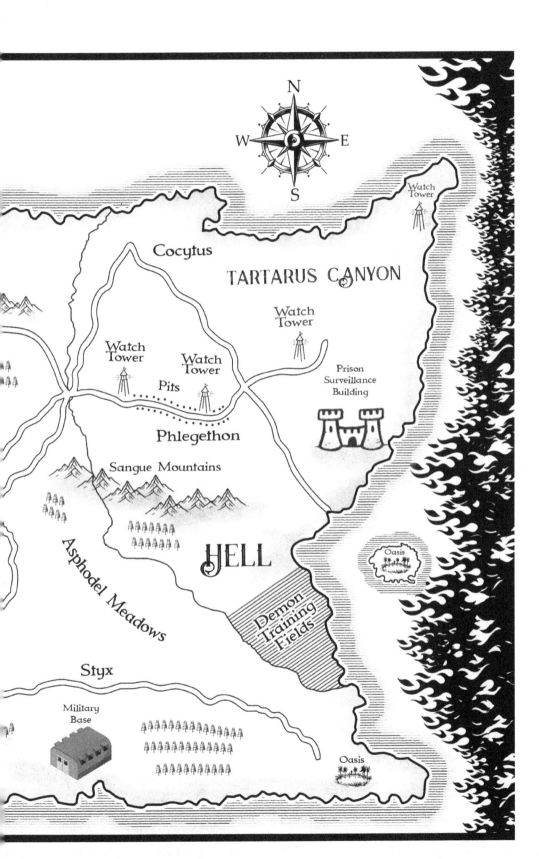

CONTENTS

PROLOGUE
PHLEGETHON'S SECRET

THE DEVIL WIPED HIS bloody hands on a clean handkerchief. The scarlet stains soiled the pale silk and calmed his raging mind, giving him a sooth reprieve to his incensed thoughts. Piles of bodies lay in an artistic fashion, strewn across the rickety wooden bridges that swayed unsteadily under the harsh conditions of Hell. Not even an artist's painting of a war-torn battleground could depict the red beauty of the scene before him. The splatters of blood and strewn coils of intestines were each delicate strokes of Lucifer's brush; he was an artist in his own right.

Lucifer slid his handkerchief over his narrow blade, smudging the blood across its smooth, metal surface. The red marks on his wrists and ankles were a painful reminder of his days as a prisoner—chained, like an animal. His bloodred eyes glared back toward his cage with a hate that could sear through flesh and bone. The metal bars of his cell were twisted and coiled, no longer the proud and robust structure that hindered his escape for hundreds of years.

A gap between the start and end of the wooden bridge to his prison marked the path to where he now stood. The lower demons, purely animalistic fiends that guarded his cell, were torn to shreds and discarded into Phlegethon, the river of fire that ran with untamed strength below Hell's prison cages. His other jailkeepers, the reapers, were similarly disposed of.

All but one.

"Living in a cage for the past few centuries"—Lucifer turned to watch the one remaining reaper who lay injured on the ground—"it's got me thinking." He gestured at the violence that surrounded him. "Your beloved queen posted hundreds of guards to keep me trapped. Hundreds of reapers and lower demons, but not one creature with a soul."

The wounded reaper dragged herself across the floor to be as far from the Devil as she possibly could. A deep gash cut along her side, and she bled heavily onto the dirt beneath her small body.

Lucifer ignored her attempts to escape and smiled thoughtfully. "She could have ordered a demigod to stand guard—a single, measly demigod. As long as one soul existed within these walls, one soul other than my own, of course, she would know if I escaped. Instead, she chose to surround me with soulless creatures, like you." He sent a sad look to the remaining reaper. "Her loss, I suppose. Gives me a head start before she hears of my escape."

He threw the soiled handkerchief to the ground and swung the sword he'd stolen from one of his guards. The Devil strode toward the wounded reaper as if he were strolling through a park. He relieved the woman of her head with one fluid motion and kicked the body into the river of fire beneath him. The kill was simple. Clean.

He inhaled deeply as though a burden had been removed from his shoulders. "Free at last."

Heat leaped up from the depths of Hell and spread across his skin as the flames lashed out in a fury at Lucifer's escape and the blood he shed. The demon only embraced the warmth. Fire was his element, not his enemy.

The crackles of flames bounced off the auburn dirt walls of the prison. The wooden bridges swung wildly, and if not for the heat-resistant spells cast on them, the bridges would collapse in the presence of Phlegethon's rage. Smoke blew up from underneath the bridges and filled the Devil's lungs. Soot blackened his tunic. His blond hair hung lower than his shoulder blades, and a heavy beard marked his chin; he would remedy his appearance once he returned to the human realm.

Lucifer had luck on his side. Since his guards were all without souls, his prison warden would not know of their demise. The Devil's lips curled into a cruel smile as he thought of Primrose Titan, the Goddess of Death. The Queen of the Underworld. His captor.

Fate would grant him his revenge. But first, he had another task to take care of. Rumors from the land of the living slipped down into the pits of Hell and reached his ever-attentive ears. Even if he refused to believe the whispers, two nights ago, a powerful vision assaulted him while he slept. There was a plot—one to assassinate the Goddess of Death. As much as he wanted to punish Primrose for her betrayal, her death would be... untimely. Lucifer needed her alive for the future he had in mind.

He crossed the final wooden bridge of the primitive prison system and walked up the metal path that led to the Underworld's surface. His siblings, the demon twins, had surely taken care of any magical alarms and secondary guards at the exit. Nobody would be able to stop him.

The Devil's return was inevitable.

CHAPTER ONE
THE GRIMM BROTHERS

THERE IS NO SUCH thing as *happily ever after.*

The idea of so-called happy endings is nothing more than a joke—a string of words thrown together in a way that pleases the mind. Nothing more than a false rumor that managed to spread through the country like a wildfire.

All life ends with death. And in death, there is no happiness.

Fate is cruel, Destiny even more so. I knew them well. Who could ever forget their twisted smiles, bared teeth, or deranged cold eyes? Both were equipped in floor-length cloaks and elaborate ball gowns draped in lace and gems while they corrupted the futures of every naïve individual that there existed.

And humans, what can they possibly do to halt their impending doom? Their petty beliefs of fantasy and hope disgust me. Dare I say, I pity them?

No. Pity is a weak emotion in the deadly sea of life. Casting it aside like the useless waste it is—that is the only way to live. No emotion is worthy enough to wield. Especially happiness. Never happiness. Whoever trusts this false promise of something better is a fool.

I used to be one of those fools.

One of those poor souls that believed one way or another, everything would turn out all right. The end was simply another beginning. The universe was watching, and those with evil in their hearts would be punished for their wicked behavior. The passionate fires of lust and desire had addled my mind. I was no more intelligent than a simple human.

Still, round and round in circles we go. From heartless and cold, I have come back home. The passion, the light, the hope, the damned happiness—it all ended the only way it could: in bitter disappointment and self-loathing.

Never again shall I be made the fool.

I am Primrose Titan, the Goddess of Death. This is my story.

"This room is for exclusive guests only!" a short man in a red tailcoat shrieked. His gloved hands were fists, trembling in rage as he blocked the narrow doorway to my destination. The tall door behind him was locked. A key dangled from the man's belt.

I stared at him, bored with his reaction. "I am well aware."

The Gatekeeper flushed. "Then you must know, Madame, that you are not welcome! Out with you!" He made a shooing gesture and stepped threateningly toward me as if his puny human figure could do anything to stop a Goddess from getting what she wanted.

I let out a puff of air and crossed my arms. Any other invited member would kill the Gatekeeper for his ignorance. Fortunately for him, I didn't care much about attending the yearly conference.

I sensed an opportunity to escape and carefully tested the waters. "So, that means I don't have to attend?" I asked innocently, tapping my hot pink Adidas tennis shoe on the white-tiled floor.

"Exactly!"

I shrugged, looking at my fingernails. They glinted in the fluorescents of the building. "Fine. I'll take your word for it." I made my way to the glass exit of Grimm Enterprises, cautiously approaching my escape.

"Wait! Lady Primrose!" Loud, heavy footsteps followed me.

I silently cursed my poor luck and stopped in my tracks. The momentary relief accompanied by my potential retreat burned out like a candle on a cold winter night. Councilor Edgar Falls rushed to stand in the way of my path.

"Yes, Councilor?"

He bowed deeply. His graying hair and creased forehead showed his age. My left index finger twitched in irritation. His formality had been amusing the first couple of meetings, but now his behavior was aggravating. "I apologize, my lady. We have a new Gatekeeper. You must forgive him for not recognizing you."

"Is that so?" I raised an eyebrow. Ordering around a Goddess was not wise. "Am I at fault for his lack of education?"

The Councilor gritted his teeth and adjusted the red tie around his neck. Despite his frustration, the bright smile on his thin lips didn't fade. "Of course not, my lady. However, you cannot fault him for his assumptions. Your wardrobe isn't quite"—his beady eyes roamed quickly over my dress—"what someone would expect for this meeting."

I glanced down at my faded jeans and Mickey Mouse T-shirt. The Councilor himself wore an expensive black suit. A pair of silver-rimmed glasses were neatly tucked into his breast pocket, should he need to read the small print of contracts, agendas, or decrees. Councilor Falls was an exemplary model of what it meant to be professional. His bitter-smelling cologne was likely more expensive than my entire outfit.

Grimm Enterprises was the definition of lofty standards and elegance. The company building was littered with expensive details. Intricate tiles mapped the floor. Marble water fountains were posted at every corner. The stairs had a legitimate, silk red carpet lining them—not the cheap kind you could find at Target. The windows were large and square-shaped, allowing light to bounce off the pale walls, each of which held dozens of expensive paintings and pieces of art. I spotted a vase from Cairo that was worth more than the neighboring building.

Among the definition of upper class, here I was, carrying my cheap Walmart bag that bore the store's logo and dressed like a tourist. I even had the black *I Love New York* baseball cap on to complete the ensemble. "Hmm," I mused. "Perhaps, I can see your point. Though I'm not quite sure what brings on your fancy attire, Councilor."

He ran a hand over his thinning hair and lifted his tired eyes to the sky. "Lady Primrose, I have explained this to you before. These meetings are absolutely—"

"Crucial to our survival and well-being," I mimicked in a stern, baritone voice and sent him a mocking smile. "Yes, I know the mantra Erin Grimm has forced you to memorize by heart throughout your years of service. My dear Councilor, these meetings occur without fail every damned year. I doubt twelve months is enough time to ruin our entire world. But if you insist, I shall attend this"—I waved my fingers around as I struggled to describe the hours I spent here—"waste of time."

The Councilor flinched at the mention of the younger Grimm Brother. No doubt, if any servant or lower-valued individual spoke poorly of Erin Grimm, they would see the end of their days. These people failed to realize that I didn't kneel before anyone, especially not a Grimm Brother. The last thing Erin Grimm needed was a larger ego.

I spun around on my heel, and my tennis shoes squeaked irritably against the pristine flooring while the Councilor stood frozen in place, bewildered by my bluntness. Finally escaping his trance, he rushed to my side, matching both my pace and my near six-foot height.

The Gatekeeper stood aside from the ebony door. The stench of fear coated his every fiber of being. Trembling hands fumbled with his key and unlocked the door, holding it wide open. A wall of darkness, like a midnight fog, lingered in the space between this room and the next, beckoning my body to enter it.

"My ap-apologies, La-lady Primrose," the Gatekeeper said, bowing low. He stumbled over his shoes to maintain his bow.

I rolled my eyes. "Don't apologize. You almost got me out of this dreadful waste of time." I couldn't stop the attitude from trickling into my voice. This was the last place I wanted to be.

The Councilor sent the Gatekeeper a scathing glare. The smaller man flinched and cowered away from us, no longer trying to maintain the facade of the intimidating Gatekeeper he was supposed to be. Ignoring the two men and their erratic behavior, I stepped into the darkness. Once I crossed the threshold, the actual appearance of the conference room confronted me.

The abysmally large room could have fit a three-story hotel within it. The domed, marble walls stood firm, fortifying the structure and adding a Greek-like essence. Unlike the lobby of Grimm Enterprises, this portion of the building lacked decorations on the walls or in the corners. The intention was to not draw attention to the periphery of the chamber. The Round Table was near the center of the room, taking over half of the room's length. Several massive thrones were placed evenly about the table, accompanied by smaller thrones and a regular chair here and there for the mortals, like Councilor Falls. The arrangement represented the class system of the deities of the world.

A scent of cinnamon slithered through the room, like an intoxicating smoke. I crinkled my nose at the overpowering odor. Damn it, Erin. He *had* to make everything smell the way he wanted. Nothing could be left to the whims of others, nor to chance. The world would end if it didn't jump through Erin Grimm's petulant hoops.

Ignoring the silent stares of already seated attendants, I approached a colossal, midnight-black throne. The only deviation from the horrid color, or rather, the absence of color, was the red rose painted on the back of the seat.

"It's only fitting," Erin had insisted. "A rose, for Lady Primrose."

In my throne, I crossed my legs and placed my Walmart bag in my lap before removing my hat. I undid the ponytail in my hair and looped the rubber band around my wrist.

Already bored with the council meeting that had yet to start, I pulled out the book *Wuthering Heights* from my bag. My hand gently ran over the aged cover, lingering near the creases and small tears. I let my soft brown curls fall like a curtain over my face to seal me off from the rest of the room and the wandering eyes of the individuals too curious for their own good. The thick locks of hair gave me some subtle form of privacy—or at least the illusion of it.

While losing myself in the first chapter of the story, multiple High Court members entered, filling the room with light chatter and boisterous laughter. A vibrant hum reverberated across the walls and echoed into the ceiling space.

I had learned to ignore the Court members' intense gazes that landed on me each meeting without fail. Most couldn't get over the fact that I, a woman wearing a Disney T-shirt, was the Goddess of Death. In part, I couldn't blame them. A good friend of mine mentioned this preconception when describing the Goddess—or according to her, the God—of Death. In her mind, the ruler of the dead was a man. Seemed sexist and old-fashioned to me, but I had shrugged it off. The man had to be buff and tall with black hair, creepy red eyes, and wearing a cloak of darkness.

"Like the Grim Reaper from the movies," she had tried to explain.

Instead, there was me. I should have been offended by her stereotypical beliefs, but she wasn't the only one. "You just don't look like *death*," my brother, the God of Life, had claimed.

"What is *death* supposed to look like?" I had demanded. The dead could take many forms.

"Not like you. You seem... too innocent. Too alive."

In contrast, my friend claimed I had brown puppy dog eyes and that the roundness of my pale face made me appear grandmotherly and nurturing. I almost incinerated her for that. She laughed it off, claiming she was jesting. "I mean to say," my friend Elinore had interjected, "that you have delicate features. Not like a fighter, more like—"

"An elderly grandmother?"

She had giggled. "No. Like a girl who won't tell a stranger they've got ketchup on their face because she's afraid of unintentionally offending them."

Trust Elinore Fey to find the perfect way to describe everything I was not.

Hushed whispers followed a sudden silence. My eyes flew up from my book.

The Grimm Brothers were here. *Both* of them. They stood side by side, Erin Grimm taking a confident step forward, familiar with the atmosphere of the High Court. He wore his traditional predatorial smile and a bright blue Armani suit. Though slim, the younger Grimm Brother was taller than me, towering over most Court members—a trait he used as a weapon of intimidation and dominance in a political setting. The smoothness of his skin suggested a particular youth gifted to a teenager or an innocent child, but his hazel eyes cut like a knife, holding years upon years of ancient knowledge.

Erin's older brother, Atlas Grimm, I had never seen before. Legends were told, and souls gossiped, but this was the first time I was ever graced with his presence. The elder Brother Grimm never appeared at Court in the past, despite Erin's position as King of the High Court, and now that my eyes befell him, I memorized the features of a possible ally or enemy.

Though their heights were similar, their likeness ended there. Unlike Erin, his brother was more reserved—his stance more cautious. I watched him, unable to look away from his emotionally vacant face. His chiseled chin was lifted in arrogance as though perceiving himself above every member of the Court. Like every deity in the room, he didn't look a day over twenty-one, a side effect of immortality. Firm muscles and broad shoulders under his dark clothing indicated a strength Erin lacked. His dark hair held a slight curl to it, winding tastefully behind his ear. Cold blue eyes missed nothing with their calculating evaluations.

Once those piercing eyes landed on me, I instantly disliked him. His thin lips twisted in revulsion before moving on to assess another member of the Court. In his mind, I wasn't worthy of more than a second of his time. A burden gleamed in his pale gaze. My bottom lip pushed out into a disappointed pout. I couldn't read him as easily as the others.

"Great. Just what I need, more drama," I muttered and rolled my eyes. Pretending to be indifferent to my surroundings, I pushed down the heat that crept up the base of my neck. I never let anyone get to me. Not even the Grimm Brothers.

Three thumps of a staff banging against the floor signaled the beginning of the council meeting. The chatter dwindled into silence as Councilor Falls cleared his throat. His tense hand gripped the staff tightly in anticipation. "Ladies and Gentlemen of the High Court, I am to call titles, and then the meeting shall commence as per the Grimm Brothers' request." The man's weak voice echoed through the vast room.

Just keep reading, I mentally told myself as I neared the end of chapter one of *Wuthering Heights.*

"Lord Erin Grimm, King of the High Court, creator of stories, co-owner of Grimm Enterprises, and the God of Fire."

Erin stood from his golden throne, arrogantly beholding the High Court with his signature blinding smile.

"Good Fortune to thee, Lord Erin," the Court said in unison.

Luckily nobody was stubborn enough to pester me about my refusal to say the damned words and lack of direct eye contact. The last time I met his eyes, Erin Grimm felt the need to send a particularly coy wink my way.

The younger Grimm Brother sat down languidly while the Councilor continued.

"Lord Atlas Grimm, enforcer of stories, co-owner of Grimm Enterprises, and the God of Ice."

"Good Fortune to thee, Lord Atlas."

Councilor Falls introduced the remaining Gods and Goddesses of the High Court along with lower-level deities, including Ladies Fate and Destiny. The list of deities and Court members was long and tedious, but it could be worse. Despite there being thousands of deities and millions more supernatural creatures in the world, only three hundred deities made up the High Court.

Each year, members gathered to give their reports to the newly crowned King of the High Court, Erin Grimm, who attained his throne less than a century ago. Attendees filled hours upon hours with Court manners and politics accumulating to one big ego-boosting, pride-feeding rally. But could I ever get out of these meetings? Not a chance. Erin Grimm, the prodigal child of the High Court, always got what he wanted. And he never wanted the Goddess of Death to miss a conference meeting.

My eyes flitted to the vacant throne of my brother, Benjamin. As God of Life, Ben was the ruler and Gatekeeper of Elysium, a subregion of the Underworld that humans referred to as heaven or paradise. I bit the inside of my cheek hard enough to draw blood. Though Councilor Falls pestered me to remind Benjamin of the meetings, Erin could care less whether my brother was present or not.

"Your brother is a hotheaded fool," Erin once said to me in his posh British accent. "You have all the meaningful power in the family. Work a magic spell and *poof*! Someone dies."

I got his message. The meetings were his way of keeping me on a leash, albeit indirectly. A heavy breath escaped my chest as I prepared for my title to be called out. Already, I sensed the heat of a multitude of eyes bearing down on me.

"And Lady Primrose Titan, Goddess of Death, reaper of souls, Summoner of the Dead, leader and Gatekeeper of the Underworld."

"Present," I called out and kept my gaze on my book.

"Good Fortune to thee, Lady Primrose."

Bloody politics. The worst part was the condescending tone the Court held when addressing me. By God, one day, my anger would get the better of me, and I would go to war with them all. Until then, I defaulted to what I did best. Withdraw. Create a shield. Appear bored, disinterested, cold. This was the only way to outmaneuver them, the only way to come out on top.

Councilor Falls seated himself in a frail, ordinary chair next to the mighty throne of Erin Grimm. The human man cleared his throat. "With the Grimm Brothers' consent, this meeting is now in session."

CHAPTER TWO
AT LAST

ONE BY ONE, EACH attendee was called upon to speak. Yearly reports weren't meant to be formal or long-lived. Any honest, straightforward deity knew a minute was more than sufficient to update the Grimm Brothers on everything that had taken place over the past twelve months, mostly because changes hardly ever occurred. But supernatural beings were hardly honest or straightforward.

Erin Grimm, however, was a magnet for the truth. It was easy for him to decipher the fancy BS that High Court members loved to craft and interpret it in actual words of meaning. For supernatural deities, verbal manipulation was a game, even a competition. Who could make their point in the most nonsensical manner while being somewhat understood? A statement said in the High Court rarely meant what it sounded like. Double meanings, impossibly high standards, and two-faced Court members were no rarity in this room.

The verbal reports droned on and on like the annoying buzz of an air conditioner, and I was dreadfully close to finishing *Wuthering*

Heights. The twenty-ninth chapter came to an end, but the meeting showed no sign of ending.

"... indeed, I see. Lady Primrose, what is the state of the Underworld?"

I turned the crinkled page of the book, tempted to ignore Erin's question, but decided against it. "All is well. The number of dead is increasing as predicted, and the balances between life and death are as they should be. Souls are no more difficult to collect, nor are they any more secretive than usual. Per my reapers' updates, our management and operations in the Underworld have been conducted successfully over the past twelve months."

"Can you produce any evidence to support your claims?"

A drop of unexpectedness touched me. My nose wrinkled. I lowered the book gently to my lap and met the icy eyes of Atlas Grimm. "I beg your pardon?"

"Can you produce any evidence?" He repeated his question, enunciating his words as if speaking to a child. He set his lips in a hard, unwavering line and impatiently waited for my reply.

I raised an eyebrow. "Call it a gut feeling."

"That's not a reliable source."

The silence in the room was as palpable as the overwhelming scent of cinnamon. I sent a fleeting glance at Erin to catch his reaction, but the younger Grimm Brother shrugged his shoulders in amusement with my predicament. Atlas was becoming more irritating every time he opened his mouth. Like a door that wouldn't shut right.

"Why do you need evidence?" I asked, keeping my tone as neutral as possible. Perhaps his intentions were innocent enough.

Atlas narrowed his eyes and lifted his chin arrogantly. "How else do we know that you are not misleading us?"

The High Court held its breath.

"Careful, Lord Atlas," I warned. "I wouldn't let Erin's title as King of the High Court get to your head. Last I checked, before you killed the former Goddess of Ice a century ago, you were nobody important."

"Now, now, Lady Primrose," Erin quickly intervened and smiled in his charming way. "There's no need to become upset. My brother asked a fair question. It's difficult to establish the accuracy of everything you tell us."

"How about some trust?" I demanded.

Atlas scoffed. "Trust—"

"What my sister means to say is that we've never been asked for evidence before."

I almost jumped right out of my throne. At the doorway of the conference room stood my brother Benjamin, the God of Life. His brown hair had grown out since I last saw him, and he had purple bruises under his eyes from exhaustion. A hint of stubble had formed at the base of his chin. Ben's taste in fashion was as sensible as mine. He wore a green Hawaiian shirt and khaki shorts. A pair of Birkenstock sandals completed the disastrous ensemble.

My eyebrows pulled together, and I bit my lip. I fidgeted in my seat and bent the corner of the book page I was on. Ben *never* attended meetings. Never.

Something was wrong. Something terrible enough to capture the attention of not only Atlas Grimm but my brother as well. My palms were sweaty at the thought of what could have happened. Was Ben in some kind of trouble?

My brother's eyes met mine, and he gave a wry smile. "Hey, Rosy. Long time, no see."

"Ben." I swallowed the lump in my throat. Blood rushed to my face at his cheesy nickname for me. "Has the world ended, or is it about to?"

The God of Life gave a heartless laugh. "You know me too well, sister." He approached the thrones, subtly refusing to sit in his, and instead leveled his piercing gaze on Atlas Grimm. "Listen closely, God of Ice. Instead of grilling my sister for evidence on something as trivial as her yearly report, all focus should be on the crisis at hand."

The Grimm Brothers conversed silently for a second. How ironic, fire and ice knew each other so well. Their minds were in sync, surely due to the elder brother's hidden gift.

Both brothers directed their gazes toward Ben.

"What crisis?" Erin probed, his ever-present smile now absent from his face.

"You know perfectly well what crisis."

"I doubt it," Atlas said, and my brother narrowed his eyes.

Ah, there it was. A chink in the armor, a weak link in the chain. Erin and his brother were hiding a secret from the High Court. A malicious smile warped my soft pink lips as I leaned forward, placing my elbows onto the table, fingers neatly intertwined. My, my, the Grimm Brothers were quite naughty these days. What were they concealing from the High Court this time?

My brother's heavy breaths were the only sound in the room for a serious moment. "The Demon King, Lucifer, has escaped from Hell."

Gasps and surprised whispers echoed across the room. All emotion dropped from my face as it drained of color. My blood ran cold.

"So," my brother said, scrutinizing my reaction, "you should really be asking my sister about the security of her prison system in Hell, considering she's in charge of that particular subregion of the Underworld."

The conference room burst into chaos. Deities sprung from their chairs and conversations escalated to loud screaming matches. Frozen, I tried to process Ben's words. The Demon King escaped. My head was feverish yet light. Drops of sweat slid down my skin. Much time passed since I felt true fear. Lucifer's name brought it back like a wave of deadly vengeance.

"Quiet," Erin Grimm ordered. "Let's not devolve into hysteria just yet."

The room went silent, and the accusing gazes of the High Court pierced me like a hot poker. "As we know," Erin continued, "the Devil is mad. He attempted to overthrow multiple deities and treasonously plotted against the High Court. We wouldn't want such a thing to happen again, Lady Primrose. I'm sure you understand."

The High Court awaited my reaction with poorly concealed anticipation. They wanted confirmation I hadn't set Lucifer free. Though I wanted nothing more than to annoy the petty, insignificant lives of the deities seated in this scented, elegant room, freeing Lucifer was not an option. His escape harmed me more than anyone else.

Claustrophobia was theoretically impossible in a room the size of a hotel, yet I was suffocating under the pressure of hundreds of expectant eyes. Though the Court members wouldn't remain patient much longer, I stole a moment to restore my composure, breathing in through the nose, out through the mouth. The beating of my heart slowed. My eyes glazed into boredom, and my heart distanced itself from every being in the room.

I chose my next words carefully. "Are you certain he has escaped?"

Ben's forehead creased. "I have no reason to lie."

"His prison is well guarded. I have every right to contest a claim so outlandish as this, especially in the High Court."

"He appeared before me."

Shocked, I stood from my throne. My book and bag fell to the floor with a loud thump. All concern about maintaining a relaxed and collected appearance evaporated. "What?"

Ben approached the Round Table. "You heard me. After throwing my castle into chaos and killing many of my loyal servants, he left a message for you."

The beating of my heart quickened.

"What did he want?" Erin Grimm asked.

"To make her pay," Ben said, looking me dead in the eye, "and to finish what he started, but along with that, he wants her."

"What could he possibly want with her?" Erin asked.

Ben gritted his teeth and inclined his head toward me. "Why don't you ask her yourself?"

Great. The gazes of the High Court pierced me once more. I lifted my chin. "Before I imprisoned him, Lucifer was in search of a queen to rule his doomed attempt at an empire. He found me suitable. I refused."

"Oh, but you did more than refuse his advances," my brother seethed. "You refused any sort of negotiation and declared war on him."

"Negotiation?" I wasn't senseless enough to make a deal with the Devil. Even *humans*, in all their ignorance, knew better. "I don't negotiate," I said. "He didn't take no for an answer, so I hunted him down, fought him, won, and imprisoned him. I have no reason to free him."

"Why not kill him?" Atlas asked thinly.

"Gee, why hadn't I thought about that? Just kill him. Easy, right?" I scowled. "You can't kill the Demon King any easier than killing one of us. If he hadn't broken our laws, he would have had a throne here"—I pointed to the empty space next to me—"in this very room, with the rest of the High Court. I couldn't find his Soul Dagger. Only he knows where it is. As each of us is aware of where our own daggers are. Lucifer may be rash, but he wasn't stupid or naïve enough to share the location with me. And no, at that time, I didn't feel the need to go on a wild goose hunt for an unnecessary dagger."

The tension in the room tightened around me, like elastic. My toes curled. Even *I*, the Goddess of Death, couldn't reap the Devil's soul without knowing the location of his dagger. Granted, anyone could kill a deity using the proper Soul Dagger—I happened to be better at doing it than anyone else in the room.

I sat back down on my throne. "I'll take care of him."

"How can we be assured of that?" Atlas asked.

My fists clenched while my heart raced. Ben sent me a glance that said, 'cool it.' Atlas Grimm's soul was painfully easy to grasp. Fortunately for him, his Soul Dagger was not in my possession. Otherwise, our conversation would be very different right now. I dropped my scowl and let the silence engulf Atlas's words. The Devil was my problem. I didn't care about assuring anyone of anything.

Atlas's unfriendly gaze cut into my chest. The temperature in the room dropped. "All right." He coolly stood from his throne and adjusted the collar of his black coat. "To ensure that you thoroughly complete the task at hand, I shall accompany you."

I blanched and pursed my lips to keep from complaining aloud. Atlas's posture was stubborn; his words were final. He wouldn't change his mind.

I crouched underneath the table to pick up *Wuthering Heights* and my bag, stuffing one into the other. I placed the bag on the glass table, took out my *I Love New York* baseball cap, and plopped it on my head.

Ben made a noise somewhere between a snort and a laugh. In times like this, he appreciated a good dose of sass.

I smiled maliciously at Atlas. "I see. If you wish to accompany me, I cannot dissuade you. We leave at dawn."

With a dramatic flip of my hair and a twirl, I made my way to the exit. The grumbles and screeching of flimsy chairs signaled the informal end of the meeting. Several deities had yet to give their reports, but after the excitement of Lucifer's escape, nobody cared to hear anything else. Knowing my brother was watching, I tipped my hat and signaled the number two. Surely, he knew when and where to meet me.

"Thorn!"

Do not incinerate Lord Atlas Grimm, I chanted to myself. *It will not do you well.*

"Thorn!" Atlas called out again.

I gave an exaggerated sigh and stopped a few steps away from the ebony door of the conference room. A freezing hand landed on my shoulder. "Listen, Thorn."

"Primrose," I corrected, swatting his hand away from my shoulder. "Lady Primrose to you."

Insensitive eyes told me how much he cared when it came to saying my name correctly. "That name is entirely deceiving for the Goddess of Death."

A brittle laugh escaped my breath. "No offense, Brother Grimm, in no way are you"—I poked his chest—"in any place to judge appearance versus reality." Especially since if anyone googled *Grimm Brothers*, they'd get some photos of random, creepy old men.

Atlas grinned, though his eyes echoed a discrete annoyance at my touch. "I won't argue with you on that. Though you should know, my name isn't Brother Grimm. It's Atlas. Lord Atlas to you." His rugged accent held a British twang to it but was nowhere near as sophisticated as his brother's.

I folded my arms across my chest. Okay, if he wanted to play a name game, I could play. "Atlas?" I pondered aloud with an airy, preppy-dumb-girl voice. "Like the book of maps and charts?"

Atlas's eyes darkened, and he took a step closer to me, using his considerable height to tower over me.

I let my index finger rest lightly on my chin as though I were in deep contemplation. My eyes widened in mock realization. "Oh! You mean Atlas as in the incompetent man that held the sky?"

The Grimm Brother relaxed, and the tension seeped from his strong muscles. "Yes, you know of the legend?"

I smirked, this close to tweaking his perfectly straight nose. I dropped the dumb-blond voice. "What stupid deal got you into that poor position?"

"I see you aren't easily impressed," Atlas said. Humor coated his frosty eyes. "One way or another, I'll find out how you tick, *Rosy*."

Forget tweaking that perfect nose. I was going to break it. If this man owned an ancient vase from Cairo, he could afford a nose job. "Lady Primrose, moron. Say it with me, won't you? Prim-rose." I pronounced my name carefully and loudly. "You're lucky I'm letting you tag along with me on my hunt for Lucifer."

"You don't have much choice in the matter."

"Seriously?" I laughed bitterly. "You gain political power in the High Court by becoming the new God of Ice, and all of the sudden you think you can order people like me around. Think again. Death is ancient. I've been around much longer than you. Back when you were nothing but a measly Grimm Brother with the power of enforcing stories, you were an insignificant political member with limited access to the High Court. Meanwhile, I was waging wars against the most powerful deities that have existed. To me, you're still a babe. A child playing an adult's game. Oh, don't get me wrong, I won't stop you from joining the game, I only wish you the best of luck. See you at dawn, At Last." I misspoke his name with a mischievous smile on my lips.

I reached for the doorknob when a growling noise sounded behind me. "Where will we meet?" Atlas's question was strained and spoken through gritted teeth.

The antique, ebony door swung wide open. With a flourish of my arm, I gestured at the immense conference room. "Right here."

With a sloppy wink and a nasty smile, I slammed the door shut. People in the lobby of Grimm Enterprises flinched at the loud sound. Shoving past a taller man in a red tailcoat, I realized Councilor Falls recruited a new Gatekeeper before the meeting's formal start. My fists clenched in irritation. He probably had the new Gatekeeper memorize my picture for future reference. Arrogant prick.

A light buzz from my Walmart bag, followed by Britney Spears's "Toxic," signaled the ringing of my phone. Ignoring the arrogant scoffs and glares of the surrounding *elegant, upper-class* High Court members and Grimm Enterprises employees, I fished out my neon green iPhone and stared at it, frozen.

One name flashed on the screen: *Lucifer.*

I felt the rush of adrenaline before the paralysis of panic. Dozens of emotions threw me into a temporary fluster. My stomach heaved. The phone call was too soon, too planned. I wasn't ready to face the man that had brought utter chaos into my life. Heat burned my forehead and the back of my neck. A strange sound rang through my ears. My spine was heavy and close to dragging me down to the ground with its weight. But the moment passed, as did the rushed heartbeat and shallow breaths. The Goddess of Death feared nothing, nor did she fall subject to something as trivial as an emotion. The heat of my skin cooled. And just like that, the numbness, the indifference, like a USB being inserted into a computer, reprogrammed my thoughts.

Either this was a prank call, some different being whose caller ID happened to be Lucifer, or this was the real deal. If it was truly him, he wouldn't stop calling if I didn't answer. Obsessive was a suitable word for describing the Devil.

Seconds before the call defaulted to my automated voicemail, I pressed the answer button and brought the phone to my ear. "Hello?"

CHAPTER THREE
BROTHERLY ADVICE

FOR A MOMENT, ALL was silent.

And then...

"Hello?" A woman on the other side of the phone spoke. I strained my ears to hear her voice. "Hello?" she repeated, louder this time.

Last I checked, Lucifer wasn't a woman. My shoulders were lighter hearing the stranger's voice, and the pressure inside my chest lessened. "Yes? Who is this? How did you get my number?"

Silence. I almost ended the call before the next words rushed out of the woman's mouth. "Oh, thank God! I didn't know who else to turn to. I need your help! You are m-my last hope. The last sun shall set upon me t-tonight, and Death shall find her m-master," she said, weeping into the phone.

The hair on the back of my neck stood up. Blood rushed to my face. Warning bells went off like a fire alarm in my mind. I recognized her words.

"Please! You've got to help me! Oh, God! Please—"

Scuffling and the slicing of a blade meeting flesh interrupted her desperate pleas. Metal tearing through flesh made a particular sound if done quickly enough. A clean noise, like a knife cutting through an apple—but with a gross sloshing of red liquid accompanying it. A small ripple wrenched through my body. One of my reapers had taken a soul.

A face flashed before me. Then came the woman's pain and the fear she experienced before her death.

Vivian Erikson, twenty-two years of age, red hair, blue eyes, three kids, widowed, nurse, Care Hospital, Boston, Massachusetts—

I squeezed my eyes shut, and the onslaught of information ended. The rest of Vivian Erikson's life was lost in the wind. People died every day, every hour, every damn second. Over my many years as the Goddess of Death, I learned how to push the memories from my thoughts. But Vivian's death felt different, meaningful.

My mouth was dry. Still in the lobby of Grimm Enterprises, the clinical scent of the room made the sick sensation in my stomach grow. I needed fresh air.

Forcing my stiff feet to move, I sprinted to the glass door and shoved it open, still clutching my phone to my ear. The burst of air that filled my lungs cleared the slimy feeling coursing through my veins.

"Hello, Rose," came a familiar voice on the other end of the phone, and I shuddered. His deep voice was filled with the memories that we shared together. Memories I wished to forget.

I licked my lips. "Lucifer, I didn't realize cell phone service was so good in Hell."

The Demon King laughed. "Oh, Rose. How I have missed you. Did you enjoy the show I put on earlier? Do the words ring any bells?"

My face burned, and I struggled to form the angry words that poisoned the tip of my tongue. Vivian Erikson was a simple human, an unlucky nobody Lucifer picked off the street to send a stark message to me. She spoke to me the words I wrote in a letter to the Devil years ago. The letter that led him into my trap in Hell. I lured him away from the safety of his army, knowing he would do anything to save me from whatever doom came my way. His fiery eyes had revealed how betrayed he felt when I turned my sword on him.

Did the words ring any bells? "Not particularly," I lied breezily. "Tell me, what has my brother done to offend you?"

"Ah, still protective of Mister Elysium, I see."

I bit my lip and tasted blood. "What is the point of this call, Lucifer?"

Silence.

I waited. The Devil knew what tense silence did to my nerves. Waiting a few seconds more was the equivalent of pouring salt over an open wound.

"You hurt me," he said. Though he didn't convey a sense of enmity, his accusation was as clear as day. "I will hurt you back."

"Good," I countered, clutching the phone tighter. "Don't hold back this time, demon."

"You seem awfully relieved," Lucifer said. His sinister voice grappled with my nerves. "I don't believe you understand my intentions, darling. I will make you my queen. But first, some manners need to be taught."

His words left me cold inside.

Lucifer's malicious laughter rang through the phone. His low voice grated against my ears. "You thought I could hate you so easily? No, beloved. I shall always hold you dear to my heart."

"That would imply you have a heart," I snapped.

"Tsk, tsk." The Demon King scolded with a smile in his voice. "There's no need to be rude, Rose."

"Listen, psychopath, in case you didn't get the memo last time, I want nothing to do with you! Can't you pick some other Goddess to be your queen? Literally anyone but me."

Metal clanged on his side of the phone, and he sighed as if disappointed. "That would defeat the entire purpose now, wouldn't it? Any other Goddess would be weaker than you. I chose you for your strength, my love."

Unable to listen to his voice any longer, I ended the call and shoved the phone into my Walmart bag, a breath away from smashing it to pieces on the sidewalk.

Staring at the blinding sun, I cursed my poor luck. The sky was a flawless blue, and the looming clouds from this morning drifted uptown. The heat was an unbearable ninety-eight degrees, but I preferred it to the cold inside my chest. A cold that could only be created by a monster.

Hunting down Lucifer in the middle of summer with the God of Ice on my derriere was not at the top of my agenda. In a metaphorical sense, destiny had its plans.

Good thing I had one, too.

I crossed through the multitude of pedestrians walking on the sidewalk and stepped out into the road, startling a taxi driver into a sudden stop. The yellow car's tires screeched, and an insistent honking commenced.

"Are you crazy, lady?" the enraged New Yorker at the wheel yelled. He leaned his head out of the open window to get a better look at what I would do next.

Not in the mood to respond, I gripped the grubby door handle tightly and forced the car door open. I slid into the back seat. "The closest Starbucks." The door slammed shut. "Pronto."

The taxi driver turned his head to look at me, flustered. "Look, lady. I'm off for today."

I fished through the purple leather wallet in my bag and handed him a few crumpled hundred-dollar bills. "This should do it."

The man gaped at the cash with wide eyes. "Yes, ma'am."

I didn't have time to buckle my seat belt before the cab's motor sprang to life. The driver surged into the heavy traffic, honking and swerving through other cars. I gave up with the seat belt; it wouldn't do much good the way this man was driving anyway. I relaxed against the worn-out, leather car seats. Though the cab had a strong odor, my stomach stopped churning the more distance we put between Grimm Enterprises and myself.

A nagging thought spun in my mind like an annoying fly. How *did* Lucifer escape? Or better yet, where would he go next? The Devil wouldn't return to Hell. He wouldn't make it that easy for me. Leaving the Underworld was a no-brainer on his part, which meant he could be anywhere right now. For some reason, the Demon King was in Boston, picked Vivian, a random stranger on the street, and murdered her. Lucifer would be long gone by the time I made it to Boston tomorrow with Atlas in tow. Nonetheless, the hunt had to begin somewhere.

A car rushed past the back of the taxi, nearly taking out the battered bumper. The cab bounced up and down as we sped through the intersection, blazing through a red light.

"Are you trying get us killed?" I asked the driver. I held tightly to the seat in front of me as we narrowly missed crashing into another car.

The taxi driver shrugged, as the cab swerved to the side of the road near the crowded sidewalk. We came to a rough stop, and the right side of the taxi bounced up onto the sidewalk, almost taking out a stroller. My hands were the only thing stopping me from face-planting the back of the rusty passenger seat.

"We're here," the driver said.

I grumbled a thank-you and threw the door open. I was barely out of the taxi when the motor roared, and the driver sped off like a madman. Was he worried I would ask for change?

I shook my head. Humanity's greed for money made no sense to me. Maybe that was a side effect of living in the Underworld. Death was a major equalizer. Once a person died, their soul passed on to the Underworld.

However, if summoned back to the human realm, a soul pieces together the body that they had before they died. When I summoned the dead to the human realm, they came as they had appeared when they had been alive. Still, their minds were practically worthless. The bodies were like puppets, ready to listen to the Queen of the Underworld regardless of their personality or beliefs.

Shaking my head once more to clear my thoughts, I stared up at the Starbucks sign. On their own accord, my legs made their way to the café. A ding sounded as I opened the door, and the beautifully intoxicating scent of caffeine surrounded me warmly, like an embrace.

Ben was seated in a comfortable nook, a tea in his hands. The soft wood and plush couches made for a welcoming environment.

Yet judging by his crouched posture and the intensity with which my brother watched my every move, Ben had much to say. Our conversation would not be pleasant.

I hesitated near the door and considered ditching Ben while I could. I decided against it and approached the counter to order a cappuccino. A blond teenager took my order at a snail's pace, fumbling with the different keys and buttons on the cash register. Her green uniform was stained with coffee, and strands of hair had fallen from her messy ponytail.

"I'm new," she said sheepishly.

I grabbed a brown paper napkin from the dispenser and grimaced in reply. I waited a few steps away for the coffee to be prepped. Ben's foot tapped impatiently on the dark tile.

"Cappuccino for Primrose," the teenage girl called out.

I moved to receive my warm cup of coffee. Though my dread for the impending conversation with Ben weighed me down as dozens of chains would, making him wait any longer would be a mistake. The God of Life was like a hybrid between the high school quarterback and the school superintendent. Most times, Ben was cool, arrogant, snarky. A complete bum, but one that everyone loved. However, every once in a while, his words cut like a scalpel, dissecting the problem and forcefully shoving the solution down the victim's throat.

I slid into the nook my brother sat in, placing my cup on the table. I refused to let go of the drink. I hoped the heat of the coffee warmed the coldness from my encounter with Lucifer.

Ben reached out and plucked my *I Love New York* cap off my head, letting it fall upside down on the table. His lighthearted actions didn't fool me. He wanted the hat off to see my face better. To read my emotions. I shrugged off the Walmart bag from my shoulder.

"Rosy, Rosy, Rosy," my brother chanted.

"Benji, Benji, Benji," I echoed, knowing he hated my nickname for him as much as I hated his nickname for me.

I half-expected a Starbucks employee to jump out and say, "Marcia, Marcia, Marcia," followed by harmonious laughter of spectators. Unfortunately, all I received was an exasperated sigh from my brother. He moved his tea aside so that he could rest his elbows on the table.

"Listen, sister. This isn't the time for you to play dumb or run your way around the problem. You know why I came here today."

I took a small sip of the coffee, burning my tongue in the process. I leaned back into the chair, taking up a pensive posture. "You believe I had something to do with Lucifer's release and plan on becoming his queen."

Ben slammed his fist violently against the table. "Be serious, Primrose. We both know that's not true."

I flinched. He rarely ever used my full first name. Whenever he did, it meant trouble.

His shoulders moved up and down as he took deep, calming breaths. "I don't mean to upset you, but I need to know what's happening. Something has been wrong for a while now, and I want to know why."

I set my coffee down. He wasn't referring to Lucifer's escape. "I'm not sure I understand. What do you want to know, Ben?"

"The truth. When was the last time you visited the Underworld?"

His purposeful question caught me off guard. I focused my attention on his Hawaiian shirt to avoid meeting his eyes. "Two days ago. Why?"

Ben leaned in closer, refusing to let me get off easy. "Rosy, I spend most of my time in Elysium. It's my realm. It needs my care and protection. Your realm is larger and more vulnerable, yet your stays away from the Underworld have increased in length over the course of time. You only go when bringing in a powerful soul yourself. It's like you think the place is diseased!"

It is a disease, I wanted to say. *And it's getting stronger as it grows.* Instead, I kept my mouth shut and schooled my facial expressions. I figured one day Ben would bring up this concern, especially after the incident last month. Still, his reaction was stronger than I expected.

"I have an army of reapers who guide souls into the Underworld," I said. "You know how this works. If I personally reap a soul at this exact moment, it will slip into the depths of the Underworld, guided by one of my reapers. The Underworld is like a magnet. Once reaped, a soul immediately latches onto the Underworld on its own. We guide the souls to make sure nothing goes wrong, to make sure each soul ends up in the right place." I meticulously placed a napkin under my coffee to avoid my brother's eyes.

Ben's nostrils flared. "Come on, Rosy! Things go wrong all the time! If they didn't, humans wouldn't have any inspiration for their horror stories. When powerful souls get trapped in the human realm—"

"Don't you think I know that?" I snapped. "But you said so yourself, only powerful souls require carefully supervised entry into the Underworld, and guess what? When powerful souls are concerned, I *always* ensure the transition takes place smoothly. If any mistakes occur, I *always* fix them." I traced my fingers over the smooth texture of my coffee cup. "Trust me, I can take care of the Underworld."

"Right," Ben drawled, "which is why the Devil is on the loose."

Fidgeting in my seat, I calculated the potential reaction my next words would exact. I leaned forward, getting into his personal space before I could talk myself out of asking. "What is Elysium like?"

"How is this related—"

"Just answer the question," I interrupted. My voice sounded too hopeful, even to my ears. A genuine curiosity for a glimpse into paradise drove my inquisition. Perhaps to get a taste of what it was like to see someone rise instead of fall.

Ben's eyebrows knit together in deep contemplation. My brother realized how important his response was. Ben might be tough to handle, but he was just as loving. He cared about my well-being, more than he should. His lips parted. "It's a paradise, as advertised," he said. "People with souls of gold migrate there and are reunited with their memories—only the happy ones. Elysium supplies them with a new body. One that is improved. They experience what they only would in their fantastic dreams." He shrugged. "There isn't much to say. I make sure everything runs smoothly, that the proper souls enter, and nothing else comes in to disturb the peace."

"Ah, now see, that's not how the rest of the Underworld is like." Spite coated each word as it left my bitter mouth.

Ben tried to backpedal. "I know—"

"No, you don't!"

A few customers openly stared at us after hearing my raised voice.

Gritting my teeth, I sank back down into my seat and kept my hands away from my coffee, afraid that their quivering would spill the warm liquid. "You know *nothing*. You are a naïve observer from a distance, and that is not the same," I said in a low voice, shaking my head. "The Underworld is full of lost souls. These people have done nothing particularly evil, but since they aren't *saints*, they wander around like fragments in the wind with no joy or pain. There is absolutely nothing."

"I don't understand. If there is *absolutely nothing*, then what's the problem?" my brother asked. His eyes held an earnest desire to understand.

The wall of glass that regularly kept me calm and distant shattered. "Let me tell you what the problem is, Ben. Whether I reap a soul or one of my reapers does it, I see that person before they die." My voice was harsh and curt. "I feel their joy, pain, or fear—no emotion escapes me. Look at these people around us!" I gestured to the Starbucks customers who had their faces glued to their computers or phones. "When they die—and they will—I see their lives, their pasts, and their potential futures. Then, a second later, everything changes. Almost *nothing* is left of them. Do you know how mentally degrading that is? To see what they could have become if they hadn't died?"

The God of Life was silent, knowing better than to interrupt me at this point.

I looked away from his searching eyes, hurt by his lack of awareness and ashamed that he felt the need to sympathize. "Worse off, you're not the one in charge of Hell." I reached out to hold Ben's hands. "Yes, the souls in Hell get their memories back. They get a body, too. But there is no damn paradise. Hell is a place of pain, punishment, horror. Lucifer was the easiest part of Hell to manage because he was in one of the so-called impenetrable cells. Any other soul is fully exposed to the land, and the land is a never-ending nightmare that breaks those poor wretches apart, over and over again.

"Maybe they deserve it." I sighed and glared down at the table. "Maybe that first time they're torn apart is a worthy punishment for the crime they committed, but for them to be punished again and again without end? Is there no mercy?" I let out a shaky breath. "You want to know the truth?"

"Yes," Ben said immediately.

"Then here it is. I hate the Underworld. I visit when I need to, but otherwise, I stay the hell away. If you knew what it was truly like, you would, too." The heaviness in the air evaporated, and the tension melted. I let go of Ben's hands and retreated back into my cocoon. My facial muscles slackened, and my eyes glazed back to indifference. The previously shattered glass of composure somehow became whole again. I relaxed back into my chair, lifting the cappuccino to my lips to take another sip before the coffee lost its warmth.

Ben slowly massaged his temples. "Rosy, you're right. I can't possibly imagine what the rest of the Underworld is like, given I've never been to your side of the realm. But it's still your kingdom! Can you imagine a world where death is wild and uncontrolled? The rules must be enforced!"

"That's why I'm here."

My brother gave me the stink eye. "Right."

I smiled. "How else is Lucifer going to get back in his cage, dear brother?"

"Lucifer has something up his sleeve," he said, tapping his fingers on the table. "It won't be as easy as last time."

I shrugged. "Last time wasn't easy either. No doubt this time won't be as smooth since Frosty the Snowman is on my case, but I'll figure it out."

Ben's eyes grew wide, and his laughter rumbled through the Starbucks. Several customers sent curious glances or threatening glares our way, but he didn't care. That's the thing about Ben. One moment he's hot, the other he's cold—and I wouldn't have him any other way. Even the Goddess of Death couldn't help but feel the most trivial of emotions toward her sibling: love.

"Frosty the... I like that," he said, wheezing, still chuckling. "You know, that may actually be a good thing."

I grunted in disbelief.

"No, really, Rosy. Think about it. The Devil won't see him coming. Having a Grimm Brother at your side isn't a terrible strategy."

I slipped my Walmart bag back around my shoulder. "He's going to slow me down."

The God of Life grinned. "He'll catch up."

I doubted it. I'm sure my expression didn't mask my disbelief, but there had been too much excitement and argument for today. I had a limited reserve of feelings after such an emotional morning. It took a lot to exhaust me physically, but I couldn't say the same about my emotional strength.

It was all Lucifer's damn fault, him and what happened a month ago. Not that I wanted to address *that* at this moment.

I slid out of the nook and grabbed my hat. "Goodbye, Ben." I tipped my hat in farewell and made my way to the exit.

"See you later, Rosy."

The moment I was out of the café, I pulled out my cell phone to make a call. The number was saved to my contacts under an alias listed in all caps. He answered on the first ring.

"Yes?"

"Start up the forge again, Vulcan." I lifted my gaze, fixing the sun with a steely glare. "Lucifer has escaped. And I need a weapon."

CHAPTER FOUR
METRO OF DOOM

A **COOL BREEZE SWEPT** along the back of my neck and lifted strands of my hair chaotically. The chill sent a shudder of excitement down my back. Tight, flexible material surrounded my long legs, the color matching the black tank top and leather jacket I wore. A pair of daggers lined my belt, and two other pairs were hidden in my jacket. A long, slender sword was sheathed and strapped to my back. The blade was light and easy to wield, the metal enchanted to be the strongest in existence. Sharp heels supported my weight, the stilettos a licensed weapon in their own right. I killed a man once by shoving the heel through his eye.

Today, I was a huntress. And I looked the part.

I entered the Grimm Enterprises skyscraper as I had yesterday. The classical music hadn't started playing yet. Everything was dark and empty inside. Without any movement or sound, the building was lifeless. Most employees arrived at eight. It was six in the morning, but tourists were bursting at the seams outside. Deities and humans were always out of sync. A few hours behind or ahead of one another, but sadly never on the same page.

Atlas stood near the door, conversing with his younger brother. They were standing close, barely an inch apart, as they discussed what appeared to be an important, solemn topic.

The thumping of the entrance door shutting loudly attracted the combined attentions of the brothers. Their hushed conversation came to a hasty end as the Grimm Brothers took a simultaneous step back from each other, as if caught doing something they shouldn't have. Both did double takes at my appearance.

I crossed my arms over my chest, a defensive shield from their invasive gazes. "Are we going or not?"

Erin was the first to regain his composure. He straightened his tie and smiled radiantly. His eyes roamed slowly over every inch of my body as if he planned to draw it from memory later. I stifled a disgusted shiver.

"My, my, Primrose! You clean up nicely!" he said and walked toward me. His brother shadowed him closely.

Though Erin wore his traditional expensive suit and tie, his brother wore his custom battle-wear. Dark, lightweight armor lined areas of the black jacket he wore over a simple shirt and jeans. The metal blended with the shade of his clothing, concealing it from view.

"Lucifer killed a woman in Boston yesterday." I ignored Erin's futile attempt at flattery and eyed Atlas. "That is where the search for Lucifer will begin."

"I almost think you've been playing me the fool this entire time," Erin continued and narrowed his eyes. "The true Goddess of Death is now before me. Where has she been for the last century?"

I gave him a blank stare, not knowing how to answer his question. I gestured with my head to the door and, placing my hands into my pockets, I spun around to exit the building. "I will wait outside for five minutes—no more."

Outside, I took a few lazy steps toward a small crowd of tourists, snapping photos of the Grimm Enterprises building. The tour guide wore a worn-out T-shirt with the words "Joe's Tour Group" printed across the front. The people with him, who were clearly not native to New York, wore heavy backpacks, *I Love New York* T-shirts, and baseball caps. Many held Sony cameras and trendy iPhones, which were surely accompanied by wallets full of Benjamins.

The corner of my lips lifted. I knew about these tours. Men from outside of the city came in and gave sham tours. They didn't have any approval or paperwork to do so, but that didn't stop them. People like "Joe" ached for an extra buck and didn't mind taking advantage of others. Inevitably, naïve tourists paid the fake tour guides ridiculous sums of money to get bogus tours.

The tour guide spotted me. His dull eyes lit up with obvious greed. He wiped the side of his crooked nose with the back of his hand and led the crowd toward me.

I wrinkled my nose in distaste. Great. Maybe I should've waited inside. Where was that dreadful Grimm Brother when I needed him?

The crowd moved like a blob, stirring behind Joe, who sauntered toward me. "Good morning!" he greeted, his yellowing teeth bared into a grand smile. "The crowd and I were wondering if you happened to be an employee of Grimm Enterprises?"

Grimm Enterprises was a famous entertainment company notoriously centered on fantasy stories. They produced films, books, TV shows, video games, even cheap merchandise like action figures and board games that could be found at Walmart. The company employed hundreds of thousands of people ranging from actors and directors to managers and accountants across the world. The stories they directed for their movies and shows stemmed from real life. Erin Grimm had the astounding ability to create stories. He could take a look into the future and see potential outcomes for a real individual's life.

Atlas enforced the stories. He made sure the characters—real people with real lives—followed their exact roles to perfection, without rebellion. Since Erin loved cooking up twisted drama, he always selected the most outlandish and uncharacteristic ending possible for the few poor souls he picked on. The public loved the stories.

The company stock was always growing, and everyone wanted a piece of the action, which was why Grimm Enterprises' popularity expanded with every passing day. Popularity was the Grimm Brothers' clean path of avoiding unnecessary conflict with humans. How could humans ever suspect this *beloved* company of being run by supernatural beings?

I smirked and crossed my arms. "Am I an employee?" I turned my head to gaze at the sixty-story building behind me. "No, can't say that I am."

Joe visibly deflated, and the crowd lost interest as murmurs rose. The tour guide started randomly spewing facts about the company and moved his hands animatedly to engage his unimpressed audience. He sent me another brief glance and rubbed the back of his head. "Are you sure you don't work here?"

"I'm sure. I'm more of a business partner than an employee."

The man stepped into my personal space. My nose twitched when the scent of musky cheap cologne hit me. "Have you met the CEOs?"

"Yeah. Complete pricks."

His eyes grew wide while the crowd gasped as though I said something ludicrously scandalous.

"You can't possibly mean to insult—"

"Yes, I can. Now get out of my space or I'll call the cops," I threatened.

Joe puffed up his chest like a rooster. "For what?"

"For your sham tours," I said, eyeing him. "Unless you have any paperwork giving you operating permission as a tour guide, you just might find yourself in a sticky situation, Joe."

The fake tour guide's eyes widened. Turning around like he had been zapped by lightning, Joe ushered the crowd away from me and toward a toy store across the street. He wasn't going to wait until I decided to call the police.

A whiff of a clinical scent escaped into the air. My lips twitched down into a frown. "Ready to go," I said bluntly.

Atlas Grimm's heavy presence seemed more profound when he stood behind me, out of my peripheral view. Unlike most people, he had no noticeable body heat. Rather, he drew from the heat nearby, leaving behind a distinct chill. I smelled a tinge of mint around him, along with the crispness of a cold winter morning. He was fresh and neat, but a dangerous edge surrounded him.

"You have an interesting way of making a question sound more like a statement," Atlas said.

"It wasn't a question," I bit back and gestured at the road. "We're taking the sewer portal."

"No."

I sent Atlas a cold look, which he returned with his frosty eyes. His eyes were the shade of yesterday's perfect sky, barely tainted by the pale color of ice. His intense gaze mesmerized me today just as it had at the council meeting. Not able to get a read on what emotions he was feeling, I clenched my fists.

"I wasn't asking," I said.

"No," he repeated. "I'm not going that way."

"Well, I am." Without waiting for a response, I trudged past two lost tourists and made my way out into the road. The Grimm Brother's cursing signaled his reluctant decision to follow me.

Traffic came to an abrupt stop as drivers desperately avoided crashing into us. A black Toyota swerved to the left, denting a freshly painted Corvette. A taxi turned into a fire hydrant, and water surged up into the sky, creating a thin mist over the street. Car horns blared, humans yelled at us to get off the road. I ignored it all.

In the middle of the road was a sewer access. I knelt on the ground, the hot pavement chafing against the slick material of my pants. Pressing my hand flat against the center of the filthy cover, the heat beneath my palm grew. Static thrummed through my hand and funneled around my fingers. Feeling the magic accumulate, I lifted my hand cautiously, keeping it parallel with the lid, and the sewer opening rose with my movement. Atlas grabbed the heavy metal cover as it hovered in thin air and tossed it aside like a Frisbee. I looked down into the deep, dark hole. The abyss gaped at us while it waited.

"After you." Atlas gestured for me to go ahead.

I placed a hand on my hip. "Afraid?"

His cool glare dropped the temperature by a dozen degrees. I shrugged. "Just make sure you end up in the right place."

Without another word, I jumped in and closed my eyes.

A breath later, buzzing tingles assaulted my body, and darkness cloaked me. Light dizziness descended on my head, but my mind wasn't addled. My limbs were suspended in the dark, as if I was endlessly floating through the chasms of space. Lethargy clawed at my arms and legs, like my limbs had gained weight or were being pulled down by ocean currents. A soft pressure touched the center of my chest; it bore down on me. The portal was ready for my command.

"Boston, Massachusetts," I spoke clearly. The sewer portal responded. Gusts of powerful wind engulfed my figure in its entirety, and the tingles began again. I felt like I was flying through a tube of air, ready to be spit out the other end.

As the anticipation hit its peak and the wind propelled me at its greatest strength, I opened my eyes, and it was over. I knelt on the top of a manhole in the center of Boston and in the middle of the road—my position the same as it was before opening the portal in New York.

Unfortunately, the gray minivan on the road did not stop.

Splitting pain battered my skull as the front bumper of the car crashed into my forehead. I flew back from the force of the impact, only to have the car's heavy tires run over my waist like a speed bump.

My ribs caved in with a *crack*, and my stomach felt ill. My lips barely caged a scream. The minivan kept going as if nothing happened.

"Bastard." I heaved a rough breath and remained on my back, waiting for the pain to subside. My forehead throbbed where the bumper of the car hit me, and a ringing noise echoed through my ears.

The following car screeched to a stop. The driver jumped out of his car and began hysterically waving his arms and yelling like a banshee. "Oh, my God! He ran her over!"

His shouting worsened my headache. Sharp pain in my skull and waist indicated my quick healing abilities were rushing to work. I groaned as two of my ribs cracked back into place. I sat up, wincing in pain. The driver rushed toward me. "Wait! Lay back down," he ordered. "How are you alive?! Your brains should be all over the damn road!"

I grumbled something about being a superhero-alien-robot with a hard head before staggering to my feet and hobbling to the sidewalk. A crowd of humans gathered, wide eyes watching my fast recovery in amazement, though nobody was brave enough to approach me. I stepped out of the street and toward Atlas, who casually leaned against a streetlamp, arms crossed and a smirk playing on his lips.

"How was your trip?"

I didn't bother dignifying him with a reply and instead walked with the swarms of people in the streets. Reddish-brown, rustic apartment buildings rose up toward the cloud-filled sky. Unlike yesterday's bright blue, flawless sky, ominous clouds bore down upon Boston. A dark shadow was cast upon us. The biting cold of the city's weather contrasted severely with New York's burning heat, a fact I was sure Atlas enjoyed dearly.

Patios and busy stores filled the grounds with their colorful goods and noisy vendors. The stores were crowded and small, one next to the other, without an inch of wiggle room. The light, smells, and noise from one store bled into the one next to it, making it difficult to distinguish between them. An occasional cold wind brought with it a misty scent of seawater, tobacco, and fast food. The humans on the street kept staring at me in an unnerving way.

Didn't they know? Staring was rude. I flipped off any pedestrian who stared too long, and they glanced away, creating a wide berth to walk around me.

Sewer portals were the main mode of transport for most supernatural beings, but they were limited to where they could take you. Middle of nowhere locations with no sewage systems were impossible to access with this portal system, and only certain manhole covers were spelled, usually one or two portals per big city. The Grimm Brothers strategically built their company close to a sewer portal in New York City. Boston's sewer portal was close to a subway station. Using the metro system, we could make it to the hospital where Lucifer murdered Vivian.

Atlas caught up with me. The ends of his lips were quirked upward in amusement. "I really shouldn't say I told you so, but the portal wasn't a great idea."

"It was efficient." I hastened my pace. I caught sight of the dirty stairway leading down to the metro station. "Any other means of transportation would have taken too long."

"You're lucky your spine wasn't injured. We'd lose an entire day before you healed enough to get back on your feet."

"Well, guess what? My spine wasn't injured, so no need to pointlessly worry yourself, Lord Atlas."

"Right," he drawled. "Well, the least you could do is wipe that blood off your face."

I wrinkled my nose and rubbed my forehead with the back of my sleeve. It came back with streaks of red. Hmm, that would explain the odd stares from the people of Boston.

Most of the pain had subsided from my waist, and all I was left with was an irritating headache and cramps, both of which would soon dwindle. My healing powers were usually quick once they started.

My chest swelled with elation as the darkness of the subway station came to view. My feet moved rapidly down the sticky steps. I passed by the pedestrians and Atlas's heavy steps followed me close behind. An artificial, yellow brightness replaced the natural, gloomy daylight.

Humming to myself, I skipped past the ticket booth's long line and vaulted over the ticket accepting machine and turnstile.

"Hey!" the ticket booth coordinator yelled.

I ignored him. Human authorities were irrelevant. The small sound of a crystalline structure being formed brought a smile to my face. Atlas created a coat of ice to cover the guard's mouth.

"Mmph! Mmph!" the guard called out in a muffled voice, but I paid him no mind as I sauntered down the escalator, taking two steps at a time.

The yellow train hadn't arrived yet, but I could hear the thrumming vibrations of the cars trudging across the tracks. It would arrive within the next half-minute, maybe less.

Humans nearby gave me strange glances, assessing my threat potential, but concluded that the guard at the ticket booth was an incompetent bastard that planned on hassling poor little me. It should upset me that people didn't perceive me as a threat, but it gave me a small bit of pride. The facade I put up worked like a charm.

I stood close to the yellow line and tapped my foot. Atlas came to stand to my left.

I shot him an intrigued glance. "You froze his mouth shut." I referred to the guard who ran around upstairs like a headless chicken.

Atlas raised his dark eyebrow.

I shrugged and looked away. "You could've used mind control. Why not?"

A frozen hush engulfed us. The sound of the approaching metro grew with a hum.

"How did you know?" His cold eyes watched me warily, as if unsure whether to kill me or congratulate me for figuring this out. His surprise seemed naïve to me. What secret could someone hide from Death?

I smiled crookedly. A bright light shined into the station. "The dead share their secrets with me, Lord Atlas. Though Erin Grimm may have the ability to concoct possible futures for humanity through his peculiar visions, I sometimes wonder where your power came from. How do you enforce the stories? Enforce is such a broad term—it could mean anything really."

Metal squealed as the train came to a stop. "All of those people," I said. "The ones that you control the endings of—they *do* share their memories with me when they die. The state of the human mind, just before it enters the realm of death, is vulnerable and honest. Sometimes, I realize their minds are not their own. People do or say things that don't match their personalities and considering the billions of memories I've seen and experienced, this fact raised a warning flag in my mind. Humans are creatures of habit."

The train doors opened with a squeak, and I stepped inside, Atlas a step behind. The car was gray on the inside. Spotting two empty chairs near a dark window, I made my way and sat near the smudged glass. Atlas sat frigidly next to me. His jaw was clenched, and a vein in his neck twitched.

I leaned back into my seat and fidgeted with the end of my sleeve as though I were bored with the topic. I reveled in the neutrality of my expression and toyed with the silence until the subway doors closed. The car moved forward.

"Truth is, I've been biding my time. Hoping to catch a moment alone with you, itching for this confrontation. Aching to say, I know your secret. You"—I pointed at him—"Atlas Grimm, have the power to control minds." I left out the part where he could also read people's thoughts. There was no victory in pushing him further than I already had. "Which makes complete sense. Otherwise, your power as CEO would be rendered useless. Without you, Erin's efforts to control people's futures are in vain. So, you both compromise. The connection between the two of you as brothers must contribute to your inability to control his mind. Still, I must wonder—simply out of curiosity, I assure you—have you ever tried to control my mind?"

Atlas's heavy gaze burned a hole in me. I knew the answer to my question, and it did bother me that my privacy had been disregarded. A subtle pressure in my head—that's all it took for me to know if Atlas tried to invade my mind. But my mind was strong enough to build mental walls to keep out people like him.

"Yes. I have tried to... control your mind." He refrained from mentioning he also tried to read my mind. Wasn't that assumed? If he could control someone's mind, he obviously had the ability to read their mind.

My index finger twitched. "And?"

He sighed. "What do you want me to say, Lady Primrose? That I failed? For some reason, I can't get into your mind."

I turned to face the Grimm Brother. His strong jaw was set tightly. His expression seemed carved from stone, sculpted almost, a characteristic very different from Erin, whose facial expressions always seemed in flux. Frown lines marred Atlas's smooth forehead.

He looked paler today, but it might have just been the lighting. His eyes were filled with disbelief and confusion. I remembered how reserved and emotionless his gaze was yesterday and earlier today. For him, being unable to enter my mind was a complete and utter failure on his part. A failure that irritated him beyond belief.

I smiled. "You want to know why."

Atlas paused, lingering in the transient thought of resistance before he nodded in reluctant admission.

I crossed my arms, and a spark of victory lit within me. "It takes a powerful mind to control an army of the dead, Lord Atlas." I leaned my head against the window of the subway car. "If my mind was as weak as that of a human, the dead would have control over me, not the other way around."

He opened his mouth to say something else, but the nasal screeching of the metro put a stop to his question. The subway car came to a sharp stop. We almost flew from our seats, and I braced myself on the chair in front of me.

Humans fell from their seats and lay groaning or screaming on the floor in agitation. I rose to my feet defensively and followed Atlas out, my eyes constantly shifting around the area to evaluate any incoming threat.

"We're not at the next stop," Atlas said.

"Marvelous observation, Sherlock Holmes." I unsheathed two knives from my belt and held them near my hips. "Something's wrong."

The lights in the car flickered, and the subway groaned noisily. The car jerked backward. I staggered a step back. My stomach dropped, and dread hung heavy on my shoulders. What the hell was going on? Who was doing this?

"We need to get out," Atlas warned, following my gaze. "Otherwise, we'll collide with the next train."

My breath caught. The next train...

I cursed under my breath and hooked my daggers back to my belt. "Damn you, Lucifer." My voice quivered, unable to hide the undercurrent of anxiety streaming through my mind.

I kicked out with my sharp heel and shattered a jagged hole in one of the train's windows. The ringing of glass elicited a number of screams from the hysterical humans. A man latched onto my shoulder to pull me back, and I shrugged him off. Using my elbow, I enlarged the hole, roughly knocking out more shards of glass.

"What are you doing?" Atlas demanded, grabbing my arm.

The lights flickered again, but when they came back on, a figure had appeared at the end of the car. Most of her body was covered in a black cloak, and a large shawl concealed the bottom half of her face. Long, blond curls hung loosely from the hood, and fierce, green eyes found mine.

"Satan," I said, recognizing the woman.

Lucifer hadn't escaped from Hell on his own. His little sister helped him. Atlas let go of my arm to analyze the new threat.

"Primrose," the demon growled.

"What are you doing here?"

Satan's lips pinched into a scowl as she unsheathed a sword from her back. "Protecting my brother from you."

"Oh, is that all?" I patted Atlas on the back. "You can take care of this, Lord Atlas."

The Grimm Brother glared at me. I ignored him, placing a foot on the bottom of the broken window. I pivoted and hauled myself onto the top of the subway car. A fierce current funneled through the tunneled area and lashed at my slender frame. I held tightly to the upper end of the window to avoid flying off and smashing into one of the walls. Small pieces of the remaining glass dug into my palm, but the cuts were superficial.

Adrenaline pumped through my body. My pupils dilated to adjust to the darkness. My heartbeat was loud in my ears, and the hair on the back of my arms stood up. I lived for this.

Bringing out another one of my daggers, I shoved it into the roof of the metro car. I grasped the hilt securely and steadied my position in a comfortable crouch. We approached the station we recently left from.

That's the mark. Now to avoid overshooting it.

I closed my eyes and narrowed my focus to the souls in the Underworld. Summoning the dead was like pulling up dozens of marionettes by their strings and moving them per my command. Their strings, though not tangible, proved to be palpable in the surrounding atmosphere.

Every soul of an individual who has died can be summoned from the Underworld, regardless of the exact location where they died. Sensing the billions of people that had died over the course of time, I called the souls forward to the surface of the railway, piecing together their bodies bit by bit. The train wiggled up and down as if hitting multiple speed bumps.

The car bounced up, and I lost my footing. I slid over the edge and held on to the dagger on the roof with my right hand. Sweat broke out on my cold forehead as I looked down at the sparking wheels of the train. The walls of the tunnel closed in. I latched back onto the side of the train and pulled myself back on the top of the car.

I clenched my teeth and continued to summon bodies as the front of the subway emerged into the station. My muscles were exhausted and aching, like I'd been working out for the past hour. Bringing dead bodies from the Underworld without a portal was physically draining. Each body required excellent concentration to control and pulling something out of nothing created a vacuum-like sensation within me, as I projected energy away from my body.

Metal groaned with the impact of flesh, and the train reduced its speed, but it wouldn't be enough. The flashing lights of the next incoming subway rushed toward us at a fast speed.

Wasn't it enough to hijack one train?

Fear chewed at my stomach. I swore and drew out the dagger from the roof to latch it back onto my belt. My shoulders tensed. I surged forward and ran on top of the subway's roof. I crouched low to avoid hitting my head on the concrete above. Adrenaline pulsed through my legs as I passed one subway car after another. I anticipated a crash in the next fifteen seconds.

With a huff of air, I slid off the last subway car and landed on the railway, bursting into a final run.

The oncoming train was a football field away. Its bright lights shined into my sensitive eyes. Broken bones, torn muscle, and mangled flesh became lodged in the wheels of the subway car behind me as it squealed to a bloody stop. A decapitated head rolled in front of me, and I almost tripped. A yelp escaped my lips. Goddamn dead bodies.

I came to an abrupt halt and extended my arms forward. I stepped back and braced myself for impact. Sensing the souls in the Underworld, I called upon dozens of bodies in front of the approaching subway. Flesh began to form only to be ripped apart by the power of metal. I bit my lip. The dead wouldn't be enough to stop the train.

I dug my feet into the tough ground, determined to stop the speeding subway cars. If Lucifer wanted blood, he would get it. A wry smile overtook my pursed lips.

An unexpected blow came from my left, and I was thrown onto the hard concrete of the station beside me. The moaning of metal and tinkling like bells filled the metro station. I skidded to a slippery stop and scrambled wildly to my feet.

Screams filled the air as humans ran from the two trains and to the surface. My eyes widened.

The trains were within three feet of each other. One was covered in bluish-white ice. In between the trains stood Atlas Grimm.

Beads of sweat rested on his creased forehead, and his unfriendly eyes watched me angrily. "Now *that*, Lady Primrose, was your first mistake."

CHAPTER FIVE
THE DEVIL'S LOVE LETTER

"I DON'T MAKE MISTAKES" was my automatic reply to the Grimm Brother's statement though I had no clue what he was talking about. "Did you take care of Satan?"

Atlas pulled himself from the railway and into the station. His limbs moved smoothly, like a panther on the prowl. His frosty eyes raged with an emotion I didn't recognize. A wave of ice-cold wind draped over my silhouette, and I shivered.

"She escaped while I was busy saving you," he said. "Before we finish our conversation, I suggest leaving this area. The human police will soon arrive."

I gritted my teeth to stifle my retort before nodding. Human police were never there when needed and always showed up when I wanted them out of my way. Again, not their fault; humans and deities were always out of sync.

With little effort, I used my control over the dead to return the souls deep into the Underworld and dismantle the bodies that remained out on the railway.

"Your eyes."

I gave Atlas a blank stare. "What about them?"

After leveling his gaze with mine for a short moment, he shrugged off his previous statement and dropped the subject. As I turned to leave, I caught sight of a simple white envelope taped to the ground. My eyebrows furrowed. "What's that?"

Atlas followed my line of sight to the envelope a few feet away from him. He crouched down and ripped it free from the white-tiled floor. His face became expressionless. "It's addressed to you."

I took a step toward him, but he pocketed the envelope with a sleight of hand that would have made a street magician proud. "First we leave, then we discuss."

I blinked in irritation and stormed off to the same escalator we came down on minutes earlier. Atlas wrapped his arm around my shoulders to pull me into a close embrace. My surprise didn't even have time to sink in before I slapped his chest. He staggered back a step on the escalator and held on to the railing, almost falling back down to the basement level. For his behavior, I was being gentle.

Sending him a scathing glare, I rested a hand on my hip. "What are you doing?"

He sent a meaningful glance upward. Two police officers were making their way toward the escalators with their radios in hand. I stifled a groan before taking a step down and allowing Atlas to pull me back into the same position.

"It's unfortunate to have to say this so soon in our little adventure, but I hate you," I said softly enough so that only he could hear.

"I am aware." He seemed as angry as I was.

"Next time," I continued, "we take care of this my way."

"On the contrary, there won't be a next time. And if there was, your way would be the last possible resort, short of pushing you off a cliff."

My face was red with anger. Instead of shoving him off the escalator, I growled and buried my face into his right shoulder. Fake sobs and heavy breaths escaped me, loud enough so that the entire subway station could hear. No doubt, my little show would do its job.

Coming off the escalators, the two cops stopped by us.

"She's in shock," Atlas said in a voice like honey. "If you don't mind, I'd like to take her home."

I let out a false whimper, and my knees collapsed. Right on tempo, Atlas picked me up as a husband would his wife before a honeymoon and held me close to him. The move worked like a charm. The two men awkwardly let us pass and walked away, their heavy boots hitting the ground rhythmically. Atlas carried me up the stairs until we reached the open air.

The moment we were out of the station, I rolled my head out of his embrace and sent him the most hateful, animalistic glare-scowl combination I could muster.

"Let me go," I hissed.

"No." His unyielding eyes held no room for argument. His grip around me tightened. "We are still being watched."

I elbowed him in the gut and stumbled out of his arms.

The clouds in the sky were darker than before, and birds flew low to the ground. A warm gust of wind embraced me, one that traveled down the length of my body. In that moment, I realized Atlas was like an iceberg.

I slipped my hand into my left jacket pocket and retrieved my iPhone. Unlocking it, I tapped the Maps icon to pull up directions to the hospital.

Atlas's heavy stare gained weight as he stepped closer. "What are you doing?"

"Looking up the hospital Vivian Erikson used to work at. I checked the news last night. Apparently, she was murdered in her office, and her body was found in one of the hospital elevators."

"So?"

"So, we go to her office and retrace her steps. Try to figure out what happened and where Lucifer could have gone next. The hospital is three miles away from here on foot, but I doubt we want a repeat of the subway incident."

Atlas nodded and leaned over my shoulder to glance at the map. "We go on foot. But first, we need to talk."

I pointed toward the Starbucks sign on our left. "Shall we?"

We crossed the street and entered the coffee shop. Before we settled at a table, I placed my order for a Caramel Frappuccino. Ice Man refused to get anything, claiming that I was wasting time. He wasn't wrong. Time was of the essence, but coffee calmed my nerves, which was what I needed right now. Besides, his complaint was hypocritical considering he opposed my plan to travel by sewer portal. Only once I obtained my cold, plastic cup did I sit down at the table for two. I felt like I was reliving yesterday's conversation with Ben, only with a stranger who hated my guts.

After placing my cup down on the table, I held out my palm expectantly. Atlas stared at it for a good two seconds before I lost my patience.

"The letter," I bit out. "I want to read it."

"All right, all right." Atlas pulled out the envelope from the inside of his jacket and held it out in front of me. My hand reached out to take it, but he moved it away at the last second. "I shouldn't be giving you this."

"Why not?" I leaned forward to grab it again, only to have the envelope waved away from the tips of my fingers.

"You put this entire mission at risk."

"What?" I stilled. I tilted my head to the side. "How so?" I demanded.

"Let's consider, shall we?" He flattened the letter against the table and kept his slender fingers pressed against it.

"The underground train was sabotaged by Lucifer. I don't see how I'm at fault."

"I never said the trap we walked into was your fault."

I leaned back in my chair and narrowed my eyes. "Then what *are* you saying?"

"The moment the train began to move backward, we should've left the car," he said matter-of-factly. "Why didn't we?"

I snorted. "You and I have a different idea of what should've been done."

"Clearly! Otherwise, I wouldn't have had to chase after you!"

I let out a puff of air and threw my hands in the air. "This is a waste of time. Let me read the letter."

"You've made your first mistake, Lady Primrose," Atlas said, breathing softly.

What mistake? He mentioned it at the subway station and now again. Heat crawled up the base of my neck. Apprehension twisted and curled around my limbs, and the meaning of his words became more muddled. Pressure built at my temples.

"Lucifer knows your weakness, and now so do I," Atlas said. He moved the letter across the table so that it lay before me. His hand touched it lightly as if to anchor the paper down to the granite countertop. "You care about humans."

I didn't understand what he said at first. His words were simple. Perhaps they were too simple. *You care about humans.* Really?

The previous tension that ran through me seeped out with an exhale. I wanted to laugh. This was his final conclusion? His doctorate thesis, his State of the Union address, his Revelations? An assertion as uninteresting and straightforward as this?

I was expecting him to say something dangerous. *Primrose, when you prepare to fight, you don't protect your left side, that spot below your elbow and above your hip. Now I know, so you'd better not get in a fight against me.*

Or *your mental walls are weaker when you summon the dead; I read your thoughts on the train. Now I know where your Soul Dagger is.*

Yet what he did say was so irritatingly irrelevant, I couldn't believe he'd said it in the first place. In his mind, my mistake was saving the lives of the humans on those two trains.

I rolled my eyes. "I don't care about humans."

"Then why didn't we leave the train? Why did you try to stop the crash?"

"Care is a strong word, Lord Atlas. I simply don't want any more death on my hands—well, any more than I'm already responsible for. What I did back there was for me, not for a group of humans."

"And yet you are the Goddess of Death!" he exclaimed, full of surprise and indignation as though I offended him in the obscenest of ways. His lack of understanding snapped me out of a dreamlike state and introduced me back to reality.

Did I really care about humans?

After what happened a month ago, when I entered a temple built to worship Hecate, the Goddess of Magic... something changed within me. Then the nightmares began to torment me—but to care for humans?

I swept the question from my mind and pushed aside my confusion. No. Impossible. Atlas was wrong, as usual. The Goddess of Death could not and did not care about human life. I noticed a crack in my shield—the same one I used to keep my emotions at bay, the very one that maintained my calm composure. The same shield that fell when I spoke to Ben not long ago. Or perhaps it had always been cracked and broken, only I didn't notice before. Now, I perceived it with such clarity and age-old wisdom.

"Not by choice." I shook my head, a dead look in my eyes. "I am the Goddess of Death, but I never had a say in choosing who I got to be. I see the irony of wanting to avoid death, considering the title I bear, but it doesn't bother me."

"It bothers *me*. Humans are worthless creatures," Atlas said, voicing an opinion most deities shared. "You know this! You weren't born yesterday."

His prejudice against humankind disgusted me, though I refused to let it show. I found his hate repulsive, even while I myself did not hold a high opinion of most humans. Humans may be part of a lower social class compared to deities, but they were living creatures. There were supernatural creatures without souls, such as lower demons and vampyres. Surely, humans were more significant than those creatures because of the souls they possessed. They deserved a modicum of respect.

"Well, tut-tut. I don't care what you think." I pried the letter from his fingertips. "I do care, however, about what Lucifer thinks."

I tore the envelope open and pulled out the perfectly folded paper. I unfolded it meticulously, like it was a ticking time bomb. I almost didn't want to read it. Black ink wove into intricate letters across the page. Thoughtlessly, I leaned in and caught a whiff of campfire, Lucifer's signature scent.

I scanned the cursive words on the page.

My dearest, beloved, and most cherished Rose,

Thy beauty is incomprehensibly innocent and regal; thy blood permits it. Yet thy roots are clouded in the muck, strewn by the first. Guard thy delightfully complex mind with not only thy shields but thy sentries as well.

Beloved Rose, if thou hast ever been as fragile as a flower, I would've crumpled thy silky petals in my hand. I know thy strength.

All the same, behold, beyond the flaming Phoenix's pretty wings, the sun sets and casts a shadow. I await thee there. Where art thy precious steel? Hidden well? Thou would hope so, and as do I.

The world has not enough time nor enough words to express my love toward thee. My precious Rose, 'til we meet again.

With all my love, mend this decaying heart,
Lucifer

I scowled. "Why can't this imbecile write in anything other than riddles?"

The letter was promptly—and rudely—snatched from my hands by Atlas. Just as I was about to protest, the paper burst into flames.

Atlas hissed and dropped the letter. I frantically threw my Frappuccino over the flames to put them out and sent a few glances around the room to make sure nobody had noticed. Fortunately, most humans were glued to their electronic devices.

I rested my elbows on the table. The letter was no more. My hands began to massage my temples slowly. "He knows you're with me."

"You think?" Atlas barked. His eyes had darkened to a deep blue. He kept rubbing his fingers together as if the fire had done some serious damage, though his skin was pristine and unblemished. "Damn fire-wielder."

I smiled impishly. Though Erin Grimm was the God of Fire, his and Lucifer's magic was much different. Erin summoned fire in its purest form—a raging flame that could be called at a moment's notice and ravage territory in the blink of an eye. Once started, this wild fire could hardly be contained. The younger Grimm Brother was known for his struggle to keep a leash on the fire he manipulated.

Lucifer, too, summoned a form of fire, but it wasn't the same. The fire he wielded was much more tame, constant, controlled. Deadly— but intentionally so. Unlike Erin, the Devil couldn't surround the *entire* world in flames, but he sure as hell could whip up a fiery rage in a specific, smaller region, like a small city or a strip of road off the I-20 highway.

Still, fire was fire, and Ice Boy here hated any kind of flame.

Atlas heaved a sigh. "What did Lucifer write?"

I knew better than to trust Atlas, no matter how incompetent I believed him to be. Schooling my expression, I decided to state the basic facts of what Lucifer said in the letter.

"There was a lot of fluff in it," I said and used a few spare napkins to clean up my Frappuccino mess. "He claims I'm naïve and have to keep my guards up."

Atlas arched an eyebrow.

I shrugged. "Lucifer likes making a fuss over the fact that I'm as innocent as a lamb yet beautiful as a rose."

Atlas blinked. "Is that supposed to make sense?"

"No, not really. I'm sure you've heard the rumors; the Devil is crazy. Legit psychopath. He's obsessed with me. There's nothing more I can say." I pressed my lips together and tapped my fingers against the countertop. "There aren't many pure stalkers in the world, but the Devil is one of them." A half-laugh tapped my chest, and my eyes narrowed. "He also mentioned the rise of the Phoenix—"

"More useless riddles." Atlas slumped back into his seat, deep in thought. "Is he trying to run us off course or—"

"It's not a useless riddle," I argued, keeping a thoughtful finger on my chin. "Phoenix isn't only the name of some ancient bird. Think about it."

The elder Grimm Brother watched me with a blank expression.

"Phoenix, Arizona?" I tested the question. "Does it ring a bell? He was referring to a location."

Atlas clenched his fists, refusing to see the reason behind my words. "Or we could be chasing our own tails."

"Look, maybe we are," I said. I stared up at the ceiling while my hand played with the straw of my coffee. I hadn't taken a sip from it yet. "I believe there's value in visiting the murder site to try to catch a scent. But with all the portals and magical shortcuts, he could be anywhere. It might be more convenient to go straight to Phoenix."

"If we do find him, what do you plan on doing?" Atlas asked. "Tracking his scent will buy us time to think up a better plan than charging at him in broad daylight, which is what we'd be doing if we rushed to Phoenix."

He brought up a good point. "Without his Soul Dagger, there's almost no point in hunting him down," I said. "But if we don't hunt him down, I can tell you this. He will hunt *us* down."

My words left a bitter taste on my tongue. The silence engulfed us as Atlas waited for me to think up the next move. After all, he was just the chaperone.

I snapped my fingers, realizing something important. "Who do you think dropped the letter?"

"What do you mean?"

"Who dropped the letter for me to find. Lucifer or Satan?"

Atlas checked his watch, still not catching on. "Why does it matter?"

I rolled my eyes. Yet another stupid question. "Lucifer is trying to get to me for the purpose of making me his queen, but Satan said she wanted to protect her brother from me. I don't think they're working together."

"You think Lucifer dropped the letter?" Atlas's eyes met mine as his interest returned.

"And hijacked the trains," I nodded. "Satan wasn't supposed to be there."

"Intriguing observation. That doesn't answer the question as to what our next step should be."

I bit my lip.

"We should both carry on to the human's workplace," Atlas suggested. He was tired of waiting for me to make a decision. "The Devil's scent will surely tell us more than his riddles."

But if his scent wasn't there, we would be wasting our time. "Maybe," I mused while toying with some mental calculations, "or maybe not."

Atlas pinched the bridge of his nose.

A sudden eureka moment hit me. "We should split up."

"No." Atlas narrowed his eyes. His calculated distrust was clear by his rigid posture and stern voice. "Wherever we go, we go together."

"Why?" I demanded.

He laughed bitterly. "Because I don't trust you."

"Consider—"

"No."

I stood up. My chair flew back, screeching as it toppled over with a loud bang. Starbucks customers gasped, and whispers shot across the room like projectiles. I rested my hands on the table and leaned forward. My face was inches away from the elder Grimm Brother. Everything about my stance screamed predator, and in the surprise in his eyes, I detected a valuable wariness.

Good. His caution might have saved his life.

"Listen here, Ice Prick!" I spat. "I've been a good little Goddess and let you tag along for the last hour or so. But if you think for one second that you can control what I"—I gestured toward myself—"want to do, or that you have any say on how, when, and where I hunt down, capture, or kill Lucifer, you're either delusional or just plain stupid." I smiled. "I'll let you take your damn pick. If you want to make it through the night, I suggest you rush over to Phoenix like the good little Grimm Brother you are. I'm going to pick up his scent from where he killed the woman, and if good luck shines upon us, we'll regroup in Phoenix and take care of Lucifer once and for all. Are we clear?"

I waited for him to agree, but he only glared at me. Atlas's silence hardened my anger and heat crept up the back of my neck. "I said, are we clear?"

Though Atlas didn't lessen the strength of his glare, he nodded, and I chose to leave it at that. If he knew what was best for him, he'd stay out of my way.

I stormed out of the café and began to walk the three miles toward Care Hospital. A rustle from a nearby dumpster startled me to a stop. A black cat rose from its home. Its matted fur stood up as it watched me with its emerald eyes. It tilted its head as if it knew me, and a mewling sound escaped its small, heart-shaped mouth. I blinked, and the cat sauntered from its junk-filled home and crossed the sidewalk in front of me.

I wasn't one to be superstitious, but that couldn't have been a good sign. Black cats were bad luck in the human world, and with the way things were going, the last thing I needed was bad luck. I tried to forget the heavy nervousness in my belly as I continued my path.

No other words would be shared between Atlas and me about Lucifer's letter—for good reason, too. Lucifer hadn't simply written a bunch of fluff. I said this to throw Atlas off my tail.

Lucifer had the chance to say many things in his letter, and he chose to make a very specific statement. *Guard your mind.*

Only Atlas Grimm could read minds.

As for my *precious steel*—the very mention of it put me in a state of high alert. According to Lucifer, someone other than him was hunting for my Soul Dagger. And for some reason, my traps, spells, and alarms hadn't gone off.

CHAPTER SIX
A GIANT SNAKE

"YOU ARE RELATED TO Nurse Erikson?" the receptionist at Care Hospital asked. A hair clamp held up her hair in a messy bun. She wore a pair of khaki pants and a blue uniform polo. Her eyes were wide with confusion. Vivian and I looked nothing alike.

Vivian was red-haired and blue-eyed. Her translucent skin was peppered with heart-shaped freckles, and she was a full foot shorter than me. My hair was a dull brown unless under the bright sun when a mahogany glint brushed my roots. Unlike Vivian's ghastly pale complexion, my skin was an unblemished ivory.

Then of course the sword I wore strapped to my back surely gave the receptionist reason enough to doubt my credibility.

"Yes, we are related." I tried to sound convincing and nodded. "I'm her second cousin twice removed. Hard to keep track of, don't get me wrong, but Viv and I were close friends."

The woman scratched her head. "Nurse Erikson didn't mention having anyone named Primrose as family." She fiddled with the edge of the telephone cord on her desk. "I should probably call upstairs and have them check you out. If you're on her privacy disclosure records, I mean. Sorry, ma'am." The receptionist sent me a shy smile. Her cheeks were red. "It's just protocol."

I flashed a half-hearted smile though my index finger twitched. "I understand." Casually, leaning on the counter, my thoughts reached out to Vivian's soul in the Underworld and her private memories. "You know, I used to watch over Johnny, her youngest."

The receptionist's hand froze as it hovered over the phone. She listened while I weaved my story. "Viv was always so protective when he was around strangers. It was so hard to convince her to give anyone a bit of trust. I practically begged her to get the afternoon to babysit him, and I'm her family, for goodness sake!" I laughed, lost in a stolen memory. "I miss her."

The woman's lower lip trembled, and tears gathered at the corner of her eyes. She wiped them away hastily, smudging her mascara. The receptionist laughed shakily and sniffled. "Yeah. I miss her, too."

The receptionist stood from her rolling chair and held out her hand. "It's a pleasure to meet someone from the family. I'm Carly Grant. Viv and I were good friends."

My hand reached out to shake hers. Carly's grip was tight—only honest people had such a tight grip. Guilt twisted its blade in my chest while I smiled a pretty smile.

This was fake. The hope my presence gave Carly Grant was all a lie. Her trust in me was as unfounded as it was naïvely human. My cheeks were tight and warm with shame.

I sternly removed my hand from her grip and stepped back to distance myself. Perhaps the distance would help me organize my thoughts and give me room to breathe. I brushed a stray strand of hair from my shoulder.

Carly noticed my distance, and the awkwardness from earlier returned. She gave a tight-lipped smile. "Do you know where her office is?"

I shook my head.

She motioned for me to follow her. After walking around the counter, she made her way toward an elevator. Of the two elevators, one was cordoned off—likely the elevator Vivian's dead body was found in. Carly pressed the Up button. She sent me one last smile, forgetting my previous reclusiveness. "Third floor. Her office is room 324. If anyone asks, Carly sent you."

The elevator door pinged and opened. I entered the empty car and pressed the button for the third floor.

Carly waved and turned to go back to her desk. Though her back faced me and the metal, gray doors of the elevator started to close, I waved back, regretting I hadn't said my own goodbye.

The doors closed, and I slumped to the bars at the back of the car. My hands held on to the bars in a death grip. My head pounded and felt heavier than it should have. I breathed in deeply, but halfway through my breath, it hurt to expand my chest anymore. I let out the shallow breath. Why did it hurt to breathe?

Or better yet, why did I feel Vivian's death was my fault? Was Atlas right? *Did* I care about humans? My cheeks flushed. That couldn't be true! If I cared... Why did I care? Could it be because of last month—

Stop, I scolded myself, refusing to let my thoughts slip toward last month's events. I glared at the elevator floor. Humans were irrelevant. Humans were nothing—stupid, dead, walking bodies.

The elevator pinged and my eyes shot up from the floor. I navigated through the hospital hallway and counted the room numbers off. I hated how empty this floor of the hospital felt. It was like the building knew death had taken place.

"321, 322, 323." I stopped. Room 324.

The bronze handle wiggled with my attempt to open the door. It was locked. I shoved the handle forward with more effort and the lock broke with a *plunk*. The broken door swung to the side and hung loosely off its rusty hinges. I entered the dark room.

The silence was deafening. Anticipation inched up my spine like an uninvited insect. The dark carpet absorbed the noise my light footsteps made, and the bare minimum light from the hallway carved a small strip of brightness on the ground.

I approached a desk near the back of the room, carefully avoiding the light that marred the carpeted floor. I softly touched the brown wood of the table. Small puffs of dust smeared against my fingertips. The clean, hand sanitizer scent of the hospital engulfed most of the office. A small touch of women's deodorant caressed the airflow generated by the AC.

I started at a scuttling noise in the back corner of the room. My gaze quickly swept the entire office. Nothing. Just a bunch of packing boxes and family photos.

There was nothing useful.

With a small growl, I twisted to the desk, hoping to find information I could use. No campfire scent lingered in the room. Lucifer must have masked it.

I roughly pulled drawers from Vivian's desk, searching for a clue, a hint, something. I shuffled through the files and papers. HIPAA documents, consent forms, regulations, rules, calendars, a piece of everything, damn it, but nothing useful.

I slammed my fist on the desk. A crack formed across its wooden surface. My eyes narrowed. The desk was covered in sticky note after sticky note.

I leaned in. Prescriptions, names, phone numbers—all on green and yellow sticky notes. One sticky note wasn't green or yellow, nor was it in Vivian's handwriting. A red note lay at the center of the desk.

I tentatively reached out and ripped away the outlier from the rest. One word was written on it: Manahawkin.

After a soul was reaped, I could access the memories of the dead individual. Sometimes I accessed the memories intentionally. Other times, the memories haunted me like a bad dream. A nightmare. I brought a hand to my head and winced. Vivian had visited a family in Manahawkin, New Jersey, before.

"Manahawkin," I whispered and lifted my eyes to the ceiling. "Vivian Erikson. Room 324." My breath caught. Was it too convenient? Was I reading into something that wasn't there?

"324 Erikson Drive, Manahawkin, New Jersey." I pulled out my phone and typed in the address. Sure enough, the cozy little home was five hours away.

I crumbled the sticky note in my hand and closed the desk drawers. I knew where Lucifer awaited me. And it wasn't Phoenix.

A sharp scuffling noise attracted my attention back to that same corner from earlier. I stilled and held my breath. My heart beat loudly, disturbing the silence. Once was an outlier, but twice was no coincidence.

A small tremor rumbled through the building, not strong enough to be felt by an inattentive human, but enough to startle me into action. I vaulted over the desk and sped toward the open door.

With the booming and cracking of bricks and wood, I lunged forward and guarded my head and neck. Small pieces of drywall and a ceiling tile landed on my back. I stumbled to my knees with a silent grunt. Powder and dust flew in every direction.

I wasn't able to see anything for a few seconds. Several coughs racked my chest. I shook off the dust from my hair and shoved the ceiling tile to the side. I braced myself against the wall closest to me and rose to my feet. Using the back of my hands, I wiped the powder off my sleeves.

My eyes narrowed as I looked into the suspicious corner. Two red flashlights glared back, and I paled. Scratch that thought—two humongous red eyes were glaring back.

Slithering out of the shadows, a pink forked tongue lashed out. A reptilian head, followed by a scaly green and yellow body, emerged. The rest of the body was curled into the many rooms of this hospital floor and the one below us. The width of his body was comparable to the size of a tree trunk, two feet in diameter at least. I struggled to piece together his size.

Intelligence surrounded the creature like an aura composed of magic, and I began to respect the magnitude of what and who I was dealing with. This was no ordinary supernatural beast. This was a shapeshifter. The only shapeshifter I knew of.

"Abaddon." I stumbled back a step and unsheathed the sword from my back. The blade comfortably lashed through the air before I held it out toward Satan's twin brother.

The enormous demon snake seemed to smile at my surprise. He lunged forward with his mouth open wide. I dove to my right and landed on my back with a grunt. Abaddon's head shot above me. I sliced at his skin with my sword.

The snake's head pulled back like a rubber band, and an unearthly cry escaped him. I rolled to the side. The serpent's heavy body landed where I had been a second ago. The musky scent of dead carcass assaulted my senses.

Adrenaline pulsed through my muscles and strengthened me. I sprang to my feet and held my sword up over my head. The large beast barreled into my waist. His long body wrapped around my small figure, and his skin oozed a green slime on my clothes. The slime burned against my skin. I gagged.

I couldn't breathe, suffocating under Abaddon's grip. My bones felt strained, ready to snap. An agonizing scream ripped from my throat. My grip on my sword faltered, and I caught a glimpse of the creature's mouth. Abaddon's long fangs dripped with amber poison.

Stars blinked in front of my eyes. My mouth opened and closed, unable to get any air in or out. Lightning-like flashes played on the surface of my skin. My heart pounded, though not from fear. Streams of energy cascaded through my veins, connecting me to a home I was very familiar with. Abaddon realized what my building magic meant, but he was too late to react.

Before the serpent could uncoil himself, small circles of light lashed out through his body. Red liquid soaked me. The scaled body released me from its grip, and I fell to the floor. With a shriek of pain, the serpent shot away, fleeing with the upper part of its severed body and leaving a trail of blood as he went. My micro portals had cut Abaddon in three with their sharp edges.

He was gone before I could blink.

I groaned and sat up. The smell of blood made me sick, but the pain overwhelmed my disgust. My arms wrapped around my pounding waist. I felt as if my heart had switched places with my stomach. My breaths sounded like wheezes, and they felt even worse.

With my jacket sleeve, I wiped away the sweat covering my forehead. I was sure I smudged blood all over my face.

A heavy exhale escaped my chest. For now, the threat was averted. Abaddon likely left to hide in a dark cave and lick his wounds while he healed and reformed. Being a shapeshifter had its perks, such as quick healing. He was a powerful demon, and Lucifer was his sibling, but all magic had limits. Time was one of them.

My eyes rested on the severed snake parts that remained. Chunks of Abaddon's scaly tail and midsection lay in a red pool of blood on the floor.

I grinned. The micro portals fulfilled their purpose, and by the looks of it, a decent amount of time would pass before the demon grew his body back.

I reached for my sword, which lay just beyond my fingertips, and sheathed the blade.

One of my responsibilities, as Queen of the Underworld, was the role of Gatekeeper. This role entailed that I controlled the portals to the Underworld—portals different from the one I had taken from New York City to Boston. Unlike sewer portals, my portals could take me to and from the Underworld with almost no limitations. The type of portal I summoned also held a more physical form, appearing, at its fullest, as a large-sized oval in which I could travel through.

A portal made for a worthy weapon. Its edges were sharper than glass. Shrinking the portals in size and throwing them around as mini-Frisbees provided for a quick escape when necessary.

Abaddon should have known better than to get too close, I thought with a triumphant smile.

I pushed off the floor. With a gasp of pain, my legs collapsed. Searing agony lit up like a fuse and ran over a sharp line along my side, from my hip to the lower half of my rib cage.

My hand touched the wounded region and I grimaced when the wound flared. I drew my fingers back to find a thin line of blood smudged across them.

I inhaled sharply. The serpent's fangs must have scratched my side in the heat of the battle. If I knew anything about Abaddon, I knew of his obsession with poisons. Though only a Soul Dagger could kill a God or Goddess, a potent enough poison made an injury take longer to heal.

I shivered. The same prickles I was accustomed to feeling when a wound started healing hadn't begun yet, and the time lapse worried me. Gritting my teeth, I punched the floor next to me. This injury was not what I needed right now! I held my jacket tighter to my waist, as if hiding the scar would make it go away.

I hunched over and braced myself on a wall. My legs felt like jelly. Once on my feet, I surveyed the damage done. Vivian's office was in ruins. Her desk was nothing more than splinters with sharp, pointed ends. Walls were caved in, and ceiling tiles littered the floor. Water from the restroom next to the office leaked past the broken walls and into the room.

Guilt spread through my chest. I had decimated this poor woman's life. Beyond causing her death, my presence here caused her workplace to fall to ruin. My presence was toxic. Everything around me became damaged.

The sound of police sirens disrupted my focus. My time in this room was limited. Of course, the police would arrive *after* the battle took place. Humans were always too late to save their own. At least they tried. If I respected anything about humans, I respected their will to try.

Recalling the electrical energy to the surface of my skin, I summoned another portal. The oval expanded into the size of a full-length mirror so that I could walk through it. Blue and white energy churned around the portal's sharp edges threateningly, and the crackling noise echoed through the office.

A mirror image stared back at me from the center, as if I were gazing into a looking glass. My reflection's eyes were tired, and my slumped shoulders echoed the weariness I felt. I took a step and staggered through the glass onto the grounds of the Underworld.

CHAPTER SEVEN
JUST A CONVERSATION

THE ACRID SCENT OF decay, fear, and blood hit me like a wall from my very first step into the realm. The humid air stuck to my body like a second skin. My body trembled, weak from the pain, but despite being in the Underworld, the place I was safest and strongest, my healing abilities refused to kick in. Clutching my waist, I stumbled on a concrete path leading toward the palace.

Many living humans wondered what the Underworld was like. Fortunately for them, there wasn't some cataclysmic, mind-blowing environment meant to frighten or harm all who entered.

No, that was Hell.

Most of the Underworld, including the land that housed my palace, was rather uninteresting. The skies were covered with a thin layer of gray, undaunting clouds, and the temperature was an average seventy-two degrees Fahrenheit. The air here was as humid as the air in south Florida and the only wind flow there existed was generated by the strong current of the rivers.

Three rivers—Lethe, Acheron, and Styx—ran beside my palace, like three snakes that converged at one point near the border of Hell. They divulged into two separate rivers, Phlegethon and Cocytus, when they entered Hell's domain. Poppy flowers grew along the bank of the rivers with many of the pomegranate trees famous in human legends of this land.

Near the palace, I spotted dozens of leafless trees from which a special fruit blossomed. Within each fruit was a key that could summon portals, much like the portals I personally summoned. These keys were useful for reapers when traveling to the human realm to reap a soul or when transporting armies over long distances.

My forehead flushed with a heavy fever and my vision blurred. I tripped over my legs and sprawled to the floor. Instead of scraping my hands on the concrete, the ground beneath me grew dense with soft grass. The Underworld sensed my pain and altered itself to soften my fall. A spasm racked my torso, and a burning sensation spread up to my chest. I groaned and crawled toward one of the trees. The branches cracked and shifted, providing a cool shade.

"Get me a reaper," I said, knowing the lands heard my request. A small tremor in the soil rumbled toward the palace. Help would be on the way.

Leaning back against the tree, I lifted my shirt to look at the injury. The skin was puffy and red. I held my breath to keep the next cry of pain from escaping my lips.

Souls mindlessly passed around me. Though souls didn't have a physical appearance, I almost felt like I could see them as a translucent sheen in the shape of a human. I could certainly feel them. There was a strong sensation deep in my gut that pinpointed the exact location of the souls. They left a cold chill in the air when they passed.

"Toxic" began playing and I flinched in surprise. I kept forgetting that my phone was spelled to work in any magical realm I traveled to.

Breathing in deep, I steadied my voice and answered. "Elinore?"

"Hey, Prim! Did I catch you at a bad time?" a sweet voice asked.

"No." I grimaced and stifled a whimper as another spasm surged through me. "I'm free to speak at the moment."

"Good!" Elinore beamed. I cringed at the level of cheer in her voice. "So, you know that alarm thingy that you told me about? The one you said I should call you about if it starts flashing or acting up?"

"Let me guess. It started flashing?"

"Like you wouldn't believe," she said. "That's bad, right?"

I sighed. "Incredibly so, but don't worry. I had my suspicions."

"This happens a lot?"

"No, someone tipped me off." I thought back to Lucifer's letter. My surroundings blackened and flashing lights tore through my vision. The following spasm of pain elicited a moan of anguish from my throat.

A pause of silence followed as Elinore processed my words. "Are you okay, Prim? You sound weird."

"I'm fine!" I swallowed the pain so she wouldn't hear. "It's just... The alarm flashing is not good news."

"Should I be expecting man-eating ninjas at my door or an evil demon hunting me down?"

I laughed at her vast imagination. "I doubt it, but to be safe I'll visit you soon."

"Yeah! No worries! Today?" A microwave pinged in her apartment. Typical Elinore. Always eating.

I looked down to my wrist as if checking an imaginary watch and shrugged. "Probably."

"I'll warm up the cookies in the oven! Prepare to be amazed!"

"Elino—" I scowled. She hung up before I got the chance to properly scold her. Classic human move.

My side burned, like a knife was being shoved deeper and deeper into my flesh.

"My lady." A reaper appeared in the corner of my eye. He ran toward me and knelt at my side. "You're injured."

His head bowed low as he assessed my injury, dark hair draping over his elegant eyes.

"Cain," I gasped, relieved to see my most powerful reaper. "I was expecting Kaitlyn." I nodded toward the palace. "Or is she hiding from the repercussions of Lucifer's escape?"

Cain lifted his head. His catlike eyes watched me with as much adoration and respect as a child would his mother. A katana was strapped to his side, though he didn't need it to be a deadly adversary.

Reapers, unlike other supernatural creatures, weren't born with magic. They used to be humans when they were alive, but upon death, their souls left their bodies while their memories and mental capacity remained. Reapers were soulless, and therefore, practically dead. But they were uncannily similar to living beings. They needed oxygen, food, water, and rest to be at their best. And like humans, they could also have children if they wished, though this was very rare. Cain was an anomaly among my reapers. To me he was the most human of them all. As human as one could be without a soul.

My reaper smiled, though his eyes flashed coldly. "Kaitlyn is afraid to speak with you. She would have come if not for more urgent matters."

Kaitlyn had been assigned to take up the guard of Lucifer's prison this past month, but *apparently* an empty cage wasn't a red flag in her eyes. Or at least she didn't think that it was important enough to tell me of it. Cain knew of Lucifer's escape because he worked closely with Vulcan, the blacksmith of the Underworld. I had called Vulcan yesterday to forge the new sword I now wielded. The High Court would contain the news of Lucifer's escape and only a select group of reapers knew so far. The less people aware about the Devil's escape, the better. Otherwise, panic might spread.

Worry marred my forehead. "More urgent? What exactly is more urgent than Lucifer's escape?"

"Let me dress this wound first. Why isn't it healing?"

"Abaddon."

"The shapeshifter?" Cain's eyes widened.

I nodded. "Lucifer's brother decided to pay me a visit. Needless to say, our interaction wasn't pleasant."

Cain brought out some gauze and alcohol wipes from his pocket. "Abaddon is known for his work with poisons. This wound will cause you excruciating pain without the proper medication."

My eyes squinted as he pried open the alcohol wipes. "Do you always carry first aid kits in your pocket?"

"The Underworld sent a great quake to the palace to warn me of your arrival, and the wind echoed a cry for help. I was worried something could be wrong."

"You were right." I winced as he dabbed the alcohol wipe against my wound.

Cain pressed his lips together and shook his head. "I wish I wasn't. You need stitches. I'll take you to the hospital ward."

I grabbed his arm to stop him from carrying me. "No. There's no time."

"You're badly injured, my lady."

"Just dress the wound." I gritted through my teeth and my body jerked with another spasm. My head rang and tears blurred my vision. "I-I'll get some pain meds from th-the human realm."

Cain frowned, but he held his tongue. He pressed the gauze against the wound and blood seeped through. He brought out a bandage and wrapped a roll of gauze around my waist. "This won't last you long. You need stiches."

I grunted. The pressure applied to the wound alleviated some of the pain. "The only person I trust to poke me with a needle is myself. I'll stitch it up later, I promise. Now tell me, what is worse than Lucifer escaping Hell?"

"An attempt on your life, I fear," he said. His jaw was tight. "A cloaked spy entered your chambers this morning, armed. We believe he was searching for you."

"Believe," I echoed. Heat climbed up the back of my neck. "You don't know for sure? Certainly, he's been interrogated by now."

"The moment we discovered the dark figure, it flung itself from the balcony. On the ground, where he had fallen, there was nothing to be found but an empty cloak."

"Did it survive?" I asked. A shiver ran down my spine.

Cain shook his head. "No, my lady. Beneath his cloak was scattered dust, black as night. I am most certain these were his remains. Whatever this creature was, it was neither human nor demonic."

An assassin like this was unheard of, but he must have been powerful to make it past the guards and the magical protections outside my chambers. I never slept in the palace, and thus this creature's attempts were in vain.

"Do you think..." I paused. "I ask this because I know you well, Cain."

He nodded. His worried eyes held an earnest desire to help

"A soulless creature like this, unheard of before—do you think there could be more of them?"

"There can always be more, my lady."

At least he was honest. I liked that about Cain. He didn't lie or pretend to know something he didn't. He said what he thought and what I needed him to tell me, nothing more, nothing less.

I pulled my shoulders back into a proud posture and lifted my chin. "Help me up."

He offered his hand and helped me to my feet. The pain in my side flared and tears threatened to resurface, but I felt stronger now.

"Thank you for your report," I said. "Is that all?"

"May I make a suggestion, Lady Titan?"

I nodded. "You may."

Cain's face darkened. "Let one of us come with you as you journey to put an end to Lucifer. My fear is that whilst you hunt the demon, another will do you harm—"

"Absolutely not. A single reaper against an assassin or the God that sent him is no fair fight. I need all of you here, taming the lower demons of Hell, or out in the world, reaping souls."

Cain's face fell.

I touched his shoulder, and his eyes met mine once more. "Besides, when the time comes, I will have a special task I need you to do. Can I trust you to do it?"

He flinched. "Need you even ask, my queen?"

† † † † † †

The portals I summoned were a strange phenomenon.

I could open a portal to the Underworld from anywhere in the world, and from the Underworld, I could open a portal to anywhere I wished. But to travel from one place to another, I always needed to physically pass through the Underworld, which was why after I fought Abaddon, I first opened a portal to the Underworld instead of the address in New Jersey where Lucifer awaited. My homeland was a medium, and without it, my portals were nothing but crackling flashes of light. Every portal required a medium. Even the portal we used to travel from New York to Boston used the sewers to facilitate transport.

Most Gatekeepers had some portaling ability. Using my personal portals to travel was much easier for me compared to the sewer portal system Atlas and I used to travel to Boston. However, I knew Atlas would refuse transport through one of my portals. He would never risk passing through the Underworld.

Stepping into another God's or Goddess's domain held a promise of trouble. My power was strongest in the Underworld. Similarly, if I entered the coldest, iciest city in the world, I would be wary of Atlas, considering he was strongest there.

I released a sigh and turned away from the path that led to my palace. Cain left after I asked of him the request I desired. He was a good reaper, an even better ally.

With a flick of my wrist, I opened a portal out of the Underworld that led to 324 Erikson Drive, Manahawkin, New Jersey. I stepped out and right into a muddy puddle. It was pouring rain.

Mud clung to my stilettos in slimy chunks. I really ought to have taken a shower in the Underworld, but the weather had been prepared for my absent-mindedness. Who needs a shower when the heavens are pouring ice-cold rain over you?

Seconds later, I was drenched from head to toe. My clothing stuck to my skin, and my ponytail was heavy with wet hair. My index finger twitched, and I bit the inside of my cheek. Oh, what a beautiful day.

I stormed up to the sidewalk and kicked off the muck from my stilettos. I followed the paved path up to the chestnut doorway of a one-story, cozy little home. The red brick building sat sturdily on 1,500 square feet, give or take. The slanted roof withstood the impact of the rain, standing firm and strong. The small windows of the home were shuttered, though a hint of light shined through them. Somebody was home.

It was warm outside, despite the coldness of the rain. Knowing my luck, hail would hurl from the daunting gray clouds if I waited outside any longer. I approached the door and knocked twice, waiting sullenly. The window on the door wasn't shuttered like the rest, but the design blurred the inside of the home. I hunched over and placed my hands around my eyes, trying to make out anything beyond the door.

No... Too blurred. I knocked again, this time banging my knuckles on the door as loudly as I could without throwing the door off its hinges. A sharp pain ran through my midsection, and I hissed, stepping away from the door to lean on the brick wall. If my side kept ailing me like this, how was I to confront Lucifer properly?

Hearing footsteps on the inside of the house, I ignored the pain and circled back to face the door again. The door creaked open. In its way stood a tall man. His sleek, tan body was dressed in an unbuttoned dark trench coat and slacks, both of which fit him well. He wasn't very muscular, but his features were perfectly drawn, like a faery, meant to attract every desire of women and men. His thin build fit that of a professional dancer. The man before me reeked of sensual pleasure, lived off of it and absorbed it into his physique, like Cupid himself. Many referred to him as Cupid, but he was no God of Love. Golden eyes bore down upon my figure, lingering on the tightness of my clothing and giving me the most implied once-over anyone could give.

I crossed my arms over my chest to hide from his gaze. "Asmodeus."

The demon of Lust smiled knowingly. "Primrose." My name on his lips sent a quick blush to my cheeks. He stepped out into the rain, aware of what his closeness was capable of doing, and said, "What would my brother say if he knew the way your eyes ravaged me now?"

I shrugged and stood my ground. "I could ask you the same."

"Still brittle as ever, I see." Lust craned his neck toward the clouded skies. "Or perhaps it is simply the poor weather that has gotten on your nerves."

I delivered an unamused stare. "Why are you helping Lucifer?"

The demon stepped closer so that his cheek hovered beside mine. My stomach fluttered with nervousness. I struggled to maintain my stance, but with steady motivation, I resisted stepping back. Demons enjoyed the thrill of prey that ran. I would not give him that satisfaction.

Lust inhaled my scent and heavily breathed out in reply. A shiver ran down my spine like a thin-legged spider. "How could I refuse to aid my brother in indulging his inner Lust?" he purred seductively.

I stiffened, ready to fight him off. My fingers grazed over the hilt of my scimitar. Instead of satisfying my beliefs, Asmodeus stepped around me and walked further into the torrential rain and out to the street. My eyes widened.

"Where are you going?" I demanded.

Lust turned and sent me a wicked smile. His scorching gaze burned a hole into my chest. "My debt has been repaid. My brother is on his own from this point forward. But I'm touched to see you care."

My cheeks flushed. I spun around and rushed into the home, out of the rain. The warmth enveloped me immediately. My skin regained some of its color, and I stopped shivering. The smell of a live fireplace touched the tip of my nose. The home gave off a cottage feel, and I could appreciate its appeal. Wooden bars lined the ceiling, and the cream walls bore family portraits and paintings. The cabinets and drawers were stained a dark color, and a comfy sofa leaned back on the wall opposite to the fireplace. The floor's fiery wood was laminated and sleek. This was a home Lucifer would like, one that he might live in... That was why he chose to come here today.

My legs moved mindlessly, approaching my foe. I could smell his campfire scent throughout the entire home—the scent of oxygen being consumed and the release of smoke into the air. I heard his relaxed breathing in the kitchen. When I entered through the doorway, time stopped. Nothing else existed, not the pain from my injury or the cold rain that soaked my clothes. Not the assassin in my chambers nor the foolishness of Atlas Grimm.

My heart pounded in my chest, driven by panic and melancholy. I knew I'd find him here, but in no way did I feel prepared to face the monster haunting me.

In the middle of a homey little kitchen stood the cause of my troubles. The nightmare plaguing my dreams, the murderer of innocent humans, and a man who was once my friend—maybe more. Someone I once respected, trusted even.

Lucifer.

Lucifer was a warrior, in every aspect of the word. His strong build towered over mine. Powerful muscles rippled underneath his dark shirt. He wore a pair of worn-out jeans. He had no weapons strapped to his side—not that he needed any. His legs were crossed as he casually leaned onto the granite countertop next to him. A red coat, most certainly his, was draped over a chair. His skin was a warm, lively color. He must have shaved away his beard and cut his hair after his escape. His strong jaw was relaxed, and his blond hair was swept to the side, meant to reveal his eyes, though in this moment, I did much to avoid meeting them. A commanding presence surrounded him like a suit of armor.

Demons had their own hierarchy, much like Gods and Goddesses. Lower demons were at the bottom, and Lucifer and his siblings were at the top, just as powerful as any other supernatural deity. This was why the High Court feared the Devil. He was an unwanted equal.

"Look at me," the Devil challenged. His husky voice hit me like a beam of light, offending my ears with its dripping pride. But that was who he was. The demon Lucifer. The demon of Pride.

I bristled but kept my gaze locked on his chest. "I am looking at you."

"Look me in the eyes, Rose." His voice lingered on my nickname, tasting it fully and toying with it on the tip of his tongue. "Or are you afraid?"

Though his accusation was childish, I foolishly lifted my eyes to meet his in defiance. Two gorgeous red opals regarded me with such intensity I almost averted my gaze, a sure sign of weakness in his mind. His eyes gleamed as he noticed my acceptance of his challenge. Dozens of emotions lived in his stare. Betrayal, anger, amusement, lust. Pride. Always Pride. I could get lost in the lifetime of memories reflected in his eyes. His emotions tore right into me, and I wanted to scream at him like I'd done the night I imprisoned him. I felt numb as the memories threatened to serve as a cruel reminder.

He thought I betrayed him. But he betrayed me.

A twisted smile marred Lucifer's features. "Oh, Rose, you are utterly and fascinatingly predictable. You know that, right?"

I kept a mask of disinterest on my face. My lips were set in a hard line of silence. If I opened my mouth with the scream that lay in my throat, who knew what would come out?

My eyes roamed his figure, searching for the familiar glint of a Soul Dagger but there was none. If his cage in the Underworld couldn't hold him, there was no point in trying to lock him back up. That was assuming I could drag him back to Hell on my own. I swallowed the lump in my throat. The best I could do now was to play his games and hope to manipulate him into doing something stupid.

Lucifer walked away from the countertop, toward me. "You could never leave a challenge untouched."

"I should say the same for you." My chin rose in defiance.

"Such a spitfire!" the Devil remarked jovially. "Tell me, kitten, when will you realize your sharpened claws and bared fangs are all for naught when fighting a metal monster?"

"Another pointless riddle."

"Merely a truth, Rose." He took one large step and came face-to-face with me. I craned my neck upward to maintain eye contact. "You're fighting a war you cannot win because you rely on the wrong kind of weapons." His hand rose to gently move away a wet strand of my hair.

I slapped it away before he could touch me. "Where's your Soul Dagger?"

Lucifer belted out a curt laugh and stepped around me, circling me like a predator. "Right to the point, my darling? All right, I shall oblige. I'll tell you where my Soul Dagger is when you tell me where yours is."

I sneered. "Why? To kill me?"

"*Au contraire, ma chère,* you are not to be trusted with it. I only mean to keep you alive. A task you seem to struggle with."

A heavy flush made my head heavy under his scrutiny. I opened my mouth to deliver a biting remark only to notice his gaze zero in on my recent wound. The jacket I wore had moved aside, leaving my bloodied tank top visible. My hand self-consciously hovered over the injury.

Lucifer stilled, and his eyes darkened. "My brother seems to have... left his mark already." He rushed past me toward his coat and brushed my shoulder. I tripped back and braced myself against the countertop. My fingers gripped the edge, and I muffled a gasp as pain seared through my side.

Lucifer glanced at my stilettos. "How on earth are you able to walk in those?"

My muscles tensed as he fiddled with his coat pocket and pulled out a small white vial. "Practice makes perfect," I said. "Besides, with supernatural males as tall as they are, a woman must alter her appearance to be taken seriously."

"I doubt that," the Devil said, though his lips echoed a faint smile. He stepped toward me, and I took a step back to preserve the distance between us. I reached for one of my daggers.

He held both hands up in surrender. "I mean you no harm. My brother's poisons are"—Lucifer clenched his teeth—"paralytic. Even to Gods. Let me help you."

Lucifer hadn't verbalized any tensions between him and his siblings before. But perhaps I'd overestimated the connection between Abaddon and Lucifer. I maintained my tense position for a short moment before nodding in reluctant agreement. I blinked and he was already removing my jacket and lifting up the edge of my tank top. His warm hands burned against my cool, drenched skin and committed my stomach into doing wild loops of unwelcome excitement. Lucifer carefully unwrapped the bandages and removed the bloody gauze.

He swore loudly, and I lifted an eyebrow. Lucifer hardly ever swore, at least in my presence. The Devil breathed in deeply before letting the air out slowly. "This wound needs to be cleaned, and you need stitches."

"The wound is clean, and I'll stitch it up later on my own time, thank you very much."

"You don't understand. My brother is desperate to hurt you. Otherwise he wouldn't have used this poison."

My gaze landed on the wound. Most of the bleeding had stopped, but blood still oozed out at a slower rate. "How bad?" I refused to let any emotion drip into my question.

"The worst. Ancient hunters once used it to torture supernatural beings. Aside from causing pain, the poison weakens the muscles and counters any magical healing powers. I believe the hunters called it King's Bane."

I huffed. "Good thing I'm a queen then."

His grip tightened around my clothing. "Not funny, Rose." His voice held a deadly edge to it. "My damned brother is attempting to put an untimely end to you. He'll be after your Soul Dagger soon enough. With my sister's help, he might succeed."

"They want to keep you safe from me." I remembered Satan's words from on the subway car.

He scowled. "I don't need their protection. We had a deal contingent on my escape, and now they've both decided to go their own way. To put a stop to you."

"Not part of the plan, am I right?"

Lucifer said nothing in response. Holding on to my shirt, he used his other hand to unscrew the cap of the vial and poured some salve on his wrist. "Abaddon used to prank my siblings and me. Often we found ourselves writhing in pain from the poisons he used—"

"You and I have a much different definition of the word 'prank.'"

The Devil sent me a blank stare. He was in a forgiving mood today. He used his index finger to apply the thick liquid to my wound. My muscles tensed. Bracing myself for the pain, I was surprised to feel cool relief upon the remedy's application. I barely refrained from sighing, though I refused to give Lucifer the satisfaction of knowing how much he'd helped me. The sharp pain faded into a dull ache. He rebandaged my torso.

"I developed a personal salve and carried it on me ever since," Lucifer said. "It won't heal your wound. Time is the only remedy to a poison of this magnitude, but the salve shall dim the pain."

"Right," I drawled and flashed him a cute smile. "Can't have your queen writhing in agony, can you?"

Done with my wound, he cupped my cheek with his hand. His eyes bored into mine, softening in the moment. "Would that be so terrible, beloved? For you to be my queen?"

I snarled and jumped back from his touch. "You're a murderer, Lucifer. A damned murderer."

His stare hardened as he closed himself off. "Then I suppose we are alike in that aspect."

"Your Soul Dagger?"

"Like yours." His mocking grin returned. "Hidden."

"I'll find it," I vowed. My fists trembled. "I'll find it, and I will kill you. No more innocent lives will be lost at your hand."

Lucifer laughed. "Remind me again, why does the murder of humans bother you? Before we became enemies, you'd spend hours lecturing me on the balances between life and death. Hours! Humans die. 'Tis the nature of things. Why do you care if I kill a few poor souls or not?"

"I..." My voice faltered. Atlas's words came to mind. *You care about humans.* How could that be possible? How could the Goddess of Death care? "No!" I yelled. "You're wrong. I don't care about humans."

A knowing spark lit up in the Devil's eyes. "I never said you did."

"There is nothing natural about murder," I said through my teeth. "There's no honor in killing innocent people. You can manipulate what I've said in the past all you want, but it doesn't change the fundamental truth."

"And she's back, ladies and gentlemen! Give a round of applause for Lady Primrose! Returned to her ice-cold self!" Lucifer's lips twitched in cruel amusement. "Speaking of ice, how is Lord Atlas doing, by the way? Does he enjoy working with you?"

"None of your damn business!" I snapped. My eyes widened. How much did he know about me and Atlas? "Make this easier on all of us, and get back in your cage, and stay there!"

He strode into my personal space once more, his nostrils flaring. "Cage or death, Rose? Choose one, but don't toy with your words. This isn't a game."

"I'll let you choose! If you willingly walk back into Hell where I lock you up and cast enough binding spells to last a thousand lifetimes, I won't kill you. If not, the only thing left of you will be your Soul Dagger when I'm finished using it."

"You're a real tool. You realize that don't you, *Lady Primrose?* You are being used—"

"On both sides, yes, I know. I'm not an idiot!" My head pounded mercilessly, and raging emotions ravaged my body.

For the first time since we had met, Lucifer's eyes held a touch of pity in them. How dare he feel sorry for me? "Oh, kitten," he said with a sigh as if it pained him to speak. "You don't know the first of it."

My restraint broke. I whipped out a dagger and sent it flying his direction. He leaned out of the way, and the blade flew past his cheek, leaving no mark. The dagger buried itself in the wall behind him. A second later, he was gone.

An inhumane cry left my lips. Every frustration, grievance, emotional stress from the past two days enveloped my scream as it rose to the ceiling. The home caged my rage, sparing the outside world of it. My skin boiled, and I felt the Underworld echo my cry.

When all breath had left me, I pulled my tank top over my bandaged wound. I held my jacket close to my body and hugged myself tightly, as if this feeling would make me feel any less alone. I knew the truth. No one would come and save me. There was no superman or hero in my story.

My head spun. Thoughts and images flew through my mind, landing on a person and a place. I opened a portal into the Underworld and once I entered my homeland, I opened yet another portal back into the human realm. Except this time, instead of visiting an enemy, I was visiting a friend.

CHAPTER EIGHT
NIGHTMARES

GRAY AND ILL-DEFINED WAS the fog that surrounded me. A faded dullness cast a shadow over my eyes, obscuring all sense but touch and sound. My skin vibrated with life at the gentle touch of a man's arm around my shoulders.

"I love you," he whispered in my ear. His voice was coarse and filled with static as if he were miles away, using a radio to speak to me.

His warm lips touched mine. I melted into his embrace. Warmth enveloped me and joy became my greatest partner. Stolen moments in the dark, with none to judge or see us, were more beautiful than the palace of a king or a mountain made of gold.

I brushed a lock of hair out of his face, unable to see his features clearly as if they were distorted by the fog's sheen. His green eyes were like two emeralds, bright and magical. Full of light and hope. In his eyes lived a promise of a future together, a future I wanted.

"I love you more," I countered with a grin. My voice came out as hoarse and full of static as his was.

Before the man could argue my mouth met his.

The scene faded from my grasp, and I was suddenly pulled out from behind, plucked from a beautiful dream. I struggled, fighting an unknown foe until my feet hit solid ground, and I began to run with a vengeance.

The fog parted, revealing a path. I didn't know where I was going, but my destination pulled at my soul like a string on a puppet.

My breath came in short puffs, and strands of my hair lashed at my face wildly. The wind swept the sheets of fog back into my path and pushed me back, daring to slow me down. My bare feet beat against the hard ground, and twigs and weeds scratched at their soles. My white nightgown was stained with the green of grass and my own scarlet blood, but I was numb to the pain.

I was hysterical, mindless. A wild animal, driven by an inexplicable primitive instinct. Dread latched onto my heart like a leech and fed itself with the very core of my soul and the essence of my being.

The path in front of me steeped upward, and I ran past the peak of a hill.

A corpse came into sight, and a terrible cry flew from my lips. I collapsed over the deformed body of my love. His beautiful, warm hair was mottled with crimson blood and his face was unrecognizable, even now as his features were no longer blurred. I never felt pain like this. An iron fist clutched my heart as if to pull it from my chest.

I knew this broken body belonged to the man I kissed, the man I professed my love to. Two green eyes no longer gazed into mine— they had blinded him, robbing him of his eyes. A churning sensation was the only warning I received before the contents of my stomach built up in my throat. I vomited violently, facing away from the man as not to stain him with the mess I made. Acid burned the back of my throat as I gasped for air and returned to sob over the body of my love. I caressed his face and comforted him with a broken, weeping voice.

I knew the truth. He would not recover so long as Pain and Fear existed. My love was only human.

"Where are they?" I choked out with my static voice.

My question was so urgent and desperate I couldn't bear to not have the answer. The man barely had any energy to shake his head. The fog hissed, my question having offended it. The grayness surrounded us, blinding me of what was before me.

"Where are they?!" I yelled.

I sat up suddenly. The same words echoed through my ears like a ringing siren. *Where are they?* The problem was that I had no clue who 'they' were.

My head whipped around wildly. There was no human man dying on the floor. No evil fog, no gut-wrenching sorrow. Instead, I sat in a dimly lit room, on Elinore's bed underneath what appeared to be three blankets.

I had woken up from a dream. A nightmare. Nothing more.

My scalp was damp with what I at first thought was sweat. I brought up a few strands of hair to my nose. My hair smelled like peach shampoo, like the one Elinore used. My hair was damp from the shower I took before falling asleep.

My heart rate calmed with my breathing. I glanced at the clock sitting on the drawer beside the bed. The time read 5:13 p.m. Considering Atlas and I left Grimm Enterprises around six this morning, it was safe to say today had been a busy day.

"You okay?"

Elinore stood in the doorway of her room. She munched on some popcorn in a red, flimsy bowl in her hands. She grabbed another handful and held her fist toward me. "Want some?"

My fingers held the bridge of my nose briefly as I tried to ward away a headache. I let out a deep breath and stood from her twin bed. "No, thanks."

When I happened upon the doorstep of Elinore's apartment in the early afternoon, she answered the door with a platter of cookies, only to drop it after seeing the blood on my clothes. She ran over to the pharmacy to buy a suture kit, bandages, and pain medication, and I stitched together the wound. Elinore demanded I take a shower and throw my clothes into her washer and sent me straight to bed. I crashed in her bedroom for nearly four hours, having to borrow her terribly childish PJs with little monkey figures on them. Hopefully my clothes were dry by now.

I did feel better rested and less spent, but I hated closing my eyes for long periods of time. I never made it through the night without terrible dreams—ever since what happened last month.

"... you get what I mean? And that's why—wait, you're not listening to me, are you?"

I blinked. "I always listen."

Elinore rolled her eyes and tucked a strand of honey-colored hair behind her ear. "I know that, silly goose. But it all goes through one ear and out the other. You sure you're okay?"

Okay? What did that mean? I'd forgotten how to respond to this question with a real answer. I could always say, 'Sure, I'm fine.' That would be a lie. I felt anything but fine. I felt sick, tired, conflicted, and alone.

With a heavy sigh, I met Elinore's inquisitive stare. "I don't know how to answer that question. Am I okay? If by okay you mean, am I feeling well? Then... no." My tongue dried. The next words stuck to my throat. "I'm"—I swallowed—"not okay."

My friend smiled upon hearing the truth ring through her bedroom. "That looked painful to say."

"It was."

Elinore laughed and left the room to go sit at her kitchen table, where a few textbooks lay open. I followed her like a shadow.

The stitches I sewed in earlier now itched, and my injury throbbed like a dull ache. "Do you have any pain meds?" I asked.

"Yeah." She grabbed the bottle off the counter and handed it to me. "It still hurts?"

"Not as bad as before."

She nodded. "Well, if you want to vent or something, I'm here. And anyway"—Elinore pointed a finger at me—"you've got some explaining to do, missy! You can start with what's troubling you and then segue into the whole alarm thingy, and what it means." My friend raised a meddlesome eyebrow. "Just because I agreed to help you without asking any questions back then, doesn't mean that I don't want answers now."

"I know." I grimaced. She deserved answers, especially after guarding one of my most precious secrets.

Elinore Fey encompassed humanity at its finest. Her respect and courage impressed me, which was how we first met. I traveled to a rural city in New York to collect the soul of a foreign prime minister in a car wreck. Elinore witnessed the crash and dove to the car to save both the prime minister's wife and child as I approached the scene. After reaping the prime minister's soul, I was to leave.

Elinore, some way, somehow, saw me while I used my powers. Most humans ignored magical events because they refused to believe in something greater than science. This way, magic remained impossible in the minds of modern society's educated members.

Elinore was different. She saw me reap a soul that day, but instead of screaming in horror or calling me out for the monster I was, she accepted me with kindness and promised to keep my secret. Normal laws of the High Court ordained that I either kill her or make her out as an insane individual under the public eye, but I did neither. She respected me, and thus I respected her. For a human, she was the best there was. And I loved her like a sister.

"How is your father?" I probed to change the subject. Elinore's father was a biologist, and she wanted to follow in his footsteps to conduct lifesaving research. "Does he like that new lab he's working at... Is it Cures for All?"

"Actually, it's called Creative Cures. He's doing fine, and he definitely loves it there. Thanks for asking. But don't think I'm going to let you change the subject."

I sat on the green couch next to me and rolled my shoulders. "Where to start?"

"With what's troubling you," Elinore said and turned a page from one of her open textbooks.

"Dreams," I muttered, feeling like I was speaking to an amateur psychologist. "Nightmares, mostly. Ever since last month, I've been having them each time I sleep."

"Is that why you haven't been sleeping?"

I lifted an eyebrow, and my friend snorted. "Come on, Prim. I'm not stupid. Anyone can see that you haven't slept for weeks. No wonder you're always so moody."

I bit my cheek to refrain from retorting, mostly because she was right about the sleep loss. The moody aspect was debatable.

"Yeah, well, about a month ago, I entered an ancient temple named Calliope to collect a human soul that ventured there by accident. I usually don't reap regular human souls, but the temple's magic would not let my reapers pass the entrance to do the work themselves. I'm surprised the human was allowed entry in the first place. Ester Calliope was an ancient queen that once worshiped the Goddess of Magic, Hecate. I assume the temple was built in her name. There was a dark stone in the center of the room, and out of curiosity, I guess, I touched it. There was a powerful aura to the stone."

My throat was parched as I tried to explain. I remembered the feeling that the stone belonged to me—the feeling that I had to reach out and grab it from its pedestal. "I suppose I thought to admire it more closely—"

"Dude, have you not watched *Indiana Jones* or something?" Elinore interrupted. Her arms flailed wildly, and she spilled popcorn all over the kitchen floor. "The bloody thing could've been booby-trapped!"

"Call me 'dude' one more time…" I warned, and she stuck out her tongue.

I blew out a puff of air. "In any case, upon touching the stone, flashes and visions assaulted my mind. When I stopped touching the stone, it dissolved into dust along with its pedestal and the visions stopped. That is, until I went to sleep that night. My mind is heavily guarded at all times; it has to be for the sake of controlling the souls of the dead, but the old magic of the stone slipped through my shields somehow. I keep seeing this"—my mouth went dry—"man."

"Aww, sweetie!" My friend giggled like a teenaged girl. "I see men all the time in my dreams."

My eyebrows furrowed. I doubted her dreams were anything like mine. "He dies, and for some reason, his death is enough to bring me to tears and desperation. Ever since I touched that stone, I've been more sympathetic toward humans. I care more than I should when they die."

"And provided you're the Goddess of Death, this upsets you?"

I snapped my fingers and smiled in relief. "Got it in one, sport."

She shrugged.

"You're not surprised?" I demanded.

"You were bound to have a moral dilemma sooner or later. If it's not a big deal, then it'll probably go away, like any other phase."

"If it doesn't?"

Elinore was quiet for a good moment. The wheels in her mind turned furiously. "Then maybe you're meant to remember something, and these dreams won't go away until you do."

My shoulders fell in disappointment. "These dreams, there's always something missing. Information I should know but can't seem to fully grasp. Maybe if I find out what I'm missing, I can reason why the dreams are happening in the first place." I shook my head and brushed aside my wary thoughts. "Nightmares aside, Lucifer has escaped Hell."

"What?!" My friend screeched and rose to her feet, spilling more popcorn. "You only mention this now?"

I leaned back into the couch and let her rant for a minute about how careless and thoughtless I was to keep such crucial information from my best friend. And how if I knew anything about friendship, I would've come to her the moment I knew my life was in danger, la la la, so on so forth.

After letting her cool off and stomp out her fury, I continued. "You done?"

Her eyes bulged as if they planned to pop out of her head. I half-expected her to pull out a baseball bat and beat me to a pulp.

"I can't speak over you," I explained, before her temper lashed out again.

Elinore took a deep breath before nodding. Her red face twitched while she struggled to keep quiet.

"Lucifer escaped Hell. He attacked my brother, and now he's keen on making a fool of me." I laughed dryly. "The High Court demanded I deal with him."

"Why though? I don't get this High Court spiel! Can't you just flip them the bird and ignore them? They can't say anything if you go on with your normal life."

My lips melted into a grin at her naivety. "If only it were that simple. See, if I let Lucifer unleash his wrath upon the deities, chances are they would go to war with me out of mere spite. And as much as I would love to test their capabilities as leaders, or lack thereof, Lucifer is truly the largest threat to me. Even if I loathe falling into line with the High Court's priorities, the Devil must be stopped."

"You don't trust the High Court?"

"Not in the slightest."

"But," Elinore tried to reason through my logic, "if you do nothing, you get screwed over by the Devil and those angry Gods and Goddesses."

"In a nutshell, yes."

"What about the alarm?" She stared at the flashing light on her countertop. The red flashes came from a button that looked like a 'that was easy' button from a cheesy game show.

"Now that's an interesting question," I mused aloud. I crossed my legs and stared at my shoes while wheels turned in my mind. "I spelled that alarm to give off a warning. If that light is flashing, then my Soul Dagger is being hunted. Whoever is hunting it has the intention of using it."

Elinore gulped, understanding the gravity of the situation. "You mean, the knife that can kill you?"

I nodded.

"You said that you already had your suspicions that someone was hunting it down." She referred to my phone call. "Why?"

I rose from the couch and brushed away some hair from my face, "Lucifer warned me that my Soul Dagger is being hunted."

"But he's the one who stabbed you, right? Isn't he the bad guy?"

Her question burned like a weight on my chest. Good and bad. Were there even such things? The line between the two concepts was so thin and muddled.

"It's not that simple," I said and shook my head solemnly. "Lucifer never caused my physical harm; his brother injured me. You need to understand, yes, Lucifer is my enemy, but so are many others. Without a doubt, he's one of the many hunting my Soul Dagger, but not with the intention of using it. He seeks to hide it from the others."

Elinore froze, a dawning realization sinking in. "If he's not hunting your Soul Dagger with malevolent intentions, then who is?"

A shiver ran down my back. The anonymity of my true hunter made me uneasy.

"Yes," I said, locking eyes with her. "Now that is the question I wish to have answered. Lucifer needs to be hunted, but regardless of what the High Court believes, my main priority is uncovering a potential usurper."

"What are you going to do?"

"Play along with the High Court." I approached a window and fiddled with the burgundy curtains. On the other side of the glass, there was a different world. Humans walked on the streets of New York City without a clue of what horror surrounded them. I envied their ignorance. "I always have a plan B."

"Aren't you afraid that the person hunting your Soul Dagger will kill you?"

I laughed. "No, my dear." I twirled away from the curtains. "Dead is dead only when I say so."

"What happens if the Goddess of Death dies, Prim?"

My eyebrows pinched together as a thought slipped my mind. I shrugged. "I suppose it would be the same as if any other deity dies. The mantle and power would be passed down to the person who killed me, and they'd be the next God or Goddess of Death. Don't worry yourself. It'll never happen."

Elinore wasn't comforted by my words.

After I spoke to Elinore, I changed into my regular clothing and left. I informed her that a reaper, Cain, would be guarding her home and accompanying her when she left the apartment. She wasn't too happy about my overprotectiveness, but I left no room for argument.

A block away from Elinore's apartment, the inevitable occurred.

Two men and a woman, all dressed in freshly pressed black suits, approached me. Three stony expressions zeroed in on mine. Their paces matched one another in perfect symmetry. They were armed and ready to use force. The leader strode in front of them and flipped out a badge. "Primrose Titan, this is the FBI. Would you come with me, please?"

The FBI rarely approached humans in this way. I knew this particular division of the agency was specifically meant for people like me. People who weren't human.

I was really not in the mood to deal with human authorities right now. Since my blank stare didn't convey the answer I wished to communicate, I answered with a word they would all understand.

"No."

The three of them reached for their guns simultaneously—the scene was almost artistic. I knocked the weapon from the arms of the agent to my right. My knee swung into his gut. Ribs cracked and the man collapsed.

Shots went off and two bullets hit my shoulder. I gritted my teeth and stumbled back with the impact. My movements blurred and the armed female agent flew back toward a brick wall. I lunged for the leader and grabbed him by his throat to make sure he didn't get any cute ideas. He released his weapon and attempted to claw my hands away from his throat. I held him in the air. His legs flailed and kicked my side. Abaddon's injury throbbed painfully. I hissed and glared at the agent.

The man I was choking started to turn blue, so I needed to make this quick. "Agent Wellsworth," I drawled in Elinore's thick southern accent. I remembered his name on the shiny badge he flipped out moments ago. "Tell Marcus that if he wants to meet with me, he will call or schedule an appointment per an official request."

The agent blubbered, but I tightened my grip. Agent Wellsworth's eyes were now bulging, and his face was purple.

"You see, he and I made a deal," I said. "We have a pact. He is well aware of my power, and I am certain he wouldn't wish to convey the thought that I am not capable of following through on those threats I dashed out several years ago." I smiled. "I would hate to make a show of my power. He knows how to reach me. Oh, and do extend my kindest greetings when delivering your message."

I let go of the human, and he fell to the ground. He gasped for air and wrapped his hand around his throat over the dark blue, growing bruise. My healing power quickly went to work on healing my bullet injuries. If only the wound Abaddon inflicted could heal that easily. Of course, Agent Wellsworth frantically kicking me didn't help. Still, with the dozen pain medications I was on, the pain had substantially diminished. Without further ado, I strolled out of the area, leaving the FBI agents to their own devices and arranging final preparations for what I was to do.

I flipped out my phone and made a quick call.

Two rings later: "How did you get this number?"

"Lord Atlas." My voice hardly concealed the animosity I held toward him. "Find anything in Phoenix?"

"No."

"Hmm, I thought not. Meet me tomorrow in Vegas, Caesar's Palace. No later than three local time."

Silence answered me for several seconds before he voiced his confusion. "Vegas?"

CHAPTER NINE
GAMBLING WITH DESTINY

DING DING DING DING ding!

"We have a winner!" exclaimed the polished slot machine as it flashed its bright lights and sang its praise. The old, white-haired woman that sat at the game fell to her frail knees and let a shout of joy escape her throat. Her wrinkled hands clawed at the golden coins that tumbled out of the machine.

Passersby stopped to stare at the scene, and some whistled and cheered. A young couple observed the woman, a few feet away from where she stood. The girl pointed at the game with a covetous expression on her face, and the boy with her went to fetch some cash or gambling chips.

My lips pulled into a crooked smile. I dipped my chin as my chest shook with laughter. Humans were strange creatures.

Caesar's Palace was a magnificent building. Aside from the casino, the mall's ceiling was painted in dark blue hues to mimic the appearance of the sky. The scents of food, drink, and perfume were plentiful. Heavy crowds surged left and right, and the sound of laughter and boisterous conversations echoed through the halls. But nothing pleased me more than watching humans spend away their fragile little lives in front of a petty game, which they had an infinitesimal chance of winning.

The casino bustled with life, smothered in envy and greed. People of all ages searched for a lucky break that could forever change their lives. And the goal? Winning that prized load of cash and leaving Vegas as rich and elite members of society.

Their pretentious beliefs were embarrassing to say the least, yet these gold-diggers didn't see themselves as anything but humble. Men and women in this room wished to achieve the American Dream through something as fickle as luck. Hypocrites. And all for not, their hope was misplaced. Lady Luck was on no one's side but her own.

"Do you play?" A cultured voice disturbed me from my observation.

The woman's words were curt, though a lulling British accent touched the vowels she pronounced, like a kitten jabbing lightly at a ball of yarn. My stomach flipped in surprise. Out of the corner of my eye, I glanced at the woman beside me. Her stiff spine and lifted chin indicated an air of superiority—strictly belonging to the upper class. Even with a pair of dark sunglasses hiding her predatory gaze, I recognized her as Destiny, a lady of the High Court. As if the British accent and imperious nature wasn't a straight giveaway.

Her red locks were gathered in loose curls and pulled elegantly out of her face. Her skin was papery pale, unhealthily so—I called it vampyre skin. An unnatural aura surrounded Destiny. Her cheekbones were too pronounced, her eyebrows too drawn, her lips too red. Though her face was white as snow, her veins didn't show. Every feature practically declared her supernatural nature to the public. All she was missing was the red eyes and bared fangs.

Destiny was a beautiful woman by human standards, but her beauty was too false, too inhumane to be truly classified as such. Too much symmetry or perfection that led to a disarming appearance. Her creator had outdone himself, and so she was unearthly.

Lady Destiny wore a floor-length, red gown that hugged her curves and attracted the attention of every mortal in the vicinity.

She always did love being the center of attention—we were different in that aspect. We were different in every aspect.

"Do you play?" she repeated. Her words were strained as she gestured casually toward a game of roulette.

I shrugged, a small smirk on my lips. "I dabble."

"Shall we?"

Her question seemed more of a demand, yet I flashed her a pretty smile and nodded. We walked toward the casino table. The attendant's eyes gleamed with excitement once his gaze landed on Destiny. No doubt he perceived her as a rich woman and big spender from whom the casino could make good money off of. His nose, however, crinkled in displeasure upon seeing me.

"Welcome, ladies!" the man beamed, smoothing his features into a congenial smile. "Ready to win today?"

"Of course," Destiny said flippantly. She moved across from me with a grace the Queen of England would envy.

I grunted, still surprised a member of the High Court had taken time out of her day to chat with me. I was especially surprised that this High Court member happened to be Destiny. We hadn't crossed paths since before Lucifer's imprisonment. Destiny was always present at the High Court meetings, but we had an unsaid, mutual agreement to keep our distance from one another ever since our little spat back in the day.

A man sitting at the game next to us widened his eyes as I shifted the sword on my back to stand comfortably. I raised an eyebrow, challenging him to say something. He quickly averted his gaze.

I turned toward Destiny, aching for some much-needed comic relief. "Nice shades. The sun bothers you at four in the morning?"

"We are inside, Lady Primrose," Destiny sniffed.

"I am well aware, Lady Destiny. Well aware."

"Bets, ladies?" the attendant interjected. His eyes hungrily assessed Destiny.

"Sorry." I grinned. "I haven't got any money on me."

"Pity." Destiny narrowed her eyes. "It's all right. I'll lend you some."

"So long as you don't expect me to pay you back anytime soon. Or ever."

"Right," she sneered. "I forgot about your particular beliefs on money, dear. Do forgive me."

"Ladies," the attendant insisted, gesturing to the game.

I smiled and waited for Destiny to mull over her important decision. As if money was worth the time and effort it demanded.

"Fine then." Her words were clipped as she finally made her choice. "I'll lend you—pardon me—*donate* to you five thousand."

I shrugged. "Suits me."

Destiny bristled at my attitude. Atlas Grimm wasn't the only one easily annoyed by my nonchalance. She flipped through her clutch and emerged with ten thousand dollars' worth of gambling chips, handing half over to me.

"You know, Lady Primrose, I cannot say that you don't have balls." Destiny removed her sunglasses, revealing two stone-cold eyes. "But you really should tread carefully. You will regret making an enemy of me."

"Ready, ladies?" the attendant asked. He sent the small ball spinning around the wheel.

"I never regret making enemies," I said and pulled the gambling chips closer to my side. I stared defiantly into her obsidian eyes. "I only regret not killing them when I had the chance."

Destiny curled her lip and bared her teeth. She turned to the attendant. "I'd like to place a two thousand dollar bet on thirteen."

"How cliché of you. Is the world's unluckiest number your lucky number by any chance?" I asked.

"And your bet?" the attendant cut in.

I tapped my fingers against the wooden rim of the green casino table. "The same amount, but I'll bet it on zero."

"A prophecy perhaps?" Destiny tittered in a light and airy voice. "An idea of what your future winnings will look like."

My right index finger twitched. I cracked my neck, to ease the strain on my muscles. "It's your money, Lady Destiny. I've nothing to lose."

"On the contrary, you have everything to lose."

I kept an eye on the small ball as it spun around the wheel.

Destiny leaned forward. "I want your title," she hissed. "You don't deserve to be called the Queen of the Underworld!"

"Straight to the point." I shrugged half-heartedly. Well, she didn't travel to Vegas for leisure. "You should've just led with that statement."

The ball landed on twenty with a resounding *clunk.* The attendant smiled. "Sorry, ladies. Better luck next time." He gathered the chips.

Destiny nodded to the man. "Another bet then."

The attendant spun the ball.

"Three thousand dollars. This time on eighteen," I said.

"Predictably random," Destiny shot back. "That's what you are, Lady Primrose."

"Predictably random? Sounds contradictory."

She laughed. "The perfect oxymoron to describe you, isn't it? Oh, I've heard from the others, darling—you're a train wreck, a guessing game on steroids. There is no rhyme or reason to how you do things. It won't be long before you run out of tricks and dig yourself into a hole you won't be able to gamble yourself out of. I should know. You see, meddling with the lives of humans is my expertise, but I am also known for meddling with the lives of Gods." Destiny smiled at the attendant. "Three thousand dollars on thirteen again, love."

The attendant flushed at Lady Destiny's comment. A tingle of apprehension ran through the back of my neck. "Just because you *somewhat* influence the decisions humans may or may not make doesn't make you all-powerful. Even Erin Grimm holds more power than you since he can definitively choose what people end up doing. Your influence is minimal."

Destiny's gaze darkened. "Do not underestimate me, my *lady.* Influence is power, no matter how minimal it is. That little voice humans hear when they're making a decision? That's *my* voice whispering in their ears. Erin Grimm might have the ability to map out the big picture of someone's future, but I decide how mortals get to their final destination. It makes me a formidable opponent. Don't you think?"

"I wouldn't know."

"Are you sure about that?" she asked with a mocking grin. "Did my darling pet not rattle you?"

Warning bells went off in my mind, and Destiny's eyes lit up, satisfied with what I realized. My chest clenched in anger. The assassin was hers.

My grip on the casino table tightened and the wood beneath my fingertips splintered. "You will regret—"

"Rosy."

I turned toward the familiar voice that uttered my nickname. "Ben?" My mouth fell open. "What—"

"Destiny," my brother addressed the member of the High Court with narrowed eyes and a cold composure. Instead of wearing his usual Hawaiian shirt and shorts, Ben wore all black and had a sword strapped to his belt.

The sound of the little ball coming to a stop brought my gaze back to the roulette game. It landed on thirteen.

My stomach sank. I'd never hear the end of it.

Destiny's eyes gleamed and a knowing smile touched her lips. "You see, Lady Primrose, all paths convene based on my will. Consistency shall always triumph over your little guessing game."

The tension escalated in the room as the temperature seemed to drop. Now that I knew Destiny sent the assassin, I could hardly mask my contempt.

"You should leave," Ben said to Destiny, his words clearly an order.

The defiance in Destiny's eyes flickered. She was smart enough to realize that fighting off two of the oldest deities to have ever existed was not within her power. Lady Destiny curtsied deeply. "Of course, my lord."

Without collecting any of her gambling chips, Destiny left.

My mind was reeling. Everything happened so quickly. Since when did Destiny decide to show her cards so early in the game and give away her advantage?

Ben grabbed my elbow and led me away from the table. "We have to leave. Now."

"What? Why?" I twisted my arm away from his grasp. My head was heavy with a sea of questions, ready to whip into a storm at any moment. "Why are you here, Ben?"

My brother's eyebrows were furrowed in worry. His movements were jittery, and his head whipped around like windshield wipers. "You're in danger."

"I always am," I shot back.

"Please, Rosy."

That's when I noticed it. There was something new in his eyes. Something I hadn't recognized before, during my confrontation with Destiny. His brown eyes were riddled with an emotion so deep it shook me to reality. Fear.

The argument I had ready for him caught in my throat. Ben's fear for me struck like a knife in the ribs, and I instantly knew something was wrong. I had to trust him on this.

"Okay." I nodded. "Let's go."

All of a sudden, hundreds of *ding ding dings* filled the air. Human screams of joy and victory assaulted my ears. A hoard of men and women rushed from side to side and barged past us to see what had happened. I shouldered my way toward Ben, and he caught my wrist to avoid being separated by the mob of humans in the crowded room.

"Primrose Titan!" a deep voice echoed above the screams and rapid beeping of casino machines.

I spun in the direction of the voice. A man stood on a casino table. His dark hair was slick with hair spray, and he wore a black suit and red tie. His skin had a sickly yellow hue. The demon reminded me of James Bond in a strange way, only not as human or nearly as cool. A foul smile warped his thin lips. Four similarly dressed men and women stood on the ground beside him.

"Mammon," I said. The Demon of Greed and Lucifer's younger brother.

Ben took a protective step in front of me, and I pursed my lips, annoyed, yet touched, by Ben's defensive gesture.

Greed laughed at my brother's actions. "Ah, though I do love giving out a good beating, I only came for the girl. Step away, God of Life, and we shall spare you years' worth of pain and regeneration."

The eyes of the four men and women beside him began to glow a deep red. Greed never walked around without a few demonic shape-shifters at his side—Hellhounds.

I grabbed Ben's upper arm and we exchanged a quick glance. I liked to think that we read each other better than Atlas could read his brother, Erin. A wicked smile crossed my face. My brother unsheathed a Scottish, two-handed sword. The claymore's broad, straight blade differed from my scimitar, which curved beautifully and broadened near the point.

The demon shrugged in mock disappointment, his smile never fading from his face. "Get them."

His four lackeys surged forward, their bloodred eyes locked on me and Ben. Their human features morphed into that of animalistic fiends, and their frames collapsed to support their weight on all four limbs. Four Hellhounds, the size of large boars, lunged toward us. Their mouths foamed as fangs erupted from their gums; fur as dark as night sprouted from their skin like thousands of thin needles to coat their newly transformed bodies. The smell of sulfur wafted toward us, and nearby humans gagged in disgust.

Ben ran to meet the hounds, blade in hand. I smiled and held my hands out as if ready to accept an embrace from a long-awaited companion. My mind grasped at the invisible strings of the souls in the Underworld, and I pulled them forward, transforming soul to flesh. Dozens of rotting corpses rose about me and jumped into action. Like a small army from Hell, they leaped toward the Hellhounds and fought them off.

Cries of fear and confusion filled the air as the mortals witnessed the supernatural battle taking place around them.

I unsheathed my sword, the metal gleaming in the dim light of the casino. Greed circled the starting battle, like a vulture waiting for a weakness to show. A Hellhound angrily ripped one of my dead soldiers to shreds, crushing tendons, ligaments, and bones in its large mouth. Its gaze locked onto its primary target. Me.

The beast attacked. My sword cut through the mutt's middle. The sound of flesh being torn grated against my ears and my stomach churned. I clenched my teeth and the nausea disappeared. Guts and gore splattered on the carpet.

The dead human that the Hellhound disemboweled started to reform. His limbs stitched themselves back together through some unseen magic.

"Zombie!" a girl wailed while running in the opposite direction of the regenerating body. Humans tripped over the tables and gold coins on the ground as they shoved past one another to leave the casino.

A beast growled from behind. I ducked and rolled forward, and the creature flew over my head. The Hellhound tumbled down before me, and I knelt on one knee to decapitate it with a clean stroke.

My brother's cry drew my attention. Of the two Hellhounds that attacked my brother, one lay dead with Ben's sword stuck in its head. Another hound latched onto his leg with its strong jaw.

I sprang into action. Vaulting over a table, I rushed to Ben's aid.

Mammon suddenly seized my sword arm in a viselike grip, forcing the blade out of my hand. I kneed him in the gut. Angered, he threw me back into a shiny casino game machine and my skull shattered the glass plate that protected the computerized device.

The slot machine blared another few *ding ding dings* in my ear. My vision went red. I ignored the blood as it dripped from the roots of my hair and snatched a large piece of glass from beside me. The shard dug into my flesh and drew blood. I lunged toward the demon and wildly swung the broken glass. It caught in his suit and tore the designer cloth.

Mammon growled. "I just bought this."

At his distraction, I brought the glass down on his left shoulder. I'd aimed for his neck, but it slipped in my hand, slick with my own blood. Nevertheless, the glass embedded itself into his skin with a satisfying *zink*.

Greed roared and moved to backhand me. I ducked under his right arm and swept his right leg from under him. He fell to the ground, his arm latching onto my elbow to pull me down with him. The stitches in my side tore and a pained hiss seethed through my teeth. The demon twisted my arm at an odd angle as he staggered to his feet, eliciting a sharp yell from my lips.

A blur of movement entered my line of sight. Ben tackled Mammon, having bested the final Hellhound with his bare hands. I brought my knee up to my chest and tore the shoe from my left foot. My brother pinned Greed to the floor, giving me enough time to shove the stiletto heel into his throat. The demon's eyes bulged, and he blubbered blood.

I removed my other stiletto and tossed it to the side. "You were never much of a fighter. Save your threats for a time when you can truly carry them out."

Ben stood and offered his hand to help me up. "Are you okay?" he asked.

"Yes. Are you?"

He nodded.

My eyes swept the casino, assessing the damage. I relinquished my hold over the dead, and the zombies dissipated into nothingness. Humans continued to run around like headless chickens while dead Hellhound parts and golden coins lay strewn across the casino floor.

I turned to Ben. "Well, it doesn't appear like we did much damage at all. From what I can see, the building is still standing."

CHAPTER TEN
SCOLD ME ONCE,
SCOLD ME TWICE

"**THIS IS COMPLETELY UNACCEPTABLE!**" Marcus yelled over the phone. "Damn it, Lady Primrose! You said you'd keep a lid on all the damage!"

"Be grateful it wasn't much worse," I countered and clutched my iPhone tightly.

"Worse! How could it possibly be any worse?!" the FBI agent demanded. His naivety impressed me, as did the swiftness to which he angered.

I almost snorted. "Pray you never find out."

"Damn you, Lady Primrose. I may be coming to clean up your mess, but I expect a damn good explanation in return!"

"In case you've forgotten, your entire job is to clean up after deities and the messes we make. I try to limit the exposure humans get to our kind and magic, but I don't make guarantees. Don't worry, you'll get your explanation. By the way, cuss me out once more, Marcus, and I'll personally send you to Hell myself."

I hung up on the human agent without another word.

Ben's gaze rested on my phone. A flash of anger flew through his eyes. "What do you hope to accomplish by associating with the human government?"

"An advantageous alliance." I shoved my phone back into the pocket of my leather jacket. Wisps of my disheveled hair flew wildly around my face, my ponytail long gone.

"They are beneath us."

"Agreed." I smiled and stuffed my hands into my pockets. "Still, we might as well avoid war with these fools when possible. If humans think that they can control us, they will leave us in peace."

The lights of a police vehicle flashed red and blue on the other side of the street. We sat at a bench across from Caesar's Palace while human authorities sorted through the situation. Chaos spilled out from the doors of the building as humans stumbled from the casino, rambling about rotting zombies and demon dogs while medics and cops desperately tried to convince them otherwise. My brother summoned his servants earlier to take the body of Mammon and imprison the demon within the borders of his kingdom.

I closed my eyes and rubbed my side, as my injury flared. A few stitches had come undone and now the dull throbbing evolved into a more obvious ache.

"Were you injured?" Ben asked. His forehead creased, and his eyes searched for signs of blood.

"Old injury. I had a close call with Abaddon."

His eyes widened. "It's taking longer to heal."

"Yes. I'm sure it's started, but it might take a few days before it recovers fully," I said. It might take longer if I kept tearing the stitches open.

"You need to be more careful," Ben scolded. "Tell me you've had it looked at by one of your reapers."

"I have! I even stitched it up. You can stop worrying." I playfully punched his shoulder.

Ben grinned. "I can't help but worry. It's my responsibility as your older brother to take care of you. If I don't keep an eye on you, you'll get into more trouble."

Touched by his sentiment, I smiled. "You are genuinely the best brother anyone can ask for. You know that, don't you?"

"Of course, I'm the best. Do you know anyone else who'd fly to Vegas last minute and fight off evil Hellhounds in his spare time?"

I tilted my head to the side. How did Ben... my eyes widened. "How did you know that Greed was coming for me?" I asked.

Ben shook his head. "I didn't."

"But you said that I was in danger. That's why you came to Vegas, isn't it?" I jumped up from the bench. "I mean, is that how you tracked me to Caesar's Palace?"

"I heard about the assassin."

I flinched. "How did you—"

"We both live in the Underworld." Ben stared at me as if I were dumb. "You do realize that Elysium is a subregion of your realm?"

I shrugged and sat back down next to him. "Yeah, but you never step foot into my territory."

"You never invite me," he said.

"Welcome to the club."

"Forget that for a second. Do you want me to answer your question, or not?"

I mimed a sealing gesture with my fingers across my lips.

Ben tried and failed to hide his annoyance with my childish behavior. "We both live in the Underworld. Your reapers guide souls into my realm all of the time."

"So?"

Ben sent me a scathing look.

"Sorry," I backpedaled. "I'll shut up now."

"A female reaper... Katy? Kathryn? Whatever her name is," my brother rushed to say when I opened my mouth to correct him. Kaitlyn. "She told me about the assassin in your palace. That's when I remembered overhearing one of my servants who served under Lady Destiny until three years ago. He recalled her boasting about how she planned to infiltrate your kingdom and kill you as you lay in your bed, deep in sleep. I decided to follow Destiny to Caesar's Palace. That's how I found you."

I shivered, although the night was anything but cold. "That's pleasant to hear. Basically, Destiny has been planning this for a while now."

Ben nodded, and I cursed under my breath.

How could I have been so stupid? This wasn't Destiny's first rodeo. She'd undertaken her fair share of devious plots and conspiracies, though rarely were they ever traced back to her. Why would she be so forward about her intentions now? I just couldn't put my finger on it.

Ben was silent. I wished I could comfort him, tell him everything would be all right. But I knew better, and besides, I didn't want to lie to him. War was coming, and blood would be spilled. However, if things went my way, the only spilled blood would be that of my enemies.

"Where is the God of Ice?" Ben asked, changing the somber subject.

A sour look crossed my face. "What, Frosty? I bet he's on his way here. Might take him a while though. He's as slow as he is dull."

"Don't talk about him that way."

My finger twitched at my brother's sudden defense of Atlas. I peeked at Ben out of the corner of my eye. "Why not?"

His eyes were full of reproach. "Atlas didn't have to come with you on the hunt to find Lucifer. He could have left you to do this alone. He's risking his life to help you. How would you like it if he said the same things about you? If his insults were as cruel?"

My cheeks flushed. While I understood Ben's logic, Atlas practically invited himself onto this quest after insulting my loyalty and capabilities as the Goddess of Death. Not to mention, if the God of Ice was so easily insulted and put off by innocent teasing, then perhaps he didn't deserve the power and respect that came with his title.

My lower lip pushed out into a pout. Ben's defense of Atlas surprised me; I didn't think he much liked the Grimm Brothers. I looked away and watched the humans make their way across the street.

"Now you're upset," Ben surmised. His tone became gentler as he considered my sulking posture.

"No," I lied.

"Yes, you are." He smiled. His good nature and patience had returned. "You never take criticism very well. Especially not from me." He bumped his shoulder against me.

My lips curled into a scowl. "What you're saying isn't criticism."

Ben paused for a moment. "Then what is it?"

I sullenly thought for an answer. "You're just telling me what to do." My response sounded lame even to me. I was grasping at straws.

Ben thought so, too, though he didn't say anything. He swallowed his laughter and turned away to hide his smile, letting me brood in silence. He'd made his point. To my dismay, he was right. I hadn't been very kind toward the God of Ice, nor would that change anytime soon.

"I think," my brother said, "you'll be safe from this point on."

I cocked my head to the side, curious. "Why do you say that?"

He nodded to his left. My eyes followed his gaze, and I froze. There, with all the glory of a vengeful angel, was Atlas, striding toward me. He was dressed professionally, not one strand out of place or wrinkle in his clothing. His steps were predatory, and dark circles adorned the skin beneath his eyes. His jaw tightened when his eyes met mine. And his eyes... His eyes bore a solemn promise of retribution.

I blanched and cursed colorfully at Frosty's untimely appearance.

Ben stood from the bench we sat on, a laugh shaking his chest. "I'll leave you two to it, then."

The God of Life left before I could convince him to stay. I cursed again.

I forced myself to look away from the angry Grimm Brother. The soft sound of his steps was threatening, though I didn't understand the cause of my sudden distress. He could do nothing to harm me.

A large hand grabbed my arm and hoisted me roughly off the bench. My legs entangled themselves due to the abrupt action, almost causing me to trip over my stilettos.

"Lady Primrose." The way he said my name sent my stomach into another round of flutters. "If you think I'm leaving you out of my sight for more than a second from this moment until we succeed in finding Lucifer, you are mistaken."

"Spare me the theatrics, Atlas." I shook off his firm grasp and stepped aside, a grimace on my face. I'd have an ugly bruise on my arm in the shape of Ice Prick's hand by tomorrow morning. "Did we not settle on three in the afternoon? How did you get here so fast?"

"I used one of those blasted sewer portals. And yes, I planned to arrive in the afternoon, but that was before you brought the wrath of a Prince of Hell upon yourself." His cold eyes were dim, blending into the night.

I had half a mind to tell him how I had confronted two—no, three—demons before Mammon but thought better of it. Atlas would make a bigger deal out of our 'splitting up' if he knew how many demons I crossed paths with.

I lifted my shoulders up and down into a simple shrug, knowing the simplicity of my actions would goad him into further anger. The temperature dropped right on cue, and I pulled my jacket closer to my body.

Atlas took a menacing step toward me. "Do you know what you've done?"

Why yes, Lord Atlas. I fought off four killer Hellhounds and one of the Seven Princes of Hell, but by no means do I expect you to congratulate me in any way, shape, or form. That would imply a maturity that you are unable of commandeering.

"What exactly is that?" I questioned innocently instead.

"You've made yet another enemy," he said. Atlas's hands fisted, and he clenched his teeth.

I laughed, unable to suppress my reaction to his ridiculous statement. "Mammon was never on my side. His brother is the demon that we are currently hunting. By default, he was always the enemy." Like Abaddon and Satan.

"And Destiny?"

An involuntary snort escaped me. "What about her?"

"I happened to cross paths with her on my way here, and she told me of your ridiculous argument. Are you foolish enough to believe she won't retaliate? Or perhaps you're foolish enough to believe you can outsmart her." Goose bumps covered my skin from the freezing cold aura that Atlas created around him. The angrier he became, the lower the temperature dropped.

"Your condescending tone doesn't flatter you, Ice Prick." I shoved my hands into my pockets to keep the shivering to a minimum. "Regardless, Destiny is no more threatening to me than your brother."

"Of whom you should feel threatened by," Atlas warned. His next step brought us face-to-face, an inch apart. Atlas's closeness filled me with the scent of mint. Despite his threatening words, I licked my lips and leaned forward.

"If anything," Atlas continued, oblivious, "Destiny holds more power than my brother. Yes, Erin can determine the final destination, the final ending of one's story, but Destiny determines the how and the why. Do you understand what this means?"

I was silent, and Atlas inhaled. "You do know. See, if Erin decided that you, hypothetically a human, were to die burning at the stake, would you rather die as Joan of Arc did, a martyr to the rest of her people? Or as those women in the Salem witch trials did, perceived as demons by their community? But you already knew that. And yet you decided to make an enemy of her."

My stomach fluttered. I grabbed a fistful of Atlas's coat and my lips grazed his ear. "Destiny's power is strong when it comes to compelling humans to do her bidding. But I am not human."

"So, you assume she can't harm you? Is your ego so blinding that you can't see a threat that lies right in front of you?"

"Don't take me for a fool! I know her power extends beyond influencing humans. I'm well aware of the abilities Destiny possesses, my lord." My breath caressed his cold skin. "But let me remind you of what *I* am capable of. It is she who should fear me, not the other way around."

"I hope you are as confident as you sound. But deep down, Lady Primrose, I think you doubt yourself." The closeness of Atlas's voice caused my heart to skip a beat.

His words aroused a silent fear I tried to keep hidden. His voice trailed off, and the silence engulfed us. I remembered the sheen of reserve in his eyes that I noticed when he first walked into the conference room at the High Court meeting—the reason his stare was openly captivating. He hid so many emotions behind a mental wall that reflected in his eyes. A wall that hid what emotions raged within him, but that wall could never hide the intensity of what he felt.

We both became aware of the closeness between our bodies at the same moment. When his lips met mine, I did nothing to stop them. His hunger took me by surprise. Mine did as well.

We melted into one being. Our mouths fought against one another, each of us desiring to dominate the other. My back slammed against a brick wall as we blindly twisted in the darkness. His arms caged me while his lips forced mine open again. His tongue met mine, and he let out a greedy moan. I hated domineering men.

I shoved him to the side, ramming his back against the wall. Irritated, a growl escaped Atlas's throat. Our lips refused to part despite our struggle for dominance. He pushed and I tugged, both of us falling down to the ground in a tumble of limbs.

"Surrender."

"Never," I vowed, a taunting smile on my lips. Never was a promise.

"Lady Primrose!" a decisively human voice called out.

My eyes narrowed, surprised to hear my name. Atlas continued his seductive onslaught, peppering kisses along my jaw line. His eyes were dark and full of such explicit lust that my cheeks heated with a heavy blush.

"Damn it, Lady Primrose!" the voice called again.

"This can't be happening," I said, shoving Atlas to the side with my elbow. The Grimm Brother sent me a lethal glare.

"Find me that wretched Goddess!" the same human voice said.

Marcus must have not seen us mingling in the shadows. Good thing, too. Whatever happened between Atlas and me... it was an accident. Never to happen ever again.

A group of FBI agents, in their black suits and ties, fanned out to search for me throughout the vicinity of the casino. The local police started to argue with the agents, upset that the Feds had breached their scene without obtaining permission. The men in black pulled out their fancy badges as if their IDs would explain everything.

I rose to my feet and shot Atlas a glare of my own. "This never happened." I was serious, too. Nobody could know. What the High Court members would do and gossip about if a deity obtained this information... It was unthinkable.

"Right," Atlas said. A coat of ice covered the ground surrounding him. How could one word sound so threatening? His eyes were heavy with lust. For a split second, I was tempted to forget about Marcus and kick off where I'd left off with the God of Ice.

No, I chastised myself. *That was an accident, remember?*

I shamefully averted my gaze and my eyes glazed over as I prepared myself to deal with the humans. I straightened out my clothing and ran my fingers through my disheveled hair. I left the shadows to approach the FBI leader across the street.

Marcus Rivers was a pudgy little man, with a lame excuse of hunched stature and a tired lump he called a stomach. His head was shaved and shiny, as if doused in baby oil. Gray whiskers poked out from his purple mouth, and his lips were always dry and cracked. He had a strong New Jersey inflection, and every time a word left his mouth, he sounded angry, no matter what word he said. He often sounded and looked like he had bronchitis—his voice was hoarse, and his nose was bright red in color. He wore a black suit and tie, much like a 007 wannabe.

When Marcus's crazed brown eyes landed on my figure, his scowl deepened. "There you are."

"Here I am." I crossed my arms in front of my chest. "What's with the scene, Marcus?"

"What's with the scene?" His face reddened and his fists began to shake. "I'll tell you what's wrong, you stupid alien!"

Ah, yes. I had forgotten he believed all supernatural creatures originated from outer space and that we'd infiltrated Earth thousands of years ago. The FBI had a special faction that dealt with the supernatural, and Marcus Rivers led this faction for the past twenty-five years. Agent Rivers and his gang made Area 51 look like child's play. His group was behind many questionable disappearances and unsanctioned government interventions.

Marcus continued his temper tantrum. "I have to answer to four different offenses because of you!"

"Which are?"

"Well, let's count, shall we?" To my surprise, he began to count on his fingers. "The subway, the hospital, my agents, and fu—forgive me, *freaking* Caesar's Palace!"

"Oh, dear." I fanned my hand in front of my face, pretending the desert heat was too much. "How dare I attack three of your agents? Such an offense is punishable with death!"

"It is," Marcus bit back. His childish tone implied a putrid hatred that I found offensive.

I took a step toward him, and he stumbled back. "Try and kill the Goddess of Death. See what good it does you. Or did you forget our little scuffle back in the day?"

A flash of fear glinted in his eyes. There had been a bloody power struggle between myself and Marcus two decades ago. The struggle lasted three days before the government decided to clean the mess they'd made, and so the start of a shaky, new alliance was born. Though we both wanted this relationship between the supernatural community and human government to work for the sake of avoiding unnecessary bloodshed, Marcus and I still hated each other.

Marcus shook his head. "Threaten me all you want, Lady Primrose! But if we're being damn serious, you should know what this kind of supernatural exposure does to communities. Especially one as large as Las Vegas!"

"I'm handling it," I growled. My hands bunched into fists. Couldn't he see we were on the same team?

"Handle it better."

"Is there a problem?" Atlas materialized beside me. His cold eyes narrowed on Marcus. Oh, for the love of God. Just the complication I needed at the moment.

The FBI agent scowled. "Another one of your freaks, I suppose."

Atlas's outrage seared through the night with a cold drop in temperature. Before the Grimm Brother could lash out and start an all-out war between humans and supernatural creatures, I threw my arms around his neck to physically rein him. "He's no one important."

Atlas stiffened, and Marcus sent me a skeptical glance like he didn't believe a word that came out of my mouth.

"Look, several... dangerous, demon-like aliens escaped Hell." I stumbled through an explanation consistent with Marcus's beliefs concerning the supernatural. My teeth chattered as the coldness of Atlas's skin soaked into my bones. "I said I'd handle it, and I will. Trust me on this one."

"A week, Lady Primrose. I'll give you a week." Marcus lifted his finger. "Fix this sh—I beg your pardon, fix this *mess* before our agency gets all over you and your supernatural alien beasts. You and I are walking on a tightrope right now, and the people I work for are just aching for one of us to trip up in the coming weeks. The deeper you get into all this crap, the less I can do about it."

"Agent Rivers." A man in black approached. "The secretary of defense is on the phone. Says he wants to speak with you."

Marcus looked to the sky as if to curse God but simply shook his head. He looked tired and helpless. Oddly enough, we were both in the same boat. Nobody wanted us to succeed. On the contrary, humans and deities alike waited on the sidelines, silently hoping we failed.

"One week," Marcus repeated. He took the phone from his fellow agent and walked away. The FBI armored cars blocked the road in front of Caesar's Palace and car horns blared as the traffic became heavily backed up.

My stiff arms fell to my side, and I placed some distance between Ice Prick and myself before I caught hypothermia. My hands trembled. Atlas truly was cold in every meaning of the word.

"What happened at the hospital?" he asked.

"Abaddon happened." I scrunched up my eyebrows and rubbed my hands together to generate some heat. A glitzy performer in a provocative outfit argued loudly with a police officer, making it difficult to focus on anything other than her screeching voice.

Atlas leaned in closer, noticing my distraction. His eyes were stern. "Any other surprises I should know about?"

Other than my encounter with Asmodeus, meeting with Lucifer, and a sleepover at Elinore's? "Nope, no other surprises."

"Right." The same word he used when I denied our recent make-out session was now said like it implied a threat. "Listen up, Rose. I don't—"

"What did you call me?" My mouth was dry, and I bared my teeth.

Atlas blinked. "Why does it matter?"

"I asked you a question," I said. The sharpness of my tone cut through the brittle air like a knife. My face grew hot.

"I called you Rose."

My breath caught, and before he could blink, I shoved him back. "Don't you *ever* call me that! You hear me?"

Several human heads turned in our direction and Atlas stared at me in open shock. He hadn't seen this side of me. I took a deep breath to calm myself and stepped away from the God of Ice.

"Sorry," I apologized through gritted teeth, "but only Lucifer calls me Rose. I'd prefer you avoid that particular nickname."

The ringing of my phone startled us both. I pulled the device out from my jacket pocket to stare at the screen. My stomach twisted, and I bit my lip, suddenly nervous. Speak of the Devil, and he shall appear. After Lucifer first called, I added him to my contacts list in case he made another phone call, and now, his caller ID flashed on my screen.

I shoved the phone in Atlas's face, and his eyes narrowed. "Speaker," he said tersely.

I nodded and answered the call. "You've got some nerve."

"Dearest Rose, it is always a pleasure to hear from you." Amusement was Lucifer's weapon of choice, as indifference was mine.

"What do you want?"

"Bellagio fountain. It's a surprise. Bring your boyfriend." He hung up before I could get out another word.

I shared a look with Atlas. "What do you think?"

He bared his teeth in a hollow grin. "Now you're asking for my opinion?"

No longer patient enough to argue with him, I spun around to leave. His hand caught onto mine before I made it three steps away. "Fine. I'm coming," he said. "Might as well, knowing the kind of trouble you get into."

I patted his shoulder, hoping to receive a reaction. "Spoken like a true boyfriend."

Two minutes later, the Bellagio Hotel was in sight along with its dazzling water fountain. For now, the lake from which the fountain sprung was quiet. However, not long ago water sprung toward the sky from a grand circle of light. It was nearing dawn, but the night sky lingered above us. In the darkness, the building was golden, and though the shows had ended hours ago, hordes of people still walked the sidewalks, stopping for pictures and chatting with friends.

Atlas and I stopped near the middle of the fountain, so as to view the man-made lake in its entirety. I looked behind me, searching through the crowds of humans for a potential enemy. A few drunken males strode by us, laughing. Lucifer's scent was nowhere to be found.

Why had he called us here?

The gurgling of liquid surprised me, and I turned back in time to see a jet of water reach to the sky. Tourists aahed and approached the fountain with smiles and laughs. Phones and cameras were out and poised for the right moment.

"I wasn't aware the fountain shows took place at five in the morning," Atlas said.

I shook my head, noticing the fountain's lights were turned off. "They don't."

We rushed forward in time to see an enormous serpent emerge from the water with a great roar of fury. For a moment, I believed Abaddon had arrived for revenge. Instead, my eyes widened as I saw the beast for what it truly was: a dragon.

CHAPTER ELEVEN
TAMING THE BEAST

THE DRAGON HOVERED OVER the fountain, drawing the eyes of every human in the vicinity. Nobody started screaming yet. Most watched the dragon with childlike wonder, mesmerized. Its red scales shined like rubies under the city lights. Leather wings, as long as those of a transatlantic aircraft, held up a strong, muscular body. Enormous talons extended from each of its four legs, barely grazing the surface of the water below it. Each talon was sharp enough to decapitate anyone if they dared approach the beast. The creature unlatched its large jaw, showcasing two rows of large, pointed teeth, and let out an ear-splitting roar. Yellow, snakelike eyes fixed themselves on Atlas and me. The beast folded its wings and dove toward us. That's when the screaming began.

Atlas reacted a second quicker than I did. He raised his arms and sent a dozen ice spears toward the dragon. The beast leaned out of the way with a magnificent grace and avoided most of the projectiles. One stray spear pierced its side and the dragon let out a cry of pain.

No, I thought numbly. That wasn't pain. The creature was angry. The ice did nothing more than scratch its glittering scales.

I broke free of my stupor and grabbed Atlas by the shoulder to pull him away from his onslaught. "The humans!" I pointed toward the crowds of people screaming and snapping photos of the angered beast. If Marcus and the FBI ever caught wind of this, supernatural beings would have worse problems than Lucifer on the loose. "Use mind control! Make them forget and leave!"

Atlas opened his mouth, ready to protest. The dragon's loud roar interrupted him. The creature lunged toward us, claws out and ready to attack. I brought out my scimitar in time to leave a bloody mark on its leg. Atlas and I ducked to avoid the dragon's deadly talons.

The Grimm Brother cursed and focused his attention to the humans. I turned to face the dragon. It flexed its strong, muscled wings and circled above us, ready to make its next move. The beast eyed Atlas and I warily, planning a stronger attack and weighing which of us was the greater foe. My mind grasped for its soul, determining whether or not the creature even had a soul or if a Soul Dagger would be needed to ensure its death.

A grim laugh escaped me as my mind felt the outline of a soul within the creature. Today, luck was on my side. No Soul Dagger would be necessary. "I can reap this one's soul. It won't be easy."

"Do it," Atlas said. Beads of sweat coated his forehead as he tired from the concentration required to control the minds of the hysterical humans. People ran in every direction to flee the area.

I widened my stance and lifted my arms toward the dragon. The tendrils of its soul expanded well beyond its body. The power of its existence was remarkable. As I began to grasp the vastness of the creature's existence, my jaw dropped. All I could do was stare. Dragons were rare, but one as intelligent and graceful as this... I felt ashamed to kill it.

I pushed aside any regret at killing the creature. Dragons didn't belong in the human world. Lucifer had summoned it from another realm, and to my dismay, I'd have to be the one to put it down. There wasn't any other alternative. I couldn't just portal the dragon to the

Underworld. The beast would tear my reapers and lower demons to shreds. I needed to end this here. Now.

My power expanded and leaped from my skin to grasp at the mighty soul of the dragon. My magic grappled with the complexity of the beast's soul, and I felt a mental click. As if a hook caught on to a small piece of thread, my magic caught on to a piece of the dragon's soul. All that was left to do was to unravel the cloth. My power pulled and tugged at the soul, bringing it down into the earth and finally into the realm of the Underworld.

The dragon's intelligence was greater than that of a simple creature. It sensed its impending demise and bellowed deeply, shaking the streets with its outrage. Its reptilian eyes locked onto my figure as it recognized me as the immediate threat. A blur of red aimed itself at my body. Unable to move without breaking my concentration, I quickened the pace at which the soul unraveled, pulling harder, as a skilled seamstress would unravel a pretty dress.

A human unwittingly ran past me. He rolled his ankle and tripped on the edge of the sidewalk, falling hard to the ground. I blinked and suddenly it wasn't a stranger lying there on the ground, it was a blond woman with gray eyes—she was wearing Elinore's face. I forced my eyes shut and when I looked again, the illusion was gone. The human man reappeared, and he struggled to get back up to his feet.

My gaze shot from the dragon to the human and then back to the dragon. My heart beat loudly in my chest. A heaviness descended on my brow, and my legs shook from the effort of reaping a soul this powerful. The dragon's maw lit up, ready to spit out a bright flame as it dove toward me.

I dropped my focus on the dragon's soul and sprinted toward the human. He tried to stand but his knees were badly bloodied. Shouldering his arm to support his weight, I threw a glance back to see fire escape the dragon's mouth. I shielded the man with my body, waiting for the flame to scorch my skin. Orange, red, and yellow lights intricately weaved between each other as the fire came closer and closer, purging everything in its path.

A high-pitched, chiming sound echoed in my ear. Cold arms wrapped around me, and a sphere of transparent ice surrounded us.

"Stay low," Atlas shouted in my ear. Never had I felt so relieved to feel his cold breath over my shoulder.

A column of flames engulfed our icy shield with its fiery rage, and freezing cold water soaked us as half the shield melted. The sheets of ice reformed as quickly as they were destroyed. I let out a huge breath, grateful for Atlas's quick thinking.

The dragon veered right, preparing for a final attack. Another blast of flames shot at us. Anticipation ate at my nerves. We didn't have much time. The beast grew desperate in its final moments, as all life did.

The dragon flew above us with aggressive speed. My lips set into a determined line, and my grip over its soul increased tenfold with my renewed focus. I let out an unearthly cry and the last bit of soul left in the dragon's body slipped straight to the Underworld.

"It's done," I said. Atlas stopped replenishing the icy shield around us and let it melt under the Vegas heat.

The red, lifeless body of the dragon spiraled toward the ground. Exhausted and angry, I lifted my hand toward the sky and opened a large portal to the Underworld beneath the falling dragon. The beast's body fell into the depths of my kingdom, where it would be taken care of by my reapers. Compared to the effort I put in to drain the massive soul of a dragon, opening a single portal to my homeland was as easy as snapping my fingers.

I huffed in satisfaction and leaned back to catch my breath.

"Why," a hoarse voice demanded, "in Hell's name did you not use a portal in the first place?"

My head pounded from fatigue. I threw my head back and laughed. First, my laughter was natural and well natured, but then it evolved into a hysterical hacking in my chest that wouldn't stop.

The God of Ice sat back and stared at me in abject confusion. He waited for my crazed laughter to dwindle. "What exactly do you find funny about this situation?"

I grinned and shook my head. "You wanted me to send a living, breathing dragon to the Underworld? God, no." My nose wrinkled.

"I like my castle and servants without damage. Dare I say I'd regret finding them lit up in flames?"

Atlas scoffed, though his lips pulled to the corner in a wry smile. "You think your reapers couldn't handle it?"

"I'm sure they could." My eyes wandered back to the human who I tried to help earlier. He was unconscious on the floor, having fainted from either fear or the mental stress of having someone control his mind and wipe his memories.

No matter how much I rejected the truth before, I couldn't continue to deny that I cared about humans. Jumping into action to save this human stranger was another shred of proof added to the pile of growing evidence. The thoughts raging through my mind were full of confusion. Why did I care about humans? Why did my mind conjure an image of Elinore when I saw the man lying on the ground?

"I guess you were right," I said.

"About what?

"I care about humans." I hugged my waist and looked up to the starless sky. "I didn't believe it before, but it's like I couldn't let the man lie there on the ground. I can't remember hesitating to help him, I just... It felt like the right thing to do."

Though the God of Ice could have used my moment of vulnerability to lob another insult, he only stood to his feet. I carefully rose to my feet as well, pausing for a second when the world began to spin. Other than the man on the ground before me, no humans remained in sight, which was good news.

Atlas shook his head, watching me as if he were seeing me for the first time. "I thought... I thought I might have imagined it before, but I was right. Your eyes do change when you perform magic."

I swallowed a heavy lump in my throat and placed my hands in my jacket pockets, growing defensive. "What do you mean?"

"Your eyes change color. From brown to green. From the moment you use your power, to the moment you stop," he said. A thoughtful expression graced his features. He smiled, satisfied that he knew something trivial that I hadn't known about myself.

I needed to put his claim to the test at some later time. I scanned the area, assessing any additional threats. In an hour or two, these streets would be filled with pedestrians and life would go on as if the dragon had never existed. Aside from the remnants of the ice sphere Atlas created, no signs of the struggle remained. In a few minutes, a puddle would be left of our icy protection and knowing the intensity of Vegas heat, the puddles would soon be dried. My clothes felt dry even though they were soaked a minute ago.

My initial concerns regarding Marcus and conflict with the human government vanished. If nobody remembered and no evidence of an attack remained, there was no need to worry. As for the pictures and videos anyone caught of the event, Photoshop and advanced technology would provide an adequate explanation if anyone started asking questions.

With this hearty conclusion, a reminder came to mind. "We need to talk," I said.

Atlas blanched in momentary surprise. His muscles tensed, as if he thought I planned to pull out a ticking time bomb. "Yes, we do."

My hand slipped into a jacket pocket and pulled out a small vial of blood. I shook it around with a sly smile for effect. "I finally have what I need to track down Lucifer's Soul Dagger."

Atlas stepped toward me to get a closer look. He examined the plastic, see-through bottle. "Whose blood?"

"It's the blood of a royal. When Benjamin first created human life, these original humans established clans among themselves. The most ancient human clan went by the name of Kovach and was ruled by a queen and a king." I touched my chin, lost in the story I weaved. "Hoping to gain power and respect among the Gods and Goddesses, the royals bowed before every whim of supernatural deities. My brother grew a grudging... respect, if you can call it that, toward the two human rulers."

I smirked at Atlas's confusion. "Yes, it seems odd that Ben had any sort of relationship with humans, but if you don't believe me, you can ask him yourself," I said.

The Grimm Brother snapped out of his shock and crossed his arms. "How is this related to finding Lucifer's Soul Dagger?"

"The connection is simple." I copied his gesture and crossed my arms in front of my chest. "To honor the actions of the humans, with the hope of encouraging other clans to willingly subject themselves to the commands of Gods and Goddesses, Ben had a powerful sorceress by the name of Fate cast a blessing upon the bloodline." I brought the vial closer to my face and tilted it from one side to another to watch the blood slip around its container. "The gist of Fate's spell is that the blood of these royals could be used to track the Soul Daggers of deities."

"You must be jesting. Your brother may be foolish, but he isn't suicidal. He'd never give humans a tool capable of endangering the lives of deities."

I shrugged. "Perhaps Ben wouldn't have done the same in this current place and time, but this spell took place back when humans lived in the Garden."

"Now I know you're lying," Atas said with a smug smile. His eyes narrowed. "Humans would never be allowed in such a sacred place."

I slipped the vial of blood back into my jacket and sighed. "Don't be foolish, Lord Atlas. Once upon a time, humans lived with Gods and Goddesses in their original land. How did humans come up with the story?" I raised an eyebrow. "You think they magically thought it up on their own? You know better."

"Which story?" Atlas asked. His interest suddenly piqued. If anyone understood that stories came forth from reality, it was a Grimm Brother.

"The oldest story of all time. The story of Adam and Eve. Ever heard of the Garden of Eden? There was a time when we all lived peacefully in the most sacred of our lands, the realm from which deities originated."

Atlas maintained steady eye contact and leaned forward. "And this peace ended how?"

"The same way all peace ends." I stepped closer to whisper into his ear. "Betrayal. Adam and Eve disobeyed God. The two ancient royals betrayed their sovereign rulers and were banished from the ancient land, never to return." My shoulder brushed past his, and my gaze landed on the Bellagio. "I require several ingredients to finish the spell to track down Lucifer's Soul Dagger, but I now possess the most important material necessary to conduct it: the blood of a Kovach royal."

Silence greeted my statement. My eyebrows furrowed and I turned toward Atlas. His lack of response was uncharacteristic of him. "Is something wrong?"

"No," Atlas said. He pursed his lips, an admission ready on the tip of his tongue. "I suppose I never realized you actually had a plan."

"What?" I chuckled darkly under my breath. "I mean, did you think I was spontaneously trekking across the country with no direction? Hey Atlas, let's go to Vegas and put Lady Luck to the test?"

My gaze challenged his, and he averted his eyes. I snorted. "That's exactly what you thought." My words came out more accusing than I meant.

Atlas said nothing. His silence irked me more than any comeback he could've come up with. It only proved that what I'd said was true—he did think so little of me. Defiance rose within my chest like a tidal wave. As the Goddess of Death, responsibility surrounded me at every nook and cranny. I couldn't get away with doing nothing or beating around the bush. I worked, I plotted, and I certainly accomplished the goals I set, regardless of what people like Atlas and Destiny believed.

"Well, for your information," I said while I held my nose in irritation, "I knew the last living Kovach royal owned a residence in Las Vegas. With a little digging, I discovered he was a compulsive gambler at Caesar's Palace, thus my presence there."

"Was."

"Huh?"

Atlas gave me an annoyed stare. "You said he *was* a compulsive gambler."

A mischievous smile warped my lips. I circled the Grimm Brother, as a predator would her prey. "How perceptive of you, my lord. See, you and I agree on one thing. Ben made a mistake when he gave humans a tool to kill us. There are other ways to trust the human race without putting our lives as deities at risk. After procuring what I needed from the only individual alive capable of being used as a tracking machine for Soul Daggers, what do you think I, the Goddess of Death, did to said tracking machine?"

Atlas paused, seeing me through a different light. His tense shoulders reminded me of a cornered animal. "You killed him."

"Bingo." I snapped my fingers and pointed to the sky. I kicked at a stray rock, and it tumbled off of the sidewalk. "Any other stupid questions?"

"Only one. What other materials are necessary?"

"Most are simple to procure." My fingers twirled a piece of hair that hung loosely over my temple. "All but one."

"Which is?"

"To track one Soul Dagger, you must have a Soul Dagger." I smiled, baring my teeth. "Yours will do just fine."

Atlas froze. Literally froze. Ice coated the area around him, and I stepped away from him before I became a block of ice. "If this is your version of a temper tantrum—"

"Believe me, Lady Primrose," he said, his voice taking on a dangerous tone and sending a chill down my spine, "you haven't seen me angry."

The coldness in the air convinced me of this. I rubbed my arms.

Atlas's jaw was tightly clenched. The vein in his temple throbbed. "You will use *your* Soul Dagger for this spell. I will not place my life at risk based on some story you weave. A story I've never heard of, much less believe."

"Why should I put my life on the line?" I argued. The last thing I needed was for the Grimm Brothers knowing exactly where to access the only weapon that could end my life.

"Because it's your problem." Atlas stepped toward me and rolled his shoulders back. I craned my neck to look up at him. His glare made me feel small as he pointed a finger at my chest. "Lucifer is your threat. A monster *you* created. Deal with him yourself."

Burning anger sent a fire through my chest.

"Fine," I spat through my teeth, "but I'll search for my Soul Dagger on my own. I won't have you accompanying me. We'll regroup after I spell the dagger."

The elder Grimm Brother nodded. He knew this wasn't an argument he could win. What I said was final. Besides, the dagger was the single ingredient I needed for the spell besides the blood. The rest of the materials that I wanted to collect would help me cast another spell. To protect me and my Soul Dagger.

"Well, isn't this quite the party?"

Atlas and I stiffened simultaneously. What the Hell was he doing here? From what I could tell, the God of Ice was as surprised as I was.

Erin Grimm sauntered toward us, a despicable grin on his face. He straightened his dark blue Armani suit and stopped in front of me. "What? Did you think I'd miss all the fun?"

CHAPTER TWELVE
A JOURNEY OF
SELF-DISCOVERY

"SO," ERIN SAID, CASUALLY adjusting his cuff links, "what *did* I miss?"

Though his tone wasn't demanding nor authoritative, Erin watched Atlas and me closely out of the corner of his eye. He'd apparently grown bored waiting on the sidelines and decided to pay us a visit. His narrowed eyes and pursed lips made him appear distrustful, though I shrugged that thought away. Why would Erin be distrustful when his own brother was making sure I didn't screw anything up?

I shot Atlas a malicious glare, daring him to make mention of my Soul Dagger to his younger brother. As if out of spite, he opened his big mouth. "Actually, there is important information Primrose neglected to mention—"

An uncomfortable ripple ran through Atlas's body. His mouth opened and closed. He looked like a fish out of water, like he was choking on his own words. The elder Grimm Brother paled and met my gaze, realizing something I hadn't.

And that's when I noticed it. My power had instinctively drifted toward his soul, pulling it into a suffocating grip. I wasn't able to move his soul any further than the borders of his body without his Soul Dagger, but that didn't mean that my tight grasp on his soul wasn't painful. I held on a second longer as a silent warning before releasing my grip over Atlas's soul. He noticeably relaxed, able to breathe again.

I turned my attention to Erin and rolled my eyes to hide the conflict Atlas and I just resolved. "What your brother wishes to say is that I discovered a means to track Lucifer's Soul Dagger. I simply require several... herbal ingredients to conduct the required spell."

The God of Fire stared blankly at me. "Okay," he said sarcastically. I wasn't shocked that he noticed my tense interaction with his brother, particularly after Atlas's profoundly disturbing reaction.

Erin turned left and right and nodded toward the empty streets. "And the dead human and random puddles—"

"The human is unconscious," I corrected. "I think he fainted."

"We encountered a dragon." Atlas regained his composure. His frosty eyes were busy throwing daggers at the back of my head, but I ignored him. It wasn't my fault that he couldn't hold his tongue.

Erin's eyes widened in disbelief. "A dragon?"

"It was a trap," I said. "Lucifer called and—"

"Lucifer called?" Erin repeated incredulously. "Why wasn't I informed of these events?"

"He called a few moments ago," Atlas said.

His reassurance didn't seem to calm Erin down. If anything, the younger Grimm Brother was barely keeping his temper at bay. He sniffed. "We had an agreement, brother. You keep me updated on all important happenings, or else I tag along. Would you care to explain to me how the search for Lucifer led you to Vegas?" He crossed his arms and lifted his chin, waiting.

I snorted. "The search didn't directly lead us to Vegas," I said. "We came to Vegas for an ingredient that I needed for the tracking spell. If it were up to Lucifer, we'd both be running around Phoenix, Arizona, like a bunch of headless chickens—"

"Phoenix?" Erin interrupted.

I gritted my teeth. "Lucifer sent a letter—"

"The Devil sent you a letter?"

"Stop interrupting me!" I snapped. "Bloody let me finish the sentence!"

Erin shook his head, more shocked by the information coming out of my mouth than by my outraged behavior. "I don't understand. When did he send the letter?"

That's when it clicked. A piece of the puzzle that I had been missing became clear. I turned to Atlas. "You didn't tell him."

I expected Atlas to jump at every chance to share the mission's details. I thought back to the High Court meeting when the two brothers conversed silently, so in tune with one another, it was unnerving. I didn't think there were many secrets between the two, at least none concerning the hunt for Lucifer. Why would there be? Yet, there was something Atlas wanted to hide from his younger brother.

Perhaps the power dynamic between the two brothers wasn't as it seemed.

"No, he didn't tell me," Erin said. "Lucifer called, something about running around in Phoenix, and now a letter?" He sent an accusing glance toward his brother. "Why would you keep this information from me?"

"Erin," Atlas began.

Then the argument launched itself in full force. Both brothers were yelling, and none of what they said made any sense.

Needing to distance myself and the two arguing brothers, I walked away from them. By the time they solved their disagreements, I could both acquire and spell my Soul Dagger.

"Hey!"

A blast of spontaneous fire appeared in my path and blew me back. The heat brought a heavy flush to my face, and I landed hard on the ground. Prickles of warmth permeated the air and dampened my clothes with the sweat my body produced in response to the heat.

My head spun, and I lay still, confused for a fraction of a second. A flash later, I was on my feet, crouched in a defensive position.

"What," I hissed at Erin, "was that for?"

He smiled coyly with a cheeky glint in his eyes. "Now that I have your attention—"

"Are you insane?" I roared and lunged for him. In the blink of an eye, I had him pinned against a tree, my arm heavy against his throat.

"Primrose, put him down."

I pressed harder against Erin's throat. Atlas's words fell flat against my ears. "We're in Vegas, idiot! Someone could have seen you!"

Erin let out a strangled laugh. "You seem quite moody, my lady. Is it that time of the month?"

"Shut up," Atlas and I said together.

"Let him go," Atlas repeated with a calm voice.

An icy coat layered over my skin. Coldness filled my body and penetrated the heat of my normal body temperature. My limbs were heavy, and I shivered as my lips chapped painfully.

I reluctantly released Erin and stepped back. Without pause, I grabbed Atlas by the collar of his shirt and pulled him close so that his face was near mine. "Don't mess with me, Lord Atlas."

"I don't plan on it," he said. His icy eyes burned with cool composure. Our eyes locked into an intense staring match.

Erin cleared his throat in an attempt to break the tension between us. We both ignored him. At that moment, Erin Grimm didn't exist, and neither Atlas nor I minded. Anger boiled through me, and a cunning chill emanated from Atlas's skin. Neither of us could control our tempers very well, and that was a problem.

"I'm leaving," I said.

"We won't stop you," Atlas said.

"We won't?" Erin demanded. "Who died and made you king?"

Without even a sideways glance toward his sibling, Atlas nodded at me with an earnest promise in his eyes. "We won't try to stop you."

His words did nothing to relieve my tensed muscles, though I understood the meaning and oath behind them. Messing with the Soul Dagger of a deity was a serious business and in most cases taboo, socially and morally unacceptable, unless for political gain. It was impossible to draw the line between acceptable maneuvers and unacceptable exploits.

I removed my hand from Atlas's collar, and I pursed my lips in reluctant acceptance of his pledge. I opened a portal to the Underworld and left Vegas.

Anger and distaste toward the Grimm Brothers dominated most of my thoughts. I hadn't forgotten Atlas's lack of cooperation in conducting the spell to find Lucifer's Soul Dagger. Nor did I forget the potential of him being an enemy in disguise.

As for Erin—what the Hell was he thinking? Using his fire so carelessly, in such a public place? Every deity knew Erin's control could slip at any time. Erin's fire was dangerously wild in nature. In fact, he slipped up more than he got things right when summoning fire. A simple mistake could literally light up the world in flames and burn all life to a pulp. It almost happened once, half a century ago. Nobody wished for it to happen again.

My eyes rose to the gray skies of my realm, landing on the thin line between Hell and the rest of the Underworld. Hell's cloudless sky was painted bright red. The heat in the subregion was unbearable for most of Hell's occupants, known for searing flesh and peeling at the minds of prisoners.

Once every year, during the summer solstice, black storm clouds loomed over the subregion, from which acidic rains and hail pelted the grounds. The treacherous storm blew heavy winds, and blinding lightning shattered the otherwise serene sky. Some years, the storm had been so heinous that multiple twisters touched the ground, and the winds lit up with Phlegethon's flames. For days, Hell's sky burned with fire.

There were five oases in all the Underworld, one of which was in Hell. An oasis was a one-story wooden cabin in which the conditions of the Underworld were nullified. Hell's fire couldn't make it past the front door because the wards were too strong. The wards that guarded an oasis were created by the Underworld, and therefore stronger than any ward created by a sorcerer or sorceress. Hell's oasis was the one place no visitor would suffer in the subregion, but it was also impossible to enter without a personal invitation from myself or an invitation from the Underworld. And the Underworld was very picky about who it liked and disliked.

The Underworld lived and breathed like any other creature, recognizing me as family of sorts. Supernatural fiends like Destiny believed themselves capable of ruling the Underworld, but they lacked the basic qualification to do so. The Underworld didn't know or respect her blood; the lands would never accept her as one of their own. The petty title 'Queen of the Underworld' changed nothing for her. Phlegethon's flames would melt her flesh, the storm would pelt hail upon her head, the ground would rumble with powerful quakes. Though I hated these lands, I would never allow a mercenary like Destiny upon them.

My right hand bunched into a fist, and another portal opened into the human world. A step later, I walked through a dull graveyard in Grindavik, Iceland. The bright noon sun shined, casting away the shadows from the stones and caskets. Seeing the names and markers for humans who were no longer in life placed me in a depressed mood. It was difficult not to linger and think of each individual's past life.

Though the sun was high, a biting chill blew with the wind. Grindavik was no desert. The Las Vegas warmth didn't reach this cold city's borders. The pathway that led to the graves was surrounded by luscious grass and green bushes. Bright blue flowers, locally known as Nootka lupine, left a distinctly sweet, floral odor in the air. The graveyard had been cleared of most tall trees, except for a few dozen birches.

There weren't many visitors today. An elderly couple solemnly stood beside a grave with their hands clasped together in prayer.

My phone buzzed, and "Toxic" started playing loudly. I held the phone to my ear. "Yes?"

"Hey, Prim! It's me!" Elinore said. She sounded as cheerful as usual, and if I hadn't known better, I would've ignored the shred of nervousness in my friend's voice. Her southern accent was always heavier and more clipped when she was nervous.

"What's wrong?" I asked.

"Oh... nothing. Nothing's wrong."

I blinked and lifted my chin, offended. "What—you think I'm stupid?"

"No!" Elinore said. "Of course not!"

"Then don't lie to me. If there's nothing wrong, why did you call?"

For a moment, there was nothing but silence on her end of the phone. "I guess that wouldn't make sense," she thought aloud. "Calling if nothing was wrong."

"So, something is wrong," I said.

"I'm not sure," Elinore said. Embarrassment colored her tone. "I guess I feel a little weird."

I held the phone closer to my ear. "Huh?"

"I feel weird," she repeated louder this time, sounding defensive.

"You feel weird?"

"Kind of."

I felt like facepalming. Great. My friend called me, not for an emergency or any troubling news—nope, she decided to give me a call and tell me that she felt 'weird.' I was at a loss for words. "Listen, Elinore." I tried to maintain my calm. "If it isn't anything important..."

"I don't know. It's just kind of weird with him following me and all," she rushed to say before I jumped to any conclusion.

The blood drained from my face, and I recoiled at the thought of my friend being in trouble. My muscles tensed. If there was someone keeping tabs on her... I made a fist, ready to open a portal. "Is someone following you, Elinore?"

"You know," Elinore insisted, "that guy you said would follow me around."

"Cain?" I cringed. My voice sounded too high-pitched, even to me.

"Yes, him."

My muscles relaxed, and my previous anxiety faded. "Let me get this straight." I pinched the bridge of my nose. "You decided to call me because you're weirded out that Cain—the guy I sent to protect you—is following you around?"

"Well," Elinore said, "when you say it like that, I guess me giving you a call seems pretty stupid."

I bit my tongue. Elinore was my friend, and out of respect for her, I resolved to listen to her full concern.

"I don't know," she said. "Him tailing me puts me on edge. He comes into all my classes and freaks out my professors." A few chatty voices in the background cut her off, and Elinore grumbled an apology. "Give me a sec. I'm out for groceries, and it's getting a little crowded in this aisle."

"Isn't it early for groceries?" The time change would put her at eight a.m. in New York.

"No. I have a class at nine. Besides, Cain doesn't let me leave the apartment after the sun sets. I need to buy groceries before my day gets busy."

I waited for her to move to a quieter place. Her grocery cart squealed as she wheeled it around.

"I mean, I feel like there's something wrong, and that's why he's following me," Elinore explained. "Is there something wrong, or is someone out to get me?"

"No," I said matter-of-factly. "If I thought you were in danger, I would've told Cain, and I would've called you right after I talked to him. You'd be on house arrest right now."

"Oh." Her grocery cart stopped moving. "That makes sense."

"You still sound nervous. What are you not telling me?" My palms grew sweaty while I waited for her response.

"I guess it's nothing. I'm a little on edge. I got a call late last night from the company my dad works at over in California. They said something about there being trouble at the lab."

The way she said the word 'trouble' made the hair on the back of my neck stand up. "What trouble?"

"They wouldn't tell me. It must've been something important though. The CEO personally took the time to give me a call. He called me close to midnight, Prim. And that's midnight in California time! It was three a.m. over here in New York. Why would the CEO call so late?"

"I don't know."

"It doesn't make any sense. And the fact that the CEO decided to make the call himself doesn't ease my mind at all. The big guy doesn't get involved unless something's insanely wrong."

I shook my head and mulled over possible explanations. A question kept nagging at my thoughts. "Why would the CEO call and not tell you anything about what happened?"

"All he said was that they were trying to contain the situation," Elinore said. "As if I knew what *situation* they were talking about. They promised to call by tomorrow at the latest and 'tell me more,' whatever that means in their messed-up dictionary."

"Did you try calling your dad?"

"Yeah, of course. But he's pretty slow when it comes to answering the phone. He always has been. He doesn't answer after dark or before noon. So, he might be fine..." She trailed off, afraid of vocalizing the other alternative of him not being fine.

I processed what she'd told me. Her father worked in a risky environment. Anything could go wrong in an experimental lab, especially a lab that dealt with infectious diseases. "Your dad's alive if that's of any consolation."

"Are you sure?"

"Positive. Goddess of Death, remember?"

"Yeah, and they would've told me if his life was in danger. They'd have to."

I nodded before realizing she couldn't see what I was doing. "I agree. It's likely an administrative issue. Or maybe the company is being sued, or your dad is being sued. It's America, Elinore. Everyone gets sued at one point."

"Exactly."

"Try not to worry too much. You'll get more information soon."

"Yes," she said. "Soon."

"Do you mind putting Cain on for a minute?"

"Sure. Is something wrong?"

"Stop being so skittish!" I ordered with a dry laugh. "I want him to give me his report while I'm on the phone with you. Why would I call his phone to ask him the same questions in a few hours when he's right there with you now?"

"Okay, okay, bossy!" I could practically see her hold her hands up in mock surrender. "I'll try and stop worrying. Hey, Cain," she yelled. "Prim wants to talk to you."

She fumbled with the phone and passed it to my reaper.

"My lady?" Cain's familiar voice put me at ease. I felt better knowing that he was close to Elinore.

"Has it been quiet over there?" I asked.

"Quiet and uneventful." A touch of sullenness stained his voice. Cain loved a good fight, and I'd stuck him with babysitting duty for the next few days. "I don't understand why you asked me to watch the girl."

"Hey! I can still hear you, you know?" Elinore's muffled voice said.

"But she can't hear me, right?" I asked Cain.

"No."

"Good." Relief flooded to my cheeks. "It's important that you watch her, Cain. Her safety is critical to the success of my plan."

I could feel Cain's frustration over the phone. "What plan?"

"I'll tell you," I promised. "Just not yet."

Cain was unhappy with my secrecy. But instead of arguing, he shifted the subject. "Kaitlyn called."

"About the dragon?"

"Yes." Amusement colored his tone of voice. "Where have you been traveling, my lady? Dragons haven't been sighted in the human realm since—"

"The Dark Ages," I finished. "Dragons still hatch in certain realms. I suppose Lucifer thought it'd be nice to summon the beast and let it terrorize the human world for a time." I made my way to an unoccupied bench at the edge of the sidewalk.

"Before you killed it," Cain said.

"Right." I flinched as a human walked past me. "And there's nothing suspicious going on over at Elinore's place?"

"Should there be?"

I sighed as I sat down. "I don't think so. Elinore received a phone call, though. Her father might be in trouble."

"If I knew the girl's involvement—"

"I know it would make your job easier," I said with a grimace. "For now, her involvement needs to remain unknown, ambiguous at most. Is that clear?"

"Yes, my lady."

His instinctive reply reminded me how lucky I was to have Cain by my side. Loyalty was rare. A loyal friend who cared was even rarer. "Good. Now, can you think of anyone you trust?"

Cain remained silent for a moment. "Yes."

I closed my eyes and nodded. "Would you send them over to check on Elinore's father? Ask her for the address and tell her it's to find out what happened to him. She'll be more than willing to help."

"I'm sure," Cain mumbled, sounding somewhat embarrassed.

I smiled, barely restraining a laugh. "She talks a lot, doesn't she?"

"I've tried to inform the girl that it's easier to do my job if she were to leave me in peace—"

Elinore raised her voice on their end of the call. I couldn't hear what she said, but Cain growled a phrase that sounded suspiciously like 'damn women' under his breath. This time I couldn't keep from laughing.

"I've been doing some research," Cain said once Elinore quieted.

My forehead creased. I didn't ask him to conduct any research. "What research?"

"About the assassin."

"I'd rather you not dig into that," I scolded as my stomach dropped. I felt more nervous about his actions than I let on. "I told you, you'll get yourself cut up into tiny pieces if the wrong person hears that you're snooping around."

"I'm not afraid." He sounded hurt. "Besides, you'll want to hear my theory."

"Okay." I watched my surroundings to make sure no one was listening in on my call. "Impress me."

"For the assassin to enter your chambers, he must have been one of two things: a magical prodigy or working with someone who is magically skilled. I don't believe the first is a valid theory. Otherwise, he would have found a way to escape without plummeting to his death."

"Okay, I agree with you so far." I stood up from the bench and looked at the gray tombstones to my right.

"He must have been working with a being who is very skilled in magic—someone so skilled that he or she could remove all of the wards protecting that room."

A lightbulb suddenly lit up in my mind. "Over a dozen wards were protecting that chamber," I said. "For someone to have busted through every single ward... There aren't that many people who can do that."

"Only a handful can," Cain agreed. "There is one being who has offered similar services on the black market in the past. Fate."

"Fate. The deity, Fate?" I mulled it over for a second. "That's a pretty big accusation."

"Yes."

A sigh left my lips. "It's possible. Fate and Destiny have worked together in the past. You know how it is. Those two deities see being a Goddess as a position higher up on the political ladder. People covet power they don't have. I don't know if you got the memo, but Destiny was behind the assassination attempt. The two of them make a powerful duo. Unfortunately, there's no hard proof."

"Not yet. My sources are reputable, I can easily dig up—"

"No more digging," I said. "That's an order. I put you in charge of Elinore for a reason. You said I could trust you with any task."

"You can," he replied fervently.

"Then prove it. Protect the girl. Make sure no harm comes to her. Now put Elinore back on."

After a quick shuffle, Elinore cleared her throat. "You two done talking about me?"

I ignored her childish question. "Cain is going to help find out what happened to your father. I'll stop by your apartment in the next day or two."

"So, there is trouble," she said. Her conclusion made sense. Why would I drop by her apartment at such a hectic time if there was nothing to worry about?

"No," I denied. "Nothing's wrong." Not yet. "There's something I need to give you. Don't worry about it yet."

"Okay... And Prim, thanks. For helping with my dad and stuff."

My expression softened. Her nervousness was warranted. After all, she loved her parents. I'd be worried sick if something happened to Ben, and Ben was a God. Elinore's father was human, and humans were very fragile. "Of course. I'll see you soon."

"Bye, Prim."

She hung up, and I put away my phone. I filed away the recent conversation to the back of my mind and shifted my attention toward another important task. I'd come to this graveyard for a reason.

I shuffled through the growing weeds, stepping between small stones and past buzzing insects. People who came to honor their loved ones frequently brought lavender and roses. The scent of these flowers perfumed this place of mourning, giving the pretty smell an intoxicating edge—like poison.

A dull numbness sat heavily on my chest and lingered painfully over my shoulders. A name came into sight.

Gavin Petreson.

The name brought a wave of sorrow that cast itself like a spell. A spell that pulled at my limbs, drew the strings of my heart into a tight bind, and bit at the edges of my mind.

Petreson. There was nothing special about the name. Nothing remarkable. But the way it rang in my ears... How familiar the name sounded when it left my bitter tongue. Yet the meaning behind the surname was lost to me.

Son of Petre, who are you?

Shadows laughed at me, taunting me with memories and images that I didn't remember but still yearned for. I remembered the questions I asked myself in the hospital elevator, on the way to Vivian Erikson's office. Why did it hurt to breathe? Why did I feel that a human's death was my fault?

The answer to both my questions was simple. Gavin Petreson—he was the reason. He was the human man I dreamed of when I fell asleep. The man with the green eyes. He was the reason I found it difficult to breathe, difficult to live, knowing that death existed only because of me. And because of how happy I was with him in my dreams, life became dull and painful in his absence. Though

I couldn't remember life being anything other than this painful, heart-wrenching mess, the possibility that it could've been more when I lived with someone I loved... that possibility drove me mad. It hurt more than any physical pain I ever felt.

I hated Gavin Petreson. Because for some sick reason, I *loved* him. A human! A dead human at that. His demise, like the broken edge of glass, cut deep into my chest to carve a hole where my heart should've been.

My hands touched my cheeks and felt them wet with tears. A flush of shame spread across my face. My knees buckled, and I fell to the ground. I cowered at the grave of a human, mourning someone I didn't know. A nobody.

Today wasn't the first time I visited his grave. The moment his image first appeared in my mind, I scoured every corner of the Underworld, looking for the one face that refused to stop haunting me. Searching for that unique set of green eyes belonging to him, and I found him. Not that it did me any good.

I coughed up a growl of anger and sent the grave a petty glare. Through the blurriness of tears in my eyes, I read the phrase, from Shakespeare's *A Midsummer Night's Dream*, engraved in the headstone.

Love looks not with the eyes, but with the mind,

And therefore, is winged Cupid painted blind.

Gavin Petreson's grave was built two and a half weeks ago, and on the same day, a human worker carved these words into the stone per my request. Gavin didn't have a grave when I first found his soul. Many humans died without the privilege of a marked grave. However, the thought of someone I once cared about having no way of being remembered didn't sit well with me. Thus, I had taken it upon myself to leave some man-made proof of his existence.

I placed my hand flat against the earth in front of the gray tombstone. I reached into the Underworld to summon the soul of Gavin Petreson. A body started to form, and my eyes stared at the man who I supposedly loved and said he loved me. A man who wasn't blessed enough to live in Elysium nor cursed enough to inhabit the lands of Hell.

I took a moment to truly look at him, to behold him in every way. The man was a few inches taller than me. Thick calluses covered his hands, suggesting a past of physical work. His broad shoulders and muscular physique reminded me of a soldier's body. He wore thick, brown mountain boots and trousers. A white tunic hung over his upper half, and a leather vest was laid on top of it. His sun-kissed skin was two shades darker than mine, making me feel colorless next to him. A thin layer of facial hair peppered his strong chin. Though Gavin lost his eyes before he died, his soul re-created his body as it was before he'd been tortured. Two green eyes shined brightly yet without any life. His facial muscles were slack and immovable.

I stood to my feet, not willing to kneel before this strange man. "Well," I asked, "have you anything to say today?"

Gavin's features remained still. Emotionless. This wasn't the first time I summoned his soul or demanded answers from him. My mind prodded into his, but as always, I found nothing. His mind, his memories, his past were not attached to his soul.

Of all the humans in the world, why could I not communicate with this one?

When someone died, their soul left their body along with their memories. A dead person was like a cabinet with two drawers. In the first drawer sat that person's soul, and in the second drawer lay his or her memories. The soul in the first drawer could never remember their previous life in the drawer beneath it, but as the 'owner' of the cabinet, I should be able to open that second drawer at any time to access that dead person's memories.

Yet this human provided no access to his mind, as if his mind didn't exist. Frustration scorched through my temples like a terrible headache. Tears threatened to resurface, but I forced them back. Of all humans, why him? Why couldn't I read his memories? I glared at the baby-blue sky while a cold wind blew my hair over my cheeks. The bright sun hurt my eyes, but it dried my tears.

I leveled my gaze with Gavin, and my expression relaxed. "You may leave."

His body sank into the ground as his soul traveled back to the Underworld. I lowered myself to the ground and dug into the soil.

Five handfuls of dirt later, my nails caught on the lid of a jar. I pulled out the green container and held it out in front of me. The contents were unperturbed. I clutched the jar close to my chest. I covered the hole and leveled the surface with the palm of my hand so that the grave and soil near the stone appeared undisturbed. Nobody needed to know that I was here.

Without another thought, I hid the small jar in one of my pockets and bunched the leather close to my body. I rose to my feet and turned to portal back into the Underworld, now ready to pick up my Soul Dagger.

A figure blocked my path, and I stopped short before slamming into his body. My index finger twitched. "Azazel," I greeted my general.

Azazel commanded one of my Four Armies of Hell. My armies guarded Hell and tamed its most horrific creatures. In times of war, the Four Armies were called forth to fight any foe of the Underworld. Azazel was no soldier. No, he was far too rebellious for such a respectful title, but he was the mightiest general I ever commanded—second only to Lucifer, who betrayed me. Instead of wearing the traditional army uniform, Azazel sported a loose shirt and torn pants. A roguish smile graced his lips, and his wild brown eyes questioned every move I made. The reapers used to call him 'the fox' behind his back, at least until Azazel found out and unleashed his sword upon those who dared utter the words.

My general did remind me of a fox. He had clever eyes, and his reddish-brown hair was always mussed up. Azazel was sharp-witted and had a sharp tongue. He was tall and lanky, though his size made him quick on his feet and even quicker with a sword.

"Lady Titan," the general said, referencing my formal title. Though his greeting appeared respectful, the distaste in his tone convinced me otherwise.

I waited for him to state the purpose of his visit. Instead, he remained silent. His mischievous smile grew as he sensed my irritation.

"Why are you here, Azazel?" I snapped.

He craned his neck to observe the ambiance of the graveyard. "I could ask you the same."

I lifted a shoulder in a half shrug. "I'll tell you my reason if you tell me yours." Arguing with Azazel only strengthened his resolve. He enjoyed our little scuffles. Negotiation somewhat bettered the situation, at least until one of us stormed away in a fury.

Azazel scratched his chin thoughtfully. "Hmm, I suppose I wished to see what business my beloved leader was attending to, only to realize—wait, she doesn't attend to actual business in her free time. She dallies through random graveyards while her reapers break their backs, sucking souls dry."

And there was that attitude. "I wonder why I put up with you."

"Because I make up for your slack."

"Don't push it," I warned, pointing my finger at his chest. "I'm in a foul mood today. I was in a foul mood yesterday. And from the looks of it, I'm going to be in a foul mood tomorrow. Shove your attitude up where the sun doesn't shine, or I'll do it for you."

"How delightful," he said. "I told you why I was here. Why are you?"

"Personal dealings concerning Lucifer's Soul Dagger. I came to collect an object I needed." I smiled, knowing my vague answer wouldn't satisfy his curiosity. "Now, if you'd excuse me, I have *business* to attend to."

"Who is Gavin Petreson? Why were you visiting his grave?"

Son of Petre, who are you? I shrugged and looked to the grave. "He's somehow related to Lucifer's little game. I'll figure it out."

The easy lie felt like a punch to the gut, but Azazel seemed to accept it. I shoved past his shoulder and stepped through a portal into the Underworld. The last thing I needed was for him to see the tears that threatened to resurface.

CHAPTER THIRTEEN
THE HALL OF THORNS

THE HOOVER DAM WAS one of the many fascinating man-made constructions in the world. Yes, I hated to admit that I thought highly of a structure created by *humans*. The Hoover Dam wasn't the first time humans impressed me. Egypt's pyramids impressed me long before the dam. Still, the immense heat the workers dredged through and the poor work conditions of the 1930s made this construction project admirable.

Today, as I walked up the path to the top of the dam, immense respect for this human accomplishment pulsed through me. Gods and Goddesses often took credit for grand monuments even though humans built these structures with their own bare hands and forged tools. Yet another perfect example of humans and deities being perpetually out of sync.

I glared up at the boiling sun and leveled my gaze with a wall of yellow-orange rock that reached up toward the bright blue sky. Light, plump clouds stretched like cotton across the sky, like white paint on a canvas. The back of my hand brushed against my sticky forehead, removing a shiny coat of sweat from my brow. My cheeks were flushed and puffy from the heat. The *whoosh* of cars driving across the Mike O'Callaghan-Pat Tillman Memorial Bridge sounded like waves crashing on the pristine sand of Miami beach.

I strode out into the dry bushes, straying from the sidewalk that led up to the top of the dam, and approached the wall of rock. My stilettos crunched against the dying plant life and dusty ground. Each step I took was heavier than the last. My advance toward the hidden location of my Soul Dagger felt like a funeral march, and a shadow loomed in my gaze despite the sun's glare. My thoughts quietly reminded me of the black cat that ran across my path not long ago.

Upon arriving near the warm stones, my hand snaked between two large boulders. In the dark, tight space between the rocks, my fingers brushed lightly over a lever. Relief eased the tension that tightened my stomach. I latched onto the handle and pulled it roughly to the side. A mechanical *click* went off, and a deep rumbling noise resonated. The boulders separated, creating a small gap for which a thin person could slip through.

My head swiveled back to get a 360-degree view of my surroundings, and my eyes scoured the area to confirm that nobody was foolish enough to spy on me. Satisfied that no one paid attention to my actions, I used my elbows to hoist myself up into the small space.

I crawled through the passageway. The darkness bled deep in front of my line of sight, and my eyes started to adjust. Only my breaths could be heard in the small space, even as my heart beat loudly in my chest.

Shortly, I came upon a sudden drop. I reached for another lever lying in a corner and pulled it roughly. Before the gap could close and crush me into a puddle of blood and bone, I rolled out of the passage. The thump of stone hitting stone rung in my ears as my feet hit the ground.

From this point forward, portals were forbidden—the wards I placed on the hidden cavern long ago made sure of this. The only means in and out was through the way I entered.

The wards of this sacred place left the room oddly empty of magic or the buzz of life. It was like a tomb, solemn and desolate, yet somewhat peaceful. There was little to no light here, and so the darkness dominated my surroundings. Despite being the Goddess of Death, I was still a living, breathing being. I could only guess what death was like for the person who died, and if I had to imagine what death would feel like, I thought it would feel like this. Empty. Dark. Full of peace.

My soft breaths echoed through the dark room, and I shrugged off my leather jacket. I searched the pockets and brought out the jar of herbs and vial of Kovach blood. I stuffed both containers into the back pockets of my pants and sealed my phone in a plastic bag before forcing it into a pocket. I folded my leather jacket neatly and set it on the stone ground before removing my stilettos.

I strode toward a cool hallway. An airy breeze blew from one end to the other, creating an eerie moaning noise. A blue light shined on the walls near the end of the corridor, and the scent of salt and moss caressed the floor. The hall wasn't very broad, maybe large enough for two people to walk through it if they stood shoulder to shoulder. I sensed my Soul Dagger. Its pull was maddening, like an itch I couldn't quite scratch. I waited at the beginning of the corridor and gazed at the walls. Anticipation made me skittish, and I started at the next moan that echoed through the corridor.

The hall vaguely reminded me of a horror movie. All that was missing was the creepy tune in the background.

I held my breath and took the first step into the corridor. My reflexes kicked in, and I rolled my shoulder back before a dark, thorn-like blade could pierce it. Not breathing, I sidestepped, narrowly avoiding two other large thorns. Unlike that on a rose, these sharp spikes were the size of short swords, making them lethal to mortals and excruciatingly painful to immortals. The thorns shot from the walls if an outside presence was detected roaming the hall.

I lunged forward and landed on my knees. I leaned back as a thorn punctured the space my face inhabited a mere moment ago. I bit my lip and watched the pointy end of the thorn with crossed eyes. I hit the blunt side of the blade with my elbow, and it clattered to the side of the hall. My hips pushed forward, and I curved my back into a bridge-like pose. My core muscles tensed and pulled me up into a standing position. A blade cut through my tank top and scraped over my old injury.

The stitches snapped apart and I yelled in pain. My forearm slammed down on the flat of the blade, breaking it in two. My other arm blocked an incoming thorn and snapped at it with the back of my fist. A burning sensation seared through my side.

My nostrils flared. Blood trickled down my lower abdomen. I'd only made it through a quarter of the hall, and already, blood had been drawn. I ignored the pain and continued down the corridor. Half a minute later, my foot finally crossed over the end of the hallway. The dangerous corridor was left behind.

A coat of sweat covered my arms, and my tank top stuck to my chest and waist like a Band-Aid. The red of blood stained the black color of my clothing. I lifted the edge of the tank top and removed the bandage to see how my older injury fared. A sharp intake of breath shook my chest.

"How?" I wondered aloud and lightly traced the wound with my finger.

I shuddered with the pain that followed. The thorn had reopened the wound that Abaddon inflicted. Most stitches were broken, and blood seeped from the break in my skin. The thin line of broken skin was bright red, though the injury was days old. The edges of the injury were rough and flaking. Small patches of skin surrounding the wound were now a purple color, as if the tissue was dying. Abaddon's poison was busy working its damage, spreading the infection to the rest of my body.

Lucifer was right. His salve would do nothing to heal me, only rid me of the pain. Cain's and Lucifer's voices echoed in my mind. *You need stitches.* Great, I needed to poke myself with a needle again later today. I rebandaged the wound, this time more tightly, and pulled the tank top back down to hide the injury. Out of sight, out of mind.

I looked back at my Hall of Thorns. The blades retracted now that the corridor was empty. Should anyone else come in, they would have to go through the same maze, only without the same knowledge I had of it.

I walked away from the hall and faced a staircase that spiraled downward into a blue-lit room. A breath of humid air escaped from the bottom of the staircase, and a damp coolness stuck to the surface of my skin. I descended the stairs, bracing myself against the railing now that the pain in my side resurfaced, and the blue light climbed up the shadow of my silhouette. The lull of soft waves wove through the cavern. As I took the last step, my bare feet sunk into the sand-covered ground and a calm sensation slammed into me like a wall. The sand was fine and soft to the touch.

A long lake spread through the room. Dark, daunting rocks hung from the walls and the roof of the cavern, ready to collapse at any moment. Their jagged edges created a dooming sort of ambiance. A small stream of water trickled from the rocks and hit the still lake with a tinkling noise. The lake's water lapped at the sandy shore with calm, slow waves.

The cold waves barely touched the tip of my toes and sent a shudder through the rest of me. I closed my eyes and walked into the water. With each step, the coldness seeped through my clothing, dragging at my limbs. My skin became soaked and trembled in the cold, clean water. The pain from Abaddon's wound became numb with the freezing temperature of the water. Once the waves reached the level of my chest, I dove under the surface. The salt burned my eyes.

I swam down toward the small opening from which the blue light came. A few strokes after passing through the opening, I floated toward the surface of the lake. My face rose above the water, and I drank up the humid air. My muscles relaxed once I waded toward the shallows and up onto the dry shore. My bare feet left light prints on the white grains of sand. In front of me stood a large, stone wall from which the blue light came. The light came from the wards surrounding the wall like an unnatural aura, moving across the wall's surface like the rapids of a chaotic river.

Dread made the back of my head hot and sweaty. I hated to break the final wards that guarded my dagger because once I did, there was no going back. These wards had taken years to fabricate, so it would be years before I'd feel secure about my life again.

I inhaled deeply and strengthened my resolve, forcing myself to approach the stone wall. With each step, my legs felt weaker and ready to buckle from underneath me. The pain in my side became unbearably hot, and I stumbled over my own two feet. My breaths were labored, and my eyelids were heavy. When I was arm's length from the wall, I collapsed. The stone wall blurred in front of me. Afraid of losing consciousness, I spotted a sharp rock near me, and my hand weakly squeezed the stone to draw blood. The red liquid dripped down my fingertips, and I reached out to smear the blood against the wall.

The second my fingers touched the stone, the eerie blue light disappeared and plunged me into darkness. With the wards now broken, my mind was no longer addled. I fumbled for my phone to turn on the flashlight.

Tiny cracks started to form along the wall. The stone recognized the blood of its owner, and a thundering boom echoed through the cavern. The cracks largened and spread, and I stumbled to my feet to duck away from the large chunks of rocks that fell. When the sand and dust settled, I rubbed my watering eyes against my arm and stepped past the rubble on the floor. The stone surface of the wall had fallen in the presence of my blood, revealing a smoother layer to the wall with a built-in keypad. I dusted off the keypad with the edge of my tank top, and nine digits became visible. I typed in the code, eight-four-eight-two-six, the five numbers that spelled out my last name, Titan. The boxy outline of a safe and its handle hid just below the keypad.

A red light flashed, and the keypad beeped. I pulled the handle, and out came the safe. I threw the heavy, metal container onto the sand and knelt down to the second keypad. A four-digit code later, the safe beeped, and I wrenched it open. The dagger's aura made the air uncomfortably heavy. I could sense its magic searching for my soul within the depths of my body though the thought immediately vanished from my mind. I stuck my hand into the safe and brought out my Soul Dagger.

Not much longer than an average steak knife, the dagger glinted in the light of my phone's flashlight. Its sleek gray blade was sharp enough to draw blood at the slightest touch, and the dark hilt of the dagger fit perfectly in my hand.

I tied the dagger to my belt beside my other blades. Without a second thought, I ran from the safe and threw myself into the water, diving deep and fast. And that's when it began. The cavern started to collapse. Elinore mentioned Indiana Jones. This was far worse.

I swam back through the opening, narrowly avoiding the boulders and bits of rock that fell into the water. The lake churned, agitated and full of tall waves. As I rose to the surface, a stone hit my shoulder. The waves thrashed over my head, and I took in water. Everything blurred. The salt stung my throat, and my chest ached painfully.

Desperate to leave the cavern, I rose again, and a burst of oxygen rewarded my efforts. Once my toes found the ground, I ran out of the water, the waves this time on my side. The rumbling of everything falling apart thundered and shook the cavern. The pain in my side worsened with my movement, and my balance faltered. A boulder fell where I just stood before my stumble. I flung myself up the staircase, forcing my feet to move despite their fatigue.

The Hall of Thorns, now inactive due to the cavern's collapse, began to close. The walls were moving inward, approaching one another and the space between them narrowed.

Before I could enter the passage, a grotesque set of claws sunk into my arm, and I found myself face-to-face with a cloaked man. I would've cried out from the sharp sting in my arm if I hadn't been so shocked by the sight of him. He had no face, only a shadow of darkness through which two milky eyes glared at me. His cloak, which hid most of his figure from my view, was riddled with thorns from the hall, and his posture slumped with weakness.

The creature had an odd scent to him, like honey. I tried for his soul but couldn't find one. Instead, I twisted the arm he'd latched onto, and the assassin howled as the bone snapped. I kicked his waist, and he fell down the staircase, hardly in control of his balance.

I didn't check to see if he tried getting back up. With little time left, I threw caution to the wind and jumped into the Hall of Thorns.

I shuffled sideways while the walls closed in. As the hallway became unbearably narrow, I burst into the opening on the other end and made a run for the lever.

With a pull, the lever clicked and the space between two boulders opened. I hoisted myself up and crawled through the narrow opening. The sound of metal squealing sent a final burst of adrenaline through me. The space between the boulders began to close. With a final push, I rolled out of the passage, and the two boulders hit one another with a deep rumble, closing the entrance to the cavern for good.

I hit the ground hard, landing on my stomach, and received a mouthful of dirt. Dry heaves racked my chest, and I coughed out the nasty taste from my mouth. Dust covered my face and stuck to my scraped and bruised arms. I turned over to lie on my back. My side twitched and throbbed, as if it had its own heartbeat. My hair lay like a curtain over my sight, and after brushing the locks away, the sun shined harshly on my face.

A human's wrinkled face popped up from the side. "Is she dead, honey?" an elderly man asked his wife, who politely waited to the side.

His wife tsked softly and shook her head. "I don't think so."

I stared numbly into the man's blue eyes. "Do I look dead?" I croaked out through my hoarse throat.

The man mumbled something like, "Don't do drugs, kid," and hobbled away with his wife. Well, that wasn't helpful.

I remained on the ground for a minute more. The sun dried the water from my skin and clothes. My minor injuries healed themselves while I waited and thought back to the assassin.

Cain was right about Fate. That scent of honey the assassin bore was specific to a rare sect of Dark Magic, and if Fate was selling magical services on the black market, she was definitely involved in the dark arts.

The image of the creature made me sick to the stomach. Without a definitive face and with clawed appendages, the creature came off as more of a fiend than the ugliest lower demons I'd come across. Whatever it was, I had never seen anything like it before, and worse, these assassins had no soul. I couldn't snap my fingers and be done with them.

I groaned and rolled over to my side. "I'm not sure the dagger is worth the pain."

And the worst part? I lost my leather jacket.

† † † † † †

I called Cain when I portaled back to New York City. He said he'd wait in Elinore's apartment for my arrival and claimed we had much to discuss. He first clarified that Elinore and I needed to 'talk privately' before he greeted me.

Before I went to the apartment, I stopped by the local Walgreens and restitched my wound in their bathroom. Though the bleeding stopped, my side cramped up every once in a while, likely an effect of the poison.

I knocked thrice against the front door of Elinore's apartment. The dust and dirt from my hands smudged against her white door. As I debated whether or not to wipe it off with the handkerchief I stole off a young man from downstairs, the knob jiggled, and the door creaked open.

Blond curls and two gray eyes peeked out from behind the slightly opened door. The worried crinkles on Elinore's forehead became more profound as she took in my appearance.

Granted, I did look like I came out of a volcano. The water from the lake made the dust, sand, and dirt stick to my skin like a powder. Plus, my leather jacket and shoes were underneath two hundred tons of rubble. Yeah, I wasn't getting those stilettos back anytime soon.

Elinore's small hand snatched at my wrist and pulled me in with unexpected strength. The door shut loudly, and I noticed her apartment was dark as night on the inside.

I raised an eyebrow, seeing my friend perfectly regardless of the darkness. "What's with the lights?"

She promptly flipped the switch and cleared her throat nervously.

"Where's Cain?" I asked.

Elinore nodded toward her bedroom. "He's waiting for us to finish talking."

An awkward silence resumed, and that's when I noticed little things about her. Her blond hair was tangled, as if not brushed this morning. Dark circles had formed under her eyes, and deep worry lines were etched into her face. Her clothes were wrinkled and disorderly, and her posture slouched.

"You look worse than I do," I said.

"Yeah, about that..." Elinore avoided my gaze and stared at my bare feet. "What happened to you? It looks like you've been through Hell."

My worry increased tenfold. Being Elinore's friend, I knew exactly when she was trying to change the subject. My face softened, and I placed my hand gently on her shoulder. She looked up at me in surprise.

"What's wrong?" I asked. "Is it about your father?"

My friend patted my hand reassuringly and gave me a tense smile. "We have a lot to talk about, Prim."

CHAPTER FOURTEEN
SUPER-SECRET SPELL

I WAITED PATIENTLY FOR my friend to continue. Her anxiety worried me, and for a brief moment, I feared the worst. Her father was alive though arguably there are worse fates than death. Elinore was always so carefree and optimistic, and to see her in this state of defeat and tiredness rattled me.

"Do you need pain meds?" she asked. Her eyes lingered on my newly bandaged injury.

Elinore's random question threw me off, and I shook my head. "No, I stopped by the pharmacy before I came here."

"You look like you're in pain."

I bit my lower lip, frustrated with her changing the subject. "I had to stitch my injury back up again, but that doesn't matter. What's wrong, Elinore? Did something happen?"

Elinore glanced away. "Maybe you should clean yourself up first. It can't feel good to be covered in dirt and blood."

"Right, so that I can give you time to come up with a fake excuse as to why you're upset." My voice took on a sharp, dangerous edge. I wanted to know what was wrong. Now.

Elinore noticed and nervously rubbed her arm. "You're right." She pursed her lips and covered her face with her hands.

A sound came from inside her chest, and my stomach tightened. When she removed her hands from her face, I could see tears fall down her cheeks. Her next sob was louder than the last, and I froze, like a deer in headlights.

Elinore never cried in front of me, not on her worst days. She never looked sad or depressed because she was always happy and funny, and now suddenly, she wasn't. The world started to spin though I stood firmly in place, and I thought back, trying to find out when everything started going so wrong. Was it back when Destiny sent her assassin to my chambers? Was it Lucifer's escape? My dreams of Gavin? Or had things been headed in the wrong direction before?

I blinked and finally left my frozen state. "Let's sit down." I placed my arm around Elinore's shoulders and guided her to her couch.

"Everything's so messed up, Prim," Elinore said through her tears. Her mascara smudged below her eyes.

"Elinore," I said. "Elinore, if you don't tell me what's wrong, I can't help. Elinore, did you hear me? Please, tell me what's wrong."

My friend nodded and wiped her tears. She sniffed and rubbed her nose against the sleeve of her blouse. Her crying dwindled, and she finally met my eyes with a broken smile. "You know how Cain sent someone to check up on my dad? Apparently, the guy stopped by Creative Cures in LA and managed to 'convince,' or I guess, beat the information out of Mister CEO, who, by the way, still hasn't given me a call yet." Her chest started shaking, and she struggled to hold the tears back.

"And?" I prompted.

Elinore shook her head and sniffed. "My dad changed labs three months ago, Prim. If he hadn't—"

The walls of the apartment seemed to suddenly cave in, and I swallowed my fear so that it didn't bleed into my voice. "I don't understand. What happened? Did something go wrong?"

"Yeah." My friend laughed, but her voice sounded all wrong. "You know, in three months, there has been absolutely no mistake. Quite the opposite. Apparently, my dad's done some good work in those three months. The CEO was planning on giving him some award at the end of the year. Everything was fine, at least until... There was a mistake."

Dread crept up the back of my neck. "What kind of mistake?"

"His coworker, Dalia. She's"—Elinore's eyebrows furrowed as she struggled for a word—"strange. I mean, I guess I only met her once, but I hate her."

"Why?" I frowned. Hate? This was Elinore, the sweetest and kindest human alive. My imagination went wild, thinking of what possibly could have happened to stir such an emotion in her.

"My father didn't make a mistake. Dalia did. She released one of the viruses he was studying into the air, and my dad inhaled it. He contracted one of the diseases he planned to cure. He's very, very sick and currently in the ICU with no visitors allowed. The CEO hasn't been clear on the phone because he doesn't want the bad publicity. They don't even know where Dalia went, only that she hasn't come back to work since."

My breathing came to an abrupt stop. I knew where the story was going, and I loathed the ending.

"He's going to die," my friend said. Her eyes lowered to the carpet on the living room floor. "And I can't do anything about it."

The implication in her voice crept up my spine. I retreated into an expressionless cocoon, where I felt safe while my thoughts worked themselves out.

I can't do anything about it, she said. I could hear her voice add, *but you can.*

Elinore's unsaid words reminded me how naïve humans could be. Humanity couldn't grasp a concept as final as death. If only death were reversible! How I wished I could stop the death of innocents with a simple thought or flick of my wrist. Nothing was that simple.

"I'm sorry about your father, Elinore." I rested a hand on her shoulder. "I wish things were different, I really do. But you know

I'm not able to save him, right? I may be the Goddess of Death, but I can't stop death. I can only cause it."

"Then what's the point?" she cried. Her pain struck me like a knife in the chest. "What's the point of causing death and not being able to stop it?"

"I don't know. Damn it, Elinore! You think I don't want to help your father? That I enjoy seeing you like this? Think! If I could stop death, nobody would die. I'd try and keep everyone alive! Nobody really deserves to die."

Elinore said nothing. Her silence cut deep. I jumped up from the couch and began to pace. I knew she expected me to offer my supernatural help, but no matter how much I cared, there was nothing I could do. Death was inevitable—the end of all things.

"There's nothing I can do," I said. Maybe if I said it enough times, she'd finally believe me.

"I know." Her words were soft yet truthful. "I just wish..."

Her incomplete sentence twisted the strings of my heart into an irreversible knot. I felt bile rise up my throat, disgusted by the feeling of complete hopelessness. Elinore's pain crushed me. This wasn't supposed to happen, not now.

"I promise you, Elinore, I will get your father the best doctors and the best hospital staff this world has to offer. He will be taken care of at no financial cost to you. I don't know if my help will be enough, but I will do everything I can to keep him alive."

My friend nodded, a glint of hope touching her eyes.

"Cain," I called out to my reaper, "you may come out."

The door to Elinore's bedroom creaked open, and Cain was suddenly at my side. "Yes, my lady?" His pale eyes were intent to serve me, to make me stronger.

"Let's go. We have work to do," I said, altering the original plan I had in mind. I turned to leave.

"Wait!"

I stopped and looked back to see my friend, who rushed toward Cain and me in confusion. "Where are you going?" she demanded.

"You don't need to worry, Elinore. Go to your father in California. Be with him. The doctors I told you of will arrive soon after I send them a message. In less than a day, they will all be at your father's bedside to give him the care he needs."

"But you said"—Elinore swallowed the lump in her throat and pointed her finger toward me—"you said that you were coming to give me something."

"I can't... rely on you now." I struggled not to hurt her feelings. "What you're going through, nobody should ever have to go through that. The last thing I want to do is add to your stress—to your worries."

"You don't get to decide that!" Elinore snapped, startling both Cain and me with the ferocity of her response. Her hands fisted in rage. "I'm your friend, right?"

"Right."

Her face turned a bright pink color. "Then, for God's sake, let me help you! Trust me."

I flinched at her tone. It wasn't a matter of trust. Of course, I trusted Elinore to keep my secrets safe and come to my aid in times of need; however, her life didn't deserve another burden. Elinore was already in so much pain. Still, by the sternness in her eyes, I knew that leaving her here, feeling as helpless as she felt now, would do nothing but harm our friendship, which was the last thing I wanted.

"What I'm going to ask of you is not an easy task," I said. "You need to understand what you're getting into before you agree to help."

Elinore bowed her head in acknowledgment, regret flashing in her eyes. "I know you mean well, Prim. But I really can help. I need to help."

Her conviction was convincing, too convincing. Elinore felt helpless in light of her father's condition and needed something to do. She needed to make a positive difference in a world that had suddenly turned her entire life upside down. Elinore always put others first, even when she couldn't take care of herself. Her personality shined through the darkest of times throughout her life, and for that reason, I became her friend.

Sensing her determination, I removed the Soul Dagger from my belt and displayed it to her. Having the dagger at my side for the last few hours made its aura less unsettling, but as the blade glinted in the light, uneasiness gnawed at my stomach.

"Care to guess what this is?"

"My lady." Cain's voice came out in a strangled breath.

Elinore's eyes grew as wide as oranges. "Is that..." Her mouth opened and closed, like a fish out of water. "The hell are you doing with that out in the open? Put that thing away!"

I rolled my eyes and tightened my grip around the dagger's hilt. "I can handle my own Soul Dagger, but I think you can handle it better."

My friend froze. She stood, not blinking or twitching—just watching me with surprised intensity. Realizing it would take her a moment to comprehend the meaning of my words, I crossed my arms and waited. My gaze slipped toward Cain to garner his reaction. His expression was stone silent, giving nothing away, which usually meant he was either in profound thought or a second away from blowing a gasket. Cain never threw temper tantrums, but he did this weird thing where he'd start asking questions and make me feel stupid about my decision.

"But," Elinore began and then shut her mouth. She blinked once, then twice. "I can't do that. The dagger..."

"Years ago, a wise friend once told me, you need to give trust to get trust. You didn't let me leave the room because you wanted me to trust you. Here is me trusting you."

"Did you just quote me?" Elinore's eyebrows shot up, but then she shook her head. "That's not the point, Prim. I can't protect that dagger!" she exclaimed and waved her arms around, frantic to convince me. "I'm just me! I'm not a ninja. I've got no superpowers!"

"That's why nobody would expect you to have it. Everybody knows you either have your dagger hidden in some secure location, or you physically have your dagger in your possession—you never leave your Soul Dagger with someone else. People are prone to betrayal and corruption. Immortal beings would never trust their lives with someone else, especially not a human. Still, I want to trust my life to you."

A flicker of pride lit up in Elinore's stormy eyes before her face crumpled into discontent. "But what if I let you down?"

I shook my head. "Accepting the burden of my Soul Dagger might be the decision that saves my life. Besides, you're not completely on your own. Cain will be here every second from now to the moment I return."

Elinore looked at Cain before biting her lip, hesitant. "I don't know."

"If it comforts you, a spell shall be cast over the dagger. I don't believe it to be necessary, but I've learned you can never be too careful when protecting your life." I sent Elinore a sideways smile. "Believe me, you're well suited to the task."

She shook her head as if to wake from a daze. My trust threw her off guard, and Cain was just as surprised.

"Are you afraid of the dangers the dagger may bring?" I asked, my voice gentle.

Elinore looked away, and her cheeks warmed. "More like I'm afraid I won't be able to fight the dangers off. The last thing I want to happen is for your life to land into the hands of the biggest, baddest people in this world because I wasn't strong enough."

"Physical strength is not what I need right now. I need someone I can rely on."

"Then why not trust the dagger to your reapers?" she asked.

I laughed. "Because it's predictable! The Underworld, my reapers—that's the first place my enemies would check. A human's cruddy apartment in New York City is the last place they'd think to search."

Elinore looked down at her hands before raising her gray eyes to meet mine. "Did you say that you would spell the dagger?"

I nodded.

"Does that mean even if I fail, you would still be okay?"

I hesitated. "Not necessarily okay, but I would live to tell the tale. Again, dead is dead only when I say so."

"Except when it comes to Soul Daggers," Elinore said.

"Everything has an exception. I could sit here all day listing out every exception in the book, or you could *trust* me when I say I'll be fine."

My statement put Elinore in a bind. She couldn't ask for my trust and not return the favor when the tables were turned. My friend dipped her head in acceptance. "If Cain is here every second of the day and you put that funky spell on the dagger, then I'll do it. Just... be sure you want to really leave it with me. I'm only human."

"I'm sure," I said.

"A word, my lady." Cain spoke for the first time since I revealed my plan.

Elinore made a shooing gesture when I checked to see if she was okay with me leaving her alone. "Begone, terrible friend of mine," she joked, a half-hearted smile on her lips. "I have a million thoughts to sort through after everything you said."

I followed Cain into Elinore's bedroom. He shut the door and stared at me. "This was your plan?"

My hands were clammy. Here came the questions. "Yes."

"To leave your Soul Dagger, the Soul Dagger of the Goddess of Death, arguably the most powerful dagger in existence," he said, "in the hands of a human child?"

"She's twenty."

Okay, maybe that wasn't the best answer to his question. Cain narrowed his eyes. "Compared to the deities who have millennia on her, she is a child, wouldn't you agree?"

Cain might have been right, but that wasn't the point. "If the dagger is on me, I'm in more danger than if the dagger is with her."

He shook his head, not seeing my point. "How so?"

"I'm under constant attack by people who are aching to get their hands on the dagger. Only a few hours ago, in the cavern where my Soul Dagger was hidden, another assassin revealed himself." *Itself.* That *thing* was no man.

Cain blanched. "How is that possible?"

"I don't know." I crossed my arms in front of my chest, and he mirrored my actions. "The creature must have followed me there, which shouldn't have been an easy task. I didn't walk over to Hoover Dam on foot. I used a portal. Now, I have to ask myself how he knew where I planned to open a portal. The reason I defeated him so easily was because of his weakness. The Hall of Thorns had ripped into him good enough. He could barely stand by the time he got his claws into me."

My reaper gritted his teeth and paced to the other end of the room. "Why are these assassins a step ahead of us?"

I didn't have a good answer to his question. "The dagger is safer with Elinore," I said. "The assassins will track me or search for my dagger back at the palace. Listen, I know you don't like this plan, but if the assassin hadn't been as weak as he was in the cavern, he might have succeeded in his task."

Cain's eyes almost popped out of his head. A vein pulsed in his temple.

"Or he might've managed to actually harm me," I offered. "The assassin's presence took me by surprise. I froze up at the sight of him. If he had been a second quicker, my Soul Dagger would have been in his hands."

"You couldn't sense his presence," Cain deduced, "because the creature didn't have a soul."

"Exactly. And these creatures aren't as big or bulky as lower demons. The assassins can stealthily sneak up on me. With Fate on their side, they could be anywhere. No wards seem powerful enough to hold them back."

"Speaking of Fate, I have news." Cain's jaw tightened. "I sent a reaper named Owen to California to learn of the girl's father. I trust Owen with my life, so I am certain his observation is accurate. He spotted Fate in Nevada."

An eerie sense of being watched made me turn my head to make sure nobody was behind me. "Near the Hoover Dam?"

"I can't say for sure. Fate may have been close enough to the dam to conduct a spell if she wanted. Even if she wasn't as close as he estimated, magic tends to overcome physical boundaries without much resistance."

I never believed in coincidences. If Fate was in Nevada around the same time an assassin attacked me, there was a sure connection between the two. I sank down into Elinore's plushy mattress with a deep sigh. "That's just great."

We both let the silence roll along for a moment while our thoughts caught up to reality. My fingers traced the polka dots on Elinore's bedsheets.

"Why did you retrieve your dagger in the first place, my lady?" Cain inquired. "It was safe in the cavern so long as nobody knew it was there."

"Natkont's spell."

Cain's eyes flashed, and he nodded as if suddenly everything made sense. "The tracking spell."

"Yes, and as you know, the spell requires a unique set of ingredients—otherwise, the dagger would have remained in the cavern." I smoothened out the corner of Elinore's bedsheet. "You see, the dagger must stay with the girl. To the world of supernatural creatures, Elinore is meaningless. A nobody. Who would ever suspect that she has the dagger?"

"I don't like this plan," my reaper admitted.

"Do you have a better one?"

"No. It's a sound plan—a good plan. I just don't like it."

I snorted. "Tell me about it."

"I don't wish to speak out of line, my lady—I'm not referring toward your plan to leave the dagger with the girl. My concern is toward something else." Cain interrupted himself upon seeing the exasperated look on my face. "I wish to speak with you about General Afreet."

General Afreet? Who the hell was General Afreet? I blinked a few times before I figured out who he was talking about. "Azazel?" I'd forgotten that my general even had a last name.

Cain nodded. "General Afreet—"

"Please call him Azazel," I cut in before he could make his point. "There's no need for the formal reference when speaking to me about him."

"I was patrolling the girl's neighborhood yesterday when General *Azazel* came to me. We exchanged some... words." My reaper swallowed his distaste. He disliked Azazel as much as I did, maybe more. Azazel and I had a complicated relationship. We tolerated one another, at best.

"By words, you mean insults."

"I tried to remain collected and formal in my responses," Cain added apologetically.

I swallowed my laughter, though a small smile broke through. "Don't worry about it. Azazel bumped into me as well, and we traded a few insults. If it's of any consolation, he's trying to mess with me more than you. I think he figures since you're closer to me than any other reaper, you make an easier target."

"It may not be my place to comment, but why do you let him speak to you in such obscene ways?"

I bit my lip. "He's a good general, and until I find a better general, I'm stuck with him. We both are." I slipped off of Elinore's mattress. "Enough of this discussion for now. I best get to work if I don't wish to dally here all day." I knelt to the floor, ready to prepare the setup for the spells to come. "The dagger needs to be spelled twice."

"Is one of those spells what I think it is?"

My chin lifted toward Cain, and I bared my teeth into a wide smile. "Be ready for anything."

I placed my Soul Dagger on the bedroom floor. Elinore never liked carpet in the bedroom, so the flooring in this room was a slick, laminated redwood material. I opened the jar of herbs and placed them artistically around my Soul Dagger—a trick I learned many years ago from a cunning man who had avoided Death once, almost twice. The small, yellow-green cut-up leaves were dispersed correctly and ready for the spell. A magical chant felt heavy on my lips. I repeated the words under my breath and a lively buzz built up in the air.

The handle of a small switchblade left an imprint in my hand. With the sharp end of the small knife, I cut my palm to draw blood. The red liquid spilled to the hardwood floor, and I let it fall upon the herbs until a circle of blood was complete. I continued to chant as the blood on top of the herbs sizzled, and the room trembled as though a minor earthquake were shaking the building. My blood, guided by the spell's soft whispers, traveled from the herbs toward the dagger, which lay in the center of the circle. The red liquid coated the blade, and the stench of decaying plant life became profound. The quaking suddenly ended.

My forehead heated with a fever, and the room spun. With each word I spoke, the red layer of blood on the dagger faded to a light pink and then to the metal's usual gray color. The dagger, now spelled, appeared normal and uninteresting to the untrained eye. My hands trembled, and the gash in my palm remained visible though the bleeding stopped.

"You look pale, my lady. Is the spell finished?" Cain asked. His eyebrows were pinched into a worried expression.

I nodded and placed the back of my hand against my forehead. Though my brow felt sticky with sweat, the fever was gone. "The first spell is complete."

Shifting my attention to the next spell, I removed the vial that contained the royal blood of the last living Kovach from my pocket and popped open the lid. I poured the first drop onto the tip of my Soul Dagger. With great care, I poured the remaining royal blood in a straight line along the center of the dagger, dividing the blade into two equal halves. When the last drop slipped out of the vial, a fiery hand clasped itself around my center, and a shudder ran through my body. My head was thrust back, and I couldn't breathe. I opened and closed my mouth to no avail, and a pit grew deep in my stomach.

Black spots blocked my line of sight, and the darkness enveloped me—I was suddenly blind. Pressure built at the base of my skull, and for a second, I felt like I was floating in space, incapable of determining which way was left, right, up, or down. Oxygen finally found its way to my lungs, and I could breathe again. Before the sensation of numbness set in, my chest began to burn, like someone decided to light a fire inside of me. I clenched my teeth to avoid a cry of pain and seethed silently on my knees. Slime filled my throat, and I bent at the waist to hurl the contents of my stomach onto the hardwood floor. My foot slipped on the vomit with my attempt to stand, and my hip banged against the sharp corner of Elinore's drawer.

Cain was at my side in an instant. His arm wrapped around my waist while my hand blindly latched onto the top of Elinore's drawer to pull myself to my feet. The sudden weakness and blindness weren't unexpected, but I hadn't performed Natkont's spell in a long time.

Cain guided me to lie down on Elinore's mattress. "The effects will soon subside."

"I know."

The darkness continued to surround me until I saw a small light. At first, the white light seemed negligible, a dot in the distance. But the dot grew in size until it became a sphere of light that lay an arm's length away.

The sphere of light surged toward me and entered my chest. I choked on my scream as the light seared through my flesh and imprinted itself into my body. My head pounded while my heart threatened to burst from beneath my rib cage. The pain left as soon as it came, and in its wake lay an internal compass—a vague map. Lucifer's Soul Dagger was now mine to track. The connection between myself and his dagger gave me the ability to sense the remnants of his soul. I could feel his dagger lingering in the distance, far from me now, but soon, I would find the tool to Lucifer's destruction.

Small slivers of my vision returned. Cain waited patiently. He dabbed a cloth to the corners of my mouth to clean the dried vomit and gently brushed the strands of hair from my face. Once my sight returned, I rose from the bed too quickly, and lightheadedness threatened to send me tumbling toward the vomit-covered floor.

Cain caught my wrist to stop my fall, and I almost jumped out of my skin. The echo of magic left me skittish, and I smiled apologetically toward my reaper, who watched me apprehensively. "Are you all right, Primrose?"

"Yes." My voice came out as a whisper. I cleared my throat. "I'm fine. The pain has subsided."

"Do you feel his dagger?"

My internal compass set off a noticeable vibration at the mention of Lucifer's Soul Dagger, and I stifled a shiver. "Yes. It's south of here. I'll need to travel on foot if I want to track it effectively."

"No more portals."

"Not if I want to keep the signal current and accurate. You know how the tracking spell is. Nonspecific. Vague. It gives me a sense of direction, not a single, pinpoint destination on a map. Using a portal, I'd waste my time guesstimating where I need to go and then repeatedly getting the location wrong."

"If I recall correctly, after you use a portal, you lose the signal for twenty-four hours as the spell recalibrates, so to speak," Cain said.

My lips pulled into a smirk. "You think they'd upgrade these spells. I could use a fancy GPS to track the Devil down."

Cain held my gaze, and a flash of sympathy clouded the paleness of his eyes. He touched my hand and smiled weakly. "It's never that simple, my queen."

I shook my head with a wry smile. "No, it never is."

"When will you leave?" Cain asked. He wanted badly to accompany me on this journey, to make sure nothing happened to me. I hated disappointing him, but Cain was more useful to me if he guarded the one weapon that could end my life. I hadn't forgotten that he addressed me by my first name a minute ago—none of my reapers dared speak to me in such an informal manner—but Cain genuinely cared about my well-being. His emotions clouded his judgment.

"I'll leave after I take a shower, change my clothes, and grab a bite to eat. Elinore's fridge is always full."

Cain's face became expressionless. "So soon?"

"Yes." Time was of the essence. Like a hound dog, I had been given the scent of blood. Now all that was left to do was to follow.

CHAPTER FIFTEEN
AN ACCIDENTAL SCRIMMAGE

"BELIEVE ME, ELINORE," I said at the threshold of her apartment unit. "You'll be fine, and so will your father. I called the doctors and clinicians I spoke to you about, and they'll all arrive at the hospital where your father resides within the next twenty-four hours." *If they didn't, they'd have hell to pay.*

"Are you sure you don't need to take the dagger with you to track Lucifer?" Elinore asked for the millionth time.

I leaned against the doorframe and shook my head. "No. I only needed my Soul Dagger to establish a connection between myself and Lucifer's dagger. Think of it this way, all Soul Daggers are connected because they are made of the same material, the metal of a Soul Altar. The connection between two Soul Daggers—I established that same connection between myself and Lucifer's Soul Dagger through the use of an intermediate, the blood of Kovach royalty. I'm now connected to his dagger. I no longer need my Soul Dagger to track him. I know it can be difficult to understand."

Elinore's eyes welled up with unshed tears. She nodded and swallowed the lump in her throat. "I guess that makes sense. I'll take good care of *it*."

She said the word 'it' in a tentative, hushed whisper as if invoking the words 'soul' and 'dagger' in the same sentence would somehow summon all the evil in the world to her apartment. For a brief second, I considered my present situation from the perspective of an all-powerful, snotty deity. My Soul Dagger, the only weapon capable of killing me, was now in the hands of a blond millennial with a southern accent.

I imagined Ben's disappointment if he knew. *Trusting a human.* His voice would be full of disgust and surprise. He'd be astounded if I didn't die within the next three days.

"You might not hear from me for over a week," I warned. "My journey will take time, but Cain will stay with you until I return."

Elinore gasped. "That long? Hunting down Lucifer's dagger could take more than a week?"

"Unfortunately, yes. I'll be busy catching buses, stealing a car here and there. Eventually, I'll have to track the Soul Dagger on foot, so yes. That long."

"Why don't you just take a portal to where Lucifer is at?"

I stared blankly at her. "I can't."

"Why not?" she asked.

"For a number of reasons. First off, the dagger's location is vague at best. It's not like I have a pinpoint location of his Soul Dagger or some coordinates I can pop into a GPS. Part of how the tracking spell works is that I gain a general sense of direction. I know to travel south for now, and as I near the Soul Dagger, its presence becomes more profound. The closer I get to it, the more specific and accurate the tracking spell becomes. Portals would become counterproductive. You know how your phone loses signal sometimes?"

"Yes."

"If confused, the tracking spell can lose its signal as well. It's like an algorithm. A formula. It calculates the distance between myself and Lucifer's Soul Dagger to provide me with that sense of direction I was telling you about. If I take a portal, the spell has to recalibrate. In essence, every time I pass through a portal, the signal is lost, and the tracking spell becomes obsolete for twenty-four hours. Thus, portaling from one place to another would only waste my time, especially since I don't know the exact location of the dagger. My sense of direction points me south, but where south? If I portal to Mexico, let's say, I lose the signal for twenty-four hours. Then what if the tracking spell points me back north? Lucifer could be in Texas for all I know. But where in Texas? El Paso, Dallas, Abilene... I'd be wasting my time with a guessing game. Traveling by bus or car is much more efficient."

"Magic is so complicated," Elinore grumbled. "A week is a long time to be gone. Stay safe, Prim. Be careful."

I surprised Elinore with an awkward hug goodbye. "Take good care of yourself, too," I mumbled into her ear. We shared a moment of comfort in each other's arms before I backed away and left.

Cain walked me out of the building. He kept rubbing his eyes, and his cheeks were hollow and pale. I was half-tempted to ask him what the matter was, but I already knew why he was upset. Cain worried about my safety, and he knew that the next time he'd see me, I'd either be triumphantly parading around with Lucifer's Soul Dagger or in a body bag.

I pulled him to the side for a final word. "Watch her carefully." I referred to Elinore.

Cain winced as if I'd slapped him. "Do you doubt me, my lady?"

"No. I don't doubt you. I could never doubt you. I have this bad feeling is all," I said and touched his shoulder apologetically. "Like something's wrong. As if somebody's watching me. There's always someone out to get me. I know that much. It's just... that eerie feeling here and there—it's gotten worse recently."

Cain stared at me indifferently before suddenly becoming very serious. "You don't seem to understand, Primrose."

I stepped back, surprised when he addressed me by my first name again, this time deliberately and with purpose.

He stepped forward and grabbed my arms to shake some sense into me. "Your life *is* in danger. I don't know if you understand what that means, and so I'll say it again: your life *is* in danger. People are trying to kill you. Someone out there, friend or foe, will always covet the power you possess. There is never a moment when you are alone. You are always watched and carefully inspected for weakness. Now more than ever, you must be alert, cautious, and exemplify a strength you may or may not feel inside."

"What are you trying to say?" I demanded and pulled my arms away from his grip.

"You *should* be afraid of the war that is to come."

I shook my head as my cheeks flushed angrily. "You go too far."

"This war isn't like the ones you have fought before." Cain's voice rose to defend his position. "The enemy will not fight you on a battlefield with an army that you can see from miles away. The enemy hides in the shadows while she sends her assassins to test your mind and body. As you hunt for Lucifer, your enemies sit together and plan an unforeseeable trap."

"I've lived in the shadows for a long time." My voice trembled with rage. "I'm no longer afraid of what hides in the dark."

"With all due respect, my lady, you've never fought a war against shadows. The wars you've fought were full of swords, blood, bodies, and magic. Armies against armies. This war will be nothing like we've faced before!" Cain lifted his chin. "Nobody contests that your magic is derived from the shadows; I know the darkness feeds the power coursing through your veins. You may be a creature of the shadows, but you've been in the light for a long time, my queen. The darkness shifts with every day, and the creatures born of the darkness are different now than what they used to be. Are you ready to face this new darkness?" he asked. "Are you ready to face a threat you cannot see, feel, or prepare for?"

"I am."

I replied the instant the question left his lips. My voice sounded stronger than I felt. I hugged my arms to keep them from shaking. I hoped my eyes had that glossy indifference reflected in them, the apathy that I had so diligently trained myself to portray to the outside world. I refused to admit it, but Cain's emotional tirade frightened me. His words rang true, and the fact that I couldn't contest any of his claims lent to another stream of worry. The feeling that my world was falling apart left me paranoid and angry.

"I *am* ready," I said again.

Cain nodded with a sad smile on his lips. "That is what everyone must believe."

"Goodbye, Cain."

I rushed to leave the apartment, unable to stand the presence of my most powerful reaper, my favorite reaper—the only servant that cared about my well-being more than anyone else. Ben's remark from earlier in Vegas resonated as clear as bells in my mind. *You never take criticism very well.*

Yet neither Ben nor Cain were criticizing me. Their words weren't an attack on my character. They were giving me advice out of love. Advice that could be the key to whether or not I made it out of this ordeal alive. I realized that now.

As I walked down the streets of New York City, the summer's warmth faded into a light chill. The skies were cloudy and gray, making the buildings appear duller than usual. I missed feeling the sun's glare on the top of my head.

An uncomfortable feeling of incompleteness grew in me as Lucifer's Soul Dagger pulled me toward its location. Though my final destination was unknown and unclear, a path had been lit for me to follow.

I traipsed through the city, barely getting a comfortable feel for the new connection to Lucifer's Soul Dagger. As my sense of direction strengthened, I headed toward the subway system and took a train out of the city and toward the suburbs. All High Court meetings were held in New York, so I knew the transportation system like the back of my hand. Beyond the bustling city's staleness lay the green mountains and hills that ran through the countryside.

At two in the afternoon, I boarded a bus out of the state and watched the hills roll by until we passed Virginia's northern border. The vehicle came to a stop in the city of Fairfax, and I stepped off for a snack and break at the local Chick-fil-A.

In the parking lot, I spotted a red Dodge Ram with the keys in the ignition. As the truck's owner argued with the staff inside of the restaurant over the wrong size of his waffle fries, I left the building and strode nonchalantly toward the perfectly available car. I drove down Route 286 with my newly acquired truck. For the next twenty miles, I didn't ease off the accelerator. The truck's engine made a weird gurgling noise if I tried speeding faster than 120 miles per hour, and by the low fuel indicator on the dashboard, the owner hadn't yet filled the tank of his car before I took the vehicle off his hands.

I stopped by a different gas station, unscrewed the truck's license plates, and replaced them with the plates of the car behind me while the driver was inside the store for a restroom break. Hopefully, switching the plates would give any police officers tracking the vehicle a harder time finding me. I fueled up and hit the road again.

A few hours into my road trip, a generic sense of where I was heading set in. My inner compass was drawing me to Georgia or Florida. As midnight came and went, I fiddled with the car radio and blasted some upbeat music at max volume to keep myself awake. I passed through Atlanta as the sun began to rise. Hours later, I crossed the Florida state line and rolled the car windows down just in time for the taste of salty beach air to touch my dry lips.

I ditched the truck in Orlando, leaving it at some old junkyard, and hopped on a separate bus to Miami. The bus wasn't too shabby. The paint on the exterior was only a little scratched, and the smooth sides of the bus had not one dent in them. The seats didn't smell too bad, and the people inside were either excessively tired or intensely preoccupied with their own world. I liked having two seats to myself when using public transportation. I picked a row near the front of the bus, leaned my back against the window, and let my boots sit on the aisle seat. After my ruined stilettos incident, I borrowed a pair of Elinore's black combat boots and a black *cardigan*—since the words 'leather jacket' were not in my friend's vocabulary. I also borrowed a V-neck and a new pair of jeans.

Prior to leaving the station, the driver gave me a stink eye when he noticed my muddy boots were soiling his not too smelly seats, but he let it slide when he saw the scimitar strapped to my back. My sword had that effect on people.

The bus engine roared as the driver left the station. After fidgeting to find a comfortable position, I scrolled through the apps on my phone, bored. The Wi-Fi was really bad, so I couldn't even conduct a proper Google search. I contemplated giving Atlas a call but decided against it. I knew I said we'd regroup after I spelled my Soul Dagger, but I changed my mind. We were always at each other's necks anyways.

Tires screeched and the bus pitched forward. The bus hit something hard and veered to the right. Humans screamed, and I whipped my head around, trying to see what happened. Glass shattered and suddenly everyone was airborne. The bus flipped, and I fell to the roof of the vehicle with a grunt. Metal groaned, making an unstable noise. My hand latched onto a chair before the bus tipped to its side.

The vehicle came to a stop, and I stood to survey the damage. The humans suffered minor injuries, cuts, and bruises, and panic was evident in their hysterical screams. The chuffing of a helicopter materialized, and the sound of sirens filled the air.

I stared out the back window of the bus. Red and blue lights of police cars flickered from behind a dozen armored vehicles. Large, bulletproof vehicles surrounded the bus. I crouched to the ground and carefully sorted through the glass of broken bus windows to find my phone. I hid my phone in one of my combat boots and shrugged the shoe back on just in time for the front windshield of the bus to shatter. My ears rang from the noise, and the bus driver who cowered behind his seat cried in fear as men and women, dressed in black, rushed into the vehicle. The passengers shrunk into their seats as the agents pointed their assault weapons at me.

I was going to kill Marcus.

"Hands in the air!" one of the FBI agents yelled at the top of his lungs and shook his gun as if to make his point more aggressively. "Do it! Now!"

I showed him my hands and slowly lifted them to the air.

"Stand up! Move!"

Instead of complaining, I gritted my teeth and stood. The man grabbed the scruff of my neck and shoved me toward the front of the bus. Before I regained my balance, another agent pushed me out through the opening, where the front windshield used to be. I stumbled to the ground, and my jaw hit the asphalt. I tasted blood in my mouth. My cheeks and forearms were scraped, though, in a few seconds, the scrapes were gone.

My wrists were cuffed together, and I barely resisted the urge to reap the souls of those around me.

While they had me on the ground, one of the soldiers patted me down, and my sword and daggers were confiscated. I kept an eye on the car my weapons were taken to and committed the license plate to memory.

I was hoisted up from the ground and led to an armored car. A group of agents waited inside the car to secure my transfer into the bulky vehicle. There wasn't much room inside the car, and once I squeezed in, half a dozen assault weapons were trained in my direction. I could smell the sweat that reeked from the soldiers' uniforms—they were afraid. I sat still while a female agent chained my wrists and ankles to a set of metal bars on the floor of the vehicle. I bit my cheek to silence the remarks on my mind. I could break these chains with a flick of my wrist. I could close my eyes and unweave each soul in this car before the second passed.

How easily the humans forgot the war I had waged against them, a war that took place only two decades ago. Did they not teach these new agents what happened the last time the FBI attacked me? Or was the bloodshed of their brothers and sisters not enough to convince them to stay away from me?

The armored car lurched into motion, and we were soon on our way to what I assumed to be a 'secure' facility. I reached out toward Marcus's soul with my magic to confirm that we were headed toward the mastermind himself. My gaze became unfocused, and my eyebrows pulled together into a confused frown.

We weren't headed toward Marcus. In fact, Marcus's soul was still back in Las Vegas, and these armored cars were heading south.

I sent the men and women in the vehicle a pointed glance. The soldiers held their guns tightly in response to my intense glare, but I didn't mind their fear. These agents weren't wearing suits and ties, like Marcus's 007 wannabes. These agents wore full head-to-toe riot gear, including the helmet and goggles.

The letters 'FBI' were inscribed on their bulletproof vests, and these soldiers had the same assault weapons that Marcus's agents liked to bear. But something was wrong with this picture. These soldiers arrived with the police. Marcus hated involving the local police. He'd never approve of a mission like this.

My best guess? Marcus didn't even know about this mission. I checked to see if my internal compass pointed in the same direction that we were heading. As long as I remained on track to finding Lucifer's Soul Dagger, I didn't mind catching a ride with these agency rogues. But the moment these cars deviated from my intended path, these agents were in for a big surprise.

CHAPTER SIXTEEN
A MIAMI BEACH STROLL

THE ARMORED CARS CONTINUED heading south, never straying from the path to Lucifer's Soul Dagger. During my time in the vehicle, I hypothesized the possible locations my internal compass pointed me toward. The more I considered it, the more I believed the tracking spell was leading me to South America.

There was a *Glass* in Argentina. There were five Glasses across the world, one in Bulgaria, Japan, Tanzania, Australia, and the closest to my current position was in Argentina. Like any portal, a Glass connected two different worlds through a medium. All Glasses connected the modern, human-occupied world to the ancient land—the Garden of 'Adam and Eve.' All life is derived from the ancient land. After humans were banished, several Gods and Goddesses moved to the human realm for the sake of entertainment. Once the first deities crossed over to the human realm, the rest of the supernatural world followed like a flock of sheep.

Though I couldn't know for sure, Lucifer may have hidden his Soul Dagger in the ancient land, which would explain why the Glass in Argentina might be the target of the tracking spell.

The armored cars came to an abrupt stop in downtown Miami. Two soldiers maneuvered my chains and hoisted me out into an underground parking lot. Their grips were tight, though humanly weak. With every step we took, another set of machine guns was pointed at my head.

A small group of agents jogged forward to open a door. The harsh, artificial light made me squint as we entered the building. The walls were cream-colored, and the room smelled like too much bleach had been used to disinfect the dark, tiled floors. The garage entrance was heavily surveilled by a dozen or so cameras. We walked down a wide hallway and stopped in front of a desk.

There was a middle-aged man sitting at the desk. He wore a checkered dress shirt and tie. His salt-and-pepper hair made his brown eyes look pale and bored. The name tag clipped to his breast pocket read 'Carter.'

"Yes," Carter greeted with his lazy voice.

"We need to make a transfer to one of the interrogation rooms," one of the agents beside me said.

Carter grudgingly turned his gaze to the computer screen and typed up some characters. "There are currently no available inter-rogation rooms."

"Make one available."

Carter stared at his computer and yawned. "Room two is finishing up. I can take her fingerprints in the meantime."

This proposition left the agents in a state of unease like they didn't know what they were supposed to do. Their orders were probably to set me down into an interrogation room until the proper authority figures arrived, but to take fingerprints, they'd have to remove my cuffs.

I lifted an eyebrow at the soldiers that held tightly to my arms.

Carter pointed to the fingerprint machine, impatient. "Thumbs first, like in the picture. See there?"

"We'd have to remove her cuffs," the agent to my left objected. His voice didn't sound as strong as it had a minute ago.

"Unless you plan to break her arms at her elbows to take her fingerprints backward, then yes," Carter said, bored again. "You have to take her cuffs off."

"Can't you make a room available, and we go there straight away? Without fingerprints?"

Carter, now annoyed, gritted his teeth. "No fingerprints, no interrogation room. It's that simple. We follow protocols here, boys."

The agent to my right scowled, and his nails dug into my skin. "We'll hold her arms." He removed a key from his pocket and poked at my cuffs. "Tighten your grip," he instructed his partner, "in three, two, one." The cuffs were off.

The human grip on my arms felt like Jell-O, and I almost laughed. I settled on a goofy smile, and Carter narrowed his eyes. "Place her thumbs on the—"

I shrugged off the soldier's grip easier than shrugging off a loose piece of cloth and threw the fingerprinting device at Carter's stupefied face. He sprawled back and fell off his chair while I curled my arm around the neck of the soldier to my left and held him in front of me like a human shield.

"Drop your weapons." Over a dozen guns were pointed in my direction, but not one of them fired. "I'll snap his neck," I threatened, "like opening a can of soda. It's just that easy."

One agent stepped forward. I tightened my grip around the soldier's neck, and he gasped for air. I pressed my lips against his ear. "Tell them to stand down."

"Shoot her," he choked out.

A curse left my tongue. Crackles of light filled the air, and a portal opened behind me. One step back, and I was suddenly in the Underworld. I released my grip over the agent I held, and he stumbled to the side with a gasp for air. He held his throat and wildly took in his surroundings.

"Fool!" I snarled. I stormed in his direction and the soldier backed away frantically. "You cost me twenty-four hours. You would rather die at the hands of your own men and take a bullet to the head than listen to me! You only had to ask them to stand down. I would have let you live. You could have gone home to your family. But no! Do you understand the gravity of what you've done? For the next twenty-four hours, my tracking spell is shot! Time is of the essence. How am I to track the Devil down now, huh? Any suggestions?"

His eyes were wide with fear and confusion, and he raised his gun to point it at me. He pulled the trigger, and the air between us suddenly became as thick as molasses. We weren't in the human realm anymore. This was the Underworld, and the land would protect me at all costs. The bullet flew toward me, but it moved so slowly that it stopped in midair. The lands turned against the human man. The soldier's boots sank into the ground until he was waist-deep in muck. A gust of wind threw his weapon from his grip, and only then, a desperate plea touched his lips. "Please," he begged. Sweat gleamed on his forehead and his breathing became shallow in his terror.

This was *my* realm; here, I was the queen. I gazed at the bullet that had frozen in midair and picked it up to hold it between my fingers. "Such a little thing, isn't it?"

Pity quieted my rage, and my creased forehead relaxed. My eyes examined the soldier. He couldn't be more than thirty, a baby, really. A child with so much anger and hatred boiling inside. Such harsh emotions toward someone he never met before today. I couldn't bring myself to kill him. While I contemplated what to do with him, a reaper waited in the corner of my vision, ready to act per my command.

"What is your name?" I asked.

The soldier hesitated, but his will to stay alive overwhelmed his pride. "Sebastian."

"Sebastian." The man's name felt bitter on my tongue. "Do you know the meaning of your name? I don't suppose you do. Men are ignorant these days. Your name is Greek. It means venerable. Venerable as in respected, looked up to, admired. None of your actions today were admirable or honorable, I'm afraid."

"Don't kill me," the man pled, wrapping his arms around his middle. His eyes frantically flitted around as he tried to understand his surroundings.

"I could have escaped without the portal," I said quietly. "Your fellow men would have riddled your body with bullets, but my injuries would heal. I could have torn their facility from the inside out at the cost of your life. At the cost of many human lives. Be grateful, for as of recent, my emotions have clouded my judgment. For causing my lapse in judgment, for being the reason I opened a portal and jeopardized my mission, you will be punished. I will let you live, but you will live at my mercy, in the Underworld. My reapers will escort you to an Oasis, where you will spend the rest of your days until you grow old and die."

I left the soldier, ignoring his curses and cry of anguish. I opened a portal out of the Underworld and back to the FBI facility's underground parking garage. A small group of agents ran around frantically, but nobody paid me mind.

Row after row of black, armored cars were lined up side by side.

My eyes landed on the license plate of the car that contained my weapons, and I jogged over to the front seat. The driver leaned into the car, sorting through the daggers I had on me from before my capture. The agent didn't hear me until I grabbed the back of her neck and slammed her forehead into the vehicle frame.

She collapsed to the concrete, unconscious, and I sifted through the plastic evidence bags for my belongings. I strapped my sword to my back as the sound of voices entered the garage. I knelt down and removed the handgun from the agent and stashed it in the back of my jeans. Her machine gun was too large and visible to carry in public. After patting down the agent and discovering a wallet full of cash, I hid it in one of my pockets.

Shots were fired, and I ducked. The bullets hit the car I hid behind. The sound of footsteps echoed from the opposite side of the vehicle. I picked up the unconscious agent's assault weapon and lay flat against the floor. Seeing the feet of the agents running in my direction, I shot at their heels and toes. Bodies hit the ground and howls of pain filled the air. The soldiers stopped shooting. In their moment of distraction, I dropped the machine gun and sprinted out from the parking lot through an emergency exit. I didn't stop running until I stepped into the alleyway behind a hotel on the shore of Miami beach, having placed several long miles between myself and the facility.

I sat down on a small set of stairs to catch my breath and take inventory of my weapons to make sure each was stashed where it needed to be. Satisfied that I wasn't missing any of my belongings, I walked out from under the dark shadow cast by the towering hotel and walked across the street toward the beach. My sense of direction was missing, and it felt like a part of me was empty and incomplete, like a void in my chest.

After the incident with the rogue FBI agents, setting a diversion for anyone on my tail seemed like a good idea. I decided to take a quick stroll along the white sands of Miami beach. The morning sun was already high in the sky upon my arrival.

The beach was overflowing with families and groups wearing swimsuits and carrying bags with beach necessities. Rainbow-colored umbrellas were set up to create a shade above the blankets on the sand. The smell of sunscreen and salty beach water touched my nose. The water near the shore appeared turquoise from where I stood. My heavy boots thudded against the sand, and I regretted not having a pair of sandals with me, especially in this heat. I scrunched up my cardigan and threw it at an annoying teenager's face.

As though my appearance brought forth a stroke of bad luck, a pained scream shook Miami's white, sandy beach. I whipped my head around, and my eyes landed on a young boy who lay limp on his back while his mother's sobs grew louder. He was newly dead, drowned. A hooded figure stepped away from the boy's small body and looked at me with gray, unfeeling eyes. It had a dreadfully pale face and gaunt cheeks. It looked to me for approval, having reaped the soul of the dead boy. No human acknowledged the figure—the spelled cloak this reaper wore made it invisible to the human eye. Not that it mattered. People only saw what they wanted to see, and nobody wanted to see the harbinger of death.

I shifted my gaze away from my reaper, unsettled by the sight of the uncaring, supernatural entity. I couldn't help but wonder if that was how my eyes appeared when I took a soul. Were they just as lifeless? As emotionless? As indifferent to the horror of death?

I turned my head back toward the boy. My reaper was gone as if it had never been there at all. All that was left in its wake was a mourning family and chaos.

Unlike Cain, many of my reapers had not retained much of their humanity after death. As similar as reapers were to humans, when a soul is reaped from a body, the memories become jumbled, chaotic, and challenging to sort through, so most reapers turned out to be emotionless and vacant. They did as they were told, and that was all. Cain, Kaitlyn, and a handful of other reapers were different because they retained some memory or emotion from before their deaths. Their uniqueness made me hopeful.

Out of the corner of my eye, I spotted a kiosk in a nearby shopping center for boat rentals. A quick idea came to mind. I strode out of the sand and toward the collection of shops.

A cluster of teens approached and walked around me. One bumped my shoulder roughly and muttered a sassy 'sorry' under her breath. I stopped and stared at my shoulder. The teens began to move away before I turned and grabbed the wrist of the girl who bumped into me.

"Hey," I said, eyeing her leather jacket. "How much for that jacket?"

The group started at my words, and a few boys guffawed. The short girl scowled, and her lip piercing twisted. "Excuse me?"

"How much for your jacket?"

"It's not for sale." The blond tried to pull away, but my grip was tighter than she expected.

I thought of the cash I lifted off of the unconscious agent from the parking lot. My lips quirked in what I hoped to be a warm smile. "I know a few dead presidents that might change your mind."

Not even a minute later, I walked away from the group of teens with a new leather jacket and a smug smile. It felt good to be back in a leather jacket once again, even a faux one. After talking to a white-haired man at the kiosk, I took the keys of an Element E16 deck boat out by a dock located a half-mile away.

I headed toward the dock on foot and walked along the water's edge to get a good dose of beach vibes. I kept far enough from the shore to ensure that the water didn't get to my boots. I stepped on a little boy's sandcastle—accidentally, of course. The scent of salt wafted through the air, and I licked my moist lips. Halfway to the dock, a heavy breeze broke through the stillness of the air, and an unsettling sensation beset itself upon the back of my neck.

Something felt off.

My hand lingered over the hilt of my sword. I leaned to the right suddenly and felt the wind of a dagger that barely missed my neck. I unsheathed my scimitar and turned.

A blond demon twirled another dagger between her fingers behind where I stood. She wore a pink, breezy dress. Her hair was loosely curled, and a twisted smile played on her lips. "Thought you could lose me so quickly, did you?" The maliciousness of her voice didn't match her pretty appearance.

I pointed my sword toward Satan and smiled back. "Well. A girl can hope."

Satan glanced around and tossed one of her daggers high up in the air before catching it again. "I don't see the God of Ice here to protect you this time."

"I don't need anyone to protect me," I retorted, and my cheeks warmed. "I can do that just fine on my own."

The demon narrowed her eyes into a sharp glare. "We shall see."

She lunged at me with two daggers. I skipped back, narrowly avoiding a blow. I stabbed at her waist, and she blocked my attack with her blades. My sword swung and struck her forearm, drawing blood. Satan snarled and ruthlessly attacked. Her blows were quicker than before, and I struggled to move my long blade as fast as she swung her daggers.

I curved my sword between her arms. It clashed with one of her blades. My free hand latched onto her arm. The pommel of her dagger met my temple, and stars flashed in front of my eyes. I ducked under her right arm to brace myself on a sand dune. I rolled to the ground, her blade narrowly missing its mark. My combat boot snapped at the back of Satan's knee, and she tripped forward with a growl. She lost her grip on the daggers and dropped them. My grip on the scimitar strengthened, and I aimed the blade at her torso.

A fistful of sand filled my eyes. I gasped, temporarily blinded. A sharp pain in my side elicited a guttural cry from my throat. Satan dug her fingers into Abaddon's old injury and ripped the stitches out in one violent move. My vision blurred, and I flailed back. The handgun I'd stashed in the back of my jeans was cold against my skin as I fell to the ground. The demon sprung to grab one of the daggers she dropped. In a blur of movement, my hand grasped the gun at my back and fired a shot.

The bullet nicked Satan's shoulder and she recoiled with a howl. Before I could fire another shot, a large wave thrust me to the side in a dizzying spiral. I lost my grip on the sword, and it flew out of my hands. My head hit the sand, and a mouthful of salt burned my throat. I clawed at the water, sand—anything I could get my hands on to stop the spinning. I caught sight of the sun's light, and my fingers grazed the water's surface. My leg pushed off the sand, and I burst out of the water with a gasp. My head twisted side to side to search for the blond demon while I spluttered out water from my mouth.

Human families screamed and tried to help their loved ones who were hit by the wave. The water covered a good quarter of what used to be the beach. Lifeguards rushed from their stations. Umbrellas floated upside down on the water's surface along with other beach items.

No sign of Satan. I brushed the wet hair out of my face and turned back to look at the open sea. The wave came out of nowhere. A low growl built in my throat, and I angrily swiped at the water. I trudged toward the shore, clutching my side. The salty water burned my injury, adding another layer of pain. I spotted a child picking up my sword that washed up to the shore and snatched away the blade.

Once away from the beach and crowds, I assessed the damage Satan had done to my wound. My eyes widened in both surprise and dread. Despite the stitches being pulled out, leaving the flesh around the scar ugly and deformed, blood no longer seeped from the wound. The scar tissue was completely dry, but the purple patches of dying tissue that surrounded the wound were larger than before. For how long would the infection spread? I breathed shakily at the worrisome thought before rebandaging the wound. Since the injury no longer bled, I felt no need to redo the stitches. I sat down and pulled my phone out from the inside of my combat boot and tried unsuccessfully to turn it on. Might as well trash it. The inside of my shoes was soaked.

The rental boat at the dock was unharmed since it had been in deeper waters. Arriving at the pier, I summoned the dead body of a brunette my height. I sat her in the boat and removed a dagger from my belt. With a sharp sting in my palm, I drew blood from my hand and smudged it over the dead woman's arms and pants and in her hair so that my scent was fully exposed to the air. I used my power over the dead to puppeteer her movements. The brunette moved the boat throttle forward, and the boat sped away from the dock and hopefully toward the Bahamas—with luck, she wouldn't hit anything or get eaten by a shark. Still, the diversion was in place, and anyone hunting me would likely follow the false trail I put out. Whether that be the FBI, Lucifer's siblings, or even Atlas Grimm.

Without my sense of direction to track Lucifer's dagger, I relied on my previous guess and decided to travel to the Glass. After some research on a public computer at the community library, I found a path where I could take a series of three buses to Argentina. A few clicks later, I booked the tickets and ran to a nearby station to catch the first bus. As I boarded, I caught a glimpse of exotic yellow eyes in the distance. The woman was gone before I could hone my focus, but I recognized her eye color. Well, well, well—Lady Fate finally decided to join the hunt.

CHAPTER SEVENTEEN
INTO THE RAINFOREST

A GRAY, RICKETY JEEP sped past me on the dirt road. The car's wheels spat out a spray of dust over my clothes, and I brushed it off my newly acquired leather jacket. The buses dropped me off at the nearest city, but no other vehicle would drive into the depths of the rainforest. From this point forward, I would travel on foot. Several days passed since I left Miami, an unfortunate consequence of not using any portals, but with the time that passed, my sense of direction returned and pointed me south toward the Glass. Just as I suspected.

The cloudy sky occasionally allowed for a stroke of sunlight to grace my path, though the gloomy color and humid scent suggested a heavy rain was to come. I approached the border to the rainforest, just outside the limits of Misiones Province, a province in the northeastern region of Argentina. Deep within the thicket, the Glass awaited me. What I didn't expect to see was a man in a black suit on the side of the road, a mile away from the forest's border.

He wore a pair of dark shades, a stiff white chemise under his black trench coat, and a crisp black tie. His arms were crossed in contemplation as he watched me coolly. Apparently, the false trail I planted in Miami wasn't working as well as I'd hoped.

I stopped before passing him, as tempted as I was to continue walking. "Can I help you with anything?"

"Marcus sent me."

I raised an eyebrow at his accent. "Marcus works with British men? Foreign nationals aren't his type."

"I am not with his government," the dark-haired man said.

With renewed interest, I let my attentive gaze survey the agent's slick dress and posture. "MI6?"

"British Foreign Intelligence," he confirmed with a professional nod.

"And your name?" I stepped closer, intimidation in mind.

"I'd rather not say."

"I'd rather you do say."

The man shifted as if uncomfortable. "For my family's sake."

I bit my lip and let it go. "What does Marcus want? Why did he send you?" Besides to apologize profusely for not stopping the FBI's rogue operation from taking place.

The agent uncrossed his arms, though he remained tense. "To warn you."

My eyes narrowed. "If I have to hear another one of his petty threats—"

"Marcus has been removed from his position," the man interrupted. He rushed his words, hoping to avoid my wrath. "He is no longer in charge of human interactions with your *alien* population."

I froze. That explained earlier events. "Who is in charge?"

"A woman by the name of Savanna Hall." The agent relaxed his shoulders after noticing my surprise. His heart beat fast and loud with cautious fear.

Savanna Hall. I didn't recognize the name. She couldn't be that dangerous—humans rarely were, though I'd miss dealing with Marcus. He was old, pudgy, and a pain, but he was determined to make peace between humans and supernatural creatures. Now we were back to the same old story—humans and deities, out of sync.

"Do I really have anything to worry about?" I asked.

The agent shrugged. "Why else would I be here?"

"Because Marcus is superstitious and shady."

"That he is," the British man said with a nod, "but this time, I believe his worry is warranted. He told me to warn you that a man by the name of Levi Cronus arranged for the FBI's change in leadership."

The name clicked with sudden recognition. A curse left my lips, and I ran my hand through my hair. The air around me became tight and tense as if a rubber band had been stretched. Levi Cronus was no ordinary human. Though the human world perceived Levi to be a billionaire tech genius and cutthroat businessman, he was Leviathan, the demon of Envy, and one of Lucifer's meddlesome brothers. His interference was no doubt happening now that I hunted Lucifer.

I looked to the green forests as if to find a solution in the dense trees. My search came up empty. "Marcus can't be of much help anymore, can he?"

"Unfortunately, no," the agent admitted. At least he was honest. Marcus had ended in his usefulness, and my alliance with the human government came to a dreary end.

"Hmm," I mused. "His warning is a little late but do thank him if you are able." With my hands in my pockets, I nodded farewell and continued my path.

"That's all?" the man demanded. "No precautions? No change in plans? You take the information I give you and do nothing with it?" His statement sounded bitter and sour.

But my pace did not slow. "I stop for no one, Agent *Cole*." I stressed the agent's name. A sly smile touched my lips. The dead provided me that particular piece of information. "Anyone in my way will not remain there for long."

The man said nothing more. I suppose he figured I was either a lost cause or knew what I was doing. Hopefully the latter.

The dirt road narrowed as I neared the rainforest. A half-mile later, I breached the boundary of the forest, and the dirt road was replaced with mud and grass. Tall trees touched the sky though their builds were scrawny and thin. The sound of birds tweeting and cawing set off a cacophony of music throughout the atmosphere.

The sweet scent of flowers and fruits swept with the wind around the trunks and branches of the trees. Insects buzzed in a constant drone, and the humid air gave my hair a frizzy texture.

At least it wasn't raining.

Thunder rumbled. I subconsciously slapped myself upside the head. Brilliant. I jinxed my already poor luck. It was bound to rain based on the ominous appearance of the clouds, but I thought I'd give myself a head start before chaos descended upon me.

The heaviness in the air thickened, and the droplets of light disappeared one by one while the dark clouds in the sky grew in size.

Magic was palpable in the environment, like an eerie humidity that penetrated the busy forest. The land around the Glass created its own magic and wards to protect and limit access to the region. Portals were impossible to summon within the borders of the rainforest—the wards preventing portals within this forest were like the spells I cast upon the cavern where I hid my Soul Dagger.

The Glass was at least a day or a day and a half out. Though the distance itself wasn't very long, the Glass lay behind a rocky maze and set of falls that I had to circumnavigate, which added another twelve hours to the hike. I wouldn't mind cutting directly through the mountain of rocks to save time, but I hadn't brought any rock-climbing gear with me, and if it rained in the next few hours, the jagged rocks would be twice as slippery.

The sky responded to my mental note about the impending rain. Soft pitter-patter sounds commenced, and a breath later, the wet chill of rain baptized my head and cleansed my skin. I pulled the jacket closer to my body and tucked my chin. Water poured from the sky in buckets, drenching me and my clothes.

My clothes and hair stuck to my back, heavy and cold. My teeth chattered from the sudden drop in temperature. The ground became slick and muddy, and irritation gnawed at the corners of my mind.

A low growl sounded behind me. I stilled and slowly turned my head—dread latched onto my mind. My eyes landed on a Hellhound. Its red eyes burned with rage, and the wet, matted fur on its back made the creature look rabid. The Hellhound gnashed its teeth. Near it stood another hound, crouched and ready to attack. Then another appeared, and yet another. I did a quick count, and there were fifteen beasts that I spotted—an entire pack of Hellhounds.

Why were they after me while their demon master remained captive in Ben's dungeon? How they found me, I didn't know.

The Hellhound at the head of the pack stepped forward. Well, I could stay and fight them... or not.

The wet, muddy environment wasn't well suited for running, but I needed to place as much distance between myself and the demon dogs as possible. I broke into a sprint. The angry howls of the demon dogs rang through the air and their pursuit was loud and heavy on my tail. I zigzagged between the forest trees and jumped over roots, boulders, and fallen plant life. The rain made the mud slide from under my feet. My shoes felt more like ice skates than combat boots. Lacking a sound footing, I tripped over a tree root and fumbled forward with a sick feeling of alarm in my stomach.

The Hellhounds' large paws had better traction on the forest floor than my shoes. A hound fastened his strong jaw on the fabric of my jeans. The material tore when I pulled my leg out of the beast's grasp. Snarls and gnashing jaws followed my heels.

I darted toward a rocky ledge and jumped to reach a tree branch that hovered over the stone ridge. My hand latched onto the rough bark, and I helped myself up to the ledge. One Hellhound jumped after me, almost making the ledge before its footings slipped, and the beast fell back down with a yelp. My boots gripped the stone better than the mud. I continued my race, steering clear of the edge and dodging past the jagged projections of the rocky surface.

Animalistic yips of success rang through the thick air. I turned back to watch the hounds' glowing red eyes as they emerged over the ledge and resumed their chase.

I hit what felt like a wall and went sprawling forward. The wall grunted. We both rolled over into a ditch and sharp edges of stone bit into my skin. We hit the fragile floor of a trench, and before I could get my bearings, the leaf-covered bottom of the trench collapsed, sending us further down to the rocky brink of a stream. My head ricocheted off a stone, and a spike of pain ran through my skull. My limbs felt sore and heavy with scrapes and bruises. The pouring rain stopped and was replaced by the cold water of the small stream as it spilled over my battered skin.

The pounding of the Hellhound's paws echoed overhead. They sprinted around the ditch we fell through away from us. Hopefully, they wouldn't see where I'd fallen.

"This," a pompous British voice said, "was not how I planned my encounter with you."

My hands fumbled to get a good grip on the stones of the stream to lift myself to my elbows. Did my ears deceive me, or did I recognize the voice that had spoken? Maybe I hit my head harder than I thought, but no matter how hard I blinked, Erin Grimm refused to disappear from sight.

Realizing that he wasn't a figment of my imagination, I shot the younger Grimm Brother a venomous glare.

He smiled thinly and rose to his feet. "It's good to see you again, Lady Primrose."

CHAPTER EIGHTEEN
THE PRINCE OF FLAMES

"AREN'T YOU GOING TO ask how I found you?" Erin fumbled after me as I strode past the trickling stream. I started to climb back up the sides of the ditch, using the tree roots that stuck out from the dirt as my handles. The quiet flow of the water echoed about the rocks.

"No." A scowl pulled my lips to a corner. I strained to haul my waist up to a small ledge and braced myself against it. "It doesn't matter how you found me or why. You're already here."

Erin smiled, ignoring what I said. "I had one of our technologically savvy employees hack into your phone after you left New York. We tracked you to Miami. I had to get creative after you drowned your phone on the beach—"

"You what?" I yelled.

I felt a hand on my behind and furiously swiveled back to see Erin quickly remove it and shoot me an innocent glance. "Just giving you a boost."

"You see this boot?" I let my sturdy combat boot hover over his face. "Touch me once more, and I'll break your pretty face with it."

The Grimm Brother smiled. "Oh, so you think I'm pretty? Ow!" He shook his hand, which now had my muddy footprint riddled on its surface.

"You hacked into my phone to track me?" I demanded.

Erin didn't even have the grace to look embarrassed.

"You..." I struggled to find the words. A growl left my throat, and I swallowed the curses ready on my tongue. I had bigger fish to fry. I took a deep breath and kept climbing. "Let's hope the Hellhounds aren't still up there."

"Even if they are, suck their souls dry, my lady," Erin said. "I'm sure you have plenty of experience—hey!" He rubbed his right eye. "You got dirt in my eye."

"Sorry," I said, not meaning it. "For your information"—my fingertips finally grazed the surface we had fallen from—"I cannot 'suck' the souls of lower demons. As any well-educated deity would know, lower demons don't have souls." I shot him a condescending glance before heaving myself over the side of the ditch and onto the solid, surface-level ground. Slimy mud stuck to every inch of my skin. "Hellhounds are simple creatures, unworthy of a soul. Only powerful demons, such as the Seven Princes of Hell, were gifted with souls upon their creation, and any time the Underworld grants a demon a soul, it also creates an altar of metal. Any demon with a soul cannot be killed without a Soul Dagger."

Erin trailed me closely. He wore his stupid, custom-tailored suit and tie, though his clothes were covered in mud and torn, like mine.

"So, I'm not a demonologist or whiz kid. Big deal." He sent me a flirtatious wink. "I've got better attributes to make up for it."

I bundled my wet hair together and tied it up into a messy bun. The heat ate at my skin now that the rain had stopped. The late afternoon's sunlight shined through the leaves atop the trees down to the forest floor. "Is one of these attributes a dysfunctional taste in fashion?"

"Speak for yourself. Both you and your brother have as much fashion sense as a frumpy, wrinkled old woman wearing a trash bag like a jacket dress." Erin removed his coat and rolled up the sleeves of his white dress shirt. He loosened his tie and tossed it on the forest floor, beside his coat.

I stopped and gave him a look. "You just littered."

Erin's smirk dropped into a prickly scowl.

"Lucky for us, I think we've lost the Hellhounds." I rested a hand on my hip and pursed my lips. "Am I right to say that you'll be accompanying me from this point forward?"

"Yes," Erin said.

I shrugged. "Make sure to keep up." Before he could spit out another remark, I started walking in the direction we needed to head in, and Erin matched my pace. "Where's your brother?" I asked. "You didn't bring him along, did you?"

"Not a chance," Erin said through his teeth. His voice sounded strained.

I laughed bitterly. "Why not? You two seem so close." My lips set into a pout, and I let a southern twang pamper into a jaded sympathetic voice. "Did you two get into a wittle bitty fight?"

"Knock it off."

The silence between us resumed, though I sensed that Erin had something to say. It only took a short minute for him to muster the will to break the ice once again.

"My brother has been up to something."

My forehead creased. I didn't expect him to confide in me, but now that he had, I decided to play along. "That's shocking to you?" My eyes shot upward at the cawing of two birds as they stirred the leaves.

"Not just something," Erin clarified and lowered his gaze from the birds. Frustration coated his voice, and for the first time since we met, I believed he was candid. I listened closely as he spoke. "He's been lying to me. We weren't always the closest of brothers, but we extended the courtesy of telling each other the truth." I snorted, and Erin looked at me oddly. "Not to say we haven't lied to others, but we did it together and not to each other."

"Okay." My mind slowly processed his words. "So, he's been shady. Why is that so terrible? It's not like you're the kindest, most obvious Prince of Compassion."

Erin walked quietly alongside me while deep in thought. "I have a feeling that he's hiding something. Something big." The hair on the back of my neck stood up, and a shiver crept up my spine. The younger Grimm Brother's admission made my stomach flip. "It seems," Erin said, "that he has a separate agenda that he doesn't want me to know about. Atlas has always been the quiet and brooding type, but he's been much quieter than usual these past weeks. I don't mind him keeping secrets, but I don't think this is only a secret." He nervously scratched the back of his head. "It feels like he's about to bring forth a reckoning capable of shaking the earth."

Though Erin's statement didn't surprise me, it reminded me that I could never trust another God or Goddess. Each deity had hundreds, sometimes millennia of years filled with a twisted past—a past that harkened an unforeseen and menacing future.

"Enough about my brother." Erin quickly changed the uncomfortable subject. He closed the distance between us and hooked arms like a cavalier teenager. "Let's talk about us, shall we?"

"Us?"

"Yes." He flashed me a blinding smile and nodded. "Us. You see, my brother shared some quality time with you, Primrose, more time than you and I ever spent alone together. This disappoints me greatly, especially since we make the greatest pair in all of history."

I pulled my arm away from him and quickened my walking pace into a jog, though Erin readily kept up. Gods never knew when to quit.

"Think of it," he continued without a stumble. "Who could stop us if we combined forces? You've already fallen for me."

"What?" I tripped over a shed snakeskin and stopped abruptly. A shock jolted my body with the fresh memory of the injury Abaddon inflicted.

"Yes, well, earlier when you were being chased by the hounds." Erin laughed, finding his humor clever.

I shook my head, and angry heat spread through my chest. "I fell because you were in my way!"

"Even still!" Erin carried on. "There is no better match to be made!"

"Please stop talking."

"But—"

My self-restraint broke. I punched him. Hard. The next half an hour was filled with blissful silence.

† † † † † †

"Lady Primrose—"

"What?" I demanded. Was the previous peace and quiet to be ended so quickly? Two hours of blissful silence interrupted by the sound of Erin's whining.

Erin lifted his hands in surrender. "Nothing! I wanted to ask you a question."

"Then ask it."

"How exactly are you tracking Lucifer's Soul Dagger?"

I rubbed the back of my neck, and my hand came back sticky with sweat. With a disgusted grimace, I wiped my hand against my jeans.

Erin cleared his throat. "Lady Primrose?"

My ears perked up, and his previous question slipped from my thoughts. Though everything on the ground seemed regular and bustling, as a forest should be, uncertainty stirred from above the trees.

"Are you going to answer my question?" he asked.

"Shh." I stopped and signaled for him to do the same. "Do you hear that?"

Erin looked around and shrugged. My eyes turned to the sky. There was a chuffing noise in the distance.

"It sounds..." I licked my dry lips and glanced back at him through the corner of my eye. I wrinkled my nose. "Like a *chuf chuf chuf.*"

He stared at me as if I lost my mind. "A what?"

"A *chuf chuf chuf.*"

Erin's gaze remained blank, and I rolled my eyes. "It sounds like a helicopter."

"You could have led with that," he pointed out.

I scowled. And then the forest exploded.

The blast sent me flying back, airborne and ears ringing. Ammunition rained down to the forest floor in bright bursts of light and sound. I landed and rolled to a heavy stop against a tree trunk. Something sharp snapped into my neck, and I cried out. Another explosion went off nearby, and the noise thundered through the forest with the heavy release of heat and debris.

Angry tears pricked my eyes, and I crawled to my knees. My hand trembled and touched the sharp stick that punctured my neck. Blood seeped from the wound and dripped to my sensitive fingertips. In one quick motion, I pulled the sharp edge out of my neck with a yell. My breath hitched from the heat that burned through the inflamed skin. My blood poured from the wound, and I applied pressure with my palm until the bleeding slowed. I silently rose to my feet.

Flames had singed my right leg and eaten away at the lower half of my jeans, leaving red, flesh exposed to the air. The pain from the burn made my breaths sound more agonizing than they felt. My new injuries prickled while my quick, healing power took effect. A new fire seared through me, and my rage grew beyond recognition.

Large rounds of poorly aimed bullets fired down upon the ground. One bullet hit my shoulder, another hit my thigh. I stumbled back and grimaced. My eyes caught sight of threatening flames that burst from Erin's angry figure, nearly half of a football field distance away from me. He was surrounded by two tanks and a group of humans.

My chin rose to the sky. I closed my eyes and breathed deeply while my magic reached for the souls of the living above me. There were three helicopters in the sky, each with a team of five soldiers. I sensed twenty soldiers on the ground, ten per tank. Agent Cole's warning gained value, now that humans hunted of supernatural beings seriously. How they tracked me here, I had no clue. Maybe they followed the MI6 agent and caught onto my trail in the rainforest, or they might have tracked Erin.

Today, it would rain blood.

My fists clenched, and ten souls were reaped from ten human bodies. The hum from above diminished as two military helicopters fell from the sky. I jogged toward Erin, whose flames grew, eating at the trees, humans, and their metal tanks. Crashes and metal bending and breaking unfolded behind me. I ducked, barely missing a helicopter blade to the neck. A fuel tank burst, and the small shock of its explosion brushed past me like a warm breeze. I frowned and looked back at the damage. Was I missing something?

Oh. I snapped my fingers and reaped the remaining five souls. The chuffing came to a complete end, and the final helicopter fell from the sky.

A blast of heat hit my body like a furnace, and I covered my face with my elbow to shield myself. The God of Fire was losing control of his flames. The fire burned an intense blue that rose to the sky and spread away from the human targets. This was the true, unbridled rage of the Prince of Flames. If he didn't rein in his power, the world would burn.

I ran toward Erin, only to be blown back by another heat wave and wall of flames. A wrenching sting set into the right half of my body. My skin blistered and turned bright red. Stabs of pain peeled at my skin, and I writhed on the rainforest floor in agony. This was a true wildfire. Flames so hot, they burned blue, and freedom so immense that nothing could rein the chaos in—nothing but a skill that its owner lacked.

Now I'd had enough. Though Erin's lapse in control angered me, it frightened me more than anything. If his power wasn't contained, the flames would spread and consume all in their path. *The world would burn.*

I braced myself on the forest floor and summoned my magic to come to my aid. Sensing Erin's soul, I pulled it into a tight bind as I did to Atlas's soul not long ago. When nothing happened, I began to pound at his soul, beating it over and over again. The flames flickered. I increased my grip on the Grimm Brother's soul and heard a cry of pain from somewhere beneath the vast fire. Erin's soul wouldn't travel farther than the borders of his physical body, not without a Soul Dagger, but my tight grasp was painful.

As if a black hole had been formed in the center of the chaos, the flames receded, first from the sky and then from the trees to one central point on the forest floor. The fiery ball was reduced to a man who collapsed to his knees and clutched his head as if it were to burst any second. His skin was red and flushed. The heat sunk into Erin's flesh, and the evidence of his loss of control was the charred hole in the forest and the silence in the air.

I released my hold over Erin's soul, and I felt like I could breathe again.

The pain from my burns lessened, and I was suddenly very grateful for the healing abilities that came with being a Goddess. Ben liked to say that I healed quicker than other deities, and as I took in my surroundings, I couldn't help but believe him. I wasn't certain how much damage had been done or how far the flames had gone. We were surrounded by ash and the charred forest floor.

The rainforest noises of scuffling, chirping, buzzing that used to surround us—none of it remained. Nothing survived Erin's wrath.

I stood back up to my feet with some difficulty. There were charred holes in my blouse, and sections of my jeans had melted and stuck painfully to my legs.

My gaze landed on Erin, and he flinched. His clothes were perfectly fine. He likely had gotten them spelled to be fireproof, being the God of Fire and all. Though his clothes were in perfect condition, the rest of him wasn't. Sweat covered his face, his body was shaking, and his eyes were wide. I recognized him as a broken man—a truth he tried so hard to hide behind his boastful demeanor and debonair smile. But the deep lines in his forehead and the defeated slump in his shoulders told a different story.

"What have you done?" he demanded, his voice raw.

I looked to the rainforest and all the damage that had been done to it by the rampant flames. "The better question is, what have *you* done?"

CHAPTER NINETEEN
A TWIST OF FATE

"I'VE FALLEN IN LOVE with someone I don't deserve." His breath touched the back of my neck as he held me in his arms. The heat of his human body warmed me, even as the cold night air bit at our skin. We sat on the tall mountain's ledge, with the distorted view of familiar cabins and lights belonging to a nameless village. A heavy fog sat at the borders of my vision, obscuring the details of my surroundings.

I smiled and touched Gavin's hand. "I am familiar with the feeling." Static jabbed at the words that left my lips.

"Impossible," he said. His coarse voice grated against my ears with lulling comfort.

I planted a gentle kiss on his forehead, and a smile danced on my lips. "Believe what you will, my love. As will I."

"I suppose it's futile to try to change your mind."

"Well said," I agreed, and we chuckled in unison. The gray fog receded as we spoke.

Gavin's muscles tensed, and I gazed into his hypnotic green eyes. "What is it?"

"Have you told him yet? About us?" he asked softly, knowing this was a tender subject.

I didn't answer immediately. I rested my eyes on the village lights below. The blinking of the stars and elegant moonlight shined down like a spotlight upon the most exciting stage there ever existed. This was our home, and happiness so untouchable embraced me. I never wanted this moment to end.

"No," I admitted. A melancholic hole blossomed where my heart beat. The fog's sheen closed in, warping my vision. "He still doesn't know. I'm afraid of what he would say, or worse"—my voice trembled—"what he would do."

Gavin's arms disappeared from behind me, and I abruptly tumbled from the mountain's edge into another world. The village lights disappeared, and my head was heavy with dizziness. The pretty pale face of a young girl appeared in front of me. The same green color of Gavin's eyes gazed into mine. Her brown hair was tied into two braids, and her pink smile deepened. The girl's height barely lined up with my waist, as I sat on a low bed. We were in a warm, wooden cabin that smelled of a homey chimney fire.

The young girl took my hand and twirled in her brown, woolen dress. The ends of her dress twisted through the layers of fog, warding it off like a fan. "Come, dance with me," she said. Her voice was clear, untouched by the throaty static from before. A small giggle escaped her lips.

I made to stand, but the world faded again, and the ground beneath me disappeared. I fell, and my head slammed against the hard floor. Lights flashed in front of my eyes, and I blinked them away. An unknown force jerked me up to my feet, like a puppet pulled by strings. An old woman with white hair and fearful eyes grabbed my arms with great strength. I trembled with a terror that echoed her own. She brought my head close to hers.

"He knows," her pale lips whispered in a raspy echo.

"Who?" I asked. Sinister shadows grew against the wooden walls of the room. An unnatural darkness tainted the once gray fog, and a biting cold blew into the room. Malicious whispers caressed my ears and overlapping voices spoke hushed words that I couldn't understand.

The woman shook her wrinkled head and repeated her warning. "He knows."

A fear, unlike anything I'd ever felt, hit me like a wave. I had no clue who she spoke of, but somehow, I did know. The midnight black fog that lingered in my surroundings closed in. I recoiled, wrenching myself from the woman's tight grip, and ran through the building we stood in. A howl in the distance made me shudder. Was that a wolf?

My right shoulder forcefully shoved a wooden door open, and again, I fell into the darkness with a scream. My head spun as I landed on my knees, draped across the dirt floor of a clearing in a forest. My nails clawed into the earth, and heavy tears fell from my cheeks to the ground as sobs punished my body. Rain poured from the sky. The drops of water felt like acid against my skin.

The heavens were mourning. They knew my loss better than even I did.

I lifted the palms of my hands toward my face. Instead of seeing the brown dirt from the ground, scarlet blood coated my skin. My breaths came in panicked gasps. My hands trembled as a scream built in my throat. I bit my tongue until it bled. A dark-haired girl placed her ghostly pale hand on my shoulder, and a tendril of magic passed through my skin like a shoot of electricity.

"What will you do?" the girl questioned with weary dread. She already knew but still asked.

My body shook with rage and melancholy. White flower beds in the distance caught the corner of my eye. A force unknown yet inexplicably close to my heart built like a fire in my veins. Nobody knew what strength I possessed.

"I will do what I must." My voice was unrecognizable. "Behold, the end of life shall be born from the depths of my pain—my *sorrow*."

I woke like a shock had run through my body. I lay still on the forest floor, cloaked by the darkness. My dream stoked the adrenaline that rushed through my body. Reality set in, and my heart started to calm.

The leaves I used to soften the surface of the tree roots that I laid my head on were damp with dew, and the soft hum of morning birds and insects waking before the break of dawn rang through the forest like a gentle moan. The stillness of the night had not yet left, though the pinch of morning mist bit my cheeks.

My eyes remained shut in silent rest. Erin insisted on stopping to rest a few hours ago, and though I hated agreeing with the Grimm Brother, his suggestion was enticing, especially since I hadn't gotten a blink of sleep during the bus rides to Argentina. Nearly six days passed since I left Elinore's apartment.

I didn't put it past Erin to do something sketchy under the night sky, but after his wild loss of control earlier, he didn't seem to have the energy to attempt anything sinister while I slept.

Erin's harsh whispers broke the threads of silence. My muscles relaxed, and my breathing evened as I pretended to sleep. I strained my ears to hear his hushed conversation. He was on his phone.

"I can handle it," Erin hissed.

I couldn't make out the voice on the other end of the line or what he or she was saying, but it upset the younger Grimm Brother, who replied with a thread of colorful curses.

"Listen," he said, "I've been doing what we've decided to do up to this point with very little deviation from the original plan. A little trust and respect would be nice." Erin continued his conversation over the phone but lowered his voice and stepped out of earshot.

I stirred and groaned as if waking up. My eyes fluttered open and caught Erin stuffing his phone into his pocket. His hair was brushed back to its orderly perfection, and his eyes had their old twinkle. His clothing was dirty and torn, though the wrinkles had been smoothed out. I groggily sat up, and Erin smiled.

"Sleeping Beauty is finally awake!" he exclaimed and crossed his arms. "Thought you'd never wake up." My eyebrows drew together in a glare, and Erin winked. "Come on, princess. Time to go."

"I'm no princess."

"Whatever you say, your highness."

Irritation pawed at the edge of my mind. Instead of throwing back a biting remark, I pursed my lips. "Do you even know where we're going?" I muttered as I rose to my feet.

Erin snorted. "Probably the Glass. Why else would we be in this botched country?"

I peered over at him and raised an eyebrow. "Sightseeing?"

"I may be pretty, my lady, but I'm not dumb."

I smirked. "Keep telling yourself that, Einstein."

"Have you ever considered biting your tongue instead of making an offensive comment?" Erin asked. Annoyance lingered over his brow like a shadow.

"Your face is offensive. You don't see me censoring it."

"Cow."

"Pinhead."

He narrowed his eyes. "Twat."

"Wanker," I shot back.

Erin smiled painfully, and my expression hardened. I straightened out my clothes and combed my fingers through my tangled hair before we resumed our path toward the Glass. We circumnavigated the rock maze late last night before stopping for a few hours of rest. A pinch of morning sunlight brightened our path this early in the day. We were closing in on the falls, which were another five miles out. Our journey through the rainforest could end by nightfall if we made good time.

Our rapid-fire bantering was endless. If I learned any new truth about the younger Grimm Brother during this journey, it was his delight in avoiding the silence that came between us. Barely walking the edge between playful and insulting, our verbal scuffles brought an illusion of comradery between the two of us.

"I really like these little chats of ours," Erin said, his face scrunched up in thought. "I think we're making real good progress as a pair."

I batted my lashes. "If you like our chats so much, let's suppose we breach a new subject."

Erin's mouth slammed shut, and his features melted into a poorly forged poker face. He knew precisely which uncomfortable *subject*

I wished to speak about, and I knew exactly how to pressure a response out of him.

"Were you planning to ignore the fact that you almost burned down the rainforest?" I demanded.

"I'm not talking about it." He ground his jaw in hardened resolve.

If he thought I planned to drop it, just like that, Erin had another thing coming for him. Millennia of dealing with bratty deities taught me a few tricks and subtle manipulations to get me the reaction I wanted. This confrontation between us was long overdue, and anticipation ate at my nerves. I yearned for the chance to finally put him in his place.

I shrugged and lifted my chin, hiding the intensity of my excitement behind a mask of indifference. "You lost control back there against the humans." *Puny pathetic humans*, my mind whispered. Erin's silence fueled my resolve, and my lips curled. "Your brother exerts control when he uses his power. Unlike you, he earns his title as the God of—"

"Enough!" Erin bellowed. Flames darted across his fingertips, and his eyes lit up with anger. "My brother is no better than I am."

"Really?" The critical question rolled off my tongue. We came to a stop and stood face-to-face. Erin's anger delighted me.

His nostrils flared as he sized me up. A second later, he pounced and backed me up against a tree. Erin's arms caged me against the rough bark.

"All I hear, every day, is how powerful Atlas is," Erin raged. He gnashed his teeth like an animal. "How *in control* and skilled he is. But Atlas isn't King of the High Court! I am! I was chosen. I was crowned! That unpolished boy would be nothing without me."

"Yet you would be nothing without him," I said.

Erin tightened his grip on my arms painfully, and his face came closer to mine until his breath fanned my cheek. "It's a double-edged sword, sweetheart," he growled in my ear. "If I am nothing without him, he is nothing without me. I loathe sharing my power with him. But whether or not his ability to influence stories matters, whether or not he manages his ice magic better than I ever will my flames, I have something he will never have." His warm hand gripped my chin to force my eyes to his. His pupils were dilated, and his cheeks were flushed.

"I, Erin Grimm, rule over the supernatural community of the world. Gods and Goddesses bow before me. Atlas will never belong with the High Court. I made sure to corrupt his reputation even before any Court member met him. He's as much of an outcast as you are, Primrose Titan." His teeth bared into a vicious smile. "The world will never accept you two. Acceptance is power, and it's a power I have all to myself."

I rolled my eyes, and Erin's eyebrows furrowed together. His eyes fell to my lips, and he made a move to kiss them. Disgusted, I threw my head forward, and his nose made a cracking sound.

The Grimm Brother belted out a string of colorful words, and blood trickled from his wound as he stumbled back. The red liquid dripped to his plump lips, and he glowered at me. "You broke my nose!"

"It'll heal, Casanova." I brushed off my jacket sleeves and tilted my head toward our path. "You coming or not?"

Erin's eyes went round, and he stared at me.

"What?" I crossed my arms and raised an eyebrow.

His jaw dropped. "I said all of that, and you plan on moving on like nothing happened."

"Do I look like I care about your personal problems? You're the King of the High Court, big deal. You hate your older brother because he's better than you. What's new? I wanted you to vent your anger now to avoid dealing with your emotional drama later when battling Lucifer or his siblings. Emotion is a weakness. Rid yourself of it."

I spun around and made my way through the rainforest. Erin's confused mumbling followed me. Good. Let him marinate on what I'd said. Perhaps then he would realize that his quarrel with Atlas was trivial and unimportant in the grand scheme of things. The world had larger problems than Erin could fathom, especially if all he ever concerned himself with was a family feud.

Two miles of terrain later, the scent of sweet honey burned the back of my throat. The rushing water from the falls echoed faintly in my ears. My stomach felt raw, and not from the lack of food. An eeriness lingered in the air, like spiders crawling up my back.

I unsheathed my sword and held it out in front of me.

Erin sighed. "Something the matter, Primrose?"

A gust of wind brought forth a heaviness tied to ancient magic as it prickled through the air. The overhanging branches of trees molded into sharp edges. A sinister, inky fog crept up from the shadows behind the tree trunks and stones, and the darkness forced itself to the sky, veiling our sight. A cold emptiness hit me as the fog touched my skin. It felt fundamentally evil and wrong to the touch. My skin prickled with discomfort, as if it had been slathered with slime and every ounce of me wanted to recoil. I crouched down, and my fingers swiped up some dirt. Using my index finger and thumb, I felt the moist texture of the soil tighten, and the particles were swept into the wind created by the fog-ridden atmosphere.

I stood back up. "Prepare yourself," I warned Erin.

"For what?"

I sheathed my sword and unclasped a dagger from my belt. The blade bit into my palm, and blood spilled to the ground. "Ipsum revelare."

The fog was crimson with blood and parted like the Red Sea upon my command. It swirled above our bodies and up toward the sky, opening our sight to the previously hidden surroundings.

The whisper of steps approached. Her long silver gown became visible first. The fabric looked like folded metal, and the waist of her dress was cinched in. The woman's black hair was pinned into a French twist, and a V-shaped silver crown fit perfectly on her elegant head. The pristine, dark skin of her arms was surrounded with tight, silver hoops.

I met the yellow eyes of a Lady of the High Court.

"Lady Fate?" Erin's accent thickened with bewilderment. Dare there be another deception the younger Grimm Brother was not aware of? To Erin, this seemed unfathomable. After all, he was *King* of the High Court. King of a corrupt people with underhanded agendas.

Fate was a sleek woman. Her high cheekbones defined her petite face. Her cheeks were pale, and a dark paint outlined her eyelids. Despite her title, Fate had no control of the fate of others; only Erin Grimm and Destiny could twist the future to their liking. Fate was a powerful witch, nothing more.

Unlike during any of her past appearances in the High Court, she ignored Erin, and her mouth twisted into a mismatched smile.

"Primrose Titan." She spoke my name like a spell on her lips. "You have not forgotten your Latin, I see."

The corners of my mouth twitched. "I'm not quite as uneducated as you believe."

"So, you say," the witch said, lifting her chin. "I've yet to see what is so impressive about you."

"You dare ignore me?" Erin demanded. He strode toward the youthful immortal in self-righteous arrogance, only to be blown back by a blast of magic that bound him to the forest floor.

"I shall deal with you soon enough," Fate said. "I've tolerated your insolence in silence for much too long."

A short laugh hacked my chest like a cough. "Your true colors have been revealed, dearest Fate. Can't hide your second face for long, can you?"

"Speak for yourself, Primrose." She sniffed, looking me over with distaste. Her vowels were pronounced with an Italian dialect. "Of all the deities, you are the most hypocritical."

"Destiny already gave her treasonous speech a short while back. I don't need another 'speech of defiance' from you as well. Both your attempts at asserting authority are quite laughable." A smirk pulled my lips, and I crossed my arms.

"I don't particularly care what you think." Fate maneuvered her layered dress to step around a fallen tree.

"Maybe not, but you are here, aren't you? You've been following me for a while now."

Fate's eyes flashed dangerously. "Whatever do you mean?"

I almost laughed. As if she didn't know! "The ward-breaking assassin was a nice touch."

"I'm glad you liked it."

"The risks you've taken, all to dethrone me... Consider this a point of no return. Desist now, and your life will be spared. Take the wrong step, and when Destiny falls, so will you."

Her lips parted. "I'm not afraid of you. There isn't anything special about you, Primrose. In fact, now that I truly look at you"—she stepped forward, and her eyes narrowed—"you seem weak and bland."

"Look closer." I unsheathed another dagger from my belt. "Or maybe you forgot who you're dealing with."

"A fool," Fate sneered and showed her teeth.

"How about the Goddess of Death?"

The sharp heels of Fate's shoes sank into the dirt. "A title and power you are unworthy of," she said and lifted her chin.

I shrugged and swiveled the blades in my hands. "We shall see about that."

A heat wave roared over my skin and shook the forest. I fell forward with a grunt as embers rained down from charred trees.

Damn it, Erin. He should have let me throw the first punch. A physical attack would have provoked a physical defense, and Fate was no fighter. If it was a battle of magic he wanted, it was magic he would get—from the strongest witch alive.

"I see you wish to be the first to engage in battle, Brother Grimm." Fate faced the Grimm Brother, who was now free of her magical bonds. A staff materialized near Fate, and her hand gripped it tightly. "Shall we?"

"Indeed, we shall." Flames spewed from Erin's fists.

Vines and roots wrapped around my arms, legs, and waist as I attempted to rise from the forest floor. Thorns embedded themselves in my flesh, keeping me in place, and I hissed in pain.

Mischief danced in Fate's yellow eyes. "Sit this round out, won't you, Lady Primrose?"

I struggled to use my daggers to cut the vines. With every vine I cut through, two more grew in its place. One wrapped itself around my neck, and my breath caught. The sound of magic and battle surrounded me while Fate and Erin exchanged blows. Knowing

Erin's struggle to control his fire, he wouldn't last a minute, if that long.

"Exsolvo," I choked out with the hopes that the spell would loosen the binds. The vines tightened. Stupid magic. Stupid witch.

I closed my eyes and relaxed my muscles. Instead of struggling, I drew upon my magic over the dead. Corpses of deceased humans rose to the surface with roars of rage. A few attempted to free me from the vines, while the rest charged toward the witch. The tug-of-war with the plants was futile. The vines grew, wrapping around the dead bodies and pulling them away from me. I clawed at the vine at my neck as my vision blurred. I needed something bigger than a few dead humans.

Oh, I had something big. Big, dead, and angry.

My focus shifted to one very large soul in the Underworld. The strings of my magic sunk deep into the earth and worked at latching onto the monster I wished to summon. The energy needed to complete the summoning left a vacuum inside my body and my limbs ached with exhaustion.

"Erin!" I yelled. My voice was strained from the pressure on my throat. "Remember Vegas!"

A life-size dragon rose from the forest floor with a bellow loud enough to shake the earth. The red, leather-winged dragon that I killed in Las Vegas trained its snake eyes on Lady Fate. Her eyes widened, and her face paled. It wasn't every day a dragon bared its fangs at you. The creature was magnificent with its poised talons and long wings that punched down dozens of trees as they moved. Glee filled me at the thought that a dragon fought by my side instead of against me.

The beast flexed its muscled back and lunged for the witch, who now had one focus: escape.

The vines loosened with Fate's loss of focus, and I cut my way out with my daggers. The dragon's jaws latched onto Fate's waist and it rose to the sky with two flaps of its leather wings. Her screams were music to my ears as they faded in the distance. I smiled and stumbled to my feet.

Erin strode toward me, caution in his eyes. His face was bruised, and he looked worse for wear. "Remind me not to piss you off."

I brushed off his compliment with a casual wave of my hand. "She won't die. I haven't got her Soul Dagger on me. But I don't think we'll be seeing Lady Fate for a good while."

CHAPTER TWENTY
REAL-WORLD VAMPYRES

MAGIC CAST TO PROTECT a sacred location displays burdensome effects on interlopers. For humans, this might mean a sudden illness befalls them when they come within a certain distance of the Glass. Perhaps they start coughing blood, or a dangerous fever brings them close to death. But one fact remains true: protection magic never intends to kill, only deter.

As for the impact of that same magic on supernatural beings, the side effects were less extreme. The air began to feel heavy and stuffy. The dirt dragged at our feet, and the wind blew against us. The temperature rose to an uncomfortable heat, and I disposed of my new leather jacket. A stench of rotting corpses and raw flesh tainted the air even though there was no evidence of any bloodshed. Although it was close to midday, darkness stained the sky, and our surroundings became unclear with a sticky mist. The protections around the Glass were strong, but they weren't impossible to overcome, especially not for a deity.

"Not to discredit or insult you, my lady..."

I grimaced and kicked over a stray branch to clear my path. "Not a great start to a question, Lord Erin."

Erin smiled. We both came to an unsaid, mutual understanding of how our 'relationship' functioned. If he subdued his arrogance, I refrained from belittling him. I hadn't snapped at him for what happened with Fate earlier, nor did he further comment about being 'King' of the High Court.

"Your approach to dealing with other supernatural fiends seems out of the ordinary, if not illogical," Erin said.

I thought silently for a heartbeat, hesitant to play along with his line of reasoning. It couldn't hurt to see where he wanted to go with this. "Well." I rubbed my arm, awkwardly. "In what way do you mean?"

"Consider your interaction with Lady Fate." He brushed a stray hair out of his face and stepped over a puddle. "You have multiple armies of reapers, dead people, demons, and exceptional supernatural warriors, waiting to be summoned to do your bidding. With these armies, you could send the supernatural world a message of your strength and completely revolutionize your image. Instead, you fight Fate on your own, with a few stray souls you happen to summon—"

"And a dragon," I added. "My image is not my primary concern. I won't waste the effort or energy of summoning my army to fight a wannabe Goddess. A better player saves her soldiers for the real battle."

"Player?" Erin asked.

"Isn't this all one big, messed-up game, Lord Erin?"

His lack of response was answer enough. I knew my image did not reflect my strength. This was my intention. People often dismissed me as a threat and ignored the power I commanded. I knew better than to reveal the cards in my hand until there came an opportunity to land the pot. Nobody needed to know I had an ace until the game was over and done with. And the game was far from ending.

"When does this all end for you?" he asked, following my train of thought. "When will people stop trying to take your title and power?

You plan to save your armies and magic for the true battle, but if you remain immortal, will you ever reveal your full strength?"

"My full strength? I don't suppose I plan to reveal every trick I have under my sleeve. I like my secrets." Erin was too young to understand. He'd never seen me summon my armies.

Lucifer's demons wiped out thousands of my soldiers in battle, forcing me to order a retreat and forge a new plan. I had faced him myself, with the help of a few trusted reapers to set a trap for him in Hell. When armies weren't useful or necessary, I didn't call upon them because I'd only be wasting my time. Fate or Destiny, on their own, didn't warrant an army. Why waste my time with a show of power and the politics behind it?

Erin missed the big picture. He cared about the way people perceived him because he believed a powerful image would discourage his enemies from challenging him. I disagreed. Power attracts power, and as proven with Fate, people will only play the puppet for so long before choosing to rebel against their so-called 'master.'

I squinted my eyes to make out a pattern near the rushing of water. "We're here."

Erin studied the environment. "I can hear the river, but where's the entrance?"

"You see that?" I pointed over to the stone pattern hidden by dark green moss. "Right over there."

"Are those...?"

"Steps." I nodded. A river cut through the rainforest, and near the crossing point, the water levels nearly doubled in height. We strode toward the ancient staircase, which spiraled upward and led to a bridge that hung over the river. Erin slipped past me and took the first of the stone steps. Instead of following him, I crouched down to see a set of markings carved by a strong blade. I brushed away the dust that covered the carvings to make out the words.

"Primrose!" Erin's voice called from above. "You need to see this!"

I jumped to my feet and took two steps at a time. Once at the top of the staircase, Erin grabbed my arm and gestured past the bridge. "There it is."

An ancient bridge connected the human world to the Glass. On the other side of the river, a mirror the size of a king's bed stood upright, stained with smudged blood but smooth and uncracked. An aura of unique power surrounded the portal—a power infinitely more potent than that of the portals I summoned.

The rickety wooden bridge that hung over the river was bloodred and littered with bones and shredded clothing, though no flesh or entrails remained. Out at the center of the bridge was a skull small enough to belong to a child. I stumbled back, my eyes stinging painfully.

The water below thrashed wildly, and the stones that marked the bay were hidden by the mist that breathed on my skin. My magic clawed at the corners of my mind with the amount of death in this one single area. It was like the region's dead bodies had been dumped in the river, and the souls had not been appropriately reaped. I doubted any of my reapers would dare venture to this venue, not with the immense aura of protection magic that surrounded the Glass. Whatever souls were reaped in this area had been lost and never made it to the Underworld. It was strange how I never sensed the loss of souls in this area. The protective wards surrounding the portal made sure of that.

Whispers and echoes filled my mind, as though the lost souls were trying to speak. Their wails and cries filled me with utter anguish and despair. The mist below the bridge clouded my vision, and the iron scent of blood suffocated me in a choke hold.

A fly buzzed in my ear, and I shook my head to ignore it. The bridge commanded my attention. The strain of the Underworld's pull made my skin feel papery thin, and the current of magic rippled across my skin like electricity. I pulled at the souls, funneling them one by one into the Underworld. My body started to shake as massive chunks of energy drained from me. A sharp sting on my cheek woke me from my daze, and my breath returned with a gasp. My restraint returned, and I stopped moving souls before my energy drained completely.

I slumped forward, and Erin gripped my shoulders tightly enough to bruise them. His eyes glinted with fear. "I've been calling your name for minutes, Primrose. What happened?"

My head turned back toward the bridge, and I touched the cheek he'd slapped to bring me back to attention. "I don't know." My voice was a dazed hush. "There has been so much death here. I—" I struggled to inhale a proper breath. "It's like I can't feel anything beyond it."

"The bridge is red with blood, likely the blood of humans who ventured too close to the Glass." He tightened his grip on my shoulders and shook me slightly. "This place reeks of ancient magic. *Don't* let the Glass influence you."

Erin let his arms fall to his side, and he walked toward the bridge.

"Don't!" I warned and stepped in the way of his path. "I read a warning carved in the stone stairs. The warning was new and frantically written; if I had to guess, it had been carved a few months ago. There's something wrong here." A hollow whisper of wind blew through the trees, and I started at a soft guttural noise from below the bridge.

"This can't be more than a magical threat meant to keep humans away." Erin attempted to walk past me.

I intercepted him and placed a hand on his chest. "I have walked this world for enough years to know that magic doesn't do this. Protection spells don't kill. And that"—I pointed to whatever was left of the dead corpses on the bridge—"did not happen by accident. I doubt that those corpses belong to humans because humans wouldn't have made it this close to the Glass in the first place."

"What do you think is waiting for us on that bridge?" Erin demanded and shoved past me. I stumbled back.

The moment he set foot on the wooden bridge an animalistic growl stirred from the mist.

A shiver ran down my spine. I stilled and thought back to the warning. "Something not human and hungry for flesh."

Erin slowly but smartly stepped back as the growling became louder and developed into a cacophony of voices.

I stepped forward to stand at his side and unsheathed my scimitar. "My guess?" I glanced over to the now cautious Grimm Brother while he watched the first creature claw its way out to the surface of the bridge. "We're dealing with vampyres."

The monster in bundled rags revealed its hideous face to us. Its ashen features were melted and distorted as it bared its razor-sharp teeth. A cry similar to a roar escaped its black lips—a cry echoed by the multitude of voices from beneath the bridge.

"Vampyres aren't real," Erin said while shaking his head in disbelief. He'd been in court for so long, he didn't know what monsters existed outside his company walls. Though his mind said one thing, his eyes told him another. Flames engulfed his fists.

"Tell that to him," I said, nodding toward the deformed creature, now hunched and training its completely white eyes on us. "Though, to be honest, they behave more like zombies than vampyres. Just as ugly, too."

The monster roared in outrage and shot toward us with incredible speed. Erin lobbed a fireball that hit the beast in the chest. It fell over the side of the bridge down to its fellow friends, who were quick to disapprove of our actions.

"Great!" Erin slapped his forehead. "Now you've pissed them off!"

I punched his arm, and he yelped. "I wasn't the one who burned the messenger to a crisp!"

The growling and roaring increased in volume, and more clawed hands scratched at the bridge. I grabbed Erin's elbow and pulled him forward. "Come on! We need to cross now!"

The bridge swayed under our weight and the mass of the vampyres crawling to the bridge's surface. A clawed hand wrapped around my ankle, and I sliced it clean off with my scimitar. Erin blasted through three creatures with flames. I ducked behind him and relieved a vampyre of its head. A growl erupted beside me. I shoved my shoulder into a creature hunched next to me, and it tripped over the ropes of the bridge and fell with a yowl. I stuck my sword through the middle of another vampyre who climbed over the bridge rope. I ran to Erin's side to kick another bloodsucker off the side of the bridge and carve ourselves a path out.

The sharp teeth of a creature latched onto my shoulder. I cried out in pain and stabbed my blade deep into its belly. The bloodsucker let go of my shoulder. I swung at its head with my fist, pummeling the vampyre over the edge of the bridge. I ducked and rolled, chin tucked. We were nearly past the halfway point of the bridge. It was a miracle the rickety old thing was still standing.

I threw a rapid-fire onslaught of daggers toward the army of vampyres, and black demonic blood hit the ground. For once, the bridge was stained with another color besides red. Anger and sorrow drove me forward. A desire to avenge the innocents who had lost their lives here thrust me into a fiery rage.

My body barreled through the vampyres with greater strength than before. My blows threw them back twice as far; my sword cut off two vampyre heads at a time. My vision swam with their black blood, and I relished the feeling of it coating my skin. The last creature lunged toward me. I roared in reply. My sword arced beautifully through the misty atmosphere and sliced the beast in half.

Erin's cry caught my attention. I turned to see him fall over the side of the bridge and into the turbulent river below. The vampyres leaped after him, forgetting about me in the process. I started, ready to jump after Erin, but a whisper in my ear kept me back. I turned to face the pretty Glass, hypnotized by the ripples that ran across it. My fingers lingered over the portal's surface, sensing an alluring call from the other side. I hadn't visited the ancient land since I first left. I hardly remembered how it used to be or why I left.

What would it be like now, millennia later? My index finger stroked the surface of the mirror as if it were an old lover. And then I stepped through the Glass.

CHAPTER TWENTY ONE
CHASING RED

THE TRUE MEANING OF magic had been lost to me before my foot landed in the watery entrance to the ancient land. A loud ringing in my ears drove me to my knees. I clutched my head and groaned as the ringing transformed into a heavy headache. My vision blurred, and a wave of conflicting emotions erupted in my chest. Denial. Anger. Fear. Acceptance. Joy. I fought the feeling at first and struggled to push the emotions back down into the pit they once hid in. My efforts were all in vain, and soon, the ringing in my ears was gone, and my mind cleared. My shoulders felt light as if a burden had been lifted from them.

A refreshing wind sang across my skin. My lips parted, and for the first time, I truly took what I could classify as a breath of air. Energy pulsed inside of me, echoing the beat of my heart and amplifying the emotions I tried so hard to hide in the past. The pain and wounds from my battles faded as if the very atmosphere of the land had a healing power. My skin tingled as if I had been shocked back to life. I rose to my feet with newfound strength and stepped from the river, the water's coolness caressing my clothes. My body felt lighter and stronger than ever, like I could climb the tallest of mountains and not break a sweat or punch through a brick wall and not know the meaning of pain.

True night had not yet fallen upon the ancient land. The sky was a pristine portrait, dark blue, and cloudless. The sweet scent of wildflowers and trees kissed my nose. The trees were taller and healthier in this realm, with thick, strong trunks. The soil felt firm yet soft under my feet. And the magic, the magic was everywhere—in the air, the sky, the trees, the soil, and most importantly, in me. My senses felt out of control, trying to take everything in, unable to focus on one singular thing. To think I had once left this paradise for a world of humans completely astounded me. No sane being would ever leave.

Euphoria engulfed me, and I knew, this—this was home.

A flash of red caught my eye as I took in my surroundings. My legs burst into motion, and I chased after the stranger in the woods, instinct propelling me forward. The pace at which I ran was faster than usual, and I easily kept up with the equally quick prey I pursued.

The being came to a sudden stop and circled back to make themselves known. My feet slid to an abrupt stop, and I placed my hand on my sword's hilt.

A laugh echoed around me. The scent of campfire revealed itself to my senses, and dawning realization sunk in.

"Dearest Rose." A warm breath touched the back of my neck.

I whipped around. My sword cut through nothing but air. The Devil's resounding laughter began again. An unsettling chill crept up my spine.

"Enough!" I sheathed my blade and ran my gaze through the forest, dissecting each tree and shadow. "Reveal yourself, Lucifer! Let your games come to an end."

There was a tense silence. My body trembled and my heart pounded in my chest; no emotions were capable of being hidden any longer. I was at the mercy of my own feelings.

"Oh, Rose." The demon's voice carried through the air and sent the silence to a foreboding end. "Who said that any of this was a game?"

I pinpointed his figure as he strode through the forest toward me. A twisted smile curved his lips. His blond hair was brushed back and clean, making me feel dirty and unkempt. The red coat he wore was pressed and neat. I couldn't sense his Soul Dagger.

My eyes widened. The portal! After I passed through the Glass, I had been so enthralled by the ancient land I hadn't noticed! My tracking spell needed twenty-four hours to recalibrate, and in its place, an empty void resided. I searched Lucifer closely, trying to see if his dagger was anywhere on him. No, if I had to guess, his dagger was deep within the ancient land, not that I would know for certain until my sense of direction returned. I met his eyes, and an unwanted emotion crawled from an abyss within me.

Lucifer let his eyes analyze me without restraint. A glint of approval flashed through them. "It seems I've missed much."

"What? You didn't meet our vampyre friends back there?" I demanded and crossed my arms. "I thought my decoy would have made it more difficult for you to find me."

"The dead girl in the boat was a fine idea, but not much to distract me. As for the vampyres, I had my fun with them yesterday. Let me guess, fire boy didn't make it through."

"No," I bit back, stung to be reminded of the fact that I completely forgot to go back and help the younger Grimm Brother in his time of need. I became so caught up with the Glass and the beauty of the ancient land. Erin Grimm ceased to exist. But how did Lucifer know about Erin?

"Is that emotion I hear in your voice, my darling?" Lucifer stepped closer, and his eyes narrowed.

I laughed, though it sounded off-key. "Why? Jealous?"

"Just a bit." He was now close enough that I could feel the heat radiating off of his body. "Though, to be honest, there hasn't been this much change in you since..."

"What change?" I asked defensively. "I'm the same *cruel* Goddess of Death. Nothing has changed."

"You were never cruel," the Devil argued gently, surprising me with his tenderness. "You aren't one of them. You never will be one of them." He referred to the members of the High Court. "Still, you are nowhere near the same person I ran into several days ago."

I winced and stumbled back. Bit by bit, the ancient land and Lucifer chipped away at any discipline keeping my emotions at bay. "Upset I don't match the personality of the girl you fell in love with?"

"More so upset that I didn't cause the change." His rough voice vibrated through his chest with passion. His sarcastic tone returned. "You are the perfect light to my darkness. The purity to match my corruptness."

I scowled. "How hypocritical," I said, circling around the Devil, "considering how I can't be the cruel queen, but you can be the evil king. Why are you the corruption, not me? Why am I not the darkness and you the light?"

Lucifer's eyes darkened. The dangerous timbre of his personality grew like an aura. "We've had this conversation before, Rose."

"No, we haven't," I said. "You keep shutting me down when I try to have this conversation with you."

He laughed, which fueled my anger. Lucifer blamed me for avoiding the truth, but today I saw a man projecting his own issues.

"You never listen," I whispered, and his laughter stopped. "You never listen to what I have to say. All I ask is that you try to be the good guy for once."

Lucifer clenched his fists. "Why would I do that?"

"It's just a challenge," I barked. He frowned at the harsh tone of my voice. "One that I don't think you're up to."

"Because it's a useless challenge."

"No, because you are incapable of being good. No matter how hard you try, this is one challenge you won't accept because you know you would lose."

Lucifer glowered at me, and I glared back. There was a contest of strength and resilience in our staring match, one I did not plan to lose. His eyes broke away from mine as he started laughing again. Why was he laughing so much? Was he in a happy-go-lucky mood today? My cheeks heated. What struck him as so funny?

"Has this journey made you soft, Rose?" he howled, and his chest shook with humor. "Perhaps now you truly believe in *happily-ever-afters*, unicorns, rainbows, and true love's kiss? Or even better, do you actually care for others now?"

My blood boiled, and a heavy blush stained my cheeks. My body shook like a volcano, ready to explode. "You know what?" I blurted out, my emotions burning like hot lava. "I do care, Lucifer! I care about other supernatural beings, and I care about humans! I don't believe in happy endings, but you know what I do believe in? Miracles! As for your crappy, skeptical attitude—you can take it and shove it up your—arghhh!" I yelled and violently kicked a tree, vexed. My voice echoed loudly in the night. "I'm sick and tired of this emotionless and indifferent crap! Love is no crime, and I have every right to become a victim to it."

For the first time ever, I had surprised the Devil. *Predictable Primrose* was long gone. The color drained from Lucifer's face, and any trace of laughter disappeared. He became catatonic as he processed my words, a shell of his former self. He almost looked afraid. I fumed and huffed, waiting for a response. Part of me was ashamed of letting my emotions get the best of me, but another part of me had waited for this moment for far too long. All of the pretending, the lies, and for what? An attempt to lead a couple of idiot deities astray? They could ridicule me all they wanted. What did I care?

"You..." Lucifer paused. The tough guy facade flickered. "You can't be serious, Rose."

I stepped closer to him. I didn't know what my feelings or emotions toward the Devil were, but there was no shame in feeling something. "That's the thing, Lucifer." I stood within reaching distance and looked to the ground. My eyebrows furrowed. "For the first time, I am serious. I've pretended for millennia to be cold, distant, uncaring." My brown eyes met his red gaze. "I'm done pretending."

"You can't lose your hard exterior," Lucifer said angrily. "Especially not now! Don't you understand? They'll eat you alive!"

"Who? The High Court?" I shook my head. "If they wish to judge me, let them. I encourage any challenge on their part. Failure and death will meet them with open arms."

The Devil stood frozen for a good minute. His forehead creased, and his eyes filled with doubt. His expression hardened. "Emotions are a weakness in this world. Today, I will prove that to you."

He lunged toward me, taking me by surprise. His fist landed a heavy blow to my stomach. I grunted, gasping in pain, and sidestepped to avoid his next attack.

I unlatched a dagger from my belt and swiped at his torso. Using his wound as a distraction, my elbow hit his chin. I swept underneath his arm and backed away. I was crouched and ready to pounce.

A flash of desperation flickered through his eyes so quickly, I thought I imagined it.

"Stop." I lashed out at the empty air between us with my dagger in warning. "This is nonsense."

Lucifer shook his head, stern and serious. "This is necessary."

I knew he believed it.

The Devil charged forward. My dagger moved again. His arm twisted skillfully, breaking the blade out of my grasp. A second later, he shoved me back, and I zigzagged around him evasively.

"Come on!" he yelled. "Fight me!"

I avoided his attacks and defended against his blows when he threw them. The fight I gave him was weak, and we both knew it. I had no cruel words or defense. For once, I didn't want to fight.

"We can end this now, Lucifer." My whisper made his eyes go wide. "There doesn't need to be a fight between us. You're not the bad guy in my story." I thought back to a time when we were friends. A time with no enmity between us. Why couldn't things go back to the way they were? Screw the High Court and their agenda.

"That's where you're wrong." Lucifer let his harsh words cut me. He brought out a blade and drove it toward my neck; the metal bit into my skin. I stumbled back, and my mouth went dry with surprise. Blood gushed from the deep wound, and the wet liquid pooled in my throat. I choked and held a palm against my neck to slow the bleed.

A gurgling noise escaped my lips. Whatever I thought him of being incapable of doing had come to pass.

He held the dagger up to strike me again. I backed up a few more steps. Fear made my knees buckle.

Lucifer shook his head. "You don't know me as well as you think, beloved."

He brought the blade down, and a blinding blast of energy came off my skin. The white wave blew the Devil away, and I fell to my back with the impact. My skin buzzed with power, and my chest felt heavy with magic.

I instinctively touched my throat again to keep pressure on the wound, only to sense that it was gone. Not a scratch remained. Confusion sunk in. I was a fast healer, but Lucifer's blade had cut deep—it should've taken at least a minute before the scar tissue was formed and longer before the scar disappeared. I sat up hesitantly and lifted my hands to my face. I turned them over to see my palms. Both of my hands glowed white with the energy that had vanquished Lucifer. The white light faded, and I was left staring at the uninteresting palms of my hands. This magical release within my body felt as if I had discovered a piece of me that was missing. The foreign magic was familiar—as if I had felt it, once upon a dream.

I looked up, searching for Lucifer. He was nowhere in sight.

I finally understood why I left this so-called *paradise* long ago. This realm amplified the volatility of my emotions and thus made me uncomfortably vulnerable to my enemies. A minute ago, I truly believed that the Devil had changed. That he would understand the whirlwind of chaos within me. How could I have been so stupid? If not for the wave of foreign magic, who knew how debilitating Lucifer's next blow would've been?

The energy and power running through me... it was something new. It had to be. I would've remembered having extra magical powers from before my migration into the human realm. For now, all I knew was that the new magic had something to do with me crossing the official border into the ancient land.

CHAPTER TWENTY TWO
CONFESSIONS AT DUSK

I ROSE TO MY feet, confused by Lucifer's disappearance. Considering the note we left off on, I expected him to surge toward me, sword in hand. Our fight was far from over, and this time, I was ready to give him hell. A ruffle of leaves and the sound of footsteps was all the provocation I needed. My scimitar was in one hand, a dagger in the other.

My face creased in confusion. When did Lucifer have time to change into a black set of clothes? I loosened my grip on the blades, and recognition dawned on my face when the figure came out of the shadows. "It's you."

"Yes." His cold voice froze the air around us. The temperature dropped, chilling my skin. "It's me."

I'd never seen eyes hold so much hatred, frustration, and insolent arrogance all at the same time. A week ago, Atlas Grimm watched me storm away to retrieve my Soul Dagger. I remembered the tension when we argued then. Today, as we stood in the forest of the ancient land, even as we simply stared at one another, waves of tension came off of him, stronger than ever before. Atlas was a ticking time bomb. His posture was refined and stiff. He wore what he had the day we parted.

Atlas didn't approach me. He waited for me to say the first word. I sheathed my sword and dagger. My face was numb from the cold he brought with him. My torn jeans and short-sleeved shirt provided no protection against the freezing temperature.

I rubbed my hands together and inhaled deeply. "If you're waiting for an apology, forget it."

The air became terribly thin as the coldness grew. Atlas took his first step toward me, and the ground froze where his foot landed. "I know better than to expect anything from you, Lady Titan."

My index finger twitched upon hearing my formal title. "I've had a rough day," I bit back and rubbed my arms. "Save your lecture for another time."

I turned my back to him to walk deeper into the forest. Big mistake. My feet became heavy, numb, and very much stuck to the ground. I looked down to see them literally frozen into blocks of ice.

"Did you think that I would let you walk away?" Atlas purred.

I blinked. After all that I'd been through with Erin and Lucifer, I didn't need Atlas's crap on my plate. However, his anger had festered and now needed to be released. The best thing to do was to let him vent his rage like Erin had. But the idea of Atlas venting his anger out on me sent my stomach into a whirlwind of chaos.

The crunch of boots on an icy forest floor approached me. My back was turned toward the God of Ice. The skin on the back of my neck froze with the feel of his breath, and his cold hand touched my right cheek and turned my head to face him. His nose almost touched mine. Ice formed where his fingers lingered.

"You were to contact me after you retrieved your Soul Dagger." Atlas's touch became painfully cold, and my breath caught. "Then, and only then, the hunt for Lucifer was to resume. You and I were intended to work together as a team."

I grabbed his arm and wrenched it away from my cheek. His eyes were frigid with anger.

"How can you blame me?" I demanded. My jaw ached from clenching my teeth. "You were a jerk from day one and an unwanted addition to my hunt. You, Lord Atlas, were never supposed to enter my life, and as far as I was concerned, you did not *exist* before that day in High Court. So, *forgive me* for ditching you the first chance I got."

I regretted the words as soon as they'd left my mouth. If the God of Ice wasn't angry before, he was now. I just lit the match that started the fire.

Atlas gripped my arms tightly and shoved me to the frozen dirt floor. The ice that held my feet frozen in place broke off at my ankles in one painful motion, and I tumbled to the ground. Cold mud stuck to my back and hair. Atlas prowled toward me, and I backed away, attempting to preserve the space between us. With another step, he pinned me to the floor.

His lips hovered over mine as he posed his angry questions. "How about now, Primrose? Do I finally exist in that pristine little world of yours?"

I elbowed him in the gut, hoping to get a reaction, but Atlas only grunted and tightened his grip. "Let me go," I warned. He was crossing a line.

"Why should I?" His question cut through the frozen air. "I am the dreaded Ice King," he spat. "My mind can manipulate the strongest of deities with a simple thought. What makes you think *you* can challenge *me*?"

My head rose so that my mouth barely touched his ear. "I am the Goddess of Death, *your royal highness*. Whatever magic you possess doesn't hold a light compared to mine."

"And how is that?" Atlas's voice had a dangerously sharp edge to it, one that could cut through flesh.

"I control a very Dark Magic," I retaliated without a moment of breath. "There is nothing eviler than what I am made to do."

The silence engulfed us like a shroud. Our breathing stopped in unison.

And then his lips were on mine. Hungry and nostalgic. I echoed his emotion and gave in to the feelings that boiled inside of me. I

spent minutes memorizing the taste of him and finally acknowledged the fact that I missed this blasted son of a bachelor. My fingers
ran through his dark hair, pulling him closer to me, and he moaned
in approval.

The God of Ice wrapped around my finger.

His hands explored my figure, but I stopped him short. "We can't."

"Why not?" His lips were quick to attack mine again. If his plan
was to distract me with his kisses, it was a pretty solid plan.

But if there was something I wasn't ready for, it was a relationship with the sketchy God of Ice. I broke away and provided the first
excuse that came to my mind. "You're angry at me, remember?"

"Not currently."

I placed my hand on his chest and created a small distance
between the two of us. My eyebrow lifted in question, and his chest
rumbled in reply.

"Besides," he said with a dead seriousness in his voice, "I don't
believe I can ever truly be angry with you."

The memory of the look in his eyes when he found me earlier
haunted me. Hatred, frustration, arrogance. "Liar."

Atlas chuckled, and the tension in the air melted. He held me
close. I needed to change the subject before he continued where we
left off.

"If you're going to tag along for the rest of the journey, there
is much you need to catch up on." My suggestion sent the wheels
turning in Atlas's mind.

He stroked the side of my head and moved away a strand of hair
with a lopsided grin. I thought he might ignore what I'd said. My
stomach came alive with butterflies at the thought that he might
lower his lips and kiss me again. I scolded myself silently, upset that
my mind even ventured close to that direction. But then Atlas stood
to his feet and gave me a hand to help me rise.

The ice had melted.

"What did I miss?" Atlas asked.

A lot. He most definitely missed a lot, though I couldn't tell him
everything. Some secrets needed to remain just that. I still didn't
trust him. Nobody in this blasted game could ever be trusted. We

stood facing each other. To shift his focus away from information I didn't want to reveal, I needed to trap his attention elsewhere.

"Lucifer's Soul Dagger is within the ancient land." I started with a truth. "My tracking spell became... confused, once I entered the Glass, and it will take a day before I regain my sense of direction. My guess is that his dagger is south of this forest. I traveled to Argentina and ran into Greed's Hellhounds along the way. You wouldn't believe who I bumped into—"

"Who?"

I almost smiled though I was forced to hide my grin under a face of stone. His attention was hooked, now to set the trap. "Your brother, Erin."

The chill that accompanied Atlas's arrival was revived. I mentally applauded my organization of speech. Atlas's face was devoid of emotion, but his emotions spoke through the aura around him.

My face scrunched up in thought. "Didn't you know? I thought he would've told you. He's been on my tail for quite some time now; we've faced several trials together."

"Is that so?" Atlas asked through his teeth. "I was not informed."

"Really?" I said in faux surprise and shifted my weight to my right leg. "Now, that's odd."

"Where is my brother now?"

I shrugged in honest ignorance. "Lost him while crossing the bridge. The vampyres are keeping him occupied."

"I see." A gleam of satisfaction warmed Atlas's eyes. Well, well, well, Erin's hatred toward his brother was echoed with equal intensity.

"Erin had a lot to say." I steered the conversation toward a sour topic. "Seems the two of you have a not-so-friendly relationship."

"Let me guess. *Golden boy* is frustrated about not being the best at everything." Atlas spat out the words as if they were particles of dirt in his mouth.

"Yeah." I laughed under my breath. "I was also lectured on of how Erin is King of the High Court, and how I will never amount to his status and power."

Atlas studied me carefully. "What did you have to say about that?"

I thought for a second. His question was a test. Avoiding it would only increase Atlas's already infinite distrust of me.

"Well," I tsked, "I don't want to be like the other members of the High Court, arrogant and cruel. To be honest, I never belonged there. Before anyone met me, they decided that I would be an outcast." I smiled and pointed toward myself. "My face doesn't scream scary Goddess of Death. To add to that, I was never much for posh or elegance. It's hard to fit in with a group of people who already formed their opinion of you before you even opened your mouth to speak. Besides, nothing they say is truly what they mean. Even a compliment from one of them can be an insult if interpreted in the proper context."

"You're not alone." Atlas surprised me with his admission. "My reputation does all the speaking for me. Millennia away from the High Court does nothing more than foster rumors and alienate other deities. Ignoring the fact that Erin's the charming"—he rolled his eyes—"golden boy of the court, I was put at a disadvantage by isolating myself from the other Court members. Adding Erin's charming manipulation worsens the entire situation. His words are like poison."

"We don't fit in, big deal." I shrugged and brushed a hair out of my face. "Why does it matter?"

"Don't you ever wish the current hierarchy would change?"

Warning bells went off in my mind with Atlas's treasonous question. Luckily for him, I wasn't like other deities because a question like that only meant trouble for him. Our society had a very strict class system, humans at the bottom, deities at the top. I doubted Atlas cared about human status; he likely cared about how power was assigned among the deities of the High Court. The system of power, the workings of the High Court, were as ancient as the old Gods. From when Ben brought to life the first few dozen deities, there became a council to oversee the supernatural communities. Did Atlas realize what he was suggesting? To uproot a system that has existed for tens of thousands of years, long before the creation of humans... was impossible.

I pursed my lips. "The hierarchy you refer to... I assume you mean within the High Court."

"Yes. Come now, Primrose, it's an age-old system in dire need of modernizing. Imagine what changing the hierarchy would mean for people like us," he said. He lifted his chin proudly, and his lips quirked into a mischievous smirk.

"I can't say I've never considered it," I said. "Why is it such a big deal to you?"

Atlas's smirk melted into a scowl. "Erin hasn't always been the kindest brother. During my absence from the court, he spread many of the unflattering rumors that there exist about me. He hides the secrets he knows will benefit him in the long term. Needless to say, his betrayals have been numerous." A muscle in Atlas's jaw twitched.

I wished I had something kind or reassuring to say, but Erin's behavior was trivial of a member of the High Court. "That shouldn't come as a surprise to you."

"I wish it didn't," he said quietly. "But part of me wishes he'd treat me like a brother instead of a competitor."

I couldn't imagine his situation. Ben was always a good brother to me. If he was half as cruel as Erin, I didn't know what I would do. We were two halves of the same whole. Incomplete if separate.

"Aren't you able to use mind control to sway the minds of deities?" I asked. "Get rid of the rumors your brother maliciously spread?"

Atlas shook his head. "Changing the mind of one deity is already a challenge. Their minds are stronger than that of humans or lesser supernatural creatures. It's nearly impossible to change the minds of all deities in the High Court, not without my secret being exposed." His voice lowered in warning. "I trust you won't share the knowledge of my power with others."

"I haven't so far," I said, and warmth rushed to my cheeks. "I've known for decades, but it's not my secret to tell."

Atlas's eyes softened, and I struggled to hide my surprise when he touched my hand. "You shouldn't have continued the hunt without me, Primrose. Though this might come as a surprise, enemies—we are not. We have more in common than you might believe. This makes us a strong pair, you and me."

Or one destined for failure.

Still, I felt a connection between us that never existed before. We were tied by some combination of fate and a twisted past. It was nice to have someone know what it was like to be an outcast, alone and unwanted. Ridiculed by those weaker than us and unable to fight the system that chained us.

"I think I believe you," I said. "Which is why from this point onward, I won't be hunting alone."

CHAPTER TWENTY THREE
A FESTIVAL OF MAN

ATLAS AND I WALKED through the dense forest. The blue sky melted into obsidian, glittering stars sprinkled about its fabric. Without my sense of direction, we headed south at a slow pace.

"How does the tracking spell work?" Atlas asked, breaking the silence. "You said the spell became confused when you crossed into the ancient land."

"After using any sort of portal, it takes twenty-four hours for the tracking spell to recalibrate," I said. "It's been a few hours since I passed through the Glass, so I'd say in twenty hours or less, my sense of direction will return."

The sound of fast, heavy footsteps stopped us in our tracks. I unsheathed two daggers, and Atlas's sword materialized in his hand.

Two laughing children burst from the bushes, one chasing the other. The blond girl caught the boy's arm, and they fell in a tangle of limbs on the forest floor. The boy's eyes landed on us first, and he froze. The girl tugged playfully at the boy's shirt sleeve, but his attention was held captive by fear.

"Elise, stop." He pointed at us, and the girl, Elise, stopped to stare as well.

My eyes landed on the two daggers I held. I hid the blades, and Atlas sheathed his sword. What were these human children doing in the ancient land? As bizarre as it was to fight vampyres while crossing an ancient bridge, it was nothing compared to humans stumbling upon us in the oldest realm in existence.

The children hopped to their feet as if struck by lightning and brushed the dirt off their garments. They shared the same blond hair and brown eyes. The girl was slightly taller than the boy, and she stood more confidently, clearly the eldest of the two. Her chin was sharp, and her features were more defined than her brother's. She wore a knee-length dress, while the boy wore a white shirt and trousers.

The girl stepped into a deep bow. "Your royal highnesses, it is good to see you! I am Elise, and this is my brother Remi."

Remi broke out of his trance and bowed. "Greetings."

He frantically looked back at Elise, unsure of what to do next. His sister gave him a glare and pointed back toward where they came from. The boy turned beet-red and ran in that direction.

I shared a confused glance with Atlas. He shook his head, as unsure of what was happening as I was. The children must have confused us for someone else because we never met them before today.

I stepped forward and nodded in hello. "There must be some mistake."

Elise rushed forward with excitement and shook her head. She spread her arms in welcome. "Hardly! You are magic wielders, are you not?"

"We are," Atlas said with narrowed eyes. Distrust stained his tone. "And this is relevant in what way?"

The girl laughed as though his question was silly. "Come, you two! The village shall prepare a festival in your honor. Your presence is truly an occasion to be celebrated." Elise stopped short as if seeing me for the first time. Her head tilted in question. "Have you visited before, my lady? You seem familiar."

"Huh?" I shook my head, still shocked by what was happening. "No, I don't believe so. I'm Primrose Titan. The Goddess of Death."

Elise's eyes grew wide. I half-expected her to shrink away in fear, considering my title wasn't quite the introduction that made people feel warm fuzzy feelings inside. Instead, the child's lips morphed into a crocodile smile. "What news! A Goddess, here, to visit our village! Kloe will be pleased to hear this news."

Who is Kloe?

I was about to ask, but then Elise ran to Atlas, practically trembling with happiness. "You must be a God."

"Of Ice," Atlas finished frostily.

"How wonderful!"

I sidestepped to stand beside Atlas and elbowed him in the ribs. He glared at me. "Be nice," I whispered in his ear. We still didn't know what was going on, but to find out, it wouldn't hurt to play along.

Elise smiled so widely I was shocked her face didn't explode. "Absolutely marvelous to meet you both! Come!"

She skipped out to where her brother had gone. I moved to follow her, but Atlas's hand latched onto my arm.

"Wait. This could be a trap," he warned.

My gaze followed the girl, who stopped to look back at us with worry. "I don't think this is a trap," I said. "This is something else."

Atlas's grip loosened reluctantly, and I followed Elise, who clapped her hands in renewed excitement. Atlas shadowed me warily. Perhaps the children were a threat to us—who was I to say they weren't? However, Elise and Remi seemed trustworthy, or at least, they didn't seem dangerous. I felt comfortable around them. My eyes furrowed in puzzlement at the thought, considering how rarely I trusted others.

Elise led us through the forest, knowing every nook and cranny better than any tour guide I ever had the misfortune of encountering. She was quick to advise where not to step and how not to lose an ankle. Apparently, losing limbs was relatively common in this part of the forest.

"It is good Remi and I found you! There are many traps set for animals around the village when hunting is good," Elise explained.

"We wouldn't want you to step into a trap, since you are our guests. You must also watch out for the Deatheri flower beds." Elise pointed toward a bed of white flowers in the distance.

"Why?" I asked.

"The Deatheri flowers are very dangerous," said Elise. "They can put you into a coma and cause eternal paralysis. The adults say that the Deatheri flowers are the bringers of eternal peace."

I shivered. "Doesn't sound very peaceful."

"Oh! Well, I really don't think it's peaceful either. But mother says the flowers bring peace because once you are paralyzed by their touch, you don't feel any pain or sorrow. I wouldn't worry much about it. The flower beds are only found on the outskirts of our village."

Though Atlas didn't say anything about Elise's warnings, his eyes went through an entire monologue of how stupid I was for trusting random strangers in the woods and how I'd probably end up missing a limb or in a deep coma if we didn't turn back now. I ignored him for most of our silent conversation.

The trees abruptly became much less dense as a clearing came into way. The walls of what appeared to be a fort came into view. The tall stone that formed the walls stood strong and ominous, expressing years upon years of history. There were several entrances into the walled village, but the largest was wide and tall enough to fit a dragon through it.

At the entrance of the village stood a crowd. Hundreds of humans waited with frozen smiles on their faces. They were dressed in clothing that befit the centuries of the past. The women wore ankle-length gowns, and men wore tunics over their trousers. Sprinkled between the majority were humans who wore a mild version of modern clothing—men and women who wore pants and blouses—though they were scarce among the crowd. Humans of all shapes and sizes greeted us. Many carried flowers or gifts as they quietly watched us pass. They bowed in greeting and avoided eye contact. The scent of spices and roses swirled with the wind, reaching the tip of my tongue.

Everything about this felt wrong. The villagers were skittish with anxiety in their eyes, hidden behind rehearsed smiles. I swallowed the lump in my throat and suppressed the flood of questions and confusion that rose within me. Maybe Atlas was right. Could this be a trap?

We followed Elise through the entrance as she led us toward the village center. The village, at its periphery, had rows of wooden homes, one next to the other. Near the homes were fields of crops and animals. There was a clear path toward the center. The village center was a large gathering area on higher grounds than the periphery, at least a five-mile hike away. As Atlas and I followed Elise toward the center, the villagers accompanied us the entire path, like a flock of loyal sheep. New villagers, who hadn't greeted us at the gate, left their homes to join the crowd.

The gathering area was a large open pavilion, two football fields in size. Near the center, tables were prepared with food and drink by dozens of humans who ran left and right to ensure everything was set properly. The scents of cooked meat and sweet desserts wafted through the area. A large bonfire had been lit.

The villagers filled into the area, and the crowd's energy shifted. Women and children standing around the bonfire danced around us with dresses of beautiful, floral colors. Flowers and rice were thrown to us from the villagers and lively laughter filled the air.

A young lady came to place a crown of flowers on my head. Her smile, though filled with happiness, was unnatural. There was something off about the crowd's energy and the growing cheers.

Atlas and I were led toward an elderly woman who watched us with joyful, wrinkled eyes. The woman wore purple robes and held a wooden staff in her hands. Her hair was hidden by a red scarf, and her sun-kissed skin brought a maternal aura about her. Her face was plump, and her cheeks were red from the bonfire's heat.

"Welcome!" She greeted us with a respectful nod. Her voice was musical and pleasant to the ear. The crowd quieted.

Elise stood by her side with her brother, Remi. Her arm twirled in a flourish. "Madam Kloe Brek, may I present you to the Goddess of Death and God of Ice."

Impressed, I sent Elise an appraising glance. The wording she used was well played. By introducing Kloe to us instead of the other way around, Atlas and I were respectfully treated as high-status socialites. It was a subtle political move. At first glance, it didn't seem like much, but knowing the importance of such details in the High Court, I was familiar with these manipulations. The villagers knew how to appease a God's pride, but how would a human child be privy to this?

Kloe bowed to greet us. "An honor to be in your presence."

I smiled. "It's a pleasure to meet you, Kloe. I am Primrose Titan." I nodded toward Atlas. "This is Atlas Grimm."

"A pleasure," Atlas greeted simply, but not before sending me a scorching glare for daring to introduce him, instead of allowing him to speak for himself. Knowing his lack of etiquette at the current moment, the last thing I wanted was for Atlas to express himself. Our hosts were a rather interesting bunch, after all, what were humans doing in the ancient land? How did they know about deities and supernatural creatures?

"It is so rare to see a God and Goddess in the flesh!" Kloe exclaimed with a loud clap. "Please! Stay, eat, and rest the night." She gestured toward the villagers. "Our village has a wonderful festival in the makings for you. A feast shall be dedicated in your honor! We are here at your service."

Atlas wrapped an arm around my waist and pulled me closer, an action that annoyed and embarrassed me. "I'm afraid we must be going."

"I think we can make the time to stay a bit, *dear*," I said and shared a glance with Atlas, who narrowed his eyes.

"We can?" His arm around my waist brought a heavy chill to my spine as he tightened his grip.

"Yes." I raised my eyebrows. "I mean, wouldn't it be nice to stay the night and *observe* the festivities and so on so forth?" *So that we could figure out why there is a village of humans in the middle of the ancient land.*

My fake smile felt cheesier by the second. Hopefully, Atlas wasn't so dull that he couldn't read between the lines. There was a story behind this village, and I wanted to know more about it. Perhaps they knew something we didn't about Lucifer and why a hoard of vampyres guarded the Glass. The village's history might provide the answers we needed. Besides, my sense of direction hadn't returned. Without it, hunting for Lucifer's Soul Dagger was a guessing game.

The God of Ice picked up on my not-so-subtle hints and nodded. "Indeed. We'll take our leave tomorrow morning."

The crowd hummed in approval and cheers filled the air. On cue, the music commenced. Flutes and violins sang through the gathering area, and couples took to dancing. Costumes of various colors spun through the night as if a black-and-white drawing had been painted and come to life. I excused myself and asked if there was a good place to freshen up. Elise led me to a nearby home, where I was given a white satin gown with a deep V-neck. White was so not my color, or lack of color if technicalities were to be considered, and I couldn't remember the last time I wore a dress. Out of respect for the villagers' hospitality, I accepted the gift and went to one of the home's bathrooms to freshen up. The little cabins had what almost qualified as modern-day showers, much to my surprise. Though the village was deep in the woods, certain elements of modern human culture and technology seeped into the ancient land. I showered and cleaned the dirt and blood off my skin. I brushed my hair and let the curls spread across my back to dry in the warm air. The white dress gifted to me was a tad large, so I borrowed a white ribbon to tie around the waist, and Elise helped me pin up the neckline and underarms.

Before we walked back outside, I caught a glance of myself in the mirror and stumbled in shock. I didn't recognize the Goddess in the mirror. My eyes looked warm and animated, like chocolate, instead of empty and indifferent. My skin looked less pale and, even in the dark, had a subtle tanned glow to it. My cheeks were soft and rosy, like Ben's nickname for me. Without being covered in blood, I appeared to be welcoming.

What surprised me the most was how the confident accent of my posture and freedom in my smile gave me a dangerous edge I'd never seen in myself before. When I looked in the mirror, a brave woman gazed back at me, and an odd thought stirred at the back of my mind. Did I really have to compromise my happiness for the sake of being the strongest warrior in the field? Because the image I now had imprinted in my mind proved the opposite. That I could be kind, happy, and even wild with freedom while maintaining my courage and strength.

I barely paid attention to my surroundings as Elise led me outside. Each step I took felt light and airy as if I were in some dream instead of reality. Everything was a haze, a time-lapsed mess. My attention was everywhere, yet nowhere, until my focus honed in on one small girl. She sat quietly, bundled in dark blankets on the floor. She leaned against a home, far on the other end of the plaza, yet her pale blue eyes were set on me. The flames of the bonfire left shadows on her face and embers playing through her eyes. There was something eerie about her gaze, something ancient.

My heart skipped a beat, and I furrowed my eyebrows. Did I recognize her from somewhere?

"Lady Primrose?"

I turned to the voice that called my name to see Kloe approach me with her purple lips in a grand smile. "What are you doing over here? In the periphery? Come!" She touched my arm to guide me and pointed toward the dancing and food. "Join us at the center! The heart of the festivities is meant for you and your companion."

I shied away from her encouragement and clasped my hands together. "Thank you, Kloe, for your hospitality. I do appreciate it, though I'd prefer to watch from here."

Kloe tilted her head to the side as if hearing me for the first time.

"I don't enjoy being the center of attention," I said.

"Why not? Lord Atlas seems to be taking it quite well."

My eyes landed on the God of Ice, who soaked in every praise and cheer. His lips warmed into an honest smile as dancers surrounded him, and gifts were laid at his feet. He seemed to be enjoying himself.

"I suppose I feel out of place," I said, uncomfortable with her inquisitive nature. "Besides, I can hardly get my bearings in the midst of the festival you've hosted—everything about your village is just so strange."

Kloe's eyes lit up with astonishment. She scrutinized me with an intense gaze, and I barely refrained from flinching away despite her only being human. "When my darling Elise brought you before me, I hadn't seen it then... but I see it now. There's something different about you. You are not like the other deities that have graced our lands."

"How do you mean?" I asked, fiddling with the skirt of my dress.

Kloe tsked. "Look at your companion." We both turned to observe Atlas. "You know your fellow Gods and Goddesses better than I do. They have an aura of pride and arrogance that surrounds them. They lift their chins, thinking themselves better than us." A touch of distaste leaked into Kloe's voice, and I watched her with careful surprise as she continued. "Most deities treat those around them with arrogant dismissal and scorn. Unfortunately, they aren't capable of seeing past the world they've trapped themselves in."

My breath caught, and I forced a sly smile to my lips. "And what? I'm not one of them?"

The elder tightly gripped her staff as if it were a cane. "No, you are most certainly not like them."

My cheeks flushed and I averted my gaze. Kloe's words resonated with a truth deep inside me. But looking inside myself was never a strong suit of mine. I feared what I would find if I searched deep enough. I was deathly afraid that Kloe was wrong. I thought myself different from the other members of the High Court, but what if the difference between them and me was a figment of my imagination? What if the only difference between myself and Erin Grimm lay in the fact that he accepted his lies and deceit as a part of his character and that I kept fighting an inevitable truth?

These thoughts tormented my mind, so I posed a different question, eager to change the subject. "What is a village of humans doing in the middle of the ancient land? Why are all of these humans still here?"

"Why indeed."

I expected the old woman to elaborate, but Kloe only looked at me expectantly. I rolled my eyes like an annoyed teenager and continued. "It's impossible."

"Is it? Then you've answered your own question."

I rubbed my eyes and pinched the bridge of my nose. "If anything, I'm more confused. Do you have a straight answer for me? I tire of riddles and half-truths."

"I have not lied to you, Lady Primrose. Nor have I hidden anything from the obvious," said Kloe. "You do have the answer to your question. My input is not necessary even as you search for it."

"Is that so?" I stood in sullen silence. If it was impossible for a village of humans to exist in the ancient land, how were these humans here? It seemed an oxymoron, but then it all made sense.

"Unless," I mused aloud and returned my gaze to the village chief, "you're not human." My words came out more like an accusation rather than a revelation.

Kloe only smiled as though everything made perfect sense. I suppose to her it did.

Though the night air was warm, a chill ran down my spine. I crossed my arms and lifted my chin, trying to hide my apprehension. "If you aren't human, then what are you?"

Her smile widened, and she shrugged. "What are we all, Lady Primrose, if not players in a game? A good player does not reveal her identity—"

"Until the game is good and done." I finished her saying of wisdom with a bitter taste in my mouth. "I can't blame you for your secrecy." Especially when my mode of thinking matched hers. It would be hypocritical of me to criticize her for being wary of who to trust.

"Then I believe we are at an impasse," said Kloe without any rudeness or solemn tone. She recognized that I understood her position.

"Even better," I said, holding out my hand to her, "truce?"

Kloe's eyes twinkled, and she shook hands with me. Her grip was firm and honest. "Truce. Perhaps one day, friendship."

"Don't get too sentimental on me. I'm told I don't do well with emotions."

"And what is your view on that?"

"Wish I knew," I deadpanned, and Kloe laughed. At least someone found my moral dilemmas amusing.

I searched for the girl I had seen earlier, the one who was watching me. "Kloe?" I pointed to where I last saw the girl. "There was a child over there. Blue eyes, sitting at the edge of the pavilion."

"Ah." Kloe nodded. "Yocheved. One of the village children. That's her favorite spot. She is a smart girl. Perhaps too smart for her own good."

"She was watching me," I said. An edge of uneasiness kissed my cheeks with a pink flush.

The elder lifted her head as if in deep thought. The night's stillness echoed her patience. "If there is any villager who can see things that others cannot, it is her. Both of Yocheved's parents died a year after she was born. She practically grew up in our archives and library. Every single aspect of our recorded history is known to her, and believe me, she notices more than most children at her age. And most adults as well." Kloe snapped her wrist at a moth in the darkness. "If she was watching you, there is something interesting about you being here." She touched my arm as if to tell me a joke. "I'd encourage you to ask her about it, but knowing the girl, she'll find you before you think to remember her name."

CHAPTER TWENTY FOUR
MIDNIGHT NEWS

"PRIMROSE."

My eyes flew open at the sound of a voice calling my name. I sat up suddenly in my bed. My ears listened to the crickets chirping and the otherwise quiet night. A gust of wind beat at the roof of the cabin, and the wood groaned in protest. The beating of my heart thudded heavily in my chest. Perhaps I imagined or dreamed of someone calling my name. Or it could've just been the wind.

I wrapped the bedsheets tightly around me to keep the heat close to my body and lay back in bed.

"Primrose." The eerie voice echoed in the room once more. It sounded like the voice of a child.

I threw away the sheets and stood to my feet. My hand gripped the hilt of my unsheathed scimitar. The sword's blade glinted in the dark room. "Who's there?"

Silence. I twirled the blade through the air threateningly. "Reveal yourself!"

The door to my chamber creaked open, and a chilling wind gust entered the room. I shivered. My heart skipped a beat. What in Hell's name was going on?

"Primrose." The voice moaned again, but this time from outside.

I rushed out of the room in a sprint. My white nightgown billowed about me. The soil was freezing cold against my bare feet. I stopped in front of the wooden cabin I was housed in. My head whipped, hoping to pinpoint the threat.

Nothing.

I tightened my grip on the hilt of my sword, frustrated. The cold night's wind blew harsher than before.

The child's soft voice echoed yet again, from the forest beyond the village walls. My legs moved without my consent, past the houses of the village. As I ran, everything seemed to pause. The farm animals were sound asleep, and even the wind stilled. No one else was in sight when I crossed the village border. I zigzagged about the animal traps in the forest as if I knew the entire path by heart, stopping only to listen to the voice that called me.

I was in a meadow full of flowers and grasses a mile outside the village. The clearing was familiar to me, though I couldn't recall how I remembered it. This location was south of the village, and Atlas and I had arrived from the north. But I'd been in this stretch of forest before.

My eyes landed on an old tree, the only tree in the meadow. Its trunk was thick, and its roots dove deep into the soil. This oak tree wasn't as tall as the pine or fir trees around me, though it had numerous branches sprawled in every direction with hundreds of thousands of green leaves. Oak trees made for good memory trees to preserve the memories of individuals for millennia or longer. Why did this oak tree call to me?

"Primrose." The voice that spoke my name was now strong and clear.

I turned to notice a teenage girl behind me. Her dark hair was braided, like a crown around her pale, freckled face. Blue eyes watched me though a thin glaze. The girl was short in stature, and a cream gown fit her slim figure tightly. She was scrawny, as if she had been underfed for weeks. The bones of her body stuck out, with no muscle or fat to accompany them—almost literally, she was all skin and bones. Her cheeks were gaunt, and her teeth were a pearly white color. Around her neck hung a smooth, metal necklace with a heart-shaped locket. Though the necklace's chain was gray, the locket had a deep, crimson tint to it.

The girl stood tall, with perfect posture, and a strange confidence surrounded her. Magic strummed through the air around her, and I instantly knew she was a witch. Oddly enough, she didn't have any scent or soul whatsoever, which explained why I struggled to pinpoint her location earlier, even while she spoke my name.

I pointed my sword toward the witch. "Who are you? What do you want from me?"

She tilted her head to the side, as if my question was strange to her.

Her silence left me more unsettled than before. I stepped threateningly toward her and arced my sword. "You will speak to me! I demand it!" My voice roared loud through the forest.

The girl's pale lips parted. My breath caught.

"Primrose," she said. "It is time."

The hair on the back of my neck stood up. My hands closed into fists. "Time for what? Who are you?"

The witch smiled. "You made a promise in return for a gift. My part of the deal, I have upheld. Now you are indebted to me and my prodigy."

"Excuse me?" I demanded. Now, I was upset. Who did this girl think she was? "I don't know you, much less owe you anything. I will ask you one more time. Who are you?"

"I was the tool to your metamorphosis, a healer of your pain, and the only ally you had when all was lost." Her explanation threw my mind into a storm of irregular chaos. She continued without heed, "My name would only be of consequence if your memory returned, and it hasn't. Not yet. I only wish to remind you of what you have sworn to me. Protect my descendant in her time of need, and our trade will come to a hearty conclusion."

My head spun, and darkness engulfed me like an embrace.

"Primrose."

I jumped up with a shock, wildly entangling myself in bedsheets. A young girl stood at the side of my bed, like the shadow of a ghost. "Umm, I think you were dreaming?" Her voice was soft and hesitant.

My heavy breaths began to slow. I was still in my chambers. I never left; it was only a dream. I exhaled heavily and tucked my head into my elbow to catch my breath. My heart pounded erratically like I had run several miles. Never had a dream been so vivid or seemed so real! My dreams of Gavin were always distorted by a dense fog. Nothing like my dream of the witch.

"Are you all right?" the child asked.

I flipped my hair out of my face and looked at the figure who stood by my bedside. Recognition dawned upon me. "Yocheved."

The young girl blanched. Her black hair was hidden by the brown hood of her cloak, which she wore over a thin shift similar to my nightgown. "You know my name?"

"Yes." I moved the bedsheets aside to sit up and assess the young girl. "Kloe told me about you."

"What did she say?"

"That you're a smart kid." I hung my legs over the side of the bed. "What can I do for you?"

She scratched her thin arm nervously. "I sat out most of the festivities today."

"Why is that?"

"Sometimes, the other kids are mean." Yocheved made a face. "It isn't fun to play with them."

I knew how she felt. After all, how many times did I refuse to deal with members of the High Court because they were all a bunch of jerks with attitude?

"How old are you?" I asked.

"Ten. But I feel a lot older."

I chuckled under my breath, unable to restrain myself. "Okay. And why did you come to me?"

Yocheved smiled, showing me all of her baby teeth. "I saw you at the festival today. You're pretty, nice, and there's something special about you. You remind me of Kloe." She raised an eyebrow. "But you're definitely not as grumpy."

"Kloe is grumpy?" I asked with a surprised curl of my lips. "I would have never guessed."

"Sometimes," Yocheved said and shrugged. "Especially when I want to play all the fun games with her. Personally"—she gestured toward herself—"I think she can't keep up as easily, and that's her excuse. Probably because of her old age."

"Oh." I struggled to keep a straight face. "Is that so?"

The girl nodded. "Yes." She leaned against my bed. "Would you like to play with me?"

The wheels of thought began to turn. I had to ponder her question for a minute before I understood what she was asking. "Now?" *In the middle of the night?*

"Yes, now, silly! When else?"

I squeezed my eyes shut and made a mental note that I was talking to a child. Ten-year-olds were far too young to incinerate. What was the harm of playing a short game with her? It's not like I had anything better to do, like sleeping. Besides, it was either weird dreams or this.

"Okay. I'm up."

Yocheved beamed and grabbed my arm. I fumbled from the bed, barely keeping up with her. We ran outside. Well, she did the running, and I was mostly dragged behind her. There was a small field a few houses away from the cabin I slept in. Yocheved ducked underneath the fence and slipped through the beams.

I climbed over the fence. My nightgown caught in the wood and the ends chafed against the material. Yocheved stopped under a tree. Hopefully, this was her land, and we weren't trespassing on another villager's property. The land itself looked unused, vacant of crops or agriculture. Old-fashioned lanterns were hung off the fence we crossed, though the moon and stars sufficiently lit up the night.

"So?" I rubbed my hands together. "What do you want to play?"

Yocheved placed a hand under her chin and thought for a moment. Her face lit up. "I know! We can climb the tree together!"

She turned around and latched onto the lower branches of the tree behind her. Her arms and legs moved quickly.

"That's a game?" My jaw went slack. Where did this kid find the energy to climb a tree in the middle of the night? I was still focusing my energy on standing upright.

"Yes, it is!" she called down to me, already halfway up.

I chewed on my bottom lip. My arms tensed, and I pulled myself up for the climb. The bark was coarse but not rugged nor scratchy. Yocheved stopped and sat on a thick branch close to the top. Since the tree limb seemed sturdy enough to support us both, I sat down beside her. Her head was lifted to the stars.

I followed her gaze. The star patterns in the ancient land differed from those in the human realm, but they felt familiar. I pointed to the one she looked at. "That's the Temple of Aura. See, you can tell by the pentagon."

Yocheved's eyes widened and landed on me. "You know the patterns?"

"Somewhat." I frowned, unsettled. "Is it odd that I know the pattern in the sky, but not what it means?" I leaned my head against the tree. "I've never heard of that temple, but I know how the stars represent it."

"The heart sometimes knows things the mind can't remember."

"You think I've been here before?"

"Maybe." Yocheved shrugged and broke off a small twig to play with. "Even if you've never visited this village before, you certainly lived in the ancient land at some point. It's the origin of all living beings. Perhaps you once knew the sky long ago. Now that you're back, you're starting to remember."

I nodded. Her explanation didn't seem quite right though it was better than anything I readily came up with. "Perhaps."

She pointed out past the walls. "You can't see from here, but outside the village borders are these white flower beds. If you ever cross our borders, you should avoid them."

"I noticed the flowers on our way into the village." I thought back to Elise's warning. "I've never heard of the Deatheri flowers before today. I don't believe they exist in the human realm. I guess they only grow in the ancient land."

Yocheved looked out past the wall with a yearning in her eyes. "That wall wasn't always there."

I followed her gaze out to the tall border that surrounded the village. The structure looked old and full of history. "It's new?"

"Well, not new," she amended. "It's been there for several thousand years. But Kloe says there was a time when we didn't need the wall."

"Why do you need the wall now?

"The wall keeps us safe."

Safe from what? I wanted to ask, but Yocheved turned her head away, not wanting to say any more. My blood turned to ice, spreading a chill through me.

Yocheved tensed upon noticing me open my mouth. The girl was skittish and hesitant. If I pressed her on this, she might close off completely. Instead, I bit my tongue and closed my eyes as Yocheved continued to play with the twig in her hands. A comfortable silence lapsed between us. I cleared my mind of any fears or insecurities. This moment felt like home—a home I never had but always wanted. Nothing was in the dark to disturb me: no monsters, no Gods or Goddesses, no politics. There was only freedom and the night.

"You remind me of someone." Yocheved's tiny voice made my eyes flutter open.

My legs adjusted my posture over the side of the branch. "Who's that?"

"Someone who used to live here. She was like you. The main difference is that she used to be happy."

"Am I not happy?" I asked and elbowed her playfully.

Yocheved smiled sadly and shook her head. "I don't think so. I think you're really sad."

My features melted into a strained poker face. If a child could read me so easily, then who else could tell what I was feeling? My bottom lip trembled. I bit my lip to stop the shaking.

Whoever this girl was, Kloe was right. She was too smart for her own good. I could see why some villagers disliked her and treated her poorly. Yocheved expressed such blunt honesty and those who did not appreciate her honesty would only be hurt by what she had to say.

"Your friend." I quickly changed the subject. "From the way you phrased it, she only used to be happy. What happened?"

"I don't know," she said and pressed her lips together in a hard line. "But she was never the same again. Can we climb down now?"

I blinked, getting whiplash from her changing train of thought. "Sure thing." I backed up and followed the same path down as I did to climb up.

A branch snapped. Yocheved lost her footing, and the tree bark slid from beneath her. She slipped with a yelp, and my arm lashed out to catch her. My fingers brushed over nothing but open air, and all I could do was watch as she fell, like a flower from the tree's branches. My senses returned when she hit the ground with a thump. Fear shuddered through me, and my chest flared in agony. I let go of the branch and slid down the rest of the tree, scraping my arms and knees.

I threw myself at the child's limp body and turned her over frantically. A shock ran through my veins. I gasped, seeing her skin as smooth and without injury as before and a white light fading from the surface of her skin. My breathing stopped. Whatever magic she had used, it was the same power I discovered within myself when fighting Lucifer.

Yocheved sat up, and her lower lip trembled. Her hood fell down, revealing one single, thick braid of midnight hair. "You weren't supposed to see that."

I took her hands in mine. "What was that magic?"

She shied away from my touch and avoided my eyes. "I'm not supposed to tell you."

"Please, Yocheved," I begged and held on tightly to her pale hands. My voice trembled with desperation. "I need to know. I swear, I've seen it before."

Her face went blank. "You have?"

"Yes." I paused, thinking up an excuse to aim the spotlight away from me. "I saw it in a dream once."

"You're a dream walker?"

My cheeks flushed, and I felt caught in a lie. "What's a dream walker?"

Yocheved narrowed her eyes in suspicion. "A person who can control their dreams. A dream walker can delve within the deepest corners of their own mind to unlock hidden memories or explore the meaning of dreams. They can see visions that are relevant to magic or prophecy."

"Then I'm not a dream walker," I said. "But I do have weird dreams that don't make sense, and I swear, I've seen that same magic you used in a dream once."

Hopefully, she didn't sense the lie in what I said. This magic within me needed to remain a secret until I figured out what it was and how to use it. Otherwise, it would become a liability instead of a tool. I didn't know these villagers well enough to trust them.

Yocheved looked away, and a line appeared between her eyebrows. She was still unsure of whether to trust me on this.

"Please," I repeated with the hopes of convincing her. If she answered my questions about her magic, maybe I could start to understand everything—the memories, the dreams, the tie I felt to the ancient land. I needed to know.

"It's protection magic."

I started. "What?"

"Protection magic." Yocheved crossed her arms and struggled to explain it. "Basic protection magic is like healing and shield spells."

"Like what you did earlier when you fell," I said and sat on my knees, getting comfortable. "There were no scrapes, bruises, or other injuries."

"Yes, most of us can put up an easy shield spell without really thinking about it. Besides, kids sometimes play a little rough, so the adults make sure to teach us just in case."

Smart move. Especially since there were children who were unkind to Yocheved. Protection magic evened out the playing field.

"What else can protection magic do?" I asked.

"Protection magic is meant to protect people, to protect yourself and others. Someone who trains and has years of experience can start using the elements to protect themselves, like using the earth, wind, or fire. Kloe says the weather changes based on emotions if the Guardian is super strong." Yocheved's forehead wrinkled. "But I don't know too much about that."

"That's okay." I caught on to a new term. "What is a Guardian?"

"It's what I am." She pointed to herself. "And so are Kloe and all the other villagers. Guardians are the only ones that can use protection magic. Kind of like guardian angels for humans. At least that's why we were created."

Protection magic I knew about, but Guardians? I cocked my head at Yocheved and tried to imagine that this human-looking girl wasn't a human at all. There was more to her than meets the eye. I must have looked confused because Yocheved tried to elaborate. "Guardians were initially created to protect humans, to watch over them. At first, the Guardians weren't too happy about that because the humans were superstitious and unwilling to accept our help, at least until an alliance was established between humans and Guardians. After that, our people really did want to keep humans safe, and humans readily accommodated us and our magic."

"Really?" I pulled at the grass from the ground. The blades were smooth and damp. "So, a God or Goddess couldn't exhibit this power?"

Yocheved tapped her chin twice while she pondered this. "Not unless they were a Guardian first." Her eyes cut like a knife as she watched me. "Why do you ask?"

I felt small under the sheer strength of her gaze. An alarming thought pulsed through my mind. *She knows.* I swallowed the lump in my throat and plastered on a fake smile. "I just wanted to know if the magic was exclusive to Guardians."

"Oh, okay." She accepted my explanation with more ease than I expected.

"Are there other Guardian villages out there?" I asked, hoping my voice concealed my curiosity. The knowledge I gained today from a child amounted to more than I had learned about myself in an entire lifetime. Yocheved was candid, and her honesty was refreshing.

"No," she said, her voice softening. "We are the only village left."

Tears gathered in the corners of her eyes, and I placed a hand on her shoulder. Rage lit its fire deep within me. "What happened to the others?"

"They—" Yocheved shook her head and brushed her tears away. "They don't exist anymore."

There was a heavy story tied to her admission. Something happened to the other Guardians. Something terrible.

"We should go." Yocheved stood quickly. She spun around as if looking for something or someone.

I rose to my feet and clicked my tongue. "Why? Is something wrong?"

"No," she answered too quickly. Guilt masked the prettiness of her face. "Nobody can know that I talked to you."

"Why not?"

"Because." She began to pull me back toward my cabin. "I'm not allowed to."

A minute later, we were back at the cabin. Before Yocheved left, I caught her wrist. "One more question," I pled. "You said that Guardians are like angels for humans. But how can you help humans from way over here? Humans left the ancient land millennia ago."

"We can't help them anymore," she admitted, struggling against my grip. "Not since we were banished from the human world."

"Who banished you?" I demanded, my voice fierce and unrelenting.

Her eyes widened. "I don't know." She shook her head frantically. "Nobody knows his name."

My grip tightened. I wasn't giving up that easily. "I have questions."

"Look for answers in your dreams!"

I laughed bitterly. "I tried to tell you already! I'm not a dream walker."

Yocheved squirmed under my intense gaze. "You don't have to be. Dream walking is a skill. Anyone can do it with enough practice. Please! I need to leave."

I let her go reluctantly and the young girl fled into the night. An errant thought slipped into my mind. I was right earlier when I first saw Yocheved at the festival. She did remind me of someone. In fact, she reminded me of a certain teenager from a lingering dream...

CHAPTER TWENTY FIVE

THE ECHO OF A DREAM

DREAM WALKING IS A skill.

Yocheved's words filled my head while I lay silently in bed. She'd said that anyone could do it. Anyone. That included me, right? I was a Goddess—surely dream walking was nothing a deity couldn't do.

I closed my eyes and let my thoughts drift. My dreams were always fleeting and out of my control, but what if I forced my dreams to show me what I wanted? If I purposefully searched for Gavin deep within the labyrinth of my mind, would I learn something new? Dreams provided a facet of valuable information. They were a window into what went on in my mind when my shields were down and emotions were high. Aside from hounding a ten-year-old with questions, dreams were the only way I was going to find the answers I searched for.

Sleep pulled me within its grasp, but I allowed my focus to sharpen. I repeated Gavin's name in my thoughts. This time, my dream took place inside the village walls.

There was no fog or feeling that I lacked control over my body. I strolled down a path in front of a row of wooden homes. Each cabin was nestled up, one after the other, and they all had an old, rustic appeal to them.

One home, in particular, stood out.

It wasn't far from the cabin I was housed in for the night. The house had the same wooden frame as most dwellings in the village, though the door was crooked, and the two steps to the porch were cracked and splintered. A cold kiss touched my forehead, and I looked to the sky to see white dots falling from the clouds.

Snow?

I held out my hand, and flurries of snowflakes fell onto my pale palm. I inhaled crisp winter air, and my exhale released a white mist in the air. The temperature dropped dramatically with a sweeping wind. The chill ate at my skin, and I approached the home that had caught my eye. Nerves ate at my stomach. This all felt very familiar, though I knew not why.

With one big step, I climbed up to the porch and lingered at the cabin's door, my fist poised to knock. The scent of leather escaped through the cracks in the door. Before I gained the courage to rap my fist against the wood, the old door creaked to an ominous opening. The warmth of the home beckoned me in. I nervously crossed my arms and stepped over the threshold.

"Hello?" I called out. Maybe the family living here was asleep.

The door closed behind me, and I flinched. My first thought was to leave immediately, but instinct insisted that I remain. My bare feet felt comfortable on the wooden floor. A warm fire was started in the main living room, and a homey mirror hung above the flames. Two leather boots sat near the doorway. They were men's shoes.

Who lived here?

The distinct sensation that I should know the answer to my own question made me shiver.

A door to another room swung open. A man came out from the room, and two children chased after him with their laughter. I backed into a corner and watched silently from the shadows as the girl and boy pulled at their father's arms in play. They danced around him, twirling and jumping.

My heart stopped. I knew both the man and the girl. Gavin's eyes lit up with joy as he lifted the children with his strong arms. He swung them around, and a deep laugh left his broad chest. The young girl was from one of my dreams, the one in which she asked me to dance with her.

The boy was new to me, but like the girl, he had the same green eyes as Gavin. Both children were the same height and had a similar bone structure. They looked like twins, even in the way they mirrored each other's movements. The way the children interacted with one another pulled the strings of my heart. The man loved the children as they loved him. How I longed for such a bond—a bond capable of connecting individuals together in a ring of unbreakable affection.

A shadow shoved past my shoulder and rushed to the family. I shrank back and placed a hand on my shoulder. The woman hadn't even flinched though she clearly brushed past me. How had she not seen me? Or was she aware I hid here and accepted my presence?

The brunette proceeded to embrace the boy and fuss over his attire. She mussed up his hair and began to fix the girl's braids. Gavin watched her with utter delight. The woman placed a hand on the man's face and a gentle kiss on his right cheek. Her visage was familiar from this angle.

I left the shadows to take a closer look. When she turned to face me, my breath left my chest with an utterly dry feeling of shock. The woman... I knew her. Impossible. I made another step toward her.

She was me.

The woman smiled cleverly, as if she knew something I didn't. Then they all disappeared. Each and every one of them—Gavin, the children, and the mysterious woman. Gone, as if they hadn't been here in the first place. The fire went out, and an eerie smoke escaped the hearth.

The smoke found its way to my nose, reminding me of Lucifer's scent. The room was no longer warm and welcoming. The cold of the snow outside triumphed in the home, and I felt like a stranger in a foreign land. I slowly crept toward where the family had been. There was a mirror that hung over the fireplace, and it glinted enticingly as I approached. I raised my chin to look into it, finding something strange about the glass. My own image stared back for one disappointing moment.

When two green eyes appeared suddenly, I yelped in shock. I lashed out wildly, and my arm hit the mirror, sending it flying toward the ground, where it shattered. I turned to collide with none other than Gavin himself, who stared at me with a stern expression, the same unemotional stare he always bore when I summoned his soul from the Underworld.

Fear and disbelief controlled my actions. I slid past Gavin without a word. The coolness of the outdoors led me to a door at the back of the home. I sprinted toward the exit and threw open the door, stumbling out to another porch in the backyard.

My eyes widened. The entire field of the yard was covered with a thick layer of snow. It only started snowing minutes ago. How could this be?

In the center of the yard, a gray wolf rolled through the snow playfully. Its fur was matted with the white flakes. Gavin and the two children were in the snow, wearing warm, layered clothes. The children tumbled with the wolf in play, not at all afraid of the wild animal. Gavin was different now, his bright smile made its way back to his handsome face, and his eyes were filled with light.

I felt a breeze pass by me, and I stepped back to see the same woman again, heading toward the family like she had earlier. She still looked exactly like me. Her hair was the same. She had my broad shoulders and thin waist. Her legs were as long and strong. The woman was like a ghost of me.

The wolf yipped, seeing ghost-me approach Gavin and the children. Ghost-me ran a hand through the wolf's fur, and it arched his back in approval. He smiled, looked back at me, and opened his mouth as if to speak. I waited, anticipating what he would say.

Surprise hit me when ghost-me unexpectedly disappeared, while Gavin and the children remained to look at me with expectation.

I turned away and opened the door back into the home. I stumbled through the wooden cabin. When my eyes found the door that led to the front porch, I cried with relief and lunged for my escape. The door practically fell off its hinges as I ran out of the house. I tripped down the broken steps of the porch and ran as if my life depended on it.

The heavy steps of someone or something followed me closely, and I sprinted faster than I ever had before. This was like the nightmares children had, with a big bad monster chasing after me and fear so strong I couldn't muster the courage to look back and face whoever followed me. With my growing fear, the gray fog from previous dreams crept around my surroundings. The village homes blurred as I passed them, and my chest ached from the cold wind that whipped against my figure. A frozen lake came into sight, and I quickened my pace.

Once my feet touched the ice, I sprawled forward and fell on my stomach. Despite the slipping and sliding, I sprung back to my feet and shakily continued my path, afraid of being caught by the ghosts that haunted me.

"Rose!"

I stopped suddenly, hearing Gavin call out my name. He didn't speak it like Lucifer did. The way Gavin said 'Rose' stirred a yearning within me, a connection between the two of us that I didn't know existed. My body froze only to turn toward the human. He strode out onto the ice, unafraid even while pieces of ice began to break under his weight. He was sure in his path toward me, without one single shred of doubt in his entire being. My stomach flipped in circles, and the hole in my chest slowly started to mend with every step he took. The fog threatened to consume him, but I forced it back with a glare. It hissed, but this was my dream now. I was in control.

When he reached me, Gavin's arms wrapped around me lovingly, in the warmest embrace I had ever known. I melted into his arms as if that was where I belonged. His chest was warm as though he were a living being, and he rested his chin on my head. I closed my eyes and held on to him, afraid he would disappear as suddenly as he had appeared. At that moment, I never felt more loved. This was happiness. This was heaven. This was my home, and I never wanted to leave.

The ice beneath us made a tinkling noise, and before I could open my eyes, we fell into the cold water below. The freezing water pierced my skin, and fear buried me into a suffocating grasp.

This time when I awoke, there was no startle or suddenness. My eyelashes fluttered open to the tweeting of morning birds, and sunlight poured in through the curtained windows. The coldness of the icy water beneath the frozen lake from the dream prickled at my skin. My arms trembled, and my chest felt cold in the absence of Gavin's warm embrace. Tears bit at the corners of my eyes, and I held them back.

Two minutes later, I was dressed and out the door with one quest on my mind. Finding that cabin.

Out in the village, people had already awakened and taken to the streets for their daily activities. The night's silence and stillness were long gone and replaced by bustling chatter and movement. The villagers smiled and said their respectful hellos when they saw me. Their smiles looked too rehearsed, and I was left with several burning questions as to why.

Elise noticed me as I scoured the streets. Her clothes were fresh and full of color, and her fair hair was braided. She waved and skipped in my direction.

"Primrose! How wonderful! You're just in time for—wait, where are you going?" she asked, as I passed by her like a ghost, ignoring her greeting.

My walk felt purposeful, methodical. The cabin needed to be close by... I stopped by a home that looked familiar.

"Lady Primrose?" Kloe arrived. Elise rushed by her side. The village chief's words were coated with caution and careful curiosity. "Is something wrong?"

I looked past the village chief, and my eyes locked on my target. My legs moved on their own accord. I walked right past Kloe and Elise as if they didn't exist. The home looked the same as it had during my dream last night. The door was crooked, and the two steps to the porch were splintered and broken.

"You are not allowed there!" Elise exclaimed though someone hushed her soon after.

I stepped onto the porch and approached the door, cautious at first. But then my fear dissolved and was replaced by hot shame. I had no right to be afraid. There was nothing beyond that door capable of defeating a Goddess, much less the Goddess of Death. I pushed open the door. There was no longer a scent of leather, nor was a fire lit.

No. The uncanniness was in the layout. The fireplace was precisely where I imagined it, and the mirror was right above it. I stalked toward the familiar glass, and the shadows in the room followed me closely.

My temper flared in anger, and I was suddenly distraught.

That cursed human. *Gavin Petreson.* A man who brought me pain and confusion. How I loathed him!

I made a motion to summon his slimy soul right out of the Underworld and show him exactly what I thought of his haunting presence when something caught the corner of my eye. In the mirror that lay above the fireplace, two green eyes shined back to meet mine. And they weren't Gavin's.

I recalled Atlas's strange words. *Your eyes change color from brown to green. From the moment you use your power to the moment you stop.*

I punched at the glass mirror, shattering it. Bits of broken glass embedded themselves in my skin and knuckles while the other pieces fell to the floor like lightly chiming bells. My breathing felt deep and labored.

I stormed over toward the back of the home and shoved open the door to the yard. My gaze roamed over the empty backyard, overrun with weeds and unruly bushes. Not a flake of snow touched the ground. No children tumbled in the yard.

A soft yip reached my ears. The movement of gray fur caught my attention. An old, frail wolf rose and limped toward me. The wolf's left paw was held close to his side as if it pained him to put it down. Despite the injury, his eyes were full of recognition and joy. Sweat broke out across my forehead, and anger festered in my chest. A flush rose along the back of my neck, but I let it die down. I closed my eyes, and when I opened them, the wolf was still there, staring at me expectantly. I nodded in reluctant acceptance.

This was my reality now and fighting against the truth would only do me harm. In the ancient land, anything was possible. Like a tidal wave, the past grew in strength and influence, and anything standing in its way would be destroyed.

I crossed my arms. "Well, are you coming or not?"

The wolf limped to my side and waited patiently. He understood.

I reentered the cabin through the back door and gave the forbidden home one last tour. The layout wasn't confusing or daunting as I'd imagined it in my dream.

When I exited the home, Kloe, Elise, and a few curious villagers waited outside. My new wolf friend followed me out.

"Where is Atlas?" I asked. My voice was calm, thoughtful. Gone were the raging emotions from earlier. My anger was unnecessary in the grand scheme of things.

Kloe's attention was held captive by the wolf beside me. "Not far from here. I can take you to him."

I followed the old woman, and her silent inquisitiveness burned through the air. Though leaving her questions unanswered might have been easier for me, the space between us was uncomfortable because of it.

I adjusted the hilt of my scimitar. "What is it?"

Kloe's eyes shot back to the wolf keeping pace with us. "Nothing you can explain, I think. Fenrir has taken a liking to you."

"Fenrir?" I tried the name on my tongue. It felt fitting.

The wolf hummed. Even he agreed to his ancient name. An honest smile graced my lips.

"Fenrir is believed to be immortal. He's been in that yard for who knows how long, waiting for something. Or someone." Kloe leaned on her staff and stopped. "Maybe you."

I shoved my hands into my pockets and bit my lip. "Who did he belong to?"

"Finally awake?" Atlas drawled, interrupting my conversation with the village chief. He approached lazily. His clothing was new and clean like mine, though he'd taken more care of finer details. He was well rested by the looks of his face. His blue eyes were less cold, and his lips were pulled into a relaxed smirk.

My lips quirked upward into a quick smile. "It seems so."

"Then it's time we leave." The Ice King took one step toward me, and Fenrir *exploded*. The wolf had been watching Atlas carefully beforehand, but the moment he came too close, Fenrir crouched into a threatening position and let out a vicious growl. He limped in front of me and stood taller than I believed an injured wolf could. The hair on his back stood up, and he gnashed his teeth.

Atlas's eyes widened. "What is this?"

My shock was greater than his. I knew the wolf was somehow connected to me, but to see him react so strongly to Atlas was unexpected. My hand rested on the wolf's forehead. "Fenrir, it's all right. Be calm now."

The wolf didn't relax, though he stopped growling and settled on pacing sullenly. His eyes never left the Grimm Brother, and his threatening posture remained.

"You've acquired a pet."

Fenrir's growl made a reappearance.

I cleared my throat, hoping to calm the wolf down. "More like a protector."

"Right," Atlas said with a skeptical click of his tongue. "Regardless, we must leave."

"So soon?" Kloe asked, disappointed. A disappointment that was echoed in me. There was so much to learn from this village. After the dream, I needed to know more. Many of my questions remained unanswered.

My thoughts raced for an excuse. Any excuse. "Shouldn't we stay? Perhaps—"

"Primrose, it's time to leave," Atlas interrupted sternly. His eyes flickered dangerously. "We have a journey to continue."

Right. A journey to find Lucifer's Soul Dagger. That's why this whole mess started in the first place. Why we were here. Only now did I realize an obvious change. I was once again tied to Lucifer's Soul Dagger, and my sense of direction had returned.

"It's back, isn't it?" Atlas asked about the tracking spell.

I nodded and shifted from one leg to another, embarrassed by the truth. It hadn't been a full twenty-four hours since I crossed the Glass, but the tracking spell was good as new, perhaps because we were closer to Lucifer's Soul Dagger than before. Suddenly, dealing with the Devil's escape didn't make it to the top of my agenda. I didn't care anymore about killing Lucifer, but it had to be done, and no one else would do it.

I met Kloe's eyes, conveying my regret but also my obligation. "We do really need to leave."

The village chief nodded, and an echo of understanding flew between us. "Our village will be here on your journey back if you wish to visit us again."

The idea of returning brought a smile to my face.

Yes, I will return.

The gasps and chatter of villagers interrupted our farewell. A man stumbled toward Kloe. He wore a satchel on his shoulder like a messenger would. His clothes were torn, and blood covered his torso and legs. A deep cut ran from his left shoulder to his right hip in a jagged pattern. Without his healing powers, this messenger would be dead.

I sent Atlas a fleeting glance out of the corner of my eye. By his narrowed glare, he now realized these villagers were not human.

"They're coming," the messenger wheezed and took another step toward Kloe. Several villagers came to support his weight when his legs gave out beneath him.

"Who?" Kloe asked calmly, though fear sparked in her eyes.

"Demons. A male and a female—siblings by the looks of it. They're assembling an army north of us to march on the village tomorrow."

The demon twins. A jolt of shock ran through me. Atlas and I shared a panicked look. "Abaddon and Satan," I said. The names left a bitter taste on my tongue.

"What do they want?" a villager behind Kloe demanded. Others echoed the question.

"They're coming." The messenger's eyes landed on Atlas and me. "For them. I don't know why, but the demons know we're harboring them."

Fear hit the crowd like a tidal wave. Shouts of anger and panic filled the air. Parents held their children close to them. Villagers openly glared and pointed accusing fingers toward me and Atlas. One large male who stood at least two feet taller than me stepped forward. "Are they willing to negotiate?"

Fenrir sent the man a low growl.

"Silence, Vasiley," Kloe barked at the bulky man, and the villagers shrunk away from her harsh tone. "We all know demons do not negotiate."

Kloe's statement wasn't entirely true. Demons negotiated in strained circumstances such as these. Vasiley's implication was bright as day, and if it were up to him, he wouldn't mind throwing us to the wolves. Heck, I don't know if I blamed him. The demon twins would kill every last villager if it meant they got to me.

"You ought to leave." The village chief turned to me with an earnest glow in her eyes. "Leave now, before they arrive. That way, you will complete your journey."

Atlas's eyes hardened when I turned to face him. He already knew what I was going to say. I waited for his reaction.

"Let me ask you this," he began, "will anything I say change your mind?"

I placed a hand on his shoulder and gave him a friendly pat. "Do you even need to ask?"

"I see," he said shortly.

"Won't you try to stop me?"

Atlas assessed me readily with cool eyes. He shook his head. "It wouldn't help."

Finally, we understood each other. I faced Kloe. "We will stay and fight with you."

The crowd of villagers murmured in surprise, and Kloe shook her head. "We cannot ask you to fight for us."

"You didn't ask; we volunteered. Let's face it, Kloe, it's our fault that the demons are here. Whether or not we leave, they'll still come and tear this village apart, inch by inch, to find us. You welcomed us into your home. We might as well help in whatever way we can. The demon twins aren't the only ones with access to an army."

The village chief appeared hesitant, and I crossed my arms. "Do you think anything you say will change my mind? I've already decided. We're staying."

"What about your important journey? You said that you must leave." Her voice was stern, and her lips pressed into a firm line.

I raised an eyebrow. "The two demons that plan to attack your village are trying to stop Atlas and me from completing our journey. What do you think they'll do after they destroy this place? Call it a day? Go home for the night?" I shrugged, and my lips pulled into a tight smile. "We're going to have to fight them regardless, whether that means tomorrow morning or a week from today doesn't change the fact that it will happen."

Kloe touched my arm with her wrinkled hand. Her eyes were filled with gratitude and palpable relief. "Thank you, Lady Primrose. And you as well, Lord Atlas. With your help, we may stand a chance."

Fenrir butted his head against my leg. A deep rumble left his chest, and I had the uncanny feeling that he was trying to say something.

I knelt down and ran my hand through his fur. "What do you think he's saying?" I asked Kloe, who watched Fenrir and me with curiosity.

Her eyes became serious, and she gripped her staff tightly. "The only thing he can say in a time like this, war is coming. And so is Death."

CHAPTER TWENTY SIX
THE FOUR ARMIES OF HELL

WHILE KLOE AND THE messenger were in deep conversation, Atlas and I awkwardly tried not to look at each other. He was still sour about my stubbornness earlier, and I didn't feel like apologizing anytime soon. Fenrir certainly wasn't helping the situation with his subtle growls and constant pacing.

Unable to stand the silence anymore, I strode toward Kloe and the messenger. Kloe's cloak swept over the man's torn rags in a comforting gesture, and she spoke to him in quiet tones. The messenger's eyes were trained on her face, and he spoke freely, trusting his village chief. A woman who tended to the man's wounds earlier now wrapped them in white cloth while he spoke. He reeked of blood, though he looked much better than before. He was less pale and sat up straight and alert.

I shrugged off the wool jacket from my back and draped it over my arm. "How long before they attack?" I inquired.

Both the messenger and Kloe turned their heads toward me. The man shot a curious gaze toward the village chief and remained seated in silence.

Kloe stood to her full height. "Less than a day." Her old hands moved to adjust her cloak. "Their army is incomplete—time is needed to prepare it."

I nodded. If the demon twins wanted to summon a force to attack two deities, they needed all the lower demons they could get. "They'll use the Argentina Glass located north of the village to portal their demon army into the ancient land. The vampyres guarding the Glass may slow them down a little. Still, we have less than a day to prepare our army," I said and undid the leather strap that held my scimitar in place. "Chances are they will attack at dawn, but we must be ready before then."

"You have an army ready to fight?" the messenger asked with disbelief. He rose unsteadily to his feet at the protests of the woman who finished wrapping his wounds.

"I am a Goddess. Of course, I have an army."

"What Zander meant," Kloe interjected, referring to the messenger, "was to ask if your army is capable of assembling so readily? I'm afraid this demon threat has been revealed with little time to prepare."

"Yes." Atlas's heavy footsteps approached. His cold breath fanned over my shoulder. "Unfortunately, the news your messenger brings comes too late to do much good. Which is why my army will not be at your disposal."

"Big surprise," I huffed under my breath. His lack of cooperation was nothing new. I tied my sword to my belt. Before Atlas could retort, I held out my palm. "Phone."

"Why would I—"

"I need to make a call." Annoyance bled into my voice. "Or would you rather I pay Hell a visit to get that army we need?"

Atlas refrained from saying anything before removing his phone from his pocket and holding it out at arm's length. I snatched it away and dialed a number.

"Your phone is spelled, right?" I asked.

"Yes," Atlas said through his teeth. "It should work, even from this realm."

My thumb hesitated over the call button before I pressed it and held the phone close to my ear. The line rang for a good minute before the fool picked up.

A lazy voice answered my call. "If this is the damn CIA calling me again, I am going to kill—"

"Azazel," I snapped. "Shut up and listen. We have work to do."

My general's irritation permeated over the phone. I heard a strange shuffle in the background and odd breathing noises before he spoke. "Oh, this'll be good. What can I do for you, my lady? Jump through more of your hoops today?"

I held my nose and closed my eyes, this close to hanging up.

"Are you still there, your royal stupidness?"

"Give me strength"—I looked at the sky—"not to kill him today. I cannot replace a general on such short notice."

"I'm still here, you know," he said bitterly.

"Or is a ten-year-old qualified?" I pondered, thinking back to Yocheved. "Perhaps with some training—"

"What do you need, Primrose?" he pressed, now curious as to why I called him. Mostly because I never called him over the phone. Azazel could usually guess when I needed him, and this time he had no reason to think war was coming. Armies were for wars, and wars were reserved for conflict between deities in the human world, not strange ancient land phenomena.

I bit my cheek before making my demand. "How fast can you make it to the ancient land?"

Silence. Well, that told me enough.

"Why..." Azazel let his sarcastic question trail off. "Never mind. Where exactly in the ancient land?"

I lowered the phone to ask Kloe, "What's the village name?" Odd that I didn't ask before.

Kloe shook her head. "Our village has no name."

"Great." I brought the phone back to my ear. "My sources tell me we are in a village with no name."

"Who the hell are your sources? Are they geographically challenged?"

"It's the ancient land, Azazel. Nothing should surprise you. How long would it take you get here? Where are you now?"

"Austria."

"Use the Glass in Belgium. That should put you... east of the village, I believe. Once you cross the Glass, head west and keep going until you get to the animal traps."

I imagined Azazel banging his head against a wall, trying to figure out how to get here before the world fell into pieces, or whatever he thought might happen if he didn't show up. "It will take me at least half a day. But—"

"How long would it take for you to get the Four Armies up here?" I interrupted, referring to the Four Armies of Hell.

Now I'd done it. Something broke over on his side of the phone. "The hell, Primrose? The Four Armies? That would take months of prearrangement!"

"Are you my general or not, Azazel?" I sharpened my tone. "Get it done. I need them here in less than a day. Do you understand?"

"You'd be *lucky* if we managed to get one regiment down there by that time."

I pulled my lips into a strained smile. "A regiment will do. By the way, I am feeling lucky today. Bring your best. Use the portal key I gave you to transport them to Belgium. From then on, you're on your own. Portals are impossible to summon within a few miles of the Glass because the land is heavily warded. Remember, the portal key is only good for fifteen minutes, so the entire regiment needs to be through by then. Also, you may or may not encounter a hoard of crazy vampyres near the Glass."

Azazel swore loudly. "There better be a damn good explanation for this."

"Yeah, yeah. I'll tell you all about it when you get here." I hung up and tossed the phone to Atlas, who barely caught it.

"Well?" Kloe asked. Her question was burdened with expectation.

I observed all those who watched me, including a crowd of eaves-dropping villagers. Too many hopes relied on my success. Too many would suffer on account of any failure. There could be no mistakes.

"My general will be here with two hundred well-trained reapers, two assassins, and a dozen trained lower demons." My smile became a little too wide. "Trust me, it'll all work out."

Atlas snorted and Fenrir growled. Those two needed to resolve their differences, though I wouldn't mind seeing Fenrir tear one out of Atlas.

Kloe bowed. "Thank you for your aid, Lady Primrose. It is much appreciated."

I touched her shoulder gently. "There's no need to be so formal. We're all friends here. I only wish we could do more. Until Azazel arrives, we can only wait and solidify the village defenses."

Kloe's eyes brightened. "Perhaps it would help for me to guide you through the village? To fight on a foreign battleground would be unwise. I could give you a tour of the borders and sensitive locations if you would like."

"I'd rather not."

"Sure."

Atlas and I spoke at the same time. He looked over his shoulder toward the wooden homes around us. "I think it would be better to scout the area on our own," Atlas said. "We would be more efficient that way."

His implication ate at my nerves. He expected me to go with him, but I had my own agenda for today. I shifted from one foot to another. "We can meet up later this evening," I suggested with an uncomfortable nod. "Getting Kloe's insight into the village soft spots might be useful."

The air cooled around us. I thought Atlas would protest, but he blinked in acceptance and left with a dark mood that hung over him like a shadow.

Kloe lingered by my side. "If you need to join him..."

"I don't." My soft words pounded through my mind like a headache. My words may have been true, but choices were never that simple. "Shall we?"

The village chief gestured for me to follow her, and I did. Fenrir trailed behind me loyally.

Kloe led me to inspect the borders, starting at the eastern wall of the village. We set a steady pace together and fell into a comfortable rhythm in which I'd share my thoughts on how to solidify weak spots in the defenses. Kloe listened to what I said and relayed the information to a group of villagers, who would then work on implementing the more robust protections. Some of the measures I suggested were simple, such as emptying the cabins near the border and moving the Guardians that lived there closer to the village center. Other measures required a greater time commitment. I asked for Kloe to find a group of volunteers to patrol the borders at staggered time intervals to ensure no attack came before we expected it.

"You seem deep in thought, Lady Primrose," said Kloe as we shifted our attention to a new segment of the village borders. "I hope your thoughts are not as heavy as they seem."

"Maybe even heavier," I joked before becoming serious. I looked down at the ground while we walked. Though I tried to focus on assessing the village defenses, my mind kept slipping toward my dreams and Yocheved's words from last night. "I suppose I'm having a Goddess's version of a 'mid-life crisis' if that makes any sense."

"I see," Kloe hummed thoughtfully. "Why do you say that?"

I hesitated. How much did I trust Kloe? I was a Guardian, like her, but she didn't know that. Elinore would laugh at my hesitation. *You have to give trust to get trust*, she'd say. On the other hand, my brother would reprimand me for sharing secrets with a stranger.

Then again, I trusted Yocheved enough to ask for answers. And Yocheved trusted Kloe. My vision blurred as I stared out into the distance.

"I thought I knew who I was," I said and met Kloe's eyes. We came to a stop while I spoke. "I have a name, a kingdom, a history, a title, and I thought that meant *something*. I thought that knowing all that I know about the world, about war, politics, life—my place in the world should be clear!" I laughed bitterly, and my fingers brushed through my hair. "What a fool I have been. I still don't fully know who I am." I clenched my fists. "How can that be? So many years of life, and I ask the same questions a child would. Who am I? What am I supposed to become? Why are things happening the way they are now?"

Kloe looked at me with age-old wisdom. "Perhaps we have no business speculating our probable identities. Instead of discovering who we are, we might be better off simply *being* who we are. Living our lives to the fullest is all we can do."

My breathing became heavy, and a squeezing pain in my chest brought a wave of agonizing melancholy. "But is that enough? To live, and not know why?"

She lifted her chin thoughtfully. I knew an intelligent woman when I met her, and Kloe was very bright. She listened to what I said to dissect the meaning behind my words.

Her silence brought forth a wave of questions I wanted answered. "I know about Guardians," I said.

Kloe didn't appear surprised. "How much do you know?"

"Hardly anything."

She smiled. "We keep our history a secret from strangers because we don't wish to make any new enemies. Nor do we wish to invite conflict. Most who visit our village already know of Guardians, but some do not."

I shook my head. "I don't understand. How could protection magic invite conflict?"

Kloe gave me a disapproving glance that made me feel infinitely more stupid for asking my question. "People always envy power they do not have—they covet what is special or magical. The last thing we want, Lady Primrose, is more attention from the outside world. I think that is one characteristic both you and our village have in common."

"Because power is the root of all evil," I concluded. People wanted to be the next Goddess of Death or harness protective spells, and they would do anything to possess those abilities.

"No. Because evil is the root of all evil. Power and greed are not intrinsically evil. A person who is greedy for food is not evil by nature. He is not evil if he works to earn his share of bread. He becomes evil when he kills his neighbor to steal a meal that does not belong to him."

Our conversation was quickly becoming more philosophical than intended. Three villagers carrying shovels and hammers marched toward us. Kloe and I made room for them to pass. I switched to another topic. "Do you get many visitors?" I asked and was reminded of my and Atlas's arrival. "You weren't surprised to see a God and Goddess in your territory."

Kloe's eyes hardened. "We don't get *many* visitors. Just enough to stir trouble." She held her scarf close to her neck, and I noticed her face was puffy from the cold. "I don't tell the story of our village to many, but this is one story that you need to hear."

I laughed. "You don't trust random strangers who come to the village, but you trust me? With all due respect, that doesn't sound very smart. I'm as much a stranger as any other visitor."

"I've told you this once already," Kloe tsked, "you are not like the others who have visited. You are different from other deities, Atlas included."

My lips pressed together, and I bit my tongue.

"Our village was created by Gods and Goddesses," Kloe started, "and we were gifted with life. Our people were created to live freely. Before the rift between the Guardians and the deities that created us, our rulers treated us like their own kind. We weren't the same, but we were almost kin, some would say. In our sister villages, and yes, there were many villages besides ours, our brothers and sisters lived and started their own families. We grew as a people. There were so many of us." Kloe's voice filled with emotion as she reminisced of times she surely couldn't remember.

"What rift?" I asked. "You said there came a rift between Gods and Guardians."

Kloe's focus shifted to me, and she smiled. "Though I appreciate your sharp attention, Lady Primrose, this is a story to be told without interruption. Your questions will be answered if you listen to my tale."

Instantly embarrassed, blood rushed to my cheeks. I impatiently waited for her to continue.

"Our village was led by a very powerful family. At its head was Kevin Petreson and his wife, Marie," said Kloe.

Petreson! I tempered my surprise and maintained an empty poker face. Was Gavin involved in the village's history somehow?

"The Petreson family was kind and loving, and they had substantial ties to the deities that ruled at that time. Every villager was treated fairly by Kevin and Marie, and so they honored their village chiefs. Before the Petreson family, the Guardians lacked clear leadership. Every village was led by a separate chief. The cause for our rift, the reason deities and our people grew apart, started before the Petreson family's unified rule. Gods and Goddesses were not fully satisfied with the world, so humans were created to satiate a hunger that many deities did not even know they had. A hunger to be served, unconditionally."

Whoosh. I ducked to avoid getting hit by a shovel. The villager carrying five shovels widened his eyes. "My deepest apologies!"

"No worries," I said with a smile. I stepped to the side as two more Guardians swooped in to help with the shovels.

"What's with all the shovels?" I asked.

"We're digging trenches up north, my lady," the villager said. "The God of Ice insisted we bring shovels at once."

"Oh?" My eyebrows shot up. Was Atlas sincerely helping? After his cold reaction earlier today, I had my doubts.

The Guardians nodded and rushed away with the shovels. Kloe hummed, "It seems your Lord Atlas is full of surprises." She cleared her throat. "As I was saying, humans were created to be the slaves of Gods and Goddesses. The creation of a people for such purposes upset many Guardians. If a human could be enslaved, then what stopped a deity from enslaving a Guardian? Our people bit their tongues at first. After all, nobody wanted to give the Gods any ideas."

I nodded. Kloe smiled warmly. "Once the Petreson family came to power," she continued, "human villages were growing alongside Guardian villages, which brought our people some grave concerns. The Kovach clan, the ruling human tribe at the time, did not have strong relations with our people, but Kevin Petreson sought to change this. Kevin called a council of Guardians together one late night to speak about humans, a council composed of previous village leaders."

I found myself leaning forward. Things were getting interesting.

"That night," Kloe said, "he made a decision that changed everything. Kevin believed in fate and that nothing was a coincidence. He claimed that Guardians were given protection magic to use it. Humans had no shield, no protection against magic, thus our people were to serve as 'Guardians' to the human race."

Let me guess. His decision didn't go over well with everyone.

"As you can imagine"—Kloe noticed the look in my eyes—"not everyone approved. Many Guardians were resentful toward the idea of helping slaves. If we were kin to deities, were the humans not our slaves as well? Why should we help them? The reactions humans had toward our offers of help only worsened the situation. Humans were wary of Guardians because we were an ancient and exotic people with close relations to deities. Most humans believed us to be in line with the Gods and Goddesses who enslaved them and refused to trust us.

"One day, a human hunting party came upon a group of young Guardians. The humans were approaching a cold winter, and they sent volunteers to hunt for wild animals—deer, rabbits—anything to fill their bellies. The Guardians they encountered were well-fed, well-dressed, and unpleasant toward the starving humans."

Kloe sighed, as if the Guardians' behavior disappointed her to this day. "A fight broke out. Our people would have been slaughtered if not for a noble human who stepped in front of his people to stop the bloodshed. This courageous human, Gavin Heitson, was brought before the Petreson family and gifted the powerful name of 'Petreson.' An alliance between humans and the Guardians was forged contingent on the marriage of Kevin's daughter, Selene Petreson, with Gavin Heitson—rather, I should call him, Gavin Petreson."

Gavin Petreson. The name echoed through my mind like a soft whisper. The memories that haunted me in this village were no coincidence after all. His history was strong here.

"Selene Petreson was not like her parents," Kloe said. "She was not as strong of a leader, nor was she kind. She believed herself to be important and expected to be treated as such."

A quick smile came to my lips. "So, she was a real priss." Kloe crossed her arms, quick to admonish me for my interruption. I laughed. "There are other five-letter words I could have used to describe her. Be thankful priss was the first to come to mind."

"As I was saying..." Kloe ignored my interruption, though I caught her smile before she regained her serious composure. "Selene thought very highly of herself. She held a distinct animosity toward anyone she believed could surpass her greatness. She had an immense dislike toward Gods and Goddesses because of their beauty and magic. Selene enjoyed surrounding herself with humans because she felt powerful around them." Kloe frowned. "Gavin was not opposed to the marriage. He knew his act would bring Guardians and humans together, and he did not dislike Selene. Selene was clever enough to hide her poor behavior when around her betrothed. But that didn't change who she was. Selene Petreson, though heir to the most powerful Guardian family, was not the belle of her home."

The wind blew, driving a chill down my spine. Kloe wrapped her cloak tightly around her figure. "There was another woman in our village. She was kind, yet wild and unruly in her behavior. Her beauty was only matched by her cleverness. The mysterious Guardian had close ties to Kevin and Marie. The day she met Gavin was the day he fell in love with her, and the day Selene Petreson became the embodiment of jealousy. In the year that followed, Selene and Gavin's betrothal was broken off, and Selene tried to kill the other woman one nightfall.

"But the woman's magic was strong. She defended herself against Selene's attack and spared the Petreson family's heir because of the love she had for Selene's parents." Kloe nodded in approval of the woman's mercy. "Selene was banished to a sister village, never to set foot in our village again. Both the Petreson and Heitson families were disappointed by the thought that an alliance would not come to pass between humans and Guardians. That disappointment soon faded when both Gavin and the mysterious Guardian woman married. A stronger, new alliance was forged."

My fists clenched. "Let me guess? They didn't live happily ever after."

"I'm afraid not." Kloe shook her head. Her eyes were full of sorrow. "The worst was yet to come. Not long after their sacred marriage, the Gods and Goddesses discovered Kevin Petreson's treasonous plan. The deities were outraged. How dare the Guardians try to take their human slaves away from them? Their outrage soon shaped into action, and a curse was set upon our people. Our sister villages began to disappear, one by one."

Fiery rage burned through my veins. How many people suffered for the sake of maintaining slavery? To feed the pride and arrogance of Gods and Goddesses?

Kloe's shoulders slumped with the heavy responsibility of delivering the end to a doomed story. "Lady Primrose, we are the last of our people. As an everlasting punishment, our village has been stripped of its name. Our people can never leave the ancient land. Gavin Petreson died many years ago, along with the mysterious woman. To this day, we remind our children of this tale so that the Petreson family may be honored and celebrated for all they did. We vow to never forget the injustices that once occurred."

I nervously chewed my bottom lip as I processed Kloe's story. "When did this all happen?"

"A long time ago."

"No, I get that." I ran a hand through my hair. "But relative to the creation of death? Because I don't remember *any* of this. If I were alive back then, I would have known about Guardians. I would have known about the Petreson family and the curse."

Kloe rubbed her hands together to warm them. "Death is not the oldest deity that exists. Once death was created, most Gods and Goddesses moved over to the human realm. I wouldn't be surprised if death came to be after these events took place."

"But that doesn't make sense either," I argued. My brow furrowed. "Are you telling me that there was a time when humans were completely immortal?"

"Without a doubt. As there was a time when all living creatures lived eternal lives." Kloe sensed my skepticism and lightly touched my shoulder. "What do you remember about the ancient land?"

I touched my brow as a merciless headache made me feel dizzy. Unwell, I squeezed my eyes shut. "I don't feel... " My throat felt dry, and my voice trailed off.

"Are you all right, Lady Primrose?" Kloe asked, though her voice sounded muffled as if I were underwater.

My head felt like lead, and I slowly sat down and kept it between my legs. Kloe sat beside me and repeated my name.

A void had been opened within the borders of my mind, and I was suddenly petrified. "Nothing," I said and opened my eyes. Even though my dizzy spell wore off, I felt deathly afraid. The pit in my stomach grew. "Nothing."

"What do you mean?" Kloe asked and held the back of her cold hand against my forehead. "You seem feverish."

"I don't remember anything about the ancient land," I whispered. "I know I came from here, but I don't remember anything about it. I should remember. I know I should."

"Be calm, Lady Primrose," the village chief commanded. "Everything has a rhyme and reason to it. Panic will do you no good."

I wanted to scream. "How can I not remember?"

"Because of a memory tree."

Both Kloe and I turned in the direction the voice come from. Yocheved stood, not far from us. She held her scarf close to her thin build. Her brown dress was torn and frayed at the edges. Green smudges of grass colored her sleeves, and she smelled of pine and sweet tree sap.

Kloe was taken aback by Yocheved's appearance. "What are you doing here?" she asked warily.

"Kloe," the girl greeted. "Am I not allowed to be here?"

I slowly looked from Kloe to Yocheved, and they both averted their gazes from me. Yocheved's posture was stiff, and Kloe's eyebrows were pinched into a stern stare. The tension between them made me unusually nervous, especially since it confused me. Kloe seemed to hold a high opinion of Yocheved when we last spoke.

"Can someone please tell me what's going on?" I asked.

"Nothing you need to concern yourself with, Lady Primrose," Kloe said, though I had a tough time believing her.

"Oh, sure. I definitely buy that," I said.

Yocheved stared at Kloe with an exasperated look on her face. "She's a terrible liar, isn't she?"

"I'm not," I protested. "Sarcasm is not the same as telling a lie."

"Yes, you are." Yocheved stepped in front of Kloe. She placed a pleading hand on Kloe's knee. "Tell her, Kloe."

"Tell me what?"

"It isn't your decision to make," the village chief argued, her cheeks red. "I told you not to speak to her."

"Why can't she speak with me?" I demanded and rose to my feet. A gust of wind blew a fistful of hair in my face, which I pushed back with an aggressive swipe. "The night we talked about her, you told me she would come to find me. To be frank, you seemed quite amused by the fact that we'd meet. Why is her speaking to me now a bad thing?"

Kloe's lips remained shut as if sealed with construction grade permanent glue, but the young girl could not keep a secret if it meant her life.

"Because," Yocheved began. Concern warped her pretty pale face. "I had a dream."

For whatever terrible answer I was planning to hear, her words fell remarkably short of my expectations. Kind of disappointing, actually. "So did Martin Luther King Jr.," I pointed out, though they probably had no clue who he was. "His dream was pretty amazing. Why is having a dream a bad thing?"

"Her dreams never mean anything good." Kloe's wrinkled face was gaunt. "She had one the night you came. After we spoke."

I jammed my hands in my pockets and raised an eyebrow. Time for a curveball. "Does this have to do with the fact she's Hecate's descendant?"

Both the elderly woman and young child froze, and time stopped. I'd watched two horror movies in my lifetime, and they were enough for me. In one of them, the head of a doll turning slowly to face its victim was the most frightening scene I'd ever seen—this coming from a Goddess who fought zombie vampyres to cross an ancient bridge while hunting the Devil. When Kloe and Yocheved turned their heads, one hundred percent synchronized, a feeling of dread clung onto me. Actually, this was worse than in the movies because this was real.

"How do you know that?" Kloe whispered and paled. She stood slowly.

I shook my head and held my hands up in surrender. "Yocheved isn't the only one who has weird dreams. Hecate visited me in a dream last night." I couldn't help but stare at the ten-year-old beside me. Her dark hair, her blue eyes, her frail build—it all held an uncanny resemblance to the woman from my dream. "She told me I had a debt to pay."

"Hecate had the power of premonition." Yocheved's words were soft, and she avoided my gaze. "She could see the future, and so can I. It would be wrong to hide it any longer. I need to tell you."

"Don't." I stopped her. "I don't need to know."

She stared up at me with wide eyes. "It's important."

"I'm sure it is. I still don't want to know."

"You don't understand—"

I raised my voice. "No means no, Yocheved."

Her bottom lip trembled, and I immediately felt bad for yelling. "Are you sure?" she asked.

I looked away from her face to contemplate her question, but I had already decided. "Yes. Things happen for a reason, and if the future changes because you tell me something I shouldn't know... then everything might change for the worse. Trust me on this."

Yocheved's hand reached for mine. Her palms were warm, and her grip was firm. "I do," she said. "Trust you, I mean." The girl wrapped me in a tight embrace. My breath left me though I moved my arms to hold her close and stroke her back. Her warmth created a deep feeling in my chest. A feeling of sincere happiness.

I lowered my head to place my lips on her hair so that she could hear my next words. "I'm sorry I yelled at you. But whatever happened in your dream, no matter how terrible you think it is, we will get through it." I loosened my embrace and lifted her chin to meet my eyes. "I promise you. I've faced hordes of terrible villains and dire situations." I rolled my eyes, and Yocheved let a small smile touch her lips. "Seriously. Things do work out in the end. Have faith."

"Yocheved." Kloe spoke from behind me in a thoughtful tone. "You mentioned the memory tree. Do you think it's responsible for her lapse in memory?"

Yocheved nodded, and Kloe sighed reluctantly. "Lady Primrose, you don't remember your time here in the ancient land, but someone must have informed you of how death came to be. How you became the Goddess of Death."

"Yes, of course," I said. Pain flashed through my eyes when I thought back to Ben's explanation of how death was created.

"What have you been told?"

"My brother used to describe the birth of the Gods and Goddesses in this way"—I became lost in my retelling of Ben's story—"in the beginning, there were the elements: earth, wind, fire, water. Together, the elements formed the physical world. From these four elements came two Gods of wind and water and two Goddesses of earth and fire. And from these four deities erupted other elemental deities of lightning, ice, metal, and so much more."

I could feel I'd caught the interest of both Yocheved and Kloe now that I immersed myself deeper into the story. They oddly didn't seem familiar with this tale. My eyes narrowed into thin slits. After all that Kloe knew about the ancient land, her *not* knowing this was strange.

"Though these deities existed," I continued, "they were catatonic and immobile—lost in their element. They were not alive. One day, a God of Flesh was made, and as the first of life, he was named the God of Life. His name is Benjamin Titan, a name he chose for himself." Speaking of Ben brought a smile to my face. "The God of Life was the first to have thought, movement, feeling, and magic. With his power, he brought to life the previously catatonic deities and many other forms of life and magic." My eyebrows furrowed together. "Evidently, he created Guardians as well, though he never told me about them. All these events took place in the ancient land."

The mood of my tale shifted toward a darker theme. "Sometime after, Pain and Fear were also born. They began to wreak havoc on the world and cause chaos. A magical being started to pity those who were sentenced to eternal pain and fear. She discovered the connection between a temple and life, so she entered it. Within the temple were unique altars made of metal that represented each distinct soul of all magical deities worthy of an altar. She carved out a dagger from the metal of one specific altar—the altar of a friend who suffered at the immortal hands of Pain and Fear. With the dagger, she *mercifully*"—the word left a bitter taste in my mouth—"ended her friend's life, and so there became death. This being was named the Goddess of Death."

A sad smile warped my lips. "I am that Goddess of Death. Life used to be immortal until the day my power was born. From that moment on"—my mouth felt dry—"life became precious. One day all of this"—I gestured to my surroundings—"will also come to an end. Anything that has a beginning must have an ending, and all that lives must die."

There was a moment of uncomfortable silence after I ended my tale. Neither Kloe nor Yocheved had anything appropriate to say. They sensed my sour mood. The story of how my power came to be was disheartening, to say the least.

"Who told you that story, Lady Primrose?" Kloe asked gently.

"My brother. Why?"

Her eyes glazed over for a brief second. "No reason. I hadn't heard it before, is all. About the memory tree..."

"I can take her there," Yocheved volunteered. "She needs to see it."

"There's very little border of the village left to show you, Lady Primrose," Kloe said, straight to the point. "I will speak to more of our villagers and give them the advice you have given me so far. Let Yocheved show you the memory tree, and then we can meet in the village center and discuss the remaining sensitive areas of our village."

A hazy image of an oak tree from my dream with Hecate resurfaced in my mind.

Yocheved tugged at my sleeve and smiled mischievously. "Let's go! You'll definitely want to see this."

CHAPTER TWENTY SEVEN
HECATE'S MEMORY

YOCHEVED LED ME SOUTH and toward a clearing a mile outside the village borders. As we passed the villagers, the Guardians gave us a wide berth and started to whisper. Their eyes held reproach and even a fiber of fear in them. Yocheved noticed my discomfort, and her electric blue eyes softened. "They're not doing that because of you."

"What do you mean?"

"They're afraid of me," Yocheved said. "That's why the other children can be so mean while the adults turn a blind eye."

"But you're a Guardian."

"And Hecate's descendant," she added, although she didn't sound sullen or upset. "In their eyes, I'm a witch."

I watched the villagers, now in a different light. I may have been an outcast in the High Court, but Yocheved was an outcast in her own home. Were Elise and Remi cruel to Yocheved as well? Charming little Elise with her beaming smile and kind words? People were not always what they seemed. The Devil was not ugly in appearance, yet he charmed his way into the lives of the naïve and manipulated them from within.

We crossed the border through a small gate in the wall around the village. The stretch of forest that we walked through became uncannily familiar. As in my dream with Hecate, Yocheved led me to a meadow full of flowers and soft grass. My gaze ranged over the center of the field, but instead of seeing an old oak tree, like in my dream, there only remained the charred stump of its trunk and the thick roots that dove into the soil beneath it.

"What happened to it?" My voice was hardly above a whisper.

"Hecate's memory tree was burned down a long time ago," Yocheved said. Though she didn't appear sorrowful or angry, she looked very unsettled. "All that's left is the stump."

"Do you know what this means?" I asked with a strained tone. My throat started to close up, and I felt sick to my stomach. "A tree stump belonging to a memory tree blocks memories. They are the strongest memory blocks that there exists."

The thought of never fully remembering my time in the ancient land sent a fire of fury through my chest, and I shifted the straps of my scimitar.

Yocheved noticed my hand creep toward my sword and sent me a disappointed glance. "Tree stumps of a memory tree can't be destroyed. You should know that."

"I deserve to remember what happened."

"And you will," Yocheved said. She sounded so confident. There was no shred of doubt in her voice.

A shaky breath escaped my lips. "How can you know for certain?"

"Your memories will come back naturally, through dreams or images—I'm sure it already started." She sent me a pointed look and then stared behind me. "You recognized the pattern in the stars last night, and Fenrir has been following you ever since I found you today."

I whipped around, and sure enough, the wolf watched me from a distance. He seemed comfortable now that Atlas was no longer in my presence. Yocheved was right about the memories, and now her connection to Hecate made perfect sense. The dreams about Gavin and the ancient land started when I entered the temple named after Calliope, an ancient queen who worshiped the Goddess of Magic, Hecate.

"Think of a memory block as boulders in a river," Yocheved explained. She bounced on the balls of her feet and bit her lip. She crouched down to pick up a few small rocks and then showed them to me. "Give me your hands."

I reluctantly placed my hands in front of me, with my palms facing upward.

The young girl set the rocks in my palms. "Try to imagine this. Boulders can change the flow of water, yes?"

"Right."

"They can determine where water will flow and where it will not. The flow of water, those are your memories. You can't access all of your memories because of these boulders." Yocheved gestured toward the small rocks in my hands. "But boulders don't stay in the same place forever. When the river floods, large surges of water can move the boulders away or overwhelm those boulders." She tossed the pebbles out of my hands. "Just like that."

"Just like that," I echoed and wiped my hands against my pants.

"You coming to the ancient land is like the start of heavy rain, and the water inside the river is starting to grow. Some boulders have begun to move, which is why you've started remembering certain memories. It's still not enough to move all of the boulders away, but that will change with time."

As odd as Yocheved's demonstration with the rocks was, her explanation made sense. I watched Yocheved's intense eyes, instantly reminded of Hecate from my dream. There was a sticky, uncomfortable feeling of guilt at the forefront of my mind, a feeling that the memory tree's existence was my fault.

"You know, there were rumors about Hecate and me," I said. "When I told you the story of how I came to be, I said that death was created to 'save' my friend from Pain and Fear—some say that friend was Hecate. The Goddess of Magic was one of the first souls to have been reaped after death was created, and she was the very first deity to die."

"You think she made the memory tree because of that?" Yocheved asked. "To plant those memory blocks in your mind so that you don't remember killing her?"

"Maybe." I shrugged. "I don't remember Hecate, much less remember killing her with the intent of creating death. I find it hard to believe that anyone would forget the first person they killed. It would take magic as strong as a memory tree to block such emotional memories."

Yocheved hesitated. "Primrose, I don't think you killed Hecate," she admitted and twiddled her thumbs while she averted her gaze. "There's something about your history with Hecate that doesn't make sense."

I smiled. The young girl proved she was more intelligent than most deities by recognizing the logic gap. "I don't disagree with you. Something has always seemed off to me about those rumors. But what?"

"I'm not sure. We're missing a piece of the puzzle. If you killed Hecate, wouldn't you be the new Goddess of Magic?" She shrugged and pushed her lips out into a disappointed pout.

"My point exactly!" I exclaimed, and Yocheved nodded. A sigh left my chest. "Maybe someone else killed her. Yet no one has publicly come forward in the last few millennia to claim her title or power. Why the secrecy?"

Yocheved positioned her fist under her chin thoughtfully and tilted her head toward the charred tree stump. "If Hecate's memory tree were still intact, I might have been able to find out what happened to her. Memory trees are very responsive to the blood of family members and a few basic spells. But Hecate had many enemies in her day."

My eyebrows pulled together into a frown. "Why do you say that?"

She nodded toward the tree. "Someone burned down her tree."

"I get your point, but Hecate was the most powerful witch that ever existed. If her memories were out in the open, accessible to anyone familiar with a few basic magic spells, then the strongest secrets in the history of magic could fall into the hands of some very nasty people."

"If that were the case, her memories could have been destroyed by simply cutting the tree down." Yocheved pointed toward the charred tree stump. "Why would someone *burn* her memory tree down, if not out of disrespect or hate?"

A shiver ran down my spine. I didn't have an answer to that. Memory trees were characteristically easy to destroy. Even a human could take an axe to the tree, and the memories would no longer exist. However, the tree stumps were a different story. Tree stumps were impossible to destroy, and that's why the memory blocks were so strong.

"I'll be honest," Yocheved said, breaking the tense silence. "I didn't only bring you here to show you the tree. I have questions. Lots of them. There's much about memory trees and death that I don't understand. How can memories be preserved after death? What happens to memories when someone dies?"

"That's a complicated question."

"I have plenty of time on my hands." The girl crossed her arms and set her lips into a stern pout. Her cheeks were red from the cold air, and her breath was visible. Her eyes never left me as she waited for me to answer her question.

I sat down on the grass and gestured for Yocheved to do the same. I shrugged off my jacket. "I'll try to explain this as best I can. Put on the coat. I can tell you're freezing your butt off."

"I'm not."

"No coat, no explanation. It's that simple."

"I'm really not cold," she said, though she took the jacket from my hands and shrugged it on.

"All right. So..." I pondered how to answer her questions. "When people die, there are three parts you need to concern yourself with." I glanced at Yocheved to see if she understood. "Three parts: the body, the soul, and the memories. If you combine these three things, you get a living being. Does that make sense?

"When a soul is reaped, both the soul and the memories leave the body. The body stays in the realm from which it was reaped, while the soul and the memories travel to the Underworld. I like to think of it this way: imagine you have a desk with two drawers."

"Like a librarian's desk?" Yocheved asked.

"Sure. Imagine a librarian's desk with two drawers. In the first drawer, there's a soul. In the second drawer, there are the memories that belong with that soul. A dead person can't remember anything— not only because they don't have the mental capacity or ability to retain memories, but also because they can't access that second drawer. Only I, the Goddess of Death, can access the memories inside that second drawer. See, though the soul and memories are kept together, they're segregated.

"To answer your question about the memory tree, if someone wishes to preserve their memories, they can tie their memories to an oak tree that they planted. Therefore, they die, the memories remain in the oak tree instead of traveling with the soul to the Underworld. Ultimately, souls and memories can be fully separated. There can be souls without their memories and memories without their souls."

"You would need to physically plant an oak tree to preserve the memories?" Yocheved interrupted to ask. "Hecate had to physically plant the tree herself?"

"Okay, two things. One, just because you plant an oak tree doesn't mean the memories are automatically preserved. Humans plant trees all the time, but that doesn't mean every time a tree is planted, a memory tree is created. Certain spells need to be cast after the tree has been planted to ensure that the transfer of memories occurs. And no, although most memory trees are physically planted by their creator, there is an alternative method. Theoretically, you could mentally 'plant a tree' inside of someone else's mind so that your memories are preserved in the safety of their subconscious, but nobody has ever tried that before."

"Let me see if I understand this," she said, counting on her fingers. "Souls can exist on their own. As can memories. A soul combined with memories is a dead person. A soul with memories *and* a body is a living person. But what happens if there's a body with a soul and no memories? Or a body with memories but no soul? Can that even happen?"

"A body with a soul and no memories is a patient with amnesia," I said, thinking of the simplest explanation to use. "A severe head injury, for example, could cause amnesia. On the other hand, a body with memories and without a soul—that's a reaper."

"A reaper," Yocheved repeated. "And reapers reap souls."

"Yes." I nodded and rubbed the back of my neck. "When a human dies, every once in a while, the Underworld chooses for them to become a reaper. And so, the memories and mental capacity to retain memories, thoughts, and everything it takes to behave like a living being are returned to the body. But when memories are returned to the body, without a soul to guide them, they become jumbled. It's like... well, you know how Kloe gave me a tour of the village borders?"

"Yes."

"Imagine if she hadn't given me a tour. If she let me try and figure everything out on my own. It would be a struggle for me, right?"

Yocheved smiled. "I guess so."

"Memories without a guide will be lost. A soul behaves like a guide. Therefore, since they don't have a soul, many reapers won't remember their past."

"But you also said that they behave like regular living beings." She wrinkled her nose, confused.

"Yes." I struggled to find the words and tapped my nails against my knee. "They don't just behave like living beings. They require and do the same things that living beings do. They need food, water, air, and sleep to function properly. Reapers can even have children, but they usually choose not to. They're like the rest of us." I stopped and then added, "Only without a soul."

Yocheved paused to process the information I threw at her. Most deities struggled to understand these concepts, but she was doing a great job keeping up so far. "I haven't heard of reapers in the ancient land," she said.

"No, you haven't, and that would be my fault," I confessed with a small smile. "Most deities in the human realm believe that the ancient land is vacant of life—myself included. I never advised my reapers to travel to the ancient land because I didn't think there would be any souls to reap."

I felt the need to defend the absence of reapers in the ancient land, though Yocheved didn't seem to hold me accountable. She only watched me with wide eyes and kept thinking through the information I shared with her.

"The Glasses, the portals between the human realm and the ancient land, dilute the magical connection between the souls of this realm and me," I said. "I never sensed the state of the souls here. Otherwise, I would have known about Guardians and my reapers would travel here regularly to reap souls."

A flash of fear sparked in Yocheved's eyes, and she stood up suddenly. "Without reapers in this realm, what happened to all of the souls of the Guardians who died here?"

I understood her concern and rushed to clarify. "Reapers aren't necessary for a soul to be reaped. A soul will be reaped with or without the help of a reaper. A reaper's most important function is to guide the soul to the Underworld. Otherwise, the soul may get lost along the way. My best guess is that the souls of people who died here have either made it safely to the Underworld or were lost along the way."

"Where can they get lost? What happens to them?" Her face paled. My words hadn't yet comforted her. A stab of disappointment pierced my chest, and a frown twisted my lips.

"They usually roam the realm they died in. Or eventually, fade away into something insignificant," I said, hoping my explanation would ease her fear. "In rare cases, they haunt the place they died due to strong, unresolved emotions such as hate or anger."

Yocheved sat back down. "If they fade away... is that painful? Do they feel lost or scared?"

"They don't feel anything," I said. "They're dead. There is no pain in death, nor fear or sorrow." *Not unless you're in Hell.* "Lost souls can be harmful to the living, in the case of hauntings, for instance, which is one reason why we want all reaped souls in one realm. Another reason is that there's a balance to everything. Souls, once reaped, go to the Underworld. If they never make it to the Underworld, certain balances are disturbed. The Underworld serves as a checkpoint, to make sure that the balance of life and death is kept within bounds."

"Are the balances of the ancient land not where they should be?"

"It's tough to say without taking a closer look at the numbers. The balances between life and death reset and cycle every decade or so. Whether or not the balances are where they should be depends on how many people have died over the past few years." I wondered if protection magic influenced how long the villagers could live. "Do Guardians live as long as humans?"

"Even longer," Yocheved said and kept her gaze on the grass. "Guardians age like humans up to the age of twenty. After that, ten human years are like one Guardian year. Kloe is almost seven hundred years old."

"Seriously?" I let my incredulousness show. That was impressive.

"Yes," she said, laughing at my reaction. "We can die of 'old age,' but Kloe would be like a sixty-five-year-old human, so she still has plenty of time left."

"Do human illnesses affect Guardians at all?" I asked, thinking of cancers, viruses, and medical issues humans contended with.

"They can, especially when we're younger. I got sick one time when I was very small, but once we grow into our magic, our protection spells usually prevent that. Guardians can die of the same things humans die of too, but our magic protects us for the most part."

"But you're not just a Guardian. You're a demigod," I said and elbowed her playfully. "Hecate was a deity, the Goddess of Magic. That makes you special."

Yocheved pulled a fistful of grass from the ground. "Being special isn't always a good thing."

No, it wasn't. Being special came at an emotional cost. People looked at you differently, some with envy, others with fear. My heart felt heavy with pity. "I never said it was."

She frowned, dissatisfied with my response. "How are demigods different from Guardians?" she asked, quick to change the subject.

My eyes narrowed. Yocheved averted her gaze and set her lips into a hard grimace. I decided not to press her on the whole 'being special' dodge. She wasn't going to talk about it even if I asked.

Instead, I shared another piece of information. "Demigods can live forever. Except there's a catch."

"What catch?"

"Anything a human can die of a demigod can die of too, like Guardians. Your protection magic gives you an advantage many demigods would sell their soul for."

"How does this all get decided?" Yocheved demanded. She finally looked me in the eye and adjusted her position. "What determines how people age or which people live forever?"

"That depends on the strength of a soul," I said. "The stronger the soul, the longer someone lives, and the harder it is to kill that person. Gods and Goddesses age normally for the first two decades. Most deities appear to be between eighteen and twenty-one. Due to our souls' strength, deities live forever unless they are killed by their Soul Dagger. When Gods have children, their children are godlings or demigods. Godlings are the children of two Gods and are completely immortal, like their parents. A Soul Dagger is required to reap their souls. Demigods, on the other hand, are descendants of Gods and humans, so their souls are weaker. A weaker soul means that an individual is more susceptible to death. There are also creatures without souls, like reapers and lower demons. Reapers and lower demons never age."

"Aren't they immortal then," Yocheved asked, "if they never age?"

I pursed my lips. "Not quite. Reapers are dead humans, remember? They can't be immortal if they're already dead. Also, if shredded into enough pieces, both reapers and lower demons won't heal for millennia. Putting someone into a coma for millennia... that sounds like death to me."

"Why do some people get Soul Daggers while others don't?"

I shrugged, unsure. My head started to throb with all the questions Yocheved asked. "It's hard to say who gets a soul or Soul Dagger—there is no hard, fast set of rules. Magic is unpredictable that way."

For a brief minute, Yocheved's mouth stopped moving, and the questions came to an end. I rolled my neck, and it made a cracking noise from the position I was sitting in. My tongue was dry from speaking. I only had such long conversations with Elinore, but Yocheved gave my best friend a run for her money. Yocheved didn't speak as much as my friend did, but she asked many questions, which left me saying more than I would if I were conversing with Elinore.

"The demons that are coming tomorrow," Yocheved said. "Do you need a Soul Dagger to kill them?"

"The two demons that summoned the army have Soul Daggers, but the rest of the army is composed of lower demons," I explained. Despite my tired tongue, Yocheved asked some pretty good questions. "The best way to face tomorrow's threat is to mortally wound each demon that attacks. A mortal wound will be enough to put the average lower demon out of commission for at least a year, maybe more. My general and reapers will make sure to dismember them after the battle is won so that they won't heal for several millennia, if ever."

Yocheved pulled my jacket more tightly around her. "You must have hurt them pretty badly, those two demons. Otherwise, they wouldn't be sending an army to attack us."

"I'm hunting their brother, Lucifer." His name left a bitter taste on my tongue. "He escaped Hell, not long ago."

A chill froze the space between us, and the sun's light flickered. Yocheved shivered as if realizing something. "You're going to kill him," she said solemnly, referring to Lucifer.

"Yes." *The Devil must die.* The reminder seared through my mind.

"Why?" Her voice sounded small.

"He's done a lot of"—my breath caught—"bad things." My stomach churned at the thought of seeing Lucifer sometime soon. "He killed many innocent people and will continue to do so unless I stop him."

"You sound like you don't want to. Kill him, I mean," she said.

I paused. My lips formed a small 'oh.' Yocheved was far more insightful than anyone I'd met. She knew me for less than a day, yet she understood me like my closest friends.

I forced the surprise to melt from my face and pursed my lips. "He used to be... a friend." I chose my words carefully. "Things changed."

"What happened?"

I looked at Yocheved, not wanting to think back to what happened several centuries ago. "Everything fell apart."

CHAPTER TWENTY EIGHT
POLITICS AND POWER

300 YEARS AGO...

The throne room was dimly lit, and most of the torches had been put out. Fire was no friend to the Devil's enemy.

Enemy. The word felt so foreign in my mind, especially associated with a man I believed was my greatest ally.

The throne room was strangely cold, and the metal throne I sat on was hard against my back. The scent of pomegranates wafted from a table set with fruit for our guests. The table was a small, lonely thing in the corner of the room. The gray cloth set on it was smudged and uneven. Nobody had given the table any care—we all knew what was coming, and it wasn't a feast.

My nails tapped against the arm of my throne, and I counted the number of diamonds painted on the ornate floor of the room while I waited. Part of me dreaded what was to come, and part of me welcomed it. My silver crown was heavy on my head, like a burden but also an incumbent reminder. There were certain things that needed to be done, and I was the only one who could do them. The black gown I wore had a long train and sleeves that dangled past my wrists. My attire filled me with the enduring sensation that I should be mourning a loss or some defeat, and I certainly felt that way after all that had occurred with Lucifer.

The reapers in the room stood guard as we waited. Cain paced near the right of my throne, his hand on the hilt of his sword. The reapers fed off of my agitated emotions, and I fed off of their tense behavior.

Earlier I demanded that all lower demons be cleared from the large room. I knew of Lucifer's experience with taming demons and would rather not have to worry about my own soldiers attacking me. I requested to have him meet me in the Underworld instead of the human realm because now I knew better than to trust him. He'd broken my trust when he killed hundreds of innocents in my name.

The tall doors to the throne room grumbled as they opened. I pulled my shoulders back and forced my chin up.

An unfamiliar, pretentious voice proclaimed Lucifer's presence: "Announcing the arrival of his royal highness. The Devil, Lord Lucifer, the Demon of Pride, King of all Demons, and Master of Hell."

My ears rang from the ridiculous entrance made by the man who introduced Lucifer. An array of servants dressed in red entered the room. They bore an interesting emblem on their clothing. There was a symbol linked in a chain, bound together as a sign of unity. I bit my tongue to not lash out just yet.

Right on cue, Lucifer entered the throne room. The coldness of the room evaporated and was replaced by an uncomfortable heat. The fire from the few torches that were lit now burned twice as strong and the scent of campfire permeated the air. Several hooded figures entered the room behind the Devil and walked to the side.

Lucifer was a picture of arrogance. He strutted in as if he already lived in my palace. He did not pause to bow or pay his respects. He strode steadily, as though we were good friends. Maybe a month ago, that was true. He stopped before reaching the steps to my throne, and Cain's muscles tensed as he unsheathed his katana.

The Devil grinned and nodded at my reaper. "Peace, Cain. I have no quarrel with you."

"I only hope it remains that way," Cain said through gritted teeth. His body was stiff, and a vein in his forehead throbbed. He and Lucifer had once been close, but that all ended when Lucifer demanded my hand in marriage. Cain was very protective and had little patience for the Devil's antics.

Lucifer's bloodred eyes locked with mine, and if I had been standing, my legs would have trembled under his intense stare. He was quite the sight to see. The Devil stood strong and tall in his armor. His hair was elegantly swept to one side, and his smile deepened. "Hello, Rose."

"Lucifer." I said his name, and my voice sounded flat. His name once brought me joy... I shook my head and forced myself to look beyond the facade the Demon King put up. To look past his pretty face and into the depths of his eyes. Past the charm and handsome gleam, there was pride, lust, anger, and a hunger for blood that existed within him.

"You look well." The Devil ignored my awkward greeting. His eyes slowly undressed me, and a blush touched my cheeks.

"And you as well."

"I was disappointed to hear that you refused my invitation to meet in the human realm," he said, impatient with my curt responses. He wasn't used to getting the cold shoulder from me. "Especially knowing how much you hate the Underworld."

The room was silent. My reapers held their breaths, and the Underworld stilled. I swallowed my rage to stop the scream that built in my throat. "Do you think I'm a fool?" Lucifer opened his mouth to speak, but I didn't wait for him to start. "After what you've done this past month, do you expect me to trust you?" My voice quivered. "To run back into your arms with an apology on my lips? Bow before you and ask for your forgiveness? Is that what you expected?"

His grin faltered. "Nonsense, Rose. What have I done to lose your trust?"

"Where do you want me to begin?" I stood up from my throne, and my reapers shifted, sensing my unease. "You asked me to marry you, in front of an audience of deities to strong-arm me into an alliance—an alliance you never took the time to ask me about first." I started walking down the steps, and Cain followed me. "You disrespected me in front of my soldiers, servants, and equals, attacking me for not answering your marriage proposal with a sure 'yes.'" I stopped at the bottom of the steps and looked into his fiery eyes. "You went on a rampage and killed my servants before you set off into the human realm and cut down life after life in your rage." I leaned in to whisper in his ear. "But the worst betrayal"—I looked at the emblem on the red uniforms of the servants that had accompanied him and pointed at one of the hooded figures in the room—"is your alliance with her."

Lucifer clenched his jaw, realizing that his covert alliance was no longer a secret. I backed away from him and took two steps toward the hooded individual. "You can wear a cloak, Lady Destiny, but you can't hide from me."

"Who said I was hiding?" the woman asked and pushed aside the hood of her cloak to reveal her red hair and dark eyes.

Lucifer grabbed my arm and twisted me back toward him. The sound of swords being drawn rang through the room and Cain's katana lay next to Lucifer's neck. "At ease, Cain," the Devil spoke, but Cain paid him no mind. Cain looked to me for direction.

"It's all right, Cain." I nodded. "Put the sword down."

Cain reluctantly moved his sword away, though he didn't sheath his weapon. I shifted my attention to Lucifer. His warm touch made my skin tingle, and my stomach twisted. "You better let go of my arm, or else Cain will be the last thing you worry about."

He reluctantly released me from his grasp. "My alliance with Destiny is unnecessary if you comply."

"If I comply."

"As for those I killed in my outrage, I owe you my deepest apologies." Lucifer bowed his head, and a glimpse of his charming composure returned. "I was surprised by your... response to my proposal and became unnecessarily angered. In my anger, I killed your servants and ended numerous innocent lives. I am sorry. I never meant to upset you."

I shook my head, wishing I could believe the sweet words that came from his mouth. "Don't pretend to be something you're not, Lucifer. You don't regret killing those people. I remember their final memories and the look you had in your eyes when you ended their lives. The love you have for that kind of bloodshed—"

"Give me a chance, Primrose," he pled. My full name slipped from his tongue.

"You had one," I snapped. "I will not be used. Nor will I tolerate the bloodshed you reap. I said a month ago that I would think about your proposal."

"Rose—"

"Well, I've thought about it, and my answer is no. I will not marry you. Under any circumstance. Not now, not ever."

He made a move to grab his sword but thought better of it when he realized where he was—my throne room in the Underworld. The land would fight him if he attacked me here. My reapers would rush to my aid if he lifted a finger.

"Now you see," I said, backing away, "why I chose to meet you here."

Lucifer knew when he was beaten. There was no way to outmaneuver me in the Underworld. "Any other place, and you would be mine."

"But we're not just anywhere." I mocked and gestured toward the rest of the room. "We're here."

"You can't hide in the Underworld forever," he warned. "I will make you my queen, one way or another. The two of us were meant to rule the world together, side by side."

"Get out."

"You can't win this war, Rose." His smile reappeared, though this time it was cruel in nature. "I won't stop until I get what I want. You know that better than anyone else."

"Get out!" I yelled, and the ground beneath us trembled with my anger. The Underworld responded to my emotions with a rage of its own, but Lucifer was beyond being afraid.

He bowed low while a shrewd gleam played in his eyes. "Until we meet again... my queen." The Devil spun around and left the room with his servants in tow.

Destiny lingered for a brief moment and let her stony stare roam the room. "Our story does not end here, Lady Primrose."

"Then it will end with your death."

Her cheeks flared, though she bit her tongue. She flung her cloak elegantly and left. When the door closed behind her, the tension in the room dissolved, and the breath I'd been holding left my chest.

"I don't understand why he killed all those people." Yocheved cut off the retelling of my memory. "They didn't do anything wrong. You didn't do anything wrong."

I couldn't answer her question. "I wish I knew. The only conclusion I can draw is that it's in Lucifer's nature. Demons lash out irrationally, and he's the demon of pride. He expected me to accept his marriage proposal immediately and without delay."

"Do you have to kill him?" she asked. "I know he did a bad thing, but everyone makes mistakes."

"Cold-blooded murder isn't a mistake. Even if I don't want to kill him, it must be done. And I'm the only one who can do it. Nobody knows the Devil like I do."

Yocheved frowned and tilted her head to the side. "Why is Atlas helping you? You didn't mention him as part of the story."

The memory, I wanted to correct her. *It's not a story. It's a memory. Stories aren't this painful to recall.* "As a member of the High Court, he insisted on accompanying me. His brother is King of the High Court."

"What's the High Court?"

"It's the governing body of the supernatural community. Every relevant God or Goddess has a place on that council. Some lower-ranking deities are also allowed to attend, but the 'ruler' of the High Court decides who can or can't attend the meetings."

"How do they decide who rules the High Court?" she asked. While we spoke, Fenrir had come closer to us and sat down between Yocheved and me. He lay his head on the small girl's lap, and she started stroking his fur.

"Either the previous king gives up their crown willingly to a successor or the predecessor is killed, and the murderer takes their place." Erin had taken the place of the previous God of Fire, Nuriel. Nuriel rarely called the High Court into session and didn't care much for politics or pleasantries, which is why I suppose Erin's arrival was so celebrated by other deities. Politics was a machine that could be used to gain power, and Nuriel knew this.

I recalled Erin's crowning. While most of the High Court celebrated the arrival of their new king, Ben and I had been wary from the start.

"Here comes the greatest pawn of them all," Ben had said to me that day. We watched the crowning from the back of the crowd. Neither of us much liked the spotlight, nor did we enjoy the event.

Nuriel and I got along fine while he was alive, and I had been filled with fury the moment his soul slipped into the Underworld. Erin searched for me by name after his crowning, but I had been long gone by the time the Grimm Brother thought to make his greeting. My loathing of Erin Grimm started long before I formally met him.

"The High Court isn't what it used to be," I said when Yocheved remained silent. "The moment Erin Grimm became king, merit and strength flew out the window and were replaced by politics and lies."

Yocheved's eyes lit up as if an idea crossed her mind. "If you could choose, who would you pick to rule the High Court?"

"Who would I choose?"

"Yes, you!" She giggled at my surprise.

My forehead creased while I considered her question. "I never thought about it before," I admitted. "Honestly, I would choose my brother, Benjamin. He's the God of Life, so everyone that exists would be nothing without him. Besides, Ben is kind and fair, and he's far more intelligent than any of those fools on their best day."

"You love him," Yocheved said with a beaming smile.

"Very much."

Her eyes became sad, and the corners of her lips drew down into a subtle frown. "It must be nice, having family. I wish I had that here."

The longing in her voice pulled at the strings of my heart. I took her hand in mine and squeezed it in a warm gesture. "You do have family, Yocheved. You have Kloe, who, despite her grumpiness, clearly loves you." I stroked Fenrir's fur, and the wolf lifted his head from the girl's lap. "Fenrir likes you, too. I'm sure he thinks that he's your family as well."

Yocheved held my hand in a tighter grip than before. "Can you be my family, too?" She stared at me intently with her pleading eyes.

I pulled her into a tight hug and whispered in her ear, "I would be honored to be a part of your family." The leaves from the trees around us bristled with a harsh wind that swept through the air. A babe's cry echoed in my ear, and I withdrew from our embrace. Fenrir's ears twitched.

"Did you hear that?" I asked.

Yocheved nodded and sprung to her feet. "No mother would take her babe this far outside the village."

I stood up. "Stay beside me. If there's danger, I want you within arm's reach." The babe's cry grew, and with Fenrir at our side, both Yocheved and I burst into a run. The cry came southeast of the village, just over a mile east of Hecate's burned memory tree. Aside from the cries, the forest had become eerily quiet. The wind stilled. The shadows of the cloudy sky cast a darkness upon the forest floor.

As we neared, I heard low guttural sounds. Above us, thick branches from the trees had been broken and lay crooked on the ground. Had something fallen from the sky? I slowed to a jog, and Yocheved did the same. My eyes narrowed into a game face, and my hand lingered near my sword. Whatever we were about to face, I was ready for it.

CHAPTER TWENTY NINE
OH GREAT ONE

A DOZEN DEMONS FEASTED on a green mound of flesh and scales, stained with crimson blood. They tore out the entrails of a dead dragon, trailing them out across the forest floor. The slain creature was a gruesome sight to see; the once magnificent wings of the dragon lay crossed at an odd, crooked angle. Its body was slumped over a group of fallen trees, and its snakelike yellow eyes lay open in death, covered by a milky sheen. Bile burned the back of my throat, and I swallowed back the urge to vomit. Melancholy rose in me like a wave, but I pushed aside my emotions before they got the best of me. The demons who busied themselves with eating the dead dragon were on all fours, like Hellhounds, but they lacked fur. Their gray skin was drawn tight against their skinny limbs, and fangs hung from the corners of their triangle mouths. The demons reminded me of small, carnivorous dinosaurs, and by the thin slits of their eyes, they looked like scouts. Demon scouts were sent by armies to spy on the perimeter of their enemy's base. Though scouts were simpleminded, a mind link connected the scouts to their leader, and through that mind link, information of landscapes and defenses were communicated. In their bloodlust, driven by the dead flesh of the green dragon, the demon scouts had ignored the baby swaddled in cloth that lay merely fifty feet away from them, nor had they noticed us approach.

Fenrir's hackles were raised, and a low growl settled in his throat.

I stared at the child, whose cries grew louder as the seconds went by. "Can you cast a protection spell around yourself and the babe?" I asked Yocheved.

She nodded. Her eyes flashed. "What will you do?"

"Kill them."

"They outnumber you," she pointed out.

"Yes, but they're mad with the scent of blood. They won't notice me until it's too late. Besides," I said with a cold smile, "how can they hope to defeat me? I am the Goddess of Death."

With that, I stalked toward the demons and unsheathed my sword. Yocheved rushed toward the child, and a blinding sphere of light surrounded her and the babe. *Her protection spell must be strong.*

My scimitar curved through the air, and I struck the demon closest to me. It squealed a warning cry, like a pig being slaughtered, as my sword cut through its neck, leaving the scout without a head. His companions swerved my way, now aware of the threat I posed. The demons pounced from the dragon's dead body and rushed toward me from all directions. Rage sharpened my focus. Demon scouts were agile and faster than most lower demons, but they were pitifully weak creatures. My sword cut through two of them at a time. My feet were forced to move quickly, and my movements were blurs. Fenrir struck out of nowhere. His jaws latched around the neck of a scout with a speed I hardly followed with my eyes. A set of claws raked across my left leg, and I stumbled back with a yell. Every time I put pressure on my leg, blood gushed from the wound. Two scouts jumped at my weakness, and I collapsed underneath their combined weight. The edge of my scimitar was the only thing keeping their fangs from snapping around my neck.

The light of Yocheved's protection spell flickered in the corner of my eye. Three demons threw themselves against the protective sphere. The magic wouldn't last much longer.

I gritted my teeth and forced the sharp edge of my scimitar through the scouts on top of me. Another set of claws ripped across my back, but determination numbed the pain. I swung my sword widely, cutting through demon after demon. Their crimson blood stained the ground and my clothes. A roar of rage left my lips and the remaining scouts that surrounded me flinched. There were three demons left, and the smallest of them turned tail to flee. Fenrir rushed after it, not allowing any room for escape. The remaining two were easy to overwhelm. I sprinted toward Yocheved, whose spell came tumbling down.

The demons that brought down the spell were quick to attack. Time moved as slow as honey as I wildly crashed toward the young girl and the babe she protected. A single thought rippled through my mind and fear of failure propelled me forward. I wasn't going to make it in time to save them.

Yocheved's hand lashed out, sending a wave of blinding light, and the demons were thrown from their feet. She cradled the child in her arms and ran, giving me enough time to reach the demons and slay them.

A desperate sort of relief calmed my racing heart. "Wait," I called after Yocheved, and she stopped running. "It is done."

The girl's shoulders sagged and her tight grip on the babe lessened. As she walked back toward me, the pain from my injuries resurfaced. My leg still throbbed, though it mostly healed. My back ached. I couldn't see how deep the claw marks were, but the tingling my skin felt was certainly a good sign. My wounds would soon heal.

"You're hurt," Yocheved said.

I shook my head. "Just a few scratches. I heal faster than most."

She paused, and her eyebrows pinched together.

A silent curse filled my head. Had I given myself away? Healing was a Guardian's power. But Yocheved was silent and gazed down at the babe, who stopped crying now that the danger was averted. She moved the cloth aside, revealing the infant's shoulder. An inky stain covered the infant's skin, like a tattoo that curled from the shoulder to the infant's fingertips.

"I know who this child belongs to," Yocheved said.

I nodded and strode toward the village. "Then we should return him."

"Not that way."

I stared at Yocheved. "Why not? Aren't we heading back to the village?"

She shook her head. "No. The babe isn't a Guardian child. We must venture deeper into the forest."

Her words left me more confused than before. I followed Yocheved as she walked further from the village. "Are we going far?"

"No. The village we're visiting, Kverst, is only a few minutes away."

"If the infant isn't a Guardian, what is he?" I asked. "And why does Kverst get a name, but your village is nameless?"

Yocheved shrugged. "Kverst isn't a Guardian village."

I threw up my hands. "Then what kind of village is it?"

The girl ignored my question and avoided meeting my eyes. She focused on her path straight ahead and held the babe tight to her chest. Her skinny arms already trembled from the child's weight.

"At least let me hold the infant. Before you drop him," I said.

"I won't drop him," she said.

"Your arms are shaking."

Yocheved stopped walking, and her lips set into a pout. "Fine, you can hold him."

I scooped the babe from her arms and held him close to me. We crossed a small stream and a fallen tree. While we walked, I grasped at the soul of the infant, hoping to see if his soul had answers to the questions Yocheved refused to answer. My eyes grew wide. The child's soul was vast, like an aura that perforated the air surrounding it. No human or Guardian soul was like this.

"We're here." Yocheved stopped by a tree.

I turned my head, searching in every direction for any sign of a village, but all I could see was the empty forest. "I don't see any village."

"They won't let us come any closer. A guard on border patrol should see us in the next minute or so. He'll take the babe to his family."

"Border patrol? In the middle of a forest in the ancient land? And who are they—the people you say won't let us come any closer?"

Yocheved didn't answer, but I wasn't going to drop the subject. "Tell me," I demanded. "What exactly have you gotten me into? This babe isn't human—that much I know. He isn't a Guardian either. So, what is he?"

"He is what I am," a new voice said.

I nearly jumped from my own skin. My gaze landed on the face of a man who appeared out of nowhere. His skin was dark, and he had a tattoo covering his shoulder and arm, like the babe. He was very large, towering over me by nearly an entire foot. His chest was broad, and his arms were as thick as my thighs. How did he sneak up on us? I should have heard him approach, but even as he moved closer toward us, his steps hardly made a sound. He was graceful in his movements.

"What are you?" I asked. My power leaped from the surface of my skin, and I touched the man's soul very lightly. I only ever felt one other creature with a soul like this. Realization struck me like a bolt of lightning. "You're a dragon!"

The man's dark eyes flickered with predatory interest. "And you are the Harbinger of Death. I felt you touch my soul."

I shivered under his intense stare. "*Goddess* of Death, but same difference I suppose. How are you a dragon when you are clearly a man?"

"Some dragons are able to shift fluidly to their human form," Yocheved finally explained. She bowed her head before the man. "My apologies for our intrusion. Will you hear what we have to say, oh great one?"

Oh great one? What kind of cheesy propaganda is this? Before I could open my mouth and make a smart remark, Yocheved dove into a story of how we'd come across a dead dragon's body and the babe in the woods. She recounted how I'd slain the demon scouts and saved the child. All the while, the dragon-shapeshifter listened with quiet contemplation. He betrayed not a single emotion. Once Yocheved finished her narrative he grumbled in approval.

"I owe you a great thanks, Reaper of Souls," the man-dragon said. "You saved one of our young today. For that we must repay you. May I see the child?"

I passed him the bundle of cloth and the babe that lay tucked away in it. He inspected the infant and nodded. "We will not forget what was done today." He turned to leave.

"Wait!" The command burst from my lips as an idea came to mind. "We could use your help. A demon army shall attack the Guardian village this coming dawn. If you wish to repay the debt you owe me, fight with us. We could use a dragon on our side." There was something about this shapeshifter male that gave him a dangerous edge. He was stronger than most creatures I encountered.

The man shook his head, and he bared his sharp teeth. "I can smell the blood of our kind on your hands. You killed one of us recently."

"No, I haven't killed—" I stopped myself. He was telling the truth. I had killed a dragon. "It was self-defense. But that dragon wasn't a shapeshifter."

"Neither am I. None of us are shapeshifters. We are all dragons. The strongest of our kind are at peace with their human form, and thus can appear as a man or a beast. I would advise you to correct your vocabulary." The dragon's nose twitched. "Be grateful that you are still alive. If your companion hadn't revealed your heroic deed today, I would have killed you."

I raised an eyebrow. "You can't kill me without a Soul Dagger."

"I appreciate you sharing that valuable information. Now I know."

I froze and the blood drained from my face, but the dragon simply smiled. "You have nothing to fear from me or my kind. When you saved the child, you more than paid back for the life you took. Our traditional law is a life for a life, but this child is special. Not many children are at peace with their human form at such a young age. I know this boy. He is destined to become the next king of our race. For saving the boy's life, we owe you one blessing. However, our rage is as fresh on our minds as the blood of our relative is fresh on your hands. Give us time for our rage to fade. Once it does, we will grant you one boon, Goddess of Death. Then, our debt will be repaid."

Before I could make another plea for the dragon's immediate help, the man and the babe disappeared deep into the forest.

Yocheved sighed. "We must turn back. Otherwise, the next patrol will catch us out here. If they smell the blood on your hands, but they don't know that you saved the life of one of their children..."

A coldness spread across my chest. These dragons frightened me more than I wished to reveal. I nodded. "Let's head back."

I followed Yocheved toward the village. Fenrir returned to us with the head of the demon scout that tried to escape earlier. He kept pace with us as we walked. My thoughts raged. Though the dragons refused to help us in the battle to come, to be granted a boon by them in the future was a valuable gift.

"What can you tell me about Kverst?" I asked.

"It's a small colony of dragons. One of the few that remain in the ancient land. No Guardian has ever seen the inside of the village. The dragons are a secretive bunch, and they are very protective of their kind." Yocheved sent me a meaningful look. "Let that be a warning to you, Primrose. Never—and I mean never—again kill another dragon. Or else you will have worse to fear than Lucifer and his siblings."

CHAPTER THIRTY
TROUBLE IN PARADISE

AZAZEL'S ARRIVAL WAS ANYTHING but quiet. His regiment approached the village from the east, unlike the demon army Satan and Abaddon summoned from the north, but I was sure any remaining demon scouts would pick up on my general's noisy appearance and report it to the demon twins. A bell tower rang, announcing Azazel's arrival at the village border. I told Kloe to inform the villagers that they didn't need to throw a celebration for my general's arrival as they had for Atlas and me. We were here for war, not a party.

The afternoon came to a weary close as the remaining light found a small clearing in the heavy clouds that filled the sky. Flocks of birds flew close to the ground, and rain was expected by nightfall.

Village children ran rampant while their parents watched them carefully, especially if they were in my presence. Now that I knew the Guardians' history with deities, the villagers' wariness made more sense.

When Yocheved and I returned, we spoke to Kloe about the demon scouts. Kloe invited me to a quick dinner to discuss defending the village soft spots, including the orphanage and religious centers. I meant to meet Atlas right after we finished sorting out the details, but Kloe insisted I finish my meal at a wooden table near where the bonfire was lit last night.

Before he found me, Azazel was in a meaningless argument with a Guardian who was minding his own business in the forest, checking the animal traps and patrolling the borders. The Guardian reluctantly brought him from the forest into the village after Azazel had demanded to speak with me at once.

The loud voice of my general interrupted my short meal with Kloe and Yocheved. "Ah, and this is where my darling queen rests before the chaos of war."

I put down the metal chalice from which I drank and dabbed a cloth to my pink lips. "Let me handle this," I said to Kloe and motioned for her to remain seated before she greeted Azazel. Guardians likely welcomed all deities with celebration and enthusiasm to avoid conflict, but I didn't want to give Kloe the impression that my general or any magical being, for that matter, merited special treatment.

I rose and turned away from the table to look my general in the eye. "You took your sweet time getting here."

Gray circles had formed below Azazel's eyes. His forehead was wrinkled, and his body was tired. Scars and fading bruises marred his skin, though I knew they would disappear within the next few hours. His armor and weapons were bunched up in a sack that hung off his back as if he'd packed everything last minute before hitting the road.

Behind him waited my regiment, not in full numbers. The reapers stood tall in my presence, though several were visibly wounded and doing their best not to collapse under exhaustion or pain. Apparently, they'd run into trouble on the way. Their faces were gray and expressionless, and cold eyes waited for further orders. Kaitlyn was among my reapers, instead of at their lead where she should have been. She shrank away and averted her eyes.

My reapers were accompanied by a dozen lower demons. The lower demons of this regiment were grotesque, animal-like creatures, and no two looked alike. Some walked on all fours, like Greed's Hellhounds. Others walked on two legs, while several possessed extra limbs such as another set of arms or legs. Two demons appeared humanlike, but their muscular bodies and gruff speech set them apart. They looked like Olympic athletes on decades of steroid treatment, and their voices sounded like sandpaper scratching against pavement. Lower demons without souls could never really be killed, but a severe injury could impair them for decades, centuries, or millennia if done properly. They were good soldiers, but once down, I couldn't count on them to make a miraculous comeback.

I noticed that a lower demon and over a dozen reapers were missing. The two assassins of this regiment were out of sight, but I sensed their presence. The assassins were usually the progeny of modern-day deities. Godlings and demigods were powerful enough to outmaneuver supernatural threats but not politically significant enough to have a presence among their parents or grandparents in the High Court. More often than not, High Court members kept their progeny as far away from them as possible to avoid possible usurpations or transitions of power. Some deities, in their bloody climb to power, ordered the execution of their offspring, and in an attempt to flee death, these children of Gods and Goddesses volunteered to fight for an army of the Underworld. All volunteers in my Four Armies of Hell were provided absolute protection from outside threats, which gave High Court members another reason to dislike me.

My general puffed his chest. "I traveled thirty miles with these soldiers into that cursed forest in Belgium. We trekked through dangerous terrain to reach that wretched bridge to the Glass, only to find ourselves outnumbered by thousands of vampyres living in the fog!"

Ah, so the vampyres were not an isolated threat to the Argentina Glass. They also appeared in Belgium.

Azazel continued his rant. "We were forced to cross the bridge in pairs, and once we crossed the Glass, we traveled yet another dozen miles before we lost a lower demon to those blasted animal traps! Not to mention the flower beds that put at least five reapers into a goddamn eternal coma! And at the end of it, here you sit at a cup of tea with your haughty little friends, reprimanding *me*—"

"I wasn't reprimanding you."

He narrowed his eyes at me. "Your first words were an insult."

I gave a dismissive wave of my hand. "I was being sarcastic. Sarcasm, ever heard of it? If you waited, I was about to tell you that you'd gotten the regiment here faster than I ever could. It took me two days to travel to this village on my own, and you traveled with a small army in a quarter of that time. That's an impressive feat."

Azazel deflated like a balloon and gaped at me. Praise from the Goddess of Death was rare—at least it used to be. I smiled crookedly and patted his shoulder before passing him to look at the weary remains of my regiment. "Soldiers, you've proven yourself today. Rest. For when dawn rises, the demon twins shall arrive with their armies, and I need you at your best. But you"—I nodded toward Kaitlyn, and her eyes widened—"you will wait to speak with me before you go anywhere." I turned to address Kloe. "If I may ask a favor of you—"

"You needn't even ask," the village chief said. "Your soldiers shall be attended to, housed, and fed, while our medics treat the wounded." She analyzed the eleven lower demons. "What do you wish to do with them?"

I understood her caution. Lower demons were known to be mindless, vicious, and animal-like creatures. Over the years I spent in the Underworld, I captured and trained all kinds of lower demons. While they indeed behaved like animals, their intelligence was far from nonexistent. As the vicious wolf had been tamed into a well-behaved, lovable guard dog, the same could be done with lower demons if treated with the appropriate time and care. Still, it would be unfair to force villagers to house foreign demons.

"They'll remain outside," I decided. "I only ask you to provide some raw meat and water so that they remain strong."

"I don't understand," Azazel interrupted.

"I wasn't expecting you to." I looked out at the growing number of villagers listening in. Instead of continuing with preparations, they dropped their work to come eavesdrop on our conversation. "Kloe?" The village chief rose from her seat and approached me. "Would you give my general and me a brief moment to speak alone?" I asked and tilted my head toward the growing crowd.

Kloe nodded and shuffled the villagers over to complete their preparations for battle. I pulled my general to the side.

"Are you finally going to tell me what this is all about?" Azazel asked with a scowl. "I don't recognize the immediate threat. If the demon twins are on their way, you need only leave before their army arrives. Alone and on foot, they won't be able to track you easily."

I nodded. "I know." That was what Atlas would have done if I hadn't gotten in his way. The smart move was to leave, but it was also a heartless move, especially after all the Guardians had done to welcome us.

Azazel's eyes looked as if they were about to pop out of his skull. "Really? You know that, and yet you dragged us all out here? For what? Your foolish pride?"

"No."

"No?" he exclaimed and then clenched his jaw.

"No," I repeated and resisted the urge to grit my teeth. "Will you let me explain the situation to you, or will you let your questions and insults get in the way?"

My general bit his tongue, though his eyes conveyed the hate and anger he felt.

"Are you familiar with Natkont's spell?" I asked.

A crease formed between his eyebrows. "The tracking spell?"

"Yes. It led me to the ancient land while tracking Lucifer's Soul Dagger. Lord Atlas tailed me, and we met up over on this side of the Glass. We discovered this village of Guardians—"

"Guardians? What the hell are Guardians?"

I sighed. Azazel rolled his eyes and made a sealing gesture over his mouth.

"They're not human is all you need to know," I said. "They welcomed us, housed and fed us, and this morning one of their messengers discovered that the demon twins were summoning an army to attack this village for harboring us."

"I still don't understand. Why are you here when you could leave? Why are the rest of us here in the first place?"

My hand gripped the hilt of my scimitar. "Because we are here to fight for these villagers."

My general was not a dull man. He pondered my words for a few seconds. There were times I said things to test his reaction. He had to wonder, was this one of those times? Seeing that my iron resolve didn't allow any deceit or doubt to leak through my composure, he concluded I was dead serious.

Azazel's hand shot out and curled around my throat. "You think me a fool, Lady Titan?" He spat out my title and tightened his grip. "To bring you an army to fight a war for peasants? I am a proud man, my queen. As general of one of the Four Armies of Hell, I was promised the glory of war in the Underworld. War fought for a regal cause or conquest, not some twisted form of philanthropy to help you sleep easier at night!"

My hands wrapped around his arm, and I dug my nails into his flesh. "You have a choice." My voice was calm, unaffected by his attack. His grip was irritating and nothing more. "Remove your hand, or you'll remain without one."

He shook me by my neck like he would a rag doll, and I drew blood from his arm. Red drops, one by one, trickled to the ground. "Tick tock." I mocked with wide eyes. "Five seconds left to decide, Azazel. Your pride or your sword arm." I checked an imaginary watch on my wrist. "Two seconds left."

Azazel let go of my neck, and I stepped back. My throat was sore, and I was sure my skin sported a new bruise. We watched one another closely. Azazel spat at my feet and set his lips into a hard line of disgust. "One day, I won't need to follow your orders anymore, my lady. Pray you'll be long gone by that day because when I get my hands on you—"

I broke out a dagger and lunged for his neck. My movements were faster than he could follow. My arm wrapped around his elbow, and

I held the dagger against his neck. He struggled but stopped when the blade bit into the sensitive skin under his chin and drew blood.

"I've been threatened too many times, Azazel," I whispered into his ear. "Lucifer, Atlas, Satan, Destiny. Even you." I trailed my blade over his skin. "There's only so much my fragile little mind can take. Do me a favor. Follow your orders and leave. Generals are uncharacteristically difficult to replace, and I'd hate to spill your blood on this sacred land."

I released him, and he stumbled forward. His fingers touched his wet throat, and he rubbed the blood between his thumb and index finger. "This time, I'll fight with you, Lady Primrose. I don't make any promises for the next time."

He stalked away.

My cheeks were warm. Antagonizing Azazel was a mistake, but I had enough of him. No matter how hard a general might be to replace, the decision would be worth the time.

The villagers already cleared away from the vicinity, thanks to Kloe. Yocheved remained, munching on some pastries. "That didn't go well," she said.

I watched the back of my retreating general. "No, it didn't. Do you know if Atlas is near?"

Yocheved stood from the wooden table we had eaten at and nodded. "He was helping the villagers fortify the northern border earlier. Fenrir is with him."

I frowned, noticing the absence of the wolf. If he'd been here, Azazel's aggression wouldn't have gone unnoticed. "Why?"

The young girl shrugged and smiled oddly. "Fenrir doesn't like the God of Ice. There must be something about him." She began to walk away. "I'll take you to him."

"Wait one moment," I said, and Yocheved stopped in her tracks.

Kaitlyn waited for me to approach her. Like Cain, she was different from other reapers, in the sense that she was more human and animated than the others. Her strawberry blond hair was pulled into a short braid. She didn't look like much at only five feet in height.

I remember how strange it felt to yell at her the first time. She was such a small thing, and with her pursed pink lips and big doe eyes, she looked like a waif. I knew better now than to lower my voice or let her get off easy. Kaitlyn was a manipulative, power-hungry reaper, which was why I placed her on duty to guard Lucifer's cell.

Guarding Lucifer's cage was no position any reaper coveted, mostly because it was the most uneventful position to hold and held no growth opportunity whatsoever. Kaitlyn, who craved positions of immense power, was absolutely livid when she first heard of her appointment as the head guard to Lucifer. The head guard of Lucifer's cage supervised Hell's prison from the outside, with a watchful eye to make sure nothing went wrong and sound the alarm if something did. But Kaitlyn never sounded the alarm.

I stopped in front of Kaitlyn and crossed my arms.

"It wasn't my fault—"

"No excuses," I snapped. "Give me a damn good explanation. Don't you shift the blame."

She grimaced and looked away. "I didn't think he would escape."

I laughed bitterly. "Obviously."

"I never wanted that job!" Kaitlyn cried and threw her hands up in frustration. "Watching Lucifer's cage, every reaper knows it's the worst position you can be assigned."

"Were you watching the prison?" I demanded with an exasperated sigh. "Were you even there?"

"No," she said through gritted teeth. "I wasn't."

"Damn it, Kaitlyn."

"If I were there, I wouldn't be here today," she said without a hint of regret. "Do you know what happened to the reapers who guarded the prison? Torn to shreds. Broken pieces washed away in Phlegethon's fiery rage. Gone for millennia, maybe forever."

I squeezed my eyes shut and pinched my nose. "I can't deal with this now," I said under my breath and opened my eyes. "When you get back to the Underworld, you will wait for me at the palace. I'll decide on your punishment once I return. Is that clear?"

She nodded, and a trace of fear creased her forehead.

Before another insult could leave my lips, I bit my tongue and followed Yocheved, who led me toward the north end of the village. Atlas was, surprisingly enough, helping the villagers, as Yocheved had said. He gave out directions like a true CEO. Every Guardian was up to their knees in dirt, shoveling out small pieces of a growing trench. Fenrir was poised nearby, watching Atlas, as if waiting for him to make a mistake. The wolf noticed my arrival, and his ears twitched.

The greatest shock was seeing Atlas himself, who rolled up his sleeves and worked alongside the Guardians. His clothes were marred with mud and grass stains. He wiped his brow, leaving a dark mark on his forehead, and lifted his chin to the sky. "A few more hours. It's the best we can do with the time we have."

The villagers mumbled tiredly. Their movements were sluggish, and they were covered in mud and sweat. They'd been working for some time. Embarrassment touched the tip of my nose, and I stepped forward. "There's no need." They all turned their heads toward me. "Please, go and rest," I said. "Save your strength. Let me deal with the trenches."

Atlas's cool eyes landed on me. While a few villagers took their leave, others hesitated. The God of Ice nodded toward them. "Go. Don't worry yourselves about finishing the trenches. You'll be more useful to the battle if you're well rested."

His approval was the sign most villagers needed to drop their shovels and walk back to their homes. A touch of jealousy poisoned my mind. These Guardians sought Atlas's approval when completing their tasks, and instead of being here to help them, I spent my time pursuing my own agenda. Uncovering a past, that may or may not matter in the grand scheme of things.

Still, the warmth of another emotion grew in my chest. To see Atlas connect with these people meant he cared about others, no matter how hard he tried to hide it. He was nothing like his brother.

The sky's daunting clouds held the burden of the unreleased rains. How I hoped the water would not fall from the gray ceiling. I sent a silent prayer to the ancient land. If the trenches were flooded, all the hard work that had been started would be for nothing.

I inhaled deeply and let my magic resurface, bringing the dead with it. Dozens of bodies surfaced from the ground and picked up the shovels the villagers put down. They began to dig.

Atlas tightened his grip on his shovel and continued hacking at the soil beneath him. Fenrir stood from his position and pranced to my side. He nudged his head against my palm, and I traced a line from his forehead to his neck with my finger. Yocheved came by my side.

"I can wait with Fenrir here," she suggested.

I took her hand and gently squeezed it in thanks. The young girl knew what I needed, sometimes before I did. I warily approached the Grimm Brother, taking small yet determined steps toward where he worked. I stopped by the edge of the trench.

"You're upset," I said.

"I'm not." He didn't look up to me when he spoke. Instead, he remained focused on his work.

I crouched down and slid into the trench with a soft thud. The mud stuck to the back of my clothes. "I'm not sure why you're upset."

Atlas stopped digging. He set the shovel aside and wiped his dirty hands against his trousers. "What is it you want, Lady Primrose?"

"I'm not sure," I answered honestly.

He raised an eyebrow, and I bit my lip. An awkward silence resumed. I disliked the feeling that I couldn't be honest with him. We'd been through so much together, though we both hated admitting it.

Atlas finally shook his head. "You really are clueless."

I stared at him expectantly, waiting for an explanation.

He scoffed and pointed a finger to my chest. "You, Primrose, are the most unreliable being in this universe. You insist we stay in this village to protect it, only to prance around with the village chief, partake in meaningless tours, and enjoy feasts. I didn't want to stay and fight the demon twins, but once it was agreed upon, I scouted out the area, I put these villagers to use, and even put myself to work. All the while, what have you done?"

My cheeks flooded with red hot shame. He was right. I should have helped more. After all, these Guardians were my people. "You're right to be confused. Confusion doesn't justify anger."

Atlas put his hands in his hair, aggravated. He began to pace.

"What I should have done and what I have been doing are two completely different tales," I said. "I am at fault for my behavior. But I'm here now."

The God of Ice stopped pacing. He refocused his sharp attention to my face.

"I'm here now," I repeated. "I'm here to help the people who live here, and I'm here for you as well."

"Do you expect me to believe that?" he demanded and picked up the shovel again.

"Yes!"

He coughed out a laugh that sounded as stunned as it did furious. He dug his shovel into the dirt. "Why?"

"Because I"—I stumbled over my words—"I... I can't explain it. I made a mistake not helping you today. I'm sorry."

Atlas threw his shovel to the side. "You're sorry?"

"I really am." My voice broke, and I swallowed the lump at the back of my throat. "We can't afford to lose tomorrow. We just can't. Too many people would die—innocent people who've done nothing to deserve bloodshed. Their deaths would be my fault, for Abaddon and Satan are hunting me in their rage. I can't live with that guilt, not while knowing that I'm powerful enough to save these villagers!"

His glare softened in response to my words. A crow's caw startled us both. The birds that once flew low now soared high in the sky. The heavy clouds from before dispersed, and the threat of imminent rain was lifted. Perhaps the ancient land heard my silent prayer.

"I need to show you something," Atlas said, taking me by surprise. He placed his foot in a small ledge in the dirt and hauled himself out of the trench. "You'll want to see this."

CHAPTER THIRTY ONE
THERE'S NO CALM BEFORE THE STORM

ATLAS LED ME NORTH, past the village border and into the forest as nightfall came to pass. We traveled a few miles out from the village, not daring to venture too far for fear of happening upon the demon army while they assembled. The moon's light replaced the sun and covered the forest in a dim shadow. The ground was dry, as rain hadn't fallen, though a slight dampness lingered in the air.

The forest was unusually quiet tonight. Perhaps the ancient land recognized the coming of war. The wind did not move the branches of the trees, and the wildlife was either fast asleep or hiding silently in the warm nooks and crannies of their homes.

"You have blood on your shirt," Atlas said. "I wanted to mention it earlier, but my anger got the best of me."

"We encountered demon scouts in the forest earlier."

"Did you kill them?"

I rolled my eyes. "What do you take me for—an idiot? Obviously, I killed them."

Atlas stopped suddenly, and I waited in his shadow. He held out his hand to the side expectantly, and I simply stared at it. Noticing my absence, he craned his neck toward me. "We need to climb this tree; let me give you a hand."

"This one?" I pointed toward the tree to his left, and he nodded.

I gave him a weird high five and ducked under his arm. I placed my foot on a rough piece of bark, and my hands found sturdy ledges. The climb up the tree reminded me of Yocheved's little game, except this fir tree was taller, and the easier-to-grasp branches were much further from the ground.

Atlas followed behind me. "You could always accept my help."

I huffed and moved my leg to a sturdy branch. "I'll accept your help when I need it."

I put more weight on the branch, and it snapped. A steady arm stopped my descent, and a curse left my lips. My leg swung up to a better position, and I regained my footing. Atlas's touch lingered, and a tingling sensation spurred through my stomach.

"You're welcome," he said.

I glared back at him. "You jinxed me right then. That was a good branch, too. Keep the bad luck to yourself."

"Where would the fun be in that?"

An easygoing smirk touched my lips. "Fair point." I hoisted myself up with greater success this time. "For the record, I would've thanked you."

"Right," he drawled. "When exactly, tomorrow?"

"Jerk."

Atlas laughed. We stopped our ascent before the branches could no longer support our weight, and we sat on two separate limbs near the same level.

"Now we wait." Atlas leaned against the bark, making himself comfortable.

I straddled the tree limb and fidgeted to find a good position. "What exactly are we waiting for?"

"You'll see."

I hummed in acceptance and rubbed my hands against my bare arms. My jacket was with Yocheved. Fenrir hadn't followed us into the woods, so I knew he'd take good care of the girl. From this height, we could easily look behind us to see the village and the forest beyond.

"I never foresaw us working together," Atlas mused.

His comment took me by surprise. "Me neither," I admitted. "I honestly thought you were a rich airhead with no decency or respect the moment I met you."

"And I thought you were a manipulative wench who purposefully set the Devil free to screw us all."

I couldn't help but laugh, and Atlas smiled. "Yeah." I moved a strand of hair behind my ear. "I guess we were both right and wrong. You definitely are a rich bum with an ego big enough to rival your brother's, and I'm unquestionably manipulative and willing to screw you all over."

"I'm charmed to see the way you think of me."

I grinned. "You are a decent man, Atlas. You respect those who respect you. That's why we got off on the wrong foot."

"How so?"

"I didn't want to respect you. I work alone, and there you were, accusing me of doing things I'd never do and insisting to come with me to make sure I got the job done. You rubbed me the wrong way because you assumed the worst of me, and I assumed the worst of you."

Atlas pondered my comment. "I suppose you're right." The silence of the night resumed for a moment. "But I know you would have never released the Devil."

I watched him curiously. "How do you know that?"

"Even if you didn't hate the Devil—and I do believe you hate him in your own way—Lucifer is a murderer. Regardless of what you wish to admit, you care for people. His release would destroy many innocent lives."

"Lives that you don't think matter," I pointed out.

"No," he admitted. "But I used to think your life didn't matter either. I used to think the lives of these villagers didn't matter. And look at what you've done." His eyes softened. "You've made me care. You've challenged me to..." He struggled to find the words. "To see beyond myself. And you've done so without directly telling me to or getting me to agree with you. I care because you care, and if I didn't, that would make a monster." He paused. "It's hard to be a monster around you."

His words touched my heart. But then a twisted thought arose in my mind; what if of the two of us, I was the monster? Atlas proved himself to be a better man today. He pushed aside his pride to help the Guardians protect their home. I had the opportunity to do the same today, but instead I spent my time pestering Kloe and Yocheved for answers.

"Do you think," I asked, "that I am weaker or stronger than when you first met me? You once said caring is a weakness."

Atlas leaned toward me. "Caring is a weakness. But when I first met you, you weren't strong. Isolated, yes. Mean as Hell, of course. Tough, you still are. Ever since you've come to this village, you've grown more comfortable in your own skin. You started believing in yourself, and that is the greatest strength anyone can have."

I didn't trust what he said about my growing strength, but my breath caught, and a flush rose to my cheeks. I thought Atlas noticed, but then he held on to the tree and stood on his branch. "Stand up."

I mirrored his motions. He pointed toward the north, and I squinted my eyes. A small flash of green light touched the sky. "Is that..."

"The Glass?" Another flash of light went off. "Yes. Every time someone uses the Glass, that light goes off. I noticed it last night."

I sent him a strange look, and he shrugged. "I don't trust people. I spent the night searching the forest and testing our surroundings. The demon twins are using the northern Glass frequently."

"They haven't finished summoning their army."

"No, they haven't. However, the northern Glass isn't my primary concern. Look east." He gestured toward our right. "Your general arrived using the eastern Glass earlier today. Are you expecting any additional regiments to arrive tonight?"

I frowned. "No."

"Ah. Then we might have a problem. The eastern Glass is being used as we speak."

My eyes landed on the sky east of the village to confirm the green flash of light that indicated the portal was being used. "The twins wouldn't waste their time traveling to Belgium if they were already using the Glass in Argentina."

"I agree," Atlas said. "Yet someone is regularly using the Glass."

"That doesn't make sense," I argued. "Who can be coming in if not the demon twins? Humans don't know of this place, nor could they make it past the vampyres. Whoever is coming in, they'd have to be..."

I let my sentence trail off. They'd have to be supernatural. To get past the vampyres, they were likely deities or traveling in large groups.

"The question is," Atlas continued, "why are they coming here?"

I met his gaze and tilted my head. "Shall we find out?"

† † † † † † †

We headed back to the village, sprinting as fast as we could. Though there was a reasonable distance between the eastern Glass and the village, if the portal was used earlier today, whoever crossed the Glass might have already infiltrated the village.

Crossing over the village border, we encountered two volunteers on patrol. The village was silent tonight. Most Guardians were resting for the battle tomorrow, though there were a few still walking the streets.

"Should we split up?" Atlas suggested. "We'll find our interloper quicker that way."

I nodded. "Let me know if you find anything."

"I will."

"Atlas." He turned from his path to hear what I had to say. "If they threaten anyone, kill them."

The God of Ice smiled wickedly. "I already planned to."

We went our separate ways. I left my scimitar in its sheath, not wanting to frighten any villagers as I patrolled the streets, though

I did unhook a curved dagger from my belt and held it close to my hips. The house lights from the cabins were mostly extinguished. Torches lit up the darkened streets. A group of young men and women bounded past me, the scent of alcohol thick on their lips.

I jogged past two fields, the animals were asleep, and no shadow seemed out of place. I wondered where Fenrir was. Hopefully, Yocheved retreated to her home by this time. Midnight approached, and dawn would arrive in close to four hours. Sunrise was always early in the ancient land. The demon twins would strike just before dawn, to catch us at our weakest point of the day.

Homes were assembled in rows from east to west. Most houses were one-story tall and distant from each other. Apart from the forest, the land was flat. There was no real high point to view all the activity throughout the village. There remained no easy way to spot trouble, so I zigzagged through the streets and headed south, toward the center of the city.

A pit grew steadily in my stomach. I headed back toward the northern border, worried I missed something. Nearly halfway through my round, I heard a loud shout from the east side of the village. I changed my course and headed in the direction of the noise with a quick sprint. A subsequent string of curses and a vicious growl followed the cry I previously heard.

A small body ran into me, and I stumbled back. My hands felt the familiar wool of the jacket I'd given Yocheved, and I hugged the whimpering figure tightly.

"Shh." I hushed Yocheved's muffled cries and placed my lips against her hair. "What are you doing out so late?" I demanded; my voice sounded hysterical.

"I was picking some flowers and fell asleep." Her voice was filled with tears. Out for flowers? Before a battle? Part of me wanted to shake some sense into her, but this wasn't the time.

"Where are they?" The words felt cold coming off my tongue.

She turned her head to look at the darkness behind her. "There."

"Stay here."

I ran in the direction she had come from and listened to the voices in the dark.

A man's voice shattered the silence. "Stay away, you wretched beast!"

Fenrir's growl raged through the night, and I applauded the wolf for his courage and violence.

"Leave him be," a commanding voice said. "The girl escaped. He got what he wanted."

A female voice cried. "Please—"

"Shut up, wench!"

"Let her go!" A loud, slapping noise filled the air.

I stopped before turning the corner and kept my back pressed to the wall. There were nine individuals beyond the corner, villagers and hostiles included. I smiled and tightened my grip on the dagger I held. I scraped the blade against the wall, eliciting a menacing screech, and turned the corner to face the five intruders.

"Hello, folks," I drawled in an American southern accent. I leaned drunkenly on the wall to my side. "How are y'all doing today?"

There were four men and a woman, though I only recognized one of the men. He was a member of the High Court. If I recalled correctly, he was the God of Messengers, Hermes. He wore casual jeans and a buttoned-down white shirt, and his platinum hair was shoulder-length. He was two inches shorter than me, though he stood taller than the men around him.

A glint of recognition tainted Hermes's hazel eyes, and he stepped back in my presence. "You."

His supernatural friends hesitated at the fear in his voice. They weren't deities. I assumed they were the progeny of Gods or Goddesses. None except Hermes required a Soul Dagger to kill. One of the other men, a short and dainty man, bore a bloody bite mark to his arm. Fenrir paced near him, though upon noticing my presence, he backed away toward me while the hairs on his back stood up threateningly. The other two men and woman held a group of villagers at knifepoint. The villager who had been slapped cowered on the floor. He'd been defending one of the women from what it sounded like. I recognized the group of young villagers to be the one I'd passed earlier.

The point of my knife lifted off of the stone wall, and I twirled the blade in my left hand. "Yes. It's me."

Hermes shifted uncomfortably under my harsh gaze. He was surprised to see me here, and the hostility that came off me in waves surely gave him reason to fear my presence.

"How did you cross the border?" I asked. The border patrols should have sounded a warning.

Hermes shrugged, though his eyes remained cautious. "I killed the man who dared try to stop me."

"Do you come here often?"

"Only to entertain ourselves. As I'm sure you know, Lady Primrose, human security and surveillance has blossomed over recent decades. We can hardly get away with killing or playing with humans as we once were able to. These Guardians are worthy substitutes."

Fenrir growled so loudly my ears hurt, but I echoed his anger. I gritted my teeth. "Fenrir, come here, love." Fenrir's side brushed against my leg, and I knelt to whisper in his ears. "Well done, my friend. I'll take it from here. Lead Yocheved back to her home."

The wolf understood though he glanced back toward me when he left. I nodded in encouragement. I could handle this on my own.

"The wolf is yours!" the bitten man spat out.

"Quiet, Cerus." Hermes regained his posture and political manners. "You stand in the presence of the Goddess of Death."

"Yeah, I know who this freak is."

A dry laugh pulled my lips up into a bitter smile. I'd enjoy killing him first.

"My apologies, Lady Primrose," Hermes said. "Cerus forgets his manners."

I smiled and strolled toward the group. "You don't need to apologize to me."

Hermes bowed his head. "Please, my lady. Let us finish our business here and leave you to your own devices. We dare not waste your time."

"I understand." I paused. "Only, you're not wasting my time. You see, I have a little business of my own, and it concerns you."

My dagger flew forward, and Cerus fell to his knees. Blood sputtered from his severed neck, while his head rolled away from the rest of his body. I sprinted forward, my heart beating loud in my ears. The woman dropped her hostage and swerved toward me. I dodged. The chill of her blade caressed my arm. My elbow rammed into her neck, and I swept her feet from under her with my heel. She fell on her back with a grunt, and I stuck her own short sword into her chest.

My ears pricked with the yell from one of the remaining men. I rose from my kneeling position with the short sword in hand and stepped back. The man squealed when the blade met his flesh. The damp feeling of warm blood seeped through my clothing.

The pommel of a blade hit my temple, and a flash of light appeared in my eyes. A ringing in my ears set in, and I stumbled and fell. The sight of steel in the corner of my eye warned me of another attack. I clapped my hands on the flat of Hermes's sword, catching his swing in midair, and thrust it forward. The hilt hit Hermes in the nose. He yelped and released the blade before retreating with a hiss. The sword clattered to the ground. My hands dripped with my own blood, but the cuts only stung a little.

The final remaining man besides Hermes held a knife up to a young woman's neck. "Don't come any closer. I swear, I'll kill—"

With a twirl of my fingers for effect, his soul left his body. He slumped forward, and the villager barely sidestepped in time to avoid being crushed under the full weight of her aggressor. I trained my eyes on Hermes, who held his bloody nose and glared at me.

"You dare attack me," he raged.

I ignored him, noticing there was one remaining soul I hadn't reaped during the fight. The woman twitched on the floor, bleeding out. I ended her then. The rest had already died the moment I went for the lethal move. Four souls now paid an unwelcoming visit to Hell.

Hermes was left. His platinum hair was stained with the blood of his comrades and his own sweat. His shirt was splattered with red. I kicked his sword aside and stalked toward him. "I can't end your life without your Soul Dagger. So let me make an oath to you, God of Messengers."

He moved to backhand me, and I swatted his hand aside. I picked him up by the collar of his shirt and thrust him back against one of the homes with a powerful yell. He staggered back to his feet, fear evident in his wide eyes.

"I swear to you that not long from now, I will find your Soul Dagger, and I will find you. Once I do, I won't kill you." I smiled, poison thick in my voice. "At least not at first. Death will only find you when you beg for it. And you will beg."

Hermes flinched.

I stepped back. "Now go. I've had enough of you."

He didn't need any more encouragement before scurrying away. As he left, I called out to him, "God of Messengers, send a message from me to those you know." Hermes stopped warily to listen. I spread my arms toward the chaos of battle. "You've seen what I can do. Warn your friends that if they come here, they shall meet the same fate."

Hearing my final words, Hermes left. I tracked his soul, making sure it truly left the village without returning.

I sent a glance to the men and women who had been threatened. Though shaken, the Guardians seemed to be fine. They'd suffered no significant injuries on account of their healing powers.

"Thank you," one of the young men said before leaving with the group.

I dropped my head in acknowledgment.

The night's activity came to a tired end. I went to work, cleaning up the bodies. After rummaging through a nearby field, I came across a flint and threw it against the pavement, where it broke into many pieces. I picked the two largest pieces and revisited the bloody scene. Striking the two stones together yielded a small spark, and the spark caught to one of the dead men's shirts. A little flame came to life and ate at flesh and clothes. With every inch it consumed, the flame grew. I set the other bodies atop of the burning man, and a bonfire came to life.

Having nothing else to do, I paced around the village. The hour was past midnight. A set of bells rang in alarm once the body of the Guardian Hermes killed was discovered. I met up with the new volunteers on patrol and explained what happened.

Atlas and I met a half hour later. We shared a knowing smile. He'd seen the bonfire. He disclosed that he would retire to bed and asked jokingly if I wanted to join him. I respectfully declined. We departed on good terms.

However, I didn't feel I could sleep, and it had nothing to do with my fear of nightmares or the daunting war dawn would bring. A dread clung to me, and I felt sick to the stomach. Sick because this village had been under attack by deities like Hermes for many years. A village I never knew existed before I stumbled upon it. A village of people like me.

The greeting Atlas and I received was a refined response to years of poor treatment from supernatural creatures to garner new visitors' sympathies. Still, I didn't understand why the attacks happened. Yocheved would know.

I walked in silence. Fenrir found his way back by my side not long after.

"Will you take me to her?" I asked.

The wolf circled around, walking back the direction he came from. I followed him. The scent of smoke strengthened as we passed the pile of burning bodies. Smoldering flesh left a disgusting taste in the back of my throat. We stopped at a cabin near the eastern border of the village. I knocked on the door. A minute later, a stern, middle-aged woman opened. Her forehead was marred with deep wrinkles, though she relaxed upon recognizing Fenrir beside me.

She pointed toward a set of doors. "Yocheved is in the second room on your right."

I thanked her and walked down the hall. The floor creaked beneath me. I was still upset that Yocheved had been caught out *picking flowers* before a battle and had some sharp words for her ready on my tongue. The door of Yocheved's bedroom was suddenly thrown open, and two small hands pulled me in. The door shut loudly behind me. Her chest trembled against me as she held me tightly.

The scolding words on my lips dissolved, and I crouched down to look into her red, tear-stained eyes. "It's okay," I said. "I'm here." I rubbed her back and her tears flowed freely. "Is it common?" I asked, referring to the supernatural visitors from earlier. "I need to know."

She sniffed and nodded. Her face was flushed, and I used my thumb to wipe her wet cheeks.

"How long has this been happening?"

Yocheved inhaled sharply and tried to steady her breathing. "Since anyone can remember. Even before I was born. We don't really know why it happens. Kloe says it's punishment for the Guardians betraying the Gods, but that doesn't really make sense. The Guardians from back then are dead. They have been for a long time."

I gritted my teeth to keep in my anger. "What do you they do when they come here?"

"They hurt people. I think... I think it amuses them. Sometimes they kill people."

How did I not know of this? Atlas hadn't known of the attacks either, and his brother was King of the High Court! Yet Hermes knew. A little, nobody deity and his demigod friends knew about Guardians while the Grimm Brothers were clueless.

"That's why," Yocheved said with a heavy voice, "you need to help us. We're all stuck here in the ancient land, and we can't cross any of the Glasses."

"How can I help you?" I demanded. "I don't know how to reverse this curse, spell... whatever is keeping you trapped here!"

She closed her eyes, and her forehead creased. "If anyone can help us, it's you. You're the only Guardian who has ever left the ancient land."

I stilled and slowly rose from my crouch to stand. "How did you—"

"Hecate knew." She knelt to the floor and began rummaging under her bed. "She came to me in a dream and told me to give you—yes! Here it is!"

Yocheved bumped her head on the bottom of her bed pulling out a simple wooden box. She rubbed the back of her head and grimaced.

She held the box up to me. The red wood was cut rectangularly, large enough to fit two hoop earrings. The box was smooth to the touch, and despite its warm appearance, unnaturally cold. My fingers pried the lid open, and the stench of bitter metal filled the air. My nose twitched in distaste. A smooth, iron pendant in the shape of a heart lay in the center. A metallic gray chain circled the main piece. I grabbed the chain and let the necklace dangle from my hand.

"I've seen this before," I muttered.

"You have," she said, not surprised.

My eyes widened, and a flash of Hecate's neck lit up in my mind. This was Hecate's necklace from my dream of her, except it wasn't red in color anymore. It was a dull, gray color now.

I shared a look with Yocheved. "Do you know what this is for?"

She shook her head. "No. But you do."

A soft sigh left my chest, and I bit my lip. I returned the wooden box to Yocheved and pocketed the necklace—a puzzle to be solved soon but not now. "You shouldn't have been so careless," I admonished. "Out picking flowers before a battle? You know better!"

"Yes." Yocheved averted her gaze. "But I didn't want to return home just yet."

"The woman who greeted me at the door—she's not your mother, is she?"

"No. She did take me in, though. To care for me. I never knew my parents," she said. "I'm a burden to her. It's better if I come home late and leave early. That way, I make life easier for her."

"I don't think you're right about that," I said. My eyes roamed around her room. She had a cozy little bed and desk near the window. "But it's still not safe for a child to stay here. Your home is on the border and not well positioned, I'm afraid. You know the guest cabin I was housed in?"

Yocheved nodded.

"Good. Fenrir is waiting outside. Take him with you to the cabin during the upcoming battle, and don't leave until I call you out. Stay put, and don't open the door for anyone else. Do you understand me?"

"Fenrir is supposed to protect *you*," she protested, but I'd hear nothing of it.

"Promise me you'll do this." I touched her shoulder when she didn't say anything. "I can't be worried about you while I'm fighting an army of demons."

She set her lips in a hard line but nodded. We left the cabin together once Yocheved spoke to her caretaker about what I said. She and Fenrir went one way, and I went another.

An hour later, I returned to the bonfire of dead flesh to see the flames, which were not as large as before. 'Twas the nature of fire. It fed and grew until there was nothing left to feed on. Then it died. As was human nature.

Darkness still clung to the sky, but I knew the time was near. Lanterns and candles were lit in several homes. My reapers sensed my anticipation, and soon my regiment would assemble. I headed toward the northern border.

My thoughts flitted back to the dying flames and burned intruders. I considered sweeping the ashes. Leaving them on the street wouldn't be proper. However, the ashes were a good warning to outsiders. Besides, when was the last time I did something the proper way?

CHAPTER THIRTY TWO
THE GOAT AND THE SNAKE

ARMOR WAS HEAVY. A nuisance, more than a means of protection, because it slowed me down and made my movements cumbersome. When Azazel came to the border at 3:30 in the morning, he brought a lighter ensemble and dropped it at my feet. He said, "Wear it or don't. I don't give a crap." He was still sour from of our last conversation.

I didn't want to wear the armor, but if we were as outnumbered as I thought we were, I would need it. I shrugged on the vest he'd brought. The material was strong enough to stop a small knife but not the full impact of a sword. The vest wasn't as heavy as traditional armor, so my movements wouldn't be as restricted.

Dawn was nearing. My regiment grouped together in less than half an hour. The demons paced around, aching for the battle, while my reapers stood at the front line, waiting for my command. The assassins were among the growing crowds of villagers preparing. The villagers had a limited supply of armor and weapons, though their protection magic would certainly help. The Guardians that would fight stood behind my reapers and demons. Satan and Abaddon's army would have to get through my regiment before they hurt a hair on their heads.

Atlas waited nearby, his eyes trained on the dark horizon. Dawn was near.

Azazel unsheathed his sword. "It's almost time."

A breath of wind blew through our ranks, and the stillness of the night came to an end. I blinked. "Give the order then."

"Attention!" The soldiers straightened. The villagers rushed to finish their preparations. "You there!" Azazel began walking around and giving orders. "The first thirty of you! Yes, you! Occupy the trench! The next fifty, spread out across that area. Hey! Did I say you can move?"

A horn sounded off in warning from the forest. "Prepare yourselves," I shouted back to the Guardians. "They're coming."

Azazel sent eighty men, women, and demons in front of the trench and resumed his position at the head of the regiment. Torches were set ablaze to light the way. The few minutes before a battle were always nerve-wracking, but I didn't feel uncomfortable in this environment. I was no stranger to war or the clashing of armies. The same couldn't be said for the villagers. They were unaccustomed to war. The Guardians looked awkward holding swords, axes, and spears. Their faces held any emotion from stark fear to wary determination. They were unevenly spread apart, some lingering close together as if their togetherness gave them comfort. My reapers stood tall and confident, relaxed with their weapons and armor. They knew war.

I looked at Atlas and held out my hand. "Are you with me?"

He smiled and clasped my hand tightly. "To the end."

We both jogged over and slid into the trench. The reapers made way for us to pass. We hauled ourselves out of the trench and walked through the front of my regiment to stand by my general.

"I brought you one army," Azazel said. "Is yours ready?"

I reached out to the Underworld. Protection magic ran through me like a burst of energy, fueling my grasp over the dead. "Oh, we're ready."

A roar burst from the forest. As supernatural beings, our vision in the dark was as sharp as during the day. From the trees came hideous demons, twisted and deformed, with sharp fangs and talons. Their skin was a disgusting maroon, and thick and muscular scars ran across their bodies. Their red eyes were like flashlights in the dark.

I closed my eyes. I inhaled, then exhaled. And inhaled again. Timing was everything.

"Draw your weapons!" Azazel commanded.

The sound of swords being drawn filled the air. Atlas did the same beside me. I spread my arms calmly.

"Any time now, Primrose," the God of Ice muttered under his breath.

My eyes opened. I grappled with the souls beneath me and summoned dozens at a time. Bodies formed in front of us and ran toward the approaching demons.

Azazel opened his mouth to give the order to charge, but I touched his shoulder. "Wait. I have a surprise for them."

His eyes flared, but he remained still. My heart pounded erratically in my chest.

I pulled some strings, summoning a powerful soul from beneath. The red dragon that I killed in Las Vegas shot from the depths of the ground. Red scales flashed through the night sky as the beast landed in front of us.

The villagers and reapers behind me balked, but I held up my hand to calm them. The dragon's snakelike eyes waited for my command.

"Demons aren't inflammable," I told Azazel. "I'll burn as much of their army as I can before we send our soldiers forward. This way I'll also draw Abaddon out from wherever he may be hiding."

My general nodded and spoke several commands to the reapers surrounding us. I approached the dragon, watching the demon army tear my undead zombies apart out of the corner of my eye. I eyed a dip in the dragon's back, directly behind his neck but in front of his wings. While he knelt to the ground, I climbed up the beast's side and settled myself on his back. His sharp scales dug into my thighs painfully despite my thick pants.

I smiled at Azazel and Atlas. The dragon spread its long wings and propelled us up into the night air. The cold wind blew my hair from my face, leaving my skin numb and cold. My arms hugged the dragon's neck tightly as we gained altitude. Below us, the demon army was making progress. The dead bodies I summoned faltered under the attack, even while I summoned more to replace them.

"There!" I pointed toward the demons who were closest to reaching our first line of defense. "Let's light them up," I told the dragon.

I shifted my weight to avoid falling as my dragon dove toward the ground. A blast of flame lit up the night, scorching anything in its path. The heat from the fire made my cheeks red and puffy, but my lips molded into a grin when I looked back to see the damage. We sailed back toward the army, readying ourselves for another attack. The darkness around us disappeared with the fire. The demons on the ground wailed as they burned. From atop my dragon, the thrill of battle excited and filled me with confidence. We were an unstoppable team, my dragon and me. Again and again, we directed the flames to eat away row after row of demons. Still, they kept coming. How many had the twins summoned?

The demons closest to the forest howled triumphantly. They made room between them for a large snake to slither through—Abaddon. The moon's waning light reflected off his scales.

Abaddon quickly outpaced his demon army. At my urging, we flew down toward the serpent. My dragon's mouth opened to release another bout of flames. The snake ended its aggressive assault to shapeshift into another creature. Its green and yellow scales remained, though four limbs sprouted from its body, and two leather wings grew from its back. Abaddon, now in the form of a dragon, swerved away in time to avoid our attack. We circled back to face him. In a blur of scales, Abaddon's claws raked across the side of my dragon, who roared in rage. We spun around and blew fire to put some distance between us. I clutched to the dragon's neck tightly. My arms and legs were scraped raw from the sharp scales.

The dragon Abaddon had shifted into was smaller than the beast I summoned. He was faster than us and nearly as strong. He flew around us with such speed he appeared like a hummingbird at a distance. His next attack hit us like a freight train and threw me from my dragon's back. The wind whipped around me as I fell. My stomach dropped as the fiery ground approached me. I sent my dragon another command. A set of talons wrapped around my waist like a band of iron and jerked me up away from the ground. I heaved, ready to throw up my dinner from the pain in my stomach. The dragon carried me past the fires of burning demons back to my regiment. He dropped me close to the ground before flexing his back muscles and meeting Abaddon again head-to-head. I hit the dirt with a grunt.

Footsteps approached as I lifted my head to see several reapers and the God of Ice.

"That," Atlas said as he crouched down beside me, "was incredibly stupid." His cold eyes were filled with worry.

He helped me up to my feet and I brushed off the dirt from my clothes. "It was effective," I said with a grin. Blood stained my clothes from where the dragon's scales cut into my arms and inner thighs. The pain ebbed away while my quick healing abilities went to work.

"I hate to ruin your glorious mood, but there are more of them," Azazel said and gestured toward the demons who approached. "Shall I give the order to charge?"

"Yes."

My general appeared satisfied with my response. He yelled out to the soldiers behind him and then surged forward with a battle cry. My reapers and lower demons charged. They rushed past me, meeting the demon army with full force. Atlas also sprinted forward. He sent spears of ice flying toward the demon creatures and mercilessly cut them down with his sword.

"Steady!" I yelled to those behind me. "Hold the line!"

The first demon broke through the reapers ahead of me. Its stench of dead carcasses made my tongue bitter with vengeance. I drew my sword and lunged forward. The curved blade cut through the demon's muscular body, above the waistline. Blood as dark as night splattered across my chest. I locked my wrist and stabbed at the next creature's gut. It screeched and lashed out with its arms. I ducked and shoved the sword so that it completely passed through the body. The demon went limp, and I stepped back. My next swing was wild, barely nicking another demon's side, but the creature went sprawling into the trenches where it was finished off. I spun, swung, stabbed, repeated, and another ten demons were down. The bodies piled around me. My leg snapped at an incoming creature, and it flew back, bumping into another.

A roar of pain brought my eyes to the sky. Abaddon sunk his jaws into the neck of my dragon. The short distraction was enough for a demon to attack. My back hit the ground in a lightning-fast movement, and my blade found itself between the fangs of a monster. With a cry, I forced the blade through its head, and blood drained itself over my face. My arms shoved the heavy body away, and I wiped the dark goo from my forehead. I fumbled to my feet and beheaded another beast. I found a rhythm, like a dance beat to move to. My sword swung instinctually, forming patterns of light that glinted against its cool metal. My thoughts retreated to a deep corner in my mind, somewhere they couldn't bother me. Nothing else existed but the metal of my blade and the demons I struck down. Another horrendous noise came again from the sky, and my focus faltered. The red dragon I summoned, now relieved of his head, started free-falling through the air and toward the villagers' side of the trench.

"Run!" I cried at the top of my lungs and motioned for the villagers to scatter. They retreated toward the cabins or ran to the safety of the trench. When the dragon hit the ground, the earth trembled with its heavy weight. Two demons launched themselves into the trench while my attention was distracted, and I turned back to the demon army.

My grip on the sword's pommel faltered. What looked like hundreds upon hundreds of demons continued to approach. Fallen reapers littered the ground in front of me. The Guardians behind me quaked with fear and their shoulders already slumped with defeat. Desperation stabbed at me as though a thorn bush grew inside my body, threatening to tear me up from the inside. We couldn't lose!

Not after everything. Atlas and I would make it out alive either way, but these villagers would die. Unless...

A deafening shriek made my skin crawl. Abaddon dove in my direction, and his maw lit up with light. Screams filled the air.

"Holy—" I sprinted toward the trench and slid in as a wall of fire passed above my head. My scimitar fell away from me.

My ankle was sprained upon impact, and I curled up into a ball as the flames lapped into the trench. My nails dug into the grainy dirt ground. The heat singed my skin and elicited a hiss from my lips, but the static energy of my protection magic leaped into use, and a cool layer spread across my skin. The screams of burning people tore at my mind. Their Guardian magic would heal them, but memories of pain were difficult to erase. My ankle prickled, already healing, and I stood.

I knew what to do, what it would take to save the lives of the Guardians. If I engaged Satan and Abaddon in battle directly and defeated them, the demon army would falter. Lower demons without a leader to command them were worthless. They'd retreat!

My chest burned from the smoke, and I stifled an ugly cough. The hair on the back of my neck stood up. Before I could turn around, a shadow shoved me, and I collapsed forward. I stumbled to my feet and frantically searched for my displaced weapon. A cloaked man with no face stood before me. A crooked scythe materialized in his hands. Though I couldn't see his lips, I could have sworn the creature smiled.

"Destiny sends her regards," he said. His voice was like chalk against a blackboard.

The assassin lunged and brought the scythe down toward me as a reaper barreled into his side. I spotted my scimitar, not far from me. My hand grasped the hilt quickly, and I ran to my reaper's side. I swung the sword, and it passed through the assassin as if he were made of nothing but air. His cloak fell to the ground, along with what looked like black dust.

My heart beat loud. I never expected the assassins to follow me into the ancient land, not with the magic that protected the Glass.

The reaper who had intervened bowed low. "My lady."

I gripped his arm in thanks and looked into his murky eyes. "What is your name?"

"Owen."

"Owen? As in Cain's friend Owen?" I asked. Ah! The reaper Cain sent to check on Elinore's father—the reaper Cain trusted.

He nodded. "Cain assigned me to this regiment to watch over Kaitlyn after she let Lucifer escape." That sounded like something Cain would do.

"I owe you my life, Owen." I smiled shakily. "Remind me to give you a promotion."

"Primrose," a sweet voice called from above. "Come out and play, would you?"

Owen moved as if to leave the trench, but I held him back by his arm. "Protect the villagers. I'll deal with her."

His eyes narrowed, and he looked ready to argue. But he pursed his lips and did as he was told.

I climbed out from the trench. The steaming ground singed my hands though the flames near the trench were mostly gone. The soil was charred, dark like the demon blood. Burned corpses of reapers and summoned dead bodies littered the floor. The villagers had also suffered, but their protection spells held strong.

"There you are," the honey-coated voice said.

My furious gaze landed on Abaddon's sister. Her hair was pulled up into a bun, and she held a long katana by her side. She wore a breastplate and forearm and shin guards. Her lips were pulled thin to reveal a deadly smile. Satan's cheekbones were sharp and defined, and she wore dark paint over them.

I lifted my chin to the sky and noticed Abaddon circling down. The demon army strayed away from the three of us. This final battle was not to be disturbed.

"I don't understand," I said and leveled my gaze with Satan. "All the time and effort spent to wage this war—for what? To kill me?" I gestured toward the violence surrounding us. "How many lives will be lost here?"

The demoness shook her head and scoffed with a wry smile. "I would normally not glance your way, Queen of Thorns. Nor would I attack a simple village. But you are to kill my brother, is that not so? And this simple village is harboring a murderer."

"What murderer?"

"You," Satan hissed. "They're harboring you!"

"And you would defend Lucifer?" I asked incredulously. "He's a monster."

"Aren't we all? And so you know, he's a monster who is stupidly in love with you, the woman who wants to kill him." She pointed her sword toward me, and Abaddon landed behind her with a growl, slowly shifting into a man. "Blood is blood," Satan continued, "and I cannot allow you to take him away from us."

Abaddon walked up to stand beside his sister. He was a head taller than her. His eyes were a unique opal color though they were hidden behind his narrowed eyelids. His eyebrows were pointed toward his strong nose, and his large lips were parted to reveal his sharp teeth.

"Let's end this." Abaddon shared a determined look with this sister. He bore no weapon, though I doubted he needed one.

I readied myself and widened my stance. Abaddon circled around me, though I knew he would let his sister strike first.

Satan twirled her katana, and the blade cut toward me. I flicked my wrist and blocked her assault. She grinned and attacked again. I parried and riposted, and she defended my counter. My feet began to move quicker, and Satan moved just as quickly. Over the years she must have trained to become stronger and faster. I barged in close to her and forced her sword out of reach with mine. My knee flew into her stomach, and she grunted and shoved me back with her other arm. Her next attack was unbridled, and her blade nicked my shoulder. I blocked an attack to the head and kicked her chest.

A hand pulled at my hair, and I cried out as I was thrown back. I hit the ground hard. My scimitar fell at a distance away from me. Abaddon kicked my ribs, and I heaved, rolling back onto my feet.

"Is something the matter, Primrose?" Abaddon asked as I staggered back. "You do notice it, don't you? The poison running through your veins." His smile was purely malicious. "Surely, you've begun to wonder why my sister nearly defeated you in Miami, or why simple demon scouts moved at a faster speed than you?"

His fist clipped me under the chin, and I flew back from the impact. His words rattled me. I hadn't considered the possibility that I was physically weaker than before Abaddon had poisoned me. I believed my enemies had gotten stronger, but now Abaddon claimed the opposite. The fact that I hadn't noticed my weakness startled me more than anything else.

"The poison I infected you with when we last fought is called King's Bane," he said while he stalked toward me. "Perhaps my brother tried to educate you on what it could do, but not even Lucifer knows this poison as well as I do. It will slow you down and weaken you, make you easy prey. Your physical wound might have healed, but the infection in your blood... that will last."

I forced myself back to my feet. The new bruises that plagued my body throbbed sorely.

Abaddon's eyes narrowed. "I could remove it. In my snake form, I could separate the poison from your blood—but see, why would I do that? Instead, I'll let the King's Bane fester in your blood, weakening you for years to come. It may take a decade before the poison completely leaves your system. I don't need a full decade to kill you."

He sent a fist my way, and I blocked his blow with my elbow. I punched his gut and cuffed him over his head.

"You'll find killing me to be more difficult than you expected," I said. I threw my shoulder into his side and ducked below his sister's sword. Satan growled.

I put up my guards and spat at my fists. "Are you ready?"

She roared and swung widely. My hand grasped her sword arm. I ducked underneath it, loosened her footing, and flipped her over my back. Her sword landed on the ground. I kicked it away.

Abaddon sent a kick to my side. I caught his leg, almost falling over. He twisted, and I let go. My feet were swept from underneath me, and Satan pinned me to the ground. Her fist broke my cheek, and I headbutted her in return. She paused, dazed, and I sent her over my head, sprawling behind me.

I kicked out my feet and flipped up. Abaddon prepared to hit me, but I was done with this sorry excuse for a brawl. Poison or no poison, I was still the Goddess of Death. I ran and tackled him to the ground, sending us both into the trenches. The trench walls scraped my skin. Dirt entered my mouth, and I coughed it away.

Two large hands wrapped around my throat and banged my head against the ground. Stars flashed in front of my eyes. "Sleepy night nighttime for you, you royal pain." Abaddon tightened his grip, and I gasped for air.

My hands went to his and began squeezing with the hopes of breaking bone. The shapeshifter changed the shape of his flesh and remained unaffected. I summoned the dead around me to beat at the demon, but his changes saved him from any harmful wound.

"You're going to stay asleep for a very long time until we beat reason into our brother's mind and find your Soul Dagger," he said. "By any chance, do you have it on you?"

I kicked him in the crotch, and he loosened his grip. Air flooded into my chest with a gasp. I slipped out of Abaddon's grasp only to be backhanded. My cheek stung.

"Low blow, Primrose." He scowled and pulled me toward him by the neck of my shirt.

I removed a small knife from my belt to pierce his arm, and he let me go with a howl of pain.

"All's fair in love and war," I said and stumbled back. My body felt black and blue, and exhaustion pressed heavily against my eyelids. I forced my focus on Abaddon. One on one, I could end this.

A sickening cry filled the air. Abaddon shot out of the trench, and I froze. My blood turned to ice while my stomach dropped. I scrambled to my feet and climbed out of the trench to see Abaddon transform back into a fire-breathing dragon and send a blast of flames toward Atlas. The Grimm Brother formed a sphere of ice around him to block the onslaught, but he retreated as soon as it became apparent the flames were too much. Satan lay on the ground where Atlas had once stood, a fist-sized wound in her chest. The grief-stricken dragon ended his assault against Atlas and lifted his sister's frail body with his talons. His large wings flapped twice, and he was airborne, flying away with Satan. Only a Soul Dagger would kill her, but I'd seen the gaping hole in her chest. Satan wouldn't be waking up for the next few years. Abaddon's roar of pain sent the demon army running back the way they came, but Azazel had been prepared for that. What remained of my regiment had regrouped to flank the demons. My general gave a signal and a group of Guardians who bore bows and arrows lit the tips of their arrows with fire before shooting them toward the fleeing demons.

Sensing the chaos among the demon ranks and the trap Azazel laid, I retrieved my sword and summoned another wave of dead bodies. Without Satan or Abaddon to lead the army, we easily cut through the lower demons, one after the other. The Guardians gained confidence and joined the offense. A wave of pity grew in me while I slaughtered the remaining demons. Their numbers dwindled, and like cornered animals, they searched for any means of escape. Azazel finished off the last of the demons, and cheers rose from the Guardians and my worn-out regiment.

The sun broke past the horizon to shine its pretty rays into my eyes. Atlas walked toward me, a smile on his face. We'd won.

We'd actually won. The Guardian village was no longer threatened by impending doom. We saved countless lives by our actions today.

I straightened my slumped shoulders and forced my lips into a beaming smile. Yes, we won the battle. Then why did I feel like we lost the war?

CHAPTER THIRTY THREE
A PHOENIX'S OATH

AZAZEL APPROACHED ME SOON after the first shouts of victory went up. He was covered from head to toe in demon blood and guts, though he didn't mind the gore. His sword, now sheathed, hung from his waist. A demon had scratched Azazel's leg though I was sure the beast paid dearly for its mistake.

"It's over now," Azazel said. "Your entire regiment deserves to be sent home."

He was right. Reapers were soulless, but like lower demons, a severe wound could put them out of business for a long time. My general would clean up the mess we'd made and take everyone home. I pried off my combat boot and picked up a portal key from inside. "These keys don't grow on trees."

Azazel took it and sent me a wry smile. "You know they do."

"Lucky for you."

He pocketed the portal key and walked away.

"Hey," I called out. My general turned, and I put down my combat boot, shrugging my foot back in. My hand found the heart necklace from my pocket, and I showed it to him. "This is supposed to be used in some kind of spell. How do you think it works?"

"How am I to know?" he asked with a scowl, though he took the necklace and fiddled with it in his hands. Azazel narrowed his eyes and pinched his fingers over some part of the heart. It suddenly opened, parting in half to reveal a sharp pin at its center. "It's a deranged brooch, I guess?" He handed it back to me.

I held the necklace carefully by the chain. "All right, then. You're dismissed. But don't forget the key only works—"

"On the other side of the Glass, after we cross the ancient bridge and leave the magical forest in Belgium."

I thought for a moment. "When you say it like that, this whole situation sounds ridiculous."

"That's because it is." Azazel shook his head. "See you around, Lady Titan." He walked away.

"And general," I called out again. He only turned his head this time. "Thank you."

He nodded and then went to work.

I watched the movement of reapers and villagers. Joy over the success of the battle permeated the air, but cleanup was a messy and thought-provoking process. For the first time, the soldiers counted the dead bodies and decided if the victory was worth it.

"Your general doesn't like you," Atlas said from behind me.

A dull ache formed at my temples. "Is it that obvious?"

The God of Ice came by my side, and I faced him. His clothes were marred with blood, though he'd taken precautions to assure none of it got on his skin. His forehead was wrinkled, and his eyes were half-closed. "We need to leave, Primrose."

"We will." I placed my hand on his shoulder in reassurance. "Give me a few minutes." I held the necklace up by its chain. "I need to return this to someone."

"It's not yours?"

"No." I shook my head and smiled. "I'll be back before you know it."

I jogged back into the village. The Guardians who noticed me bowed to pay their respect. After fighting alongside someone, it was hard to hate them. My heart warmed, and for the first time, I felt genuinely welcome among a people.

The cabin that housed me upon my arrival was in the center of the village. Fenrir sat outside, guarding the door. He yipped happily when he saw me and ran toward me. I knelt down to embrace him and held his warm fur close to me.

"Thank you, old friend. I owe you an unpayable debt." I held the wolf's head in my hands to look into his eyes. "I must go soon," I told him.

His brown eyes saddened, and he butted his head against my cheek. "I know." My voice trembled. "I wish I didn't have to. Don't worry about me." I held up the metal necklace. "I have a plan."

I knocked on the door to the wooden cabin and called Yocheved's name. She flew out like a chaotic whirlwind and embraced me. "You're okay!"

"I always will be." I laughed and held her close to me. "We won the battle. It's all over."

"It is?"

"Yes. And guess what?"

"What?" she asked.

I dangled the heart necklace she'd given me to show it to her. "I needed some help to figure this puzzle out, but I now know what to do."

Her blue eyes watched me with admiration. Did she realize I admired her just as much? "What does the necklace do?"

In my dream of Hecate, the locket was red, not the gray metallic color that it was now. I placed my finger on the sharp pin inside the locket and let the droplets of my blood fall into the metal heart. The small prick was harmless but important. My blood filled the heart until it could no more, and I closed the metal case. The heart now was crimson, and I clasped the necklace around Yocheved's neck.

"Wait," she said and touched the metal. "Isn't this necklace for you?"

I shook my head and crouched down to her eye level. "Maybe it used to be, but I don't need it. Not anymore. The Guardians may be trapped here, but I'm not just a Guardian. I'm a Goddess, too.

Leaving the ancient land for me won't be a problem. Besides, I need you to use the locket."

Yocheved recoiled and inhaled sharply. "What do you mean?"

I put my hand over my heart. "Something's going to happen. I feel it in here." I tapped my chest. "I know you feel it, too." I led her hand over her own heart. Yocheved's eyes widened. "And when it does," I continued, "you will know. I need you to go to the human world and find me after it happens. Can you promise me that you'll do that?"

Yocheved nodded solemnly. "I promise. But how will I—"

"Take Fenrir with you." I inclined my head toward the loyal wolf. "He's not bound to this land anymore, not since I returned. Trust in the necklace. Wear it at all times. As long as it is red with my blood, it will protect and guide you. No curse or spell can stop its power." My fingers lingered over the metal heart. "Blood is powerful."

"Yes, it is," she agreed. Tears touched the corners of her eyes. "Just... please don't forget us." Yocheved gestured toward the nearby homes. "Don't forget this place. We all need to be freed, not just me. You're the only one who can deliver us from the cage we live in. The Guardians are meant to protect humans. We belong in the human world as much as everyone else."

"I could never forget you." I touched her cheek. "I promise I will never forget you or the Guardians. I will free everyone here." I stood to my full height. "There's something I need to resolve before I do."

Her chin trembled, but she nodded. "I'll be ready."

"I know you will."

I walked back to Fenrir. "We shall see each other soon, old friend. Guard her. It was my oath to Hecate a long time ago." And an oath must be kept. No matter when it was made.

The wolf bowed his head. I sent Yocheved one last smile and waved goodbye. Her dark hair flew wildly in the wind, and the sun made her pale skin appear lively. Her electric eyes echoed my resolve. We would meet again.

† † † † † † †

I walked back toward the battlefield. A large group of villagers gathered together to celebrate. Kloe was with them. She pulled me aside to thank me. The village chief named me a hero, a savior, and more in front of the large crowd. I shied away from the attention. Kloe insisted I stay and celebrate, but no matter how much I wanted to revel in our victory, I had a job to do.

"Thank you for your hospitality," I said and backed away from the food, music, and colorful festivities. "But I need to leave."

The elderly woman sighed, picked up her staff, and put her wrinkled hand on my shoulder. "If you must, do what you have to do, Lady Primrose. But remember, you are one of us. You will always be welcome among our people."

Her words warmed my heart. I knew she meant them. I placed my hand over hers in thanks.

I then left but not before stopping to admit a truth. "I lied, Kloe."

The village chief inclined her head in interest.

A genuine smile graced my lips. "I lied when I said I don't know who I am. Back when we toured the village borders. I know exactly who I am. A part of me always knew."

Kloe didn't show any signs of surprise. She simply blinked and shifted her attention to the villagers and celebration. I think she knew all along as well.

And with that, our time together came to an end. Azazel was close to finishing up on the battlefield. Atlas stood in the middle of the carnage and watched the sky carefully. Something about his gaze was off, so I followed his line of sight.

A small dot of fire on the blue sky approached us. I sprinted toward the God of Ice. "What is that?"

A mighty squawk followed my question, and a bird of fire dove toward us and dropped a rolled-up piece of parchment to the ground. We ducked to avoid the flames that followed close behind. The orange and yellow fire swirled around the creature's wings and head, making it difficult to define its shape or size.

"A Phoenix," Atlas uttered in awe. "We were wrong."

"Lucifer's letter. It wasn't a metaphor." I picked up the unburnt scroll and unrolled it. The paper crackled when moved. "It says—"

"The time has come." Atlas read from the parchment. "Follow the Phoenix."

The bird squawked again and soared above the village, toward the forest south of the border. It looked over its shoulder to see whether or not we followed. It stalled and waited.

"You said you were with me to the end." I shared a glance with the Grimm Brother. "Did you mean it?"

Atlas nodded.

"Good. Then let's follow that stupid bird."

CHAPTER THIRTY FOUR
THE CANYON OF DOOM

THE PHOENIX FLEW ABOVE the trees. Any lower and the flames would set the woods on fire. The bird had a distinctive respect for the ancient land, like most creatures that lived here. Magic ran through the soil, the air, the water, and every living being. To disrespect the land was to disrespect magic, and magic had an uncanny reputation of getting even.

Even so far up above us, the flames of the Phoenix could not be missed. The creature made sure to stay within our sight and circled back around us to ensure we followed closely.

A bitter taste ran down my throat when I thought about Satan. Before and during the battle, I had been so angry with her and Abaddon. But if I had the chance to end their lives, to deliver the killing blow, would I have been able to? Were they so wrong to defend their brother? I hated to admit it, but their actions were justified. Lucifer's death was a necessary evil but killing the demon twins for trying to save the one they loved was unjust.

Atlas broke the silence. "You seem deep in thought." As the noon sun rose, the heat on our backs increased. The trees around us thinned, and the ground became rockier.

I kicked at a small stone and stepped over a broken tree limb. "I was thinking about how to kill him." Atlas knew I referred to Lucifer.

"Do you think he has his dagger on him?"

"I'm certain he does." I glared up at the sun, not happy with its scorching rays. "The direction we've been traveling in is the same direction his Soul Dagger has been pulling me. He wouldn't trust anyone else with it. Especially since he knows about my familiarity with Natkont's tracking spell."

We transitioned into a comfortable silence. A few miles later, the trees disappeared completely, revealing a rocky path. Without the cover of shade, the sun ate at our skin, tougher than before. Atlas brought a comfortable chill to the environment. The Phoenix flew lower now, unafraid of lighting anything on fire. The flames surrounding it lashed out freely.

The rocky path ended suddenly and gave way to an immense canyon. Mother Nature had taken her hunting knife and carved a crooked crevice in the earth's surface. Jagged stones stuck out from the cliffs. The bottom of the canyon lay a mile underneath us. Unlike the Grand Canyon of the human world, there was no river at the bottom. Only a dry, stone-filled death lay below.

The Phoenix dove into the maze of rocks and flew down near the bottom. It slipped away in a tiny hole marked with scarlet blood. That was the extent of Lucifer's guidance.

I crouched down and bit the side of my cheek. "I didn't bring equipment to scale a mile-long canyon."

Atlas stepped closer to the edge. "Neither did I." He flicked his wrist, and a path of ice crystallized to life toward the canyon floor. The rocks were covered with a zigzag staircase made of crisp ice.

"Wow. Impressive." I nodded and pointed toward the deadly sun in the sky. "I think you forgot about that monster."

He shrugged. "I'll make new layers of ice if I need to. Don't slip and fall in the meantime."

"Oh great." I stood to my feet. "I hadn't thought of that."

"If you want me to go first, just say so."

My legs moved toward the cliff before Atlas finished his statement. His chuckle followed me. The staircase was naturally slippery, but my combat boots gripped the ice well.

Though Atlas joked about slipping, he hovered closely. A warning touch here, a word of caution there, his worrying became irritating after a few minutes, though his intentions were good-hearted. My chest swelled and a soft smile graced my lips. Had I truly melted the heart of the God of Ice?

"I only know what your brother said about your history with Lucifer."

I placed my hand on the rock wall beside me, maneuvering past a tight corner. I wasn't sure if Atlas's comment warranted a response, so I remained silent.

"I know you hate him," he continued, intrigue tainting his previously monotone voice, "but something doesn't add up."

I sighed and leaned against the side of the cliff, finding a small relief of shade. My skin was sticky with sweat, and my eyes watered from the sun's harsh gaze. I closed my eyes and held the base of my nose. "Ask what you want to ask, Atlas. Beating around the bush won't help me answer your question."

Atlas stepped into the cool shade. His proximity dropped the temperature, and my head felt less heavy. "He wanted to make you his queen."

"I already am a queen," I noted and pulled my hair tie out.

"Yes, but an alliance with him would have grown your kingdom, your power, and ultimately gained you the blind loyalty of the Demon King, who would jump at every opportunity to please you. He might have been a murderer, but no doubt, he would have changed for you."

"See, that's the thing." I sat down on a boulder and rubbed the back of my neck. "Besides the fact that blind loyalty is wrong for so many reasons..." Atlas rolled his eyes, but I went on. "I don't want him to change for me. Change is meant to make you better, but you need to want to change for it to work that way. If he tried changing for me, the first few months, it might have worked. But then, his bloodlust would grow and his resolve would break because, at heart, he never wanted to change in the first place." I looked Atlas in the eye. "He wants me, along with my title and power, without having to change. Do you know the story of how we met?"

Atlas shook his head. "No."

"Well then, sit down, God of Ice. This is a complex tale, but I'll shorten it for your ears."

Atlas didn't sit, but he leaned against the rock wall beside me.

I recalled the memories from long ago. "I heard of Lucifer's fierce battle capabilities from my advisors. Azazel was my first general, and he vouched for the Devil, claiming he'd never seen power or strength that held a light to the Demon King. Lucifer used to hunt down and train demons, creating an army powerful enough to destroy the world if he wanted to."

"Where is that army now?"

"After he was imprisoned, the demons disbanded. Lower demons without an authority figure will disperse and go their separate ways. There's no such thing as a demon army without a leader." A black scorpion scuttled out from under the boulder I sat on. I tensed until it crawled away. "Lucifer had created this army of lower demons long before I looked his way, earning his title as the Demon King," I continued. "Before I went to speak to him about a position in my army, he came to my palace in the Underworld and demanded ownership over a piece of land in Hell—the darkest and harshest portion, which yielded the greatest number of demons per year."

Atlas crossed his arms. "And you refused."

"On the contrary, I admired his bravery and honesty." I smiled, reminiscing. "Nobody had come to *demand* anything of me, and never so boldly either. I gave him the land on the condition that he became a general in my army. He accepted this offer, though since there was no need for immediate war or military restructuring, his duties were little to none at the time." I leaned against the wall of rock behind me. "Lucifer focused on building his kingdom in Hell, and I didn't think much of him for a time. But war doesn't stay dead for long. One day, a demon by the name of Lilith was summoned by a sorcerer, Nazar."

"Nazar used to be a member of the High Court," Atlas said. He ran a hand through his hair. "I saw him there once or twice."

I sometimes forgot that Atlas and his brother had not always been permanent members of the High Court. When they were first born, Erin and Atlas were known for their powers as the Grimm Brothers—creator and enforcer of stories, respectfully. These positions granted them partial access to the High Court, as insignificant political members. That was, until the brothers went out and killed the previous God of Fire and Goddess of Ice.

"Yes, Nazar was a member of the High Court," I said. "At least until we became aware of his favorite pastime."

"Which was?"

"Murdering children, feeding on their hearts, and sacrificing whatever was left to demons. Are you aware of how demons are made?"

"Either Hell creates them, or they are summoned through blood sacrifices."

I raised an eyebrow, impressed with Atlas's knowledge on the subject. "In simple terms, yes. The Underworld has a mind of its own, as does Hell. The land can bring life to its own creatures. Demons created by Hell are often lower demons. But very rarely, the land creates powerful demons such as Lucifer and his siblings. Time and energy are devoted to the creation of these mighty creatures, and they have strong minds, bodies, and souls. Since these demons are so powerful, the land creates altars for their souls. The seven Princes of Hell, as they are often called, were smart enough to carve out their Soul Daggers before anyone could use their daggers against them.

"Back to Nazar, murdering children is an especially heinous crime, and in return, a powerful demoness, Lilith, was summoned. As demons come from Hell, which is inherently my domain, the High Court expected me to deal with the situation. Lilith, since summoned by a sorcerer, did not have a Soul Dagger herself. Instead, her soul was tied to Nazar's soul. Nazar, of course, had a Soul Dagger of his own. Between the sorcerer and his demon pet stood an army of followers and lower demons that Nazar summoned over the years. I called Lucifer into battle for the first time.

"Azazel is a good general... but nobody can live up to Lucifer's standards. Lucifer cut through Nazar's army with unparalleled skill and aggression. He brought his own army of demons into battle with him. I fought by his side and grew a fond respect toward him. I used Natkont's spell to track Nazar's dagger, and Lucifer offered his Soul Dagger for the tracking spell."

Atlas flinched in surprise. His reaction reminded me of his refusal to contribute his own Soul Dagger to the spell. In all fairness, Atlas and I had very little shared history. Lucifer was my general, and for me to use his Soul Dagger maliciously would be a crime against nature. To use Atlas's Soul Dagger against him would be considered a political maneuver by most.

"Nazar's Soul Dagger was with him," I said. In times of war, most deities kept their Soul Daggers with them. "When the time came, Lucifer fought Lilith, and I fought Nazar. Nazar's spells tore through my army of the dead, but he wasn't much of a fighter in hand-to-hand combat. However, he placed a spell on his Soul Dagger, one that helped him evade death. I thought I killed him when I plunged the dagger through his heart. I was wrong."

Atlas's eyebrows shot up. He opened his mouth to say something, but no words came out.

I grinned. "Yes, death isn't as certain as you might expect. The partnership between Lucifer and me grew through the length of the war, but my trust in him was solidified when he tracked down Nazar, five years later. Nazar lost all his memories with the spell he used, so Lucifer killed him with ease and brought me his head. I think..." I paused to ponder my next words. "I think we were good friends at that point. But as all beginnings have an end, my friendship with Lucifer also came to an end. Nearly a decade later, he came to my throne with an army and asked for my hand in marriage. I didn't agree nor refuse up front, but my lack of immediate response threw him into a rage." A sense of weariness swept over me, and my shoulders sagged.

"He killed many innocent people in his anger," I said, and my throat thickened. "For the first time, I realized his bloodlust wasn't only a side of him that came out during war. It was a part of who he was. He forged an alliance with Destiny, which is why Destiny and I can never be allies. We've been enemies since I can remember. In response to Lucifer's tantrum, I outright refused his proposal and went to war with him. My armies were devastated by this, however, and I formed a new plan to avoid any more losses. Lucifer cared for me on an emotional level, so I pulled a terrible trick. One that I regret to this day. I sent him a letter, telling him that my life was being threatened. I asked for his help, and he came. I planted my ambush in Hell, and Lucifer ran straight into my trap without an ounce of suspicion. The land abided by my command and turned on the Demon King. Even the most powerful beings in the world cannot stand against the Underworld. There are some things that are greater than both God and the Devil.

"Was Lucifer's marriage offer tempting? It was. At least before he started killing those around me to force my hand. Do I hate him for what he did?" I hesitated. "No. It's hard to hate someone you've fought alongside with, but his death is necessary. He needs to be ended before he ends anyone else."

Atlas stood still as he processed my story. "Are you sure you have it in you? To kill him?"

I stood from the stone with a grunt and looked him in the eye. "What do you think?"

His eyes dove into mine, searching for a weakness deep inside me. It seemed he came up empty. "I think the Devil is going to die today."

We left the cool shade and continued our descent. Fifteen minutes later, we were near the bottom of the canyon. The hole the Phoenix entered through was not as small as it appeared from the top of the cliff. The entrance was large enough to stand in and leveled out a few feet in. My hand hovered over my scimitar, and I glanced back toward Atlas. "Are you ready for this?"

"Ladies first."

I entered the maze of rocks.

CHAPTER THIRTY FIVE
A CAVERN OF NIGHTMARES

THE TUNNEL WAS DARK and damp. The coolness brought much-needed relief to my feverish skin. My eyes adjusted to the lack of lighting. The Phoenix disappeared somewhere down here. This place had a sacred ambiance, and the buzz of ancient magic filled the walls. Atlas shared a wary glance with me. Lucifer had chosen this place for a reason, but why?

The stone walls widened as we walked further, and our footsteps echoed dramatically. The path split into two different tunnels, one to the right and the other to the left.

"He's trying to split us up." Atlas's words echoed past the rocks.

I searched for some difference between the two tunnels but came up empty. Both were dark, ominous, and creepy.

"Then we don't split up," I said firmly. "We pick a tunnel and go together."

"Which should we choose?"

"We could flip a coin," I joked.

Atlas lifted an eyebrow. "If we had a coin."

Right. I didn't have my phone anymore, much less a coin. "Okay, then let's stick to the tunnel on our right," I decided. "We need to be able to find our way out when it's all said and done."

My words felt flat and left my mouth dry. *When it's all said and done.* The deed in consideration being Lucifer's death. I never thought the death of a demon could be something to dread, but Lucifer wasn't just any demon. He used to be my friend. Atlas sensed my unhappiness and hovered near as a comforting gesture. I appreciated his calming presence.

I stepped into the tunnel to my right with newfound courage and Atlas followed me. The path we took circled back underneath the entrance to the cavern and inclined downward. My eyes scoured every corner of the tunnel, searching for booby traps, but neither Atlas nor I found anything worth noting. The tunnel split again, into five different tunnels, each in equally separate directions. In the cavern at Hoover Dam, where I hid my Soul Dagger, I filled the path to my dagger with obstacles and traps, like the Hall of Thorns. Lucifer preferred deception and manipulation. Splitting us up, trying to confuse us.

Anger chewed at the edge of my mind. I banged the rocks beside me with the side of my fist. "It's just like that jerk to screw with us before we fight him. He knows he can't beat us in a fair fight!"

A small rumble grew through the cavern, and the rocks started to tremble.

Atlas looked at the rocks I'd touched. "How hard did you hit that wall?"

"Not that hard!"

A growl echoed from a tunnel on our left. Two red eyes of a lower demon fixed themselves on Atlas and me. Atlas unsheathed his sword and held it out in front of him. The ground shook more wildly, and the walls of the five tunnels all began closing in. My shoulders sagged, and a weary sigh escaped my lips. Yet the thought of Lucifer waiting beyond these tunnels sent a surge of new energy through me.

"Damn it!" I desperately dove into the tunnel on my right. The lower demon lunged for us. Atlas shouted after me; his fingers grazed my arm before I was out of reach. Halfway through the tunnel, the walls already pressed against my back and chest. I turned my head and struggled to move. The stones shoved against my temples, and the moment my hand grasped the end of the tunnel, in a final pull, I fell out the other end of the death trap.

The scraped skin at my temples and back stung, though no bone was broken. I steadied myself and stared back at the closed tunnel. "Hello!" I yelled at the top of my lungs. "Atlas! Can you hear me?"

The echo of my question was the only response. Either Atlas couldn't hear me, or I couldn't hear Atlas—or both. I cursed my stupid decision of running into the tunnel. The walls closing was another maneuver to separate us. This time, it worked. If only I'd listened to my own advice about sticking together.

I turned my attention to the room behind me. The tunnel I'd chosen led to a large circular room with markings on the wall and floor. A blue light covered the ceiling, forming strong wards around the room, wards like the ones that protected my Soul Dagger, only not as potent. Lucifer's knowledge of magic wasn't as extensive as mine. There was a stone door at the other end of the room. I ran to it and tried to shove it open. It was closed. The door was thick and robust—not easily broken—the entire room appeared to support its structure.

Like the rest of the cavern, this room had an eerie atmosphere to it. I approached the written words on the walls to see what they said. The walls were an ashen color, and the Latin words were neatly written in what looked like black charcoal.

"All who enter the Cavern of Nightmares, do beware," I read aloud. I touched the charcoal though it didn't smudge under my fingertips. "One memory shall be revealed, the one you wish to forget above all. Morpheus." Morpheus was the God of Dreams. He was as easy to find as it was to catch a cloud. He never attended High Court and kept to himself, like an old hermit. He must have built this cavern before he moved over to the human realm.

I shifted my attention to the center of the ground, where a set of fresh words had been carved with a knife. I knelt down to get a closer look. My fingers traced over the letters engraved in the stone.

These words were in English. My stomach exploded with anxiety as I scanned the writing.

"They're after me. I always knew the time would come, yet I never imagined it to be so soon. I didn't know who else to turn to. I need your help. You are my last hope. The last sun shall set upon me tonight, and Death shall find her master. Hell will become my eternal tomb."

My breath caught. Lucifer quoted my letter to him. The letter I once sent to lure him into my trap in Hell.

I had to get out of here. Now.

The ground started to tremble, as it did when I was separated from Atlas. I jumped to my feet and ran to the door. My heart pounded as claustrophobia set in. I tried to push the stone door open to no avail. The walls seemed to cave in around me, and gut-wrenching frustration tore through my chest. The floor split at the center of the room and small pieces fell through to the darkness that lay beneath. I threw my fist into the door though it refused to budge. I backed up and kicked with all my strength. Cracks formed against the stone door like a spiderweb, and I laughed in temporary success.

I stepped back to kick again, but instead of stepping on solid ground, my foot fell through the splitting floor. I stumbled back. My hand barely gripped the stone floor, and I dangled over the edge. Beneath me lay an abyss. My eyes couldn't see its end. The piece of flooring I held on to cracked before I could make my next move, and I fell to the darkness below.

I never recalled hitting the ground. For the longest time, all that existed was darkness. An eternal continuum of emptiness, free of emotion or thought. The nothingness didn't last long. The Latin words I read from the cavern walls repeated themselves in my mind. *Beware, one memory shall be revealed, the one you wish to forget above all.*

My mind conjured up images, and my body was no longer my own. I knew my thoughts, but nothing else was under my control. As if I were in a dream, my body traveled to depths of the Underworld.

CHAPTER THIRTY SIX
A MADMAN'S CELL

292 YEARS AGO...

I walked through the fire-filled depths of the pits of Hell. The pits were underground pockets of air, and at their bottom raged lava and the pure river of fire, Phlegethon. This place reeked of burning soil, and the air felt inadequate with the smoke billowing throughout the area. Long ago, once I exhausted the limited prison space in the deepest canyon of Hell, I built most prisons in these conditions. The dirt walls of the pits were riddled with prison cells that hung over the fire raging below. The cells were forged of Demon's Bane, a metal that paralyzed demons when it reacted with their blood. Even if the beasts didn't bleed on the metal, merely touching it seared their flesh. Between the cells were outposts, in which reapers oversaw the prisoners. A metal path connected the outposts to the surface, which was walked by lower demons at my command. Lower demons that would tear at the prisoners if they escaped and made it that far. Nobody ever had.

From the outposts, there were wooden paths that led to the prison cells. These wooden bridges were merciless and challenging to cross as they swung, tore, and caught on fire if the heat-resistant spells faltered. Crossbows were aimed toward the prisoners, and a magical alarm system was in place in case any demon escaped their cell. The alarm system notified me immediately, so even the strongest demon would be faced with the immediate threat of the Goddess of Death, should they escape.

I crossed the bridge that led to Lucifer's cell with confidence. Hell's fire lessened in my presence, the smoke cleared, and the bridge was steadied by the land surrounding me. The Devil's cell was closest to Phlegethon. He stood tall, even while he was wounded, and refused to sit or accept defeat. The cuffs around his wrist were forged by Vulcan, a talented blacksmith who created the greatest weapons there existed. The cuffs dampened the effect of magic so if Lucifer tried to use his power over fire, he would find it extremely difficult and fatiguing.

Lucifer's armor was dented and lay on the floor. The tunic he wore underneath was stained with soot and bright red blood, most of it not his own. The light emitted from the fire below dulled the color of his hair. He watched my approach, though he didn't say anything. He didn't need to.

Lucifer's silence spoke a lifetime's worth of emotions.

I stepped closer to the bars, and as did he. We both stopped when the bars were a bare inches away. A hair closer and the burning Demon's Bane metal would touch our skin.

My mouth opened and closed, though words were unable to escape. I steadied myself and finally spoke. "I did what I had to do."

Lucifer's labored breath cut off. His eyes flashed with pain before hardening with resolve. The muscles in his shoulders tightened, and he tensed like a bow ready to snap. "Tell yourself what you will, Rose. You cannot hide from the truth."

"The truth," I scoffed and turned away. "I suppose you know what the truth is?"

"Even you know it."

I faced him again. "I forget that you perceive me as an all-knowing telepath. Why don't you enlighten me? What is it I know but refuse to admit?"

The rumble of laughter shook the Devil's broad chest, though the light of humor was not reflected in his eyes. "Do you really think I'd tell you? Just like that. Make it easy on you after what you've done?"

"Like I said, I did what I had—"

"What you had to do. Yes, I know what you said. It's what you will continue to say when you thrust a dagger through the heart of an innocent fool who's done nothing wrong but love you. It is what madmen and dictators have reasoned when sending the masses to their deaths. They believed that what they did was justified and necessary, but let me be very clear, Primrose." His hands suddenly gripped the metal bars, and the flesh on them blistered, starting to melt off. "There is always a choice, and you already made it. There will come a time when what needs to be done is more costly than the crime that needs to be stopped. You don't even realize that you are on the wrong side of justice." He released the bars of his cage. The wounds on his hands bled though he did not grimace. Nothing could be worse than the pain he felt inside.

The smell of his charred flesh made my stomach churn. "There is no right or wrong," I said with a steady voice. His words shook me, though I wished I could hide it.

Lucifer bared his teeth. "Right and wrong are in the eye of the beholder. There may be no such thing as right or wrong. But let me tell you what does exist. A winner and a loser. The champion and the dead. Today, I am the one who has lost, but come tomorrow... that may change."

His words cut me inside like shards of glass. I forced my face to slacken. "Threatening me so soon, Lucifer?"

"Damn it, Rose. I thought you cared!" The Demon King's voice echoed through Hell's prison, and I flinched. "We were partners!"

"We were more than that! We were more than friends!" I yelled back with a wave of anger that didn't suit me. "Don't forget your trust wasn't the only one broken. I didn't agree nor refuse when you came to my palace that day. But that wasn't enough for you, was it?

You had to enlist Destiny's help. You had to kill innocent people. You couldn't just trust me! If you had only waited—"

"You still would have said no." Lucifer's voice calmed, and he shook his head as if to accept something he wished weren't true. "You fear commitment. You fear attachment. You hide your emotions while everyone is watching when, in reality, all you want to do is let it out. You pretend to be strong, like nothing affects you, but deep inside you're still as fragile as a rose. And one day, your pretty petals will be ruined. One day, the stress, pain, fear of everything will get the best of you, and you will fall."

I gritted my teeth. He was wrong. I was the Goddess of Death, and nothing affected me. Nothing could defeat me. Not even him. "You're wrong." My voice trembled. "I rejected you because you are a threat to me and my kingdom. And from this moment on, you will rot in this cell. Hated. Defeated. Alone."

I left to cross the bridge. My head was heavy with thoughts that didn't belong in my head.

"You know what the worst part is, kitten?" Lucifer called out. "You don't know that you care about them. You still don't understand why you're angry about me killing those humans. It eats you alive at night when you sleep. That there is something in this world capable of hurting or weakening the *Goddess of Death*. You know at heart that the reason the High Court justified sending you any additional armies to kill me is that you begged them to."

I almost stumbled on the bridge. He'd rattled me with that comment, and he knew it. I lifted my chin and continued my path out of Hell's clutches. Lucifer didn't know me. Nobody did. That was why he lost the war he waged against me.

CHAPTER THIRTY SEVEN
THE DEVIL'S RAGE

MY EYELIDS WERE HEAVY, and the back of my head throbbed as if someone had taken a Goddess-sized baseball bat to it. My back was sticky, and something sharp protruded from my waist. The flares of pain dulled the recency of my memory of Lucifer.

With great effort, I forced my eyes open. My vision was blurred. The dripping of water echoed from someplace nearby. I blinked, and everything around me cleared. I was in some sort of cavern. I inhaled deeply and touched the back of my head. Pain flared through my skull, and I flinched, bringing my hand back to my face. My fingers were painted red. Suddenly, the memory of falling from the Cavern of Nightmares crashed back into my mind. I gritted my teeth and lifted my head to look at my waist as much as I could. The bones surrounding my spinal cord pierced through my midsection, and my ribs stuck out of my skin at odd angles. My breathing was labored, and I laid my head back down. I couldn't feel anything below my shoulder blades, which I was currently grateful for considering the number of fractures I gained from my fall. However, it could take hours before my spine put itself back together, and until then, I couldn't wiggle a toe much less stand up.

"Having some trouble there, love?" Lucifer's voice rang through the cavern.

My chest tightened. I refrained from answering him. Here I lay at the Devil's mercy unless my healing power picked up the pace. With my despair rose the warmth of light inside my chest. The Guardian's protection magic strummed past my heart and down to my spine. A resounding crack echoed past the walls, followed by my cry of pain. Sensation returned to the lower half of my body like a jolt of electricity. Crack after crack, my bones shifted and changed. Minutes of agony passed while the protection magic soothed my pain as much as it could. My ribs dove back into place, and I clenched my teeth to quiet the grunt of anguish that left my chest. The magic dwindled away, leaving me renewed and ready to fight. I rolled to my stomach and braced myself against the ground. With a final push, I was on my knees and then on my feet.

Lucifer watched me with a glare of approval. "You've gotten better at that."

"I've gotten better at a lot of things." My implied threat loomed in the air.

The Devil stood at a short distance away. He wasn't dressed for battle. He wore a comfortable pair of dark pants and a red jacket over his casual shirt. A dagger was clipped to his belt, a jeweled sheath covering it. There it was, left obvious as Lucifer paraded it in front of me.

He noticed where my gaze had gone and smiled. "Are you looking for this?" Lucifer patted the dagger. "This is what it all comes down to, doesn't it? Here lies the tool to my destruction, to my death."

"You don't seem disturbed." I closed half the distance between us and stopped. "You should be. I'm much stronger than before."

"That's funny," he said. "A week ago, you would have never admitted that you had any room for improvement." Sharp, jagged edges of the cavern jutted out from above. Four torches lit up the corners around us.

I narrowed my eyes, hating that he was right. "People change, Lucifer. I changed, and you changed, too."

I noticed a glimpse of vulnerability. A stumble in the high and mighty way the Devil held himself. Maybe a sliver of humanity in the echo of his gaze. But just as it flashed before my eyes, a typical smirk of ridicule painted his lips. "A tad philosophical, aren't we, Rose?"

Any small hope of avoiding the coming fight disappeared faster than the speed of light. "More like perceptive," I snapped. "Call it what you will—doesn't change a damn thing." A small stream of water dribbled down the side of a cavern wall. The water droplets hit the floor at the constant beat of my heart, like a drum.

"Well, come on then." He opened his arms in a welcoming gesture. The fire from the torches danced across his eyes. "Do what you absolutely *have* to do. What you came here to do. Kill me, once and for all."

Well, if he was so eager. My hand touched my hip, only to find my sword and daggers were gone.

The Devil laughed, sending a shiver down my spine. "Did you really think I'd let you keep your weapons? If you want my Soul Dagger, you'll have to fight for it the old-fashioned way—with your fists."

"Put up your guards then." My hands clenched into fists, and I widened my stance. "If it's a beating you want, it's a beating you'll get."

Lucifer took that as a challenge and accepted it with a gleeful delight.

His movements were a blur, but so were mine. I blocked his fist with my forearm and swept my leg over his front arm. Lucifer's technique was elegant yet impatient. He moved from one combination to the next in unison. His attacks were successive onslaughts.

I spun, and his fist caught a handful of my hair. Pain tugged my scalp. I wrestled his arm and stepped behind him. We sparred like we had when he was my general and we were training for war. All of our emotions, the festering hatred and frustration, cumulated into a heated dance between the Goddess of Death and the Devil. My nails grazed against his cheek, leaving red marks. One of his kicks caught me in the waist, and I flew back.

"You've gotten sloppy." Lucifer stalked toward me as I shakily got to my feet. "When you trained with me, you were much faster."

I jumped off the wall behind me and kicked his neck. The Devil stumbled back as I began an aggressive onslaught. "Don't forget," I puffed between hits and threw my elbow into his chin. "I used to beat you every damn time."

Lucifer caught my knee mid-assault and flipped me back. I kicked to sweep his feet, but he jumped to avoid my legs. I rolled to my knees, and Lucifer caught me by the collar of my shirt. He threw me against a wall and forced his arm against my neck. "I was going easy on you then, darling."

I kicked his shin and thrust my palm into his nose. The bone cracked. He cursed and hit me across the cheek. I fell to the side, and the air left my lungs with a blow to my ribs. I used the momentum from his punch to put distance between us and stumbled to my feet. I hated to admit it, but Abaddon was telling the truth. His poison slowed and weakened me. Regardless of what Lucifer claimed, my normal strength was superior to his, at least it used to be! In my current condition, Lucifer was the stronger fighter of the two of us, and he knew me better than I would've liked, which made me predictable. In a one-to-one fight, without magic, he had a chance at winning. I swayed on my feet, looking for a way out.

The Devil smiled maliciously. Blood spluttered from where I hit his nose, but the pain didn't bother him. "Stuck in a rut, are we, Rose? Can't get out this time."

I summoned a few souls, and they ran toward Lucifer. He simply tore them apart, limb by limb. I tried to open a portal but wasn't surprised when nothing happened. The magic of the Glass prohibited the creation of portals within the ancient land. I summoned ten other souls. Lucifer's lower lip pulled to the corner in irritation, and he set the bodies aflame. I was only buying lost time now. The space we were in wasn't nearly large enough to summon a dragon.

I continued backing up. My eyes swept the cave. If only I could escape Lucifer for a few moments, to find Atlas and regroup! We could defeat the Devil together. There was an opening on the other end of Lucifer. Not that he'd let me get that far.

The Devil struck down the last dead human I summoned and faced me. "Enough, Rose. It's over."

In a last-ditch attempt, I placed my hand out in a stopping gesture and pulled at the protection magic in my veins to help me. I tried to blast him back with a wave of light, like I had when we fought in the forest.

Lucifer stopped his assault and stared at my outstretched arm in confusion. "What's that supposed to do?"

I repeated the gesture in frustration and achieved the same result. Nothing. Protection magic was only any good if I knew how to use it.

"You seem to be out of tricks," Lucifer said.

I readied my fists again. "Doesn't mean I'm out of the fight. I can still beat you."

"Do you really think so? You're outskilled, outsmarted, and alone. What exactly in that sweet mind of yours tells you that you stand any chance against me?"

"She's not alone."

A frosty voice filled the air, and for the first time, I was relieved to hear how cold it sounded. The temperature dropped, despite the Devil's warm presence. Atlas Grimm stood at the entrance to the cavern with a sword in his hand.

His blue eyes filled with anger. "She has me."

CHAPTER THIRTY EIGHT
THE ROSE OF DEATH

THE DEVIL HAD PREPARED for everything. Everything but the God of Ice. Lucifer's jaw clenched so hard, I heard his teeth grind together. His eyebrows pinched into an open glare, and he turned toward Atlas. "This doesn't concern you, Brother Grimm. Begone."

Atlas narrowed his cold eyes.

"See, that's just the thing," I said. Lucifer's head swiveled back to look at me. "I got it wrong the first time, too. His name isn't Brother Grimm."

"No, it isn't," Atlas said icily and strode toward us. "You've made a grave mistake attacking her."

Lucifer seemed appalled by his comment. His facial muscles slackened before a burst of laughter shook his chest.

"Oh, now, this is priceless!" he howled. "Fallen for her little trick, have you? Think she loves you or cares for you? Yes"—Lucifer nodded toward me—"she'll do that. Draw you in with her hard-to-get act and sweet innocent eyes—at least before she tries to kill you and claim it's all your fault. It's in her nature to push people away the moment they get too close. Though I'm sure you know that already."

Atlas clenched his fists though I knew Lucifer's words wouldn't rattle him that easily. We shared a glance, and for the first time, we understood one another in a way that words couldn't describe. Together, we could beat Lucifer. But we needed to work as a team. As one. An idea spun through my mind, and I was surprised by the audacity of it. This new plan could work.

I blinked and let down the surface of my guard; my thoughts leaked through the air between Atlas and me.

"You can't beat us, Lucifer." I tried to distract the Devil until Atlas figured out what I was doing. "You trying to get into Atlas's head won't work. He's above that."

Atlas tilted his head. His nose twitched as if he could smell something different in the air.

"Is that so?" the Devil purred. "Even if my words are true?"

Atlas's voice filled my head. *Cleverly done.* A moment of glee brightened my mind. Part of me knew that Atlas's mind control lent him the power to read minds, and I was glad to be right. *How did you know?* Atlas asked. He never told me about his ability to read minds.

"Everyone knows better than to trust the Devil," I snapped at Lucifer, trying to keep track of two conversations.

Deductive reasoning, I answered Atlas. *And a risky gamble, but one that paid off. After I knew about the mind control, it was easy to figure out the mind-reading part.*

He doesn't know? Atlas asked.

No, I thought silently. *But it's not worth trying to get into his head. He's too strong. If we work together, we can beat him. Are you ready?*

Atlas tightened his grip on his sword, and that was enough of a sign for me.

I threw my leg toward Lucifer's shoulder. He caught my foot, and I used the momentum to jump up and wrap my thighs around his neck. A shard of ice tore into his flesh, and the Devil threw me away from him with a cry of rage. I rolled to my feet, now on Atlas's side of the cavern. Lucifer deflected the next ice daggers that flew in his direction with a wave of flames, anger written clearly on his face.

The God of Ice by my side, we rushed toward the Devil. With my mental shields down and my thoughts fully open to Atlas, we formed a connection with each other. Atlas read the attacks I planned against Lucifer in my mind, and he complemented them beautifully with his skill. Lucifer hadn't expected us to work so well together. We cornered Lucifer, who struggled to avoid both Atlas's sword and my fist. While Atlas swung his sword, the Devil resorted to magic and disarmed the God of Ice with an overwhelming blast of fire.

The heat lashed at my skin, my protection magic rising up with a cool shield, and I burst through the flames. My fist flew into Lucifer's stomach. With each blur of movement, I expressed every single rage, frustration, desperation, and mental agony I'd felt this past week. The melancholy from my lost memories, the injustice from learning about the Guardians—it all built up. I fought with the pain brought by the world's unfairness and my lack of ability to right simple wrongs. In my cry of fury, I backhanded the Devil, and a mountain of energy exploded from the surface of my skin.

Both Atlas and Lucifer flew back with the strength of my protection magic while I relished the feeling of power as it curled around my limbs with a bittersweet caress. I never felt stronger than I did then, bathed in my volatile emotions.

The blur of a black cloak caught the corner of my eye, and before I knew it, I was thrown to the ground.

My head hit the dirt hard, but I wasn't at all dazed. Fear made me rush back to my feet to see an assassin fall from his hiding spot, high up between the rocks of the cave. When he hit the ground, there was nothing left of him but the velvet material of his cloak and the black dust that scattered beneath it.

I was light-headed as shock overwhelmed me. Lucifer lay on the floor, a familiar dagger sticking out from his heart. An assassin had been sent to kill me... and Lucifer had taken the hit.

Fear dove through my stomach, filling me with pounding dread. I knelt down and touched the dagger to confirm what I already knew. The hair on the back of my neck stood up in warning. The blade was mine... my Soul Dagger. But how? I'd given my Soul Dagger to Elinore and ordered Cain to guard her with his life. If the dagger was here...

Elinore!

A gut-wrenching cry left my lips. Pain like nothing else shattered my heart, as if it were made of glass. I would've sensed her death if her soul had been reaped, but there were worse things than death. If she was harmed—

"That bad, huh?" Lucifer huffed, mistaking my fear for Elinore's health to be fear for his well-being. With my attention back on him, my breathing stopped. Lucifer was the one who threw me to the ground. He jumped in the way of my Soul Dagger to save my life. The thought lingered in my mind like a cold tremor. "It's your dagger, isn't it?" he continued. "If it were mine, I'd be dead now." Lucifer watched my actions closely, though the feverish fight in him was no more. He lay in surrender, no longer willing to fight.

My mouth opened and closed, gasping for air and words. I narrowed my eyes and slapped him hard. "Why would you do that? You idiot!" I cried out, pure anger tainting my words. Overwhelming emotions clouded my mind. I pulled out the blade from his chest and threw it aside in a fit of rage. The metal rang when it hit the stone wall of the cavern.

Lucifer tried to laugh, but coughs shook his chest, and blood stained his lips. "Because Rose, you were right."

I stilled and watched him with wide eyes for a few seconds before slapping him again. "And the only way you could prove that was by bloody getting stabbed?"

He flinched this time and rubbed his cheek. "You were right when you said I can never turn down a challenge."

I nodded slowly, still unable to wrap my head around how the Devil saved my life. I was here to kill him! Instead, he took a knife in the chest for me.

He smiled crookedly. "But you're not always right, Rose, sometimes you're very wrong. You were wrong about one important thing."

"What?" My chest trembled with the next breath I took.

"I didn't lose this one." Lucifer touched my hand and brought it over his heart. His blood felt cold under the tips of my fingers. "I didn't lose this challenge. I am trying to be the 'good guy' here." He moved to get his Soul Dagger from his belt. The pretty blade echoed the bond to his soul. He placed the unsheathed blade in my hand, and the coolness of the metal burned my skin. Natkont's spell, finally satisfied, ended its pull toward Lucifer's Soul Dagger.

"The heart has its reasons that reason cannot understand," he said. "The only way we know truth is by the heart." His grip loosened, and he let his arms fall to his sides. "That's how I know that this—what I feel for you, whether it be love, lust, or an insane obsession—all I know is that it's true."

His beautiful red eyes spoke his honesty with the fortitude of kindness. The Devil trusted me with something more precious than his life. He bared his soul before me, leaving him vulnerable. He held his heart out on his sleeve, and the last time he did that, I hurt him. Deep down, beyond the clutches of reason and logic, my heart believed his feelings for me were more than what I had thought them to be. His intentions went beyond a crazed obsession or attempt to gain political advantage. Lucifer was a fool, and as Satan said, he was stupidly in love with me. Pity grew within my chest. More than anything, I just wanted to leave and let him be.

Tears for what I was about to do gathered in my eyes. I struggled to hold them back as I tightly gripped the hilt of his Soul Dagger and held it above his chest.

"I have to..." The rest of the words refused to leave my dry mouth. A sick sensation stuck to my tongue, and my forehead warmed as if with fever. I always did what I had to do. I did what was necessary. Wasn't this necessary? Didn't I have to do this? The Devil needed to die.

Lucifer parted his lips. "Do you? Do you really have to?"

His simple question made my hand tremble in dilemma. I tightened my muscles around the hilt of the blade to finish the deed. With a sudden movement, I dropped the dagger and rose to my feet. "No." I shook my head and backed away from the Devil. I put enough distance between us that there would be no time for regret or taking back my decision. "I don't have to do anything."

The High Court be damned. They didn't care about Lucifer back when he tried to force my hand into marriage. Why should they care about him now? I wasn't in the business of pleasing a handful of manipulative deities.

Pride and something akin to joy blossomed inside of Lucifer. The smile that graced his lips was uniquely natural, not cruel or devious. All the good memories we had in the past came crashing back to me, and I was glad to have let him live. We could start over, and things would be better than they were before.

A shadow flew past me and thrust Lucifer's Soul Dagger deep into his heart. My eyes widened as I stared at the crouched figure of Atlas Grimm. The God of Ice pulled out the bloody dagger, and I sensed Lucifer's soul drain down to the pits of Hell. His eyes dulled, and he lay limp on the floor. An inhuman, shrill scream pounded through the room. The scream had come from my lips. The Devil was truly gone. Dead.

Dead. Dead. Dead. The thought echoed in my mind. *Dead...* and not by my hands.

Betrayed, I threw myself forward, unsure of what I would do to the Grimm Brother once I reached him. A sharp, wet feeling burst through my chest, and I lurched forward to my knees. My wrists broke my fall, and cloudy confusion wrapped around my weak head.

"Tut tut, Lady Primrose. You lose." Destiny's silky voice ground against my ears.

There was no time for me to feel surprise, anger, or fear. I incoherently touched the tip of my Soul Dagger, which now pierced my heart before Destiny pulled it out.

I struggled to breathe, and blood poured from my chest. I felt so cold, even as my protection magic struggled to keep my heart pumping. Without the strength to keep my head up, I collapsed to my side and sent Atlas a last pleading look. In his eyes was stinging regret paired with self-hatred as Destiny elegantly strode toward his side.

"Goodbye, Primrose," he said softly. His words, though full of melancholy, fell flat against my ears. They were as meaningless as words to an illiterate.

"She's still alive?" Destiny asked with a tiny scowl that pulled at the side of her bright red lips. Her red hair was pinned in an intricate braid, and she wore a white cocktail dress with nude beading. Her dress was stained scarlet with my blood. "Suppose it makes sense that she gets an extra moment before she dies," she said, "her being the former Goddess of Death and all. How do you think it will feel, Atlas dear, being the ruler of the Underworld?"

Lucifer's death weighed on me like a shadow that darkened my vision. Elinore's and Cain's faces flashed in my mind. And Atlas... I trusted him and he deceived me. Everything had fallen apart in the past few minutes. The meaning of Destiny's words and actions hit me all at once, like an eighteen-wheeler. A hysterical laugh racked my chest. The pain of being stabbed in the heart finally sank in despite my shock, and my consciousness started to slip away. What they didn't realize was that their actions were all for naught.

"Do you really think this is over?" I demanded and lifted my chin in defiance for the last time. "Dead is dead, only when I say so."

Destiny's haughty stare and a guilt-filled flash in Atlas's eyes were the last two things I saw before the darkness reigned.

CHAPTER THIRTY NINE
UNFORESEEN
REPERCUSSIONS

THREE DEITIES ENTERED THE moonlit throne room. A tall figure sat on the throne and waited patiently. A mask lay on the being's
face to hide any emotion.

Fate, Destiny, and a Grimm Brother—a cunningly effective team
to lay a lethal trap for the Goddess of Death. Hundreds of years were
devoted to devising the intricate plot that finally came to pass two
days ago. A plot that had almost not succeeded on account of the
Devil's untimely meddling.

"It is done." Destiny swept forward in her paper white dress.
"Primrose Titan is no more."

The masked shadow stood from the throne and approached with
a slow, steady pace. "And her body?"

"It disappeared," said Atlas Grimm. "All that remained was her
Soul Dagger."

The God of Ice was shaken by Primrose Titan's death, but he would soon forget her. The power and political position now granted to him would one day overshadow any feelings he might have once held for the deceased Goddess.

Destiny flipped her fiery hair and lifted her head to look into the dark eyes of the masked deity. "Her power has not transitioned to me yet."

Destiny's subtle defiance did not go unnoticed. The being rested its steely gaze on the woman, and she cowered under the scrutiny. "Be patient," the masked figure said. "Primrose was the first and only Goddess of Death. To kill the Goddess of Death has never been done before. We know nothing of how the transition of power will proceed. I presume you have her Soul Dagger."

"And my old Soul Dagger," Destiny affirmed. "Until the transfer of power has taken place, I'll keep both daggers with me."

Primrose's old Soul Dagger would become Destiny's new Soul Dagger. But until Destiny's old dagger disappeared, as it should under a regular transition of power, it would be wise to carry both daggers to avoid any... complications.

The masked figure nodded. "Until the transition of power has occurred, we need Azazel to supply us with portal keys to travel to the Underworld. He has been most cooperative so far. We can pick more keys from the trees that surround the palace and use them as needed. With or without Primrose's power, you are Queen of the Underworld."

"We came across a people in the ancient land," Atlas said, expressing a mild concern. He summoned a small flame, which wrapped enchantingly around the tips of his fingers. Lucifer's power transferred to him perfectly. "They took to Primrose quite well."

"The Guardians won't be an issue," the masked deity said confidently. "I'll make sure of it. You need to take care of your brother, Lord Atlas. He's started asking too many questions."

Atlas nodded. His fingers hung over the hilt of his sword in greedy anticipation. The elder Grimm Brother had long waited to kill his younger brother, and now the time had come.

Fate closed her yellow eyes and hummed as her forehead wrinkled. "Hecate's progeny—the girl could become a threat to us. I sensed her strength when I approached the Glass."

The masked figure laughed with a derisive grin on its lips. "The girl is more Guardian than Goddess. Her blood won't let her cross the Glass, not with the curse in place. I'll send a few... friends over to the ancient land—to make sure the Guardians stay out of our way."

Atlas shook his head. "The situation isn't that simple anymore. The deities are afraid of returning to the village. She killed several of Hermes's followers."

"And now she's dead," Destiny said. She crossed her arms in childish annoyance. "How can they possibly fear a dead Goddess?"

"Enough."

Everyone was suddenly silent.

The shadowed being watched the three deities with sharp intuition. "We are still on a very tight schedule. The assassins I created should have been enough to kill Primrose Titan on their own, but we didn't anticipate the kind of help she would receive. Lucifer's escape was not part of the original plan, and we lost plenty of time convincing Primrose to hunt that fool down and use their history to kill two targets at once. Now, without delay, we must move on to the next stage."

The being turned its back to the three powerful deities and lurked toward the throne to sit.

"What's the next stage?" Atlas inquired once the silence became unbearable.

The masked figure smiled. "Hell on Earth."

EPILOGUE
REBIRTH

THE SOFT BEEPING OF machines hummed in the small, white hospital room. Doctor Lim rubbed his creased forehead with the sleeve of his white coat. He adjusted his thin-framed glasses and clicked his tongue while looking over the patient files. Quite simply, things didn't add up.

He flipped over to the next page of the lab results with a resounding *humph* and sent his patient a quick glance. The nurse placed the woman on an IV and hooked her up to oxygen three days ago when she first arrived. This morning, he'd given the order to remove the intubation tube, as the patient began to show signs of response to stimuli and regular breathing activity. It shocked him how quickly the woman recuperated, given the state she'd been found in.

Doctor Lim put down his clipboard and picked up the newspaper from a red plastic chair in the corner of the room. The headline read 'Woman Falls from the Sky.' Apparently, his patient fell from the rooftop of an apartment building with stab wounds and evidence of other trauma. The paramedics presumed her dead, twice—but without a doubt, her heart still beat loud and clear today. The stab wound was through the chest, and if Lim knew any better, he'd have said it was through the heart. At least, the entry and exit marks indicated this. Logic, however, did not justify his conclusion, and therefore he thought nothing of it. His patient was a lucky woman.

As to how she ended up on a roof, stabbed and thrown off... well, nobody knew that. Her fingerprints left no information, and the police department was unable to identify her. A special investigative force was commissioned by the Los Angeles police, but nothing turned up.

Even if the woman woke, which Doctor Lim suspected she would, given the rate of her healing, the amount of head trauma she incurred would substantially debilitate her ability to recount recent events, if anything. Data pointed toward potential mental retardation, given the condition of her most recent brain scan.

A social worker and recent graduate of UCLA, Sara White, was on her way to the hospital. Lim knew her type and scrunched up his nose in disgust. He threw the newspaper back down on the seat and picked up the patient files once more for a final review. Sara White was an idealist, but a well-backed one. UCLA would support her decisions on how to best help the patient post-treatment, and the school would surely publish her research and conclusions.

A strangled gasp startled Doctor Lim, and he spun toward the patient's bed. The woman sat up, and her brown hair wildly flew about her pale face. She looked left and right hysterically. "Where am I?"

"Please, miss, calm down." The doctor reached for and pressed the nurse's call button before approaching his patient with his arms up in a surrendering gesture. "You are in a hospital right now."

The woman stopped fidgeting, though her brown eyes widened in confusion while she brushed her hair away from her face. "A hospital? Why?"

"Can you tell me your name, miss?"

The nurse finally entered the room, and she and the doctor shared a look of disbelief. The patient was not supposed to be awake, much less speaking. But the extent of her head trauma became evident when she fumbled with her next words.

"M-my name? Name?" she muttered under her breath and a line formed between her eyebrows. Her eyes flickered, and she looked up to the doctor with newfound desperation. "I don't know my name."

Both the doctor and nurse nodded as if this made sense to them, but the woman stifled a cry of anguish. "How can I not know my name?"

"It's all right," the nurse cooed.

"No. It's not okay! Why can't I remember?!"

Doctor Lim left the room, embarrassed by the patient's reaction. The nurse would explain what she needed to know. Besides, Sara White would be here soon. She could take it from here.

† † † † † †

A young girl watched the reddish-brown hospital building from afar. It was an old building, though it was sturdy and had an old rustic charm. "There she is." She spoke to the air and pointed to the building.

Her fingers touched the red heart locket she wore around her neck, and the girl smiled. "It's time, Fenrir."

A large wolf stepped from the brush behind her. The gray fur on his back bristled with anticipation. Brown, steely eyes watched the hospital with a readiness that would frighten any onlooker. The beast yearned for blood. And he would get it.

Yocheved crouched down to the wolf's level and placed a gentle hand on the back of his neck. "Are you ready?"

Primrose will return in Book Two of
The Chronicles of the Underworld.

CAGED MAGIC

ROSALIND THORN REMEMBERS NOTHING of her past, not even her real name. Determined to move on with her life, she tries to ignore her magical connection to the dead. While a familiar stranger, Gavin Petreson, haunts her mind, Rosalind finds herself thrust into a past full of magic, supernatural creatures, and politics.

As her memories return, will Rosalind accept her former title as Primrose Titan, the Goddess of Death, or will her enemies find her before she can? With only a handful of allies at her side, Rosalind fights to stay alive and right the wrongs she committed in past years. She must prevail; after all, dead is only dead when she says so.

ACKNOWLEDGEMENTS

THANK YOU TO EVERYONE who has supported me during my journey in writing *Dark Magic*. To my sister and best friend, Kristine, I could have *never* done this without you. Thank you for reading every draft of my book and providing honest feedback and criticism to guide me. She made time out of her busy schedule as a student to fill in the holes in Primrose's story and ensure the magical world I built was sturdy and captivating.

A very special thanks to my mom and dad for encouraging me to publish. My parents helped me gain the courage to put my book out into the world and never gave up on me. My father is my mentor, and my mother is my safety net—I owe much of my success to them. To my grandparents, thank you for your compassion, kindness, and unconditional love.

I also want to thank Kevin Anderson & Associates staff for helping me prepare my book for publishing, including Mark Weinstein, Lauren Downey, and Hannah VanVels. Hannah guided me through several rounds of revisions and editing, and I am genuinely grateful

ssion for writing, I couldn't have written a 130,000-
ank you to all my high school and university English
cially Mr. Darrell Benton and Mr. David Kleinbeck

from Trinity School of Midland, for inspiring my creativity and love for crafting a story on the page.

Creating a strong female character cannot be done without being surrounded by strong women in my life. Thank you to the officer team for the Win STEM Foundation, particularly the chapter at The University of Texas at Dallas. You've inspired me with your leadership and ambition.

RALUCA NARITA was born in Romania and grew up in Southern California and West Texas. She currently resides in the Dallas-Fort Worth Metroplex and loves to travel in her free time. Raluca is the author of The Chronicles of the Underworld. For each book sold, 99 cents will be donated to the Win STEM Foundation to support women in STEM.

To learn more, visit
www.dark-magic.net
www.winstem.org.

CPSIA information can be obtained
at www.ICGtesting.com
Printed in the USA
LVHW031433150423
744095LV00007B/13/J